LOVE

CATWALK SERIES - BOOK 5

S. Q. ORPIN

Published by Wild Hibiscus Press

PO Box 1761 Lafayette CA 94549

Cover created by Fresh Design

*Love is dedicated to Shawn, for encouraging me to follow my heart and
always supporting my dreams.*

THE CATWALK SERIES

The Catwalk series was inspired by the exciting but perilous world of modeling in Los Angeles. Dream was motivated by an accident that redefined the life of the author's model-niece, Sterling. Wanting to give a voice to additional characters and in response to a 'What next?' storyline, Catwalk expanded to a five-part series. The stories encompass a deep examination of characters struggling to find meaning in life and love.

The books are written from multiple viewpoints allowing the reader to explore the diverse characters, while delving into the deep, and sometimes dark, human existence and tumultuous relationships. The series contains adult situations and language, including sex, trauma, and violence.

DREAM introduces the cast of characters and the relationship developing between Casi and Kyle. It layers the superficial world of modeling with the lifestyle of a small-town man, creating challenges and pitfalls. **HOPE** continues as reality and conflict consume the couple and supporting character storylines develop. **TRUST** explores the emotional rollercoaster of love, career, loss, and coming to terms with the past. **SEEK** reveals secrets and back story, helping the characters move forward as emotional scars are healed. **LOVE** is the final book in the series which spans five years, achieving triumph and finding meaning in life and love. The series primarily focuses on the main characters of Casi and Kyle, but supporting characters are intricately woven throughout the five books.

CAST OF CHARACTERS

Casi (Roberts): A former swimsuit model in LA. Born in Burnaby, Canada, and now living in Blackberry Falls, WA, with her husband, Kyle. She is a marketing and promotions manager for Macrae Skincare.

Kyle Jensen: A master woodworker with his own business in Washington State. Married to Casi.

Jake: Kyle's older brother and business partner. Father of Olivia, Reid, Austin, Tommy, and Charlotte.

Gail: Jake's ex-wife and mother of Olivia and Reid.

Mary Ann: Gail's best friend. Married to Tucker.

Lia: Lauren's older sister. Ex-wife of Jake and mother of Austin and Tommy.

Lauren: Lia's sister. Dated Kyle for three years. A chef in Seattle.

Fran: The mother of Lia, Lauren, and Lance.

Anna: Works with Casi at Macrae. Married to Jake and mother of Charlotte.

Georgia Jensen: Kyle's and Jake's adoptive mother.

Peter Jensen: Married to Georgia, and the adoptive father of Kyle and Jake.

Tara: Biological mother of Kyle and Jake.

Jack Roberts: Casi's father. He and his wife, Ava, own a restaurant and brewery in Bellingham, WA. Divorced from Casi's mother, Sonya.

Ava: Jack's wife and Casi's stepmother.

Sonya: Casi's troubled mother. Deceased.

Mary: Casi's mentor and Ava's close friend. Owner of Macrae Skincare.

Alix: Casi's ex-boyfriend. Celebrity, graphic artist.

Dylan: Casi's best friend and hairdresser from LA. Now in Seattle with Brian.

Earl: Peter's best friend and former partner in a plumbing business.

Grady: Kyle's best friend from high school who was killed in a boating accident.

Brian: The Jensen brother's accountant.

Amber: Kyle's high school girlfriend.

Nicole: Kyle's high school girlfriend, after Amber.

Amy: The receptionist at the wood shop. Dating Riley.

Riley: The apprentice at the wood shop.

Ray Dawson: Casi's former doorman in LA. He is an avid cook.

Dawn: Casi's best friend from high school. Married to Joey.

Katie: Casi's other best friend from high school. Married to Shane.

Joey: Casi's high school boyfriend.

Dingo: Kyle's German short-haired dog.

Jezebel: Casi's calico cat.

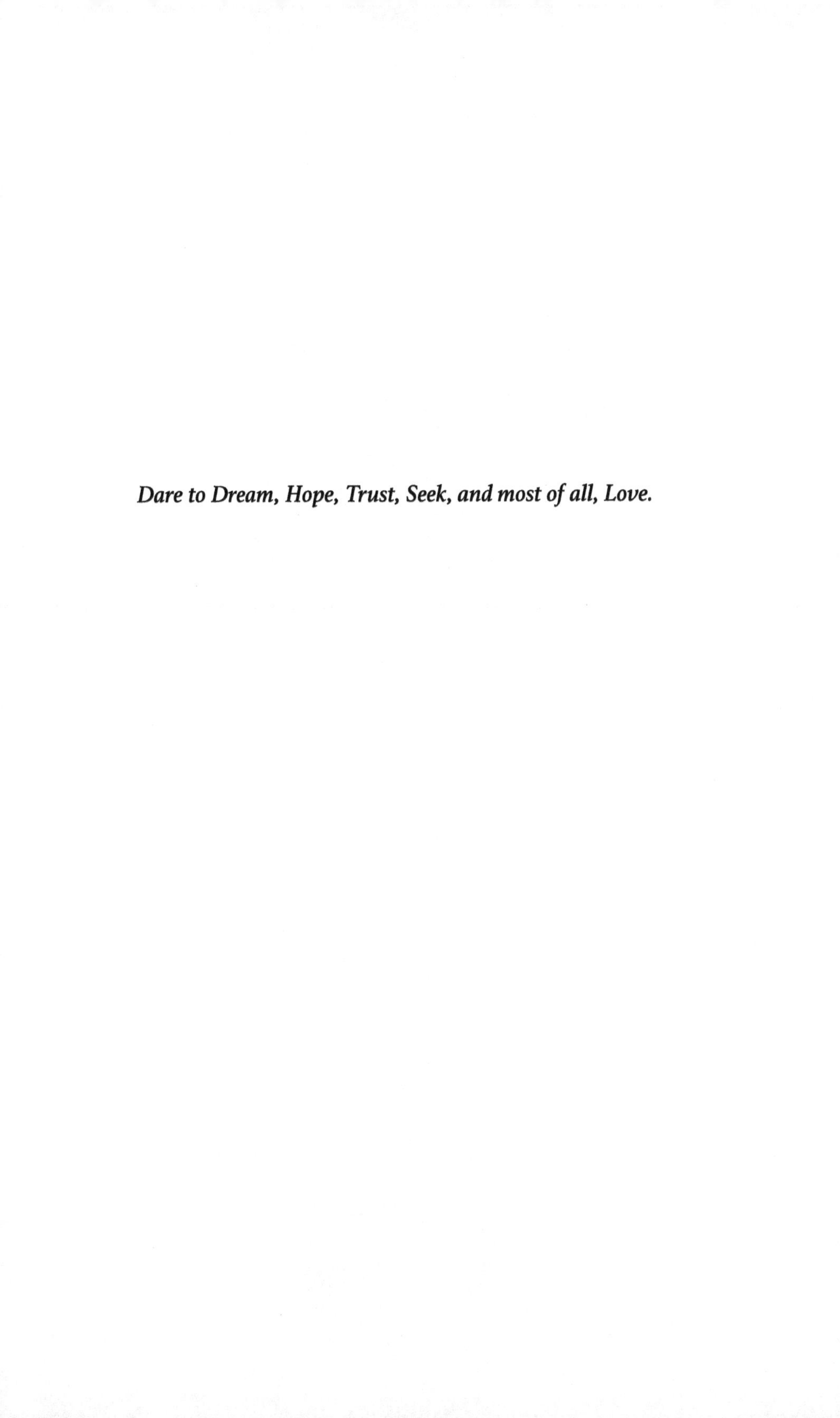

Dare to Dream, Hope, Trust, Seek, and most of all, Love.

PROLOGUE - DREAM

Cassidy Roberts had stars in her eyes when she was scouted for modeling at seventeen, on the beach in Burnaby, Canada. She moved to Los Angeles with her mother, Sonya, and changed her name to Casi. She distanced herself from her father, Jack, and stepmother, Ava, determined to reinvent her image and leave her old life behind. Sonya micromanaged Casi's career and immersed herself in the chaos of Hollywood life until Mary stepped in as Casi's mentor and redirected her to a better path. Her career blossomed in the world of lingerie and swimsuit modeling, accenting her curvaceous figure.

A dozen years later, as an experienced and in-demand model, Casi lived with her celebrity artist boyfriend of four years, Alix Grey. She created a life of excess, parties, and glamour, but was unfulfilled and petrified about turning thirty. When she met Kyle Jensen, a craftsman from Blackberry Falls, WA, she became instantly smitten. After she broke her pelvis in a car accident, her career was jeopardized and Casi spiraled down, becoming lost and confused about which direction to take. She bought a loft in Hollywood, and focused on her career, capitalizing on her success, while also finishing her business degree. She followed her heart and pursued a relationship with Kyle, ignoring the issues involved with moving to a small town, and dealing with Kyle's untrusting brother, Jake.

An opportunity to be part owner in a surfing line, Sand and Surf, with ex-boyfriend Alix, promised to be lucrative and provide extra income. Casi naively accepted the deal, assuming everything would fall in place. Passionately in love, Kyle and Casi married in Hawaii, determined to prove everyone wrong and live a happy life, with their cat Jezebel and dog Dingo, in their house on the lake in Blackberry Falls.

PROLOGUE - HOPE

Casi discovered marriage was more challenging than she anticipated. Kyle became frustrated with her living in LA while he remained in Washington. When Casi came home for Christmas she tried to tell him about the failure of her business venture with Alix, but she was rushed in for emergency surgery for a ruptured ovarian cyst. Reacting on advice from the doctor, Kyle signed for a tubal ligation, believing it was in her best interest. Feeling disconnected and angry with him, Casi fled back to LA.

Jake had a fling with Sonya on the beach in Hawaii, acting out when he felt Lia was being clingy. Lia informed Jake she was pregnant and was surprised by his reaction. When he failed to commit to her, she questioned whether she should keep the baby.

Sonya convinced Casi to do a racy editorial, not telling her about what else she planned. When Alix realized the trouble Casi was in, he called Kyle to come to LA. Jake and Kyle discovered her unconscious with signs of an assault. After a scuffle getting the pictures from the editorial, Kyle was shot and ended up in the hospital. Once returning to Washington, Kyle took charge, overwhelming Casi with his controlling behavior. She grew closer to Jake as he comforted her and confided secrets and anxieties. Mary stepped in and offered Casi a position in her skincare line, wanting her to be an independent woman. Casi's new profession suited her, and she soon blossomed into a successful businesswoman. She became close friends with Anna, the woman Jake had fallen in love with. Anna helped Casi create a professional appearance and shared her trade experience.

Casi met Kyle's ex-girlfriend, Lauren, at Lia's baby shower and was mortified to learn he kept secrets from her, while over-sharing with Lauren. After Lia gave birth to Austin, Casi convinced them not to give him up for adoption. She took care of the infant while Lia wrestled with post-partum depression. Jake also turned to ex-wife, Gail, for advice.

Casi's father, Jack, and stepmother, Ava, faced new problems as Sonya intervened in their close relationship, creating a wedge between them as she ignited past sorrows. Kyle took a stand against Sonya's meddling, settling her in the loft in LA, and away from Casi.

While Jake's love for Anna grew, he discovered Lia was pregnant again. Anna revealed she was marrying a wealthy business tycoon, which devastated Jake. Lia wanted to terminate the accidental pregnancy, but Jake insisted they should become a family and raise the two children together. They married in Vegas, realizing the union was doomed.

PROLOGUE - TRUST

Kyle and Casi settled into happily married life in their house by the lake. Casi continued to thrive in her career, traveling more and focusing on professional opportunities. Her mother claimed to be abandoned in LA once everyone dismissed her drama. Casi bought a cottage in Blackberry Falls in hopes of relocating her mother and providing a stable and safer environment. After a painful night in LA rescuing her from a nightclub, Casi realized there was little she could do to change Sonya's behavior. She called Kyle for help when she suspected Sonya would not come willingly. He rushed to her aid with Jake in tow, but instead discovered Sonya had overdosed. Alix stood by Casi while she struggled with the reality of her mother's death.

Casi insisted on walking the runway at a lingerie show to prove she left LA on her own terms. The video went viral when she dominated the catwalk with her sexy rendition. When Kyle figured out Casi had used cocaine to aid in her fearless performance, he revealed his former college party lifestyle, including using and selling cocaine. Jake was angered by the information and betrayed by his brother's secret drug use.

Kyle planned a cruise for the families to spend time together and included Anna and Charlotte, on Lia's insistence. Lies and confessions unexpectedly unravelled on the trip after Casi tried to figure out what was causing her night terrors. Kyle confessed he had been falsely accused of rape in college by a disgruntled classmate who later tried to make amends. Jack revealed the truth about his brother, Jamie, who was married to Ava. He was killed in a car accident, and Ava lost her unborn child. Ava also confided how her relationship with Jack began and the deep love she had for Casi since she was born. The truth brought the families closer, and new bonds were formed.

PROLOGUE - SEEK

Casi and her family traveled to her mother's hometown in Northern Canada to put her to rest. They discovered it was a compound with a cult-like existence, and Casi refused to leave the ashes. Ava revealed she knew more about Sonya's past than she had let on, causing Jack to question what else she was hiding. Kyle insisted Casi decide what to do with the remains, wanting closure. She settled on casting them out to sea on the coast of Vancouver. When they returned, her friends had gathered to comfort her, and she reunited with her long-lost friend Katie, who had married the local drug dealer, Shane, now reformed.

Kyle was disturbed by memories of his boating accident as the twenty-year anniversary approached. He attempted to swim to the cave where Grady drowned to see if he could have saved him, but Peter confessed Grady had been decapitated when the boat capsized. When Olivia acted out and challenged Kyle, he disclosed the truth about Tara being alive and their early years of abuse and gave Jake disturbing documentation.

Lauren began dating the heir of a winery in the Columbia Valley, Dalton. Libby announced her secret marriage to Earl to ensure she was his advocate as his dementia progressed.

Casi planned an epic trek through Scandinavia to help Kyle complete his original trip he had intended to do with Grady. Before they left, Casi received disturbing photos of her mother indicating she was murdered. She had a blow out fight with Kyle when he misinterpreted the situation. She raced to LA to confront the blackmailer while Kyle was left devastated and confused. Lauren witnessed the fight and assumed their marriage ended. Ava and Mary teamed up to cover Casi's tracks and forced her to go to Scandinavia with Jake and Kyle to keep her safe. Casi smuggled Grady's ashes in her bag, knowing Kyle would be prevented from traveling with undocumented human remains. Kyle was able to complete his mission of scattering Grady's ashes, which brough him tremendous comfort. Casi shared a disturbing journal documenting the cult her mother had grown up in and admitted she attempted to kill the blackmailer. Ava met them in Austria at Mary's home to disclose the truth about the accident in Edmonton and the lies to keep Casi safe throughout the years. Kyle was fascinated by the rituals, but they agreed it was safest to burn the journal and end Sonya's tragic tale. Jack was appalled he had been naïve to the coverup and the shocking confession Ava and Mary were sisters.

Ava and Jack accompanied them to Italy to bond as a family before the trio continued to the French Riviera. Casi discovered Deshawn Mathews at a casino and forced him to be accountable for the hit-and-run accident in LA.

Anna met them in France for the final week and indulged them in fancy hotels, dinners, spas, and a cooking class. Kyle fell in love with the European architecture and history and Casi made secret plans to purchase a spectacular antique sideboard. Anna confessed she had gone to France when she became pregnant after the rape and gave birth to a daughter. Jake proposed to Anna on the top of the Eiffel tower, and she accepted.

1

MORELS AND MOROSE

"Are you sure?" Amy hesitated at the counter as she cradled the calico cat, Jezebel. "I usually wait for Kyle to return to update him on how things went while he was away." She stroked the cat's fur. "I was looking forward to hearing about his trip to Scandinavia." Dingo sat at her side in acknowledgment of her loyalty. "I should ensure their flight from Paris hasn't been delayed. Dingo doesn't eat for another hour. I'm not sure how Kyle would feel about changing his schedule." She scanned Lauren as she bustled around the kitchen.

"I'm Kyle's best friend and I can handle feeding his dog." Lauren rolled her eyes. "He is dealing with personal issues and has not been in the mood to call or text. His absence from social media, while not unusual, is a sign he requires space." She reflected on the sudden disappearance of Casi's accounts, replaced with generic place holders, specifically noting the blank relationship status and location of LA. It could only mean the relationship had ended, and she was taking a break before announcing it to her adoring followers. She masked her inner glee at the prospect and held firm to her insistence to take over the maintenance of the beautiful lake house.

Amy shifted her stance. "I wanted to ensure the house was ready for them when they returned from such a long flight."

Stupid girl, it'll only be Kyle! The super-model wife has gone back to LA. Lauren smirked and surveyed the expansive living room with floor to ceiling windows overlooking the serene lake, and her heart expanded with joy to think it would soon belong to her. And finally, Kyle would be hers again. Mr. and Mrs. Jensen. She caught the questioning look on Amy's face and cleared her throat. "The house is tidy, and Kyle would prefer to be alone. He'll pay you at the wood shop tomorrow."

Amy checked her watch. "I'm not concerned about the money. Call me if he doesn't arrive on time. Jezebel can be fickle about who feeds her."

Who cares if the ridiculous cat eats? "Thanks for understanding. It's important we support Kyle." Lauren patted her hand and expedited her departure.

Amy gathered her things and hugged Dingo and Jezebel before she left. "Your mommy and daddy will be home soon."

Lauren squared her shoulders and regarded the picturesque view. "This is the moment I take charge of my future." She smoothed her hands over the granite slab she had personally chosen to complete the modern appeal of the kitchen, insisting the commercial fixtures would complement the Pacific Northwest style home. She bit her lip as her mind slipped back to the warm summer day when Kyle stood there beaming with a sense of accomplishment. He had gazed at her with sapphire eyes, sharing his happiness. Her heart expanded when he leaned in and kissed her; firm lips touching her own quivering mouth. She had loved him for so long, settling for the gift of his friendship while he played the field and kept an impenetrable boundary between them. The kiss shattered the barrier and let loose the floodgates of emotions hidden within her. Although the next few years held heartache and ultimately ripped her soul out when he ended the relationship, the first tender moment was her beacon of hope he had once cared for her. A shiver ran down her spine at the memory and the prospect of rekindling what they once had, as her mother predicted. Let him have his fun with the gorgeous, curvaceous woman; allow him to get it out of his system. The timing was perfect. Her ovulation kit indicated she was at her peak and the fertility pills would ensure a positive outcome. There would be no waiting like last time. No silly games. She would take him in her arms and soothe his broken soul, listening as he unleashed his anguish about the selfish wife who left him. The lovemaking would be sweet. The result would be a child. And her dreams would come true.

She busied herself preparing his favorite meal, veal parmigiana with homemade pasta and mushroom sauce. She had driven across Seattle to find the perfect morels for the dish, delicate in flavor yet earthy and robust. Thanks to Lia and another failed romance, she had to source the produce from another vendor. She sighed as she filled the pot with water. Her sister was an easy target. No man had to wait to get in her bed. Now she was dating a married man, again. Why was she such a mess? And yet, silly Lia lived in an ideal cottage with lace curtains, watching her adorable little boys play in the manicured yard. She slammed the lid on the pot. Not fair! At least she had a better job than her sister, a real career. "Kyle admires my ambition. I'm strong, smart, and independent. I own a condo and I'm excelling in the culinary field," she repeated the mantra.

She removed the cherry mascarpone tarts from the oven and set them on a rack, eyeing a long scratch on the granite. The insidious woman insisted on cutting directly on the counter. She was useless in the kitchen. For God's sake, she couldn't even make coffee! Kyle had spent so much time and money to build his dream house, and the only room his ignorant wife excelled in was the bedroom. It wouldn't matter. This time she would be the lover he desired. She had vanquished reservations about certain acts and forced herself to watch those dirty movies men liked. If he required it, she would deliver. Casi might be stunning with a perfect body, but she couldn't love Kyle the way she could. Her love was genuine and deep.

"Lauren?" Kyle approached with a smile.

"Surprise!" She spun around to face him, and the blood drained from her face. *Why was she in his arms? Clinging to him like they were about to make love! Their marriage is over! She left him...*

"Are you ok?" Kyle raised an eyebrow. "I assume you were expecting us if you were cooking."

Just you, not her. "Yes, of course. I figured you would be tired after traveling and would appreciate a home cooked meal. I didn't hear you come in."

"How incredibly thoughtful." He put an arm around her shoulders in a warm greeting before dipping a spoon in the sauce. "Perfect menu. We went on a truffle hunting excursion and did a cooking class in Italy."

"It was divine," Casi said with a knowing smile. "We had the best time discovering Italy. It was a dream vacation."

Kyle reached for Casi's hand and led her to the bedroom. "We'll take a quick shower and be out in a jiffy. I have a nice bottle of Pinot Noir to pair with the meal."

"Stupid bitch," Lauren swore under her breath. She was tempted to throw the food in the trash. She regarded the ingredients perfectly portioned for two and seethed at the intrusion.

"What?" Kyle asked as he stepped in the shower beside Casi.

"Seriously?" she laughed. "Lauren planned a romantic dinner for two. I'm not surprised my meltdown indicated our marriage was over. I'm guessing you didn't tell her we worked things out in one of your secret texts."

He kissed her forehead. "I told you every time I sent her a message. You asked me not to include anything about you. I wasn't being secretive about our relationship." He kneaded his temple. "It was unintentional to mislead her. What should I do?"

Casi put a hand to his chest. "I'll take my time getting ready. Talk to her. As much as I don't care for her, I caused this mess, and it's not fair for her to be hurt, again."

Kyle entered the kitchen with towel-dried hair and the glimmer of a god as he smiled at Lauren and opened the bottle of wine. "It surprised me to find you here."

She glanced toward the bedroom and heard a blow-dryer. "You

worked things out? I was worried your trip would be ruined with the drama." She inhaled sharply. "I didn't want you to return to an empty house after the state you were in when you left." She glanced at the ragged red scar along his forearm.

"What a shit-show. I'm sorry you had to witness it. The first few days were tough, and Casi was overwhelmed by a ton of emotional crap. After we dealt with it, the time away helped us focus on our marriage. It brought us closer, and we realized nothing will ever tear us apart. Jake was a great help since he adores Casi and is probably our best cheerleader." He blushed. "He smuggled our rings to Europe and insisted we put them back on."

"How thoughtful." Her heart shattered into a million pieces and she swallowed the bitter taste of regret.

Kyle reached past her and added a plate to the other two set on the stove to warm. "I'm sorry if my texts were unclear. I wanted to share the sites we were seeing, and Casi had asked me not to include any information on her." He noted the tears in her eyes. "I appreciate your friendship and how you're always available to help me, especially when my life implodes."

She stirred the mushroom sauce. "I'll always support you."

"Hey, guess what?" He poured the wine. "Jake and Anna got engaged. She met us in France, and we went to a bakery specializing in canelés. I bought the copper molds, and the owner gave us lessons. You should have seen the hutch she had in the kitchen." He clutched his chest. "Absolutely stunning! The craftsmanship and intricate detail were outstanding. Right, Casi?" He turned as she approached in a pink cotton dress and bare feet.

"It was elaborate and suited your unique taste. It's a shame you don't want to remodel this pedestrian style." Casi gulped at the words straight out of her mother's mouth. She shivered at the idea the woman who caused so much harm held a place inside her.

"Why would you change this perfect space?" Lauren gasped.

"Believe me, if you saw this piece you would rip these generic materials out and redesign it to complement the antique cabinet. Oh well, in another lifetime," he chuckled. "We bought dishes in Paris."

"What's wrong with the white ones?" Lauren cocked her head.

"They're white," Casi giggled. "The new ones have a similar pattern to the cabinet Kyle fell in love with." She plucked a scrap of veal from the pan and fed it to Jezebel, as the cat purred with delight. "Did Kyle tell you about Jake and Anna?"

Lauren glared at her thoughtless act. "I'm shocked Anna accepted. I figured she wasn't in a rush to get married again."

"Thank God she did." Kyle sipped his wine. "He proposed at the top of the Eiffel Tower under a full moon with a ring he bought in Italy. It would have been horrifying if she refused."

"It was the most romantic proposal," Casi chimed in.

Kyle frowned. "Better than mine?"

Casi threw her head back and laughed. "Yours was unexpected and heartfelt. I love how you planned everything so perfectly." She recalled the remodeled closet and the tiny kitten with the pink bow securing the stunning diamond ring around its neck. "You already owned my heart, so I was thrilled to give you my hand."

"Good answer." Kyle chuckled and clinked his glass to hers before turning to Lauren. "Thanks for welcoming us home. The trip was amazing, but it's nice to be back to reality."

2

DEFAULT

Fran staggered through the kitchen in disbelief of the news relayed by her daughter. "You said she threw the ring at him! Why would Kyle take her back? I figured he went to Europe with his brother to clear his head. Do you think she followed him and begged him to give her another chance when she realized no one else would want her?"

"I don't know, Mom. He was completely distraught. I've never seen him so broken. Is it possible to win a man back with sex?" Lauren contemplated the scenario, incensed by Kyle's weakness. "Lia seems to get everything she wants by being a doormat." She regarded her mother wincing in pain and directed her to a chair. "Is your knee still bothering you?"

"Your sister is a hopeless romantic. She's convinced a man will fall in love with her if she gives him a good time in the sack." Fran rubbed her leg. "The doctor said the injections aren't working anymore and surgery is the next step."

"When can they schedule it? I'll take time off work if you need me." Lauren mentally calculated the impact of being away from her job during the busy summer season.

"He has an opening at the end of the month. Lia can help me, her job is minimal, and she has Jake helping her pay the bills." Fran cocked her head. "Perhaps your sister isn't as naïve as we believe. She married a Jensen, although not the good one. I have to admit her sons are adorable even though she raises them like wild animals."

"Casi's influence."

"True. What was wrong with Dalton? I realize you're in love with Kyle, but maybe we forced the timeline. You've been taking the fertility drugs like I suggested? I would like a granddaughter from you before your biological clock runs out."

"I believed I had an opportunity to reunite with Kyle." Lauren shrugged. "I could contact Dalton and make an excuse work has been intense which is why I needed space."

"Focus on your goals, Lauren. A child is a priority and then your restaurant. Your friendship with Kyle will have to suffice for now, and Dalton is respectable enough for a husband. His family is wealthy, so perhaps you can convince him to fund your endeavor if you give them an heir."

"My relationship with Kyle will only grow stronger over time. He'll see how determined I am to achieve my goals and I could make him the godfather of my child." Lauren sat back with determination.

"Thanks for meeting me." Lauren twisted the napkin to calm her nerves. She didn't want to appear desperate and weighed her words carefully. "I was concerned our relationship might impact my career. It's difficult for a woman to be taken seriously in the culinary world and your family's association through the winery..."

Dalton reached over and clutched her hand. "My family can be intimidating. I'm glad you wanted to talk. We have a connection and who knows what kind of partnership we can create?" He left the question dangling while he sipped his wine, considering the flavor profile. His lips curled into a smile. "Our winery has been gaining popularity. Do you realize what could make it skyrocket?" Lauren shook her head. "My father is considering creating a restaurant. It was my suggestion, of course. He wants to bring in a celebrity chef from Napa, but I have someone else in mind." He gave her hand a squeeze. "Do you think you would be interested?"

"Are you serious? Why would they choose me over a celebrity? I don't have name recognition."

"I'll be honest." Dalton swirled his wine and watched the beads of cabernet drip down the sides. "There would be an investment on your part. Moving our winery to the Columbia Valley impacted our finances, and bringing in a well-known chef isn't feasible. It would be an amazing opportunity to have your own place."

Lauren smiled and considered the offer. "I appreciate your honesty and in return I want to lay my cards on the table." She altered the truth to sound sincere. "I'm at the top of my game in my career. Opening my own place is the next step and I would excel at the challenge." She smoothed the tablecloth and exhaled. "On a personal level, I want to get married and have a child. I'm at an age where I must expedite things. I sense you would be a good partner and I've reconsidered the amazing qualities you possess and how well we work together."

Dalton clinked his glass to hers. "I like a woman who knows what she wants. I've received a lot of family pressure about settling down and being more involved in the business. I believe fate has brought us back together."

❧

Jake smiled at Lia and Gail sitting together amicably at the table with the boys in the café. He hesitated a moment to watch Gail refilling Tommy's sippy cup while Lia helped Austin color in a book. They chatted good-naturedly, comfortable in each other's presence. It surprised him how much the relationships had evolved over the last few years from anger and hurt over his affair with Lia to a close bond of raising the children in a loving and supportive environment.

"Hello, Ladies." He slid in the booth beside them. "And gentleman. Did you miss me?"

"Daddy!" Tommy launched himself at Jake.

Jake kissed his cheek and cuddled him while Austin scrambled over to join. "No issues while we were away?"

Gail glanced at Lia and they giggled. "What was the impromptu relocation about? It was like Blackberry Falls evacuated on cue."

"I'll allow Casi to fill in the details, but basically there was concern about shit her mom had done and how it might affect our family and friends. You were secured in safe locations until the threat cleared," Jake relayed.

"Like a spy movie." Gail shuddered. "Is Casi ok? I noticed her Facebook page changed, and she didn't post vacation pictures. Please tell me the rumor about her and Kyle splitting up is a horrible lie!"

"Casi and Kyle are deeply in love and remain married." Jake stopped himself from stating who would have started the vicious rumor.

"What about Lauren? She didn't go anywhere," Lia said.

Jake frowned at the obvious oversight. "It was only immediate family. How did your vacation go with Shane?"

"Divine," Lia swooned. "It was amazing to have time with him out of cell range from Katie. He's so good with the boys and taught them how to play road hockey. He wants to teach them how to skate. Would you mind?" Lia grabbed a cup as Austin wrestled with Tommy, sending the contents of the table flying.

Jake considered the request. "Maybe a heads up so I don't miss out on a cool first experience. If things go in the direction we hope for, Shane will be a significant part of our lives and I'm happy to share our offspring. Did you meet his daughters?"

"They're like mini Katie clones." Lia shuddered.

Jake chuckled at the image. "Junior neurotics?"

"Katie is giving Shane a hard time about proceeding with a divorce. She won't even let him talk to a lawyer to begin the paperwork." Lia tore at her placemat in annoyance.

"Some ex-partners are so needy. I'm proud to say I hit the road the minute you women told me to." He grinned as they rolled their eyes.

He winked at Gail. "Plus, I have made myself available for reconnecting in the bedroom whenever the desire hits."

"Stop." Gail blushed and hit his arm playfully. "Lia, do the girls know their parents are splitting up?"

"We pretended to meet at the lake by coincidence. Shane kept reiterating he was best friends with my husband, which was why the boys were familiar with him."

Jake turned to the waitress and placed his order and slid the coloring book in front of himself. When the boys fought over the blue crayon, each possessing an immediate desire to fill in the sky, he broke it in half. "Now there are two."

Lia smiled at his gentle manner. "Shane's eldest was paranoid about eating. She was quoting me diet tips and freaked out when Shane bought ice cream. She asked if my husband liked chunky women!"

"I like women of many shapes and sizes," Jake confirmed.

"The middle girl was afraid of the bacteria in the water and screamed when Austin splashed her." Lia shook her head. "So obviously he kept doing it and Tommy mimicked him."

"Of course, that's what brothers do," Jake agreed.

"Shane thought it was hilarious, which pissed the kid off even more." Lia's eyes crinkled with amusement.

"He grew up with brothers. He understands the complexity of the weaker sex." Jake moved the coloring book to make room for the chicken nuggets and fries, ensuring they were split evenly. Austin stole a fry from Tommy's plate and Jake reached around him and ate one from his, making the toddler giggle.

"The youngest girl is sweet, although she doesn't talk, or verbalize, as Shane explained." Lia regarded her children. "We got lucky. I don't think I'm a great mom, but everyone seems to love our kids."

"You're an excellent mother," Gail insisted. "We help because it's what's best for the children. Selfishly, I adore these guys and I can't get enough time with them. Katie is smothering her girls and causing anxiety. It must be nice for Shane to be with the boys."

"Carefree and wild?" Lia laughed. "He gets them riled up like crazy! Austin tripped and got a bloody lip and Shane freaked out." Lia reached out and stroked Austin's cheek. "This kid laughed it off and kept on running."

"Good boy," Jake praised. "You're a true Jensen. When the world knocks you down, get back up and keep going."

"Why did you ask to meet us? Did you get lonely in Europe? You're looking super-fit, by the way." Gail lifted the hem of his t-shirt while she and Lia admired his rippled abs.

"I must decline any actions to move this forward." Jake grinned and gave them a wink. "I proposed to Anna. You should hear it from me, not the gossip channel. I comprehend how this affects you and our blended family. If you have any concerns, we can talk about them. I'm aware of my history of failures, but in this case my ill-begotten child is already on the planet and thriving without my support."

Gail grasped his hand. "We adore Anna and she's the perfect woman to keep you in line. Charlotte might not require your financial support, but little girls need their daddy."

"Will they live at the lake? It would be nice to have Charlotte spend more time with her brothers." Lia surveyed Austin attempting to fit a French fry in his brother's ear. "Unless you think they'll be too rough with her. We can arrange different days for custody."

Jake extracted the fry and tossed it to the side. "Anna doesn't jump into things. She agreed to a summer wedding at the lake. Nothing is planned, and I'm slightly concerned now she and Casi are back to work, the whole affair will be a low priority."

"I can help," Gail offered. "You know how much I love planning events and coordinating the details. Our wedding was a circus, but I learned a lot from putting together Mary Ann's."

"You excel in the planning arena," Jake agreed. "Would it be possible to phone Anna, maybe in the pretense of congratulating her and extend your offer? I'm trying not to appear anxious."

"Can I help too? I never did anything for our wedding. Vegas was cool for our temporary nuptials, but a lakeside ceremony sounds ideal." Lia's eyes lit up at the prospect.

"Let's propose meeting for happy hour with Anna and Casi." Gail marked the time in her calendar with determination.

Jake grinned as he surveyed the women bent toward each other, excitedly exchanging ideas. "It's handy to have two ex-wives to plan the details for my third wedding."

Lauren twisted the band on her finger as she walked to the front door. She pushed her annoyance aside at the fact she had to finance her own ring due to Dalton's trust fund issues. She glanced at the classic solitaire and swallowed her bitterness at the recollection Kyle had once purchased the exact one. She was surprised by the hammering and commotion penetrating the vibration of the hard rock music. Since Casi moved in, it wasn't uncommon for the house to be taken over by pop songs, but Kyle usually preferred the serenity of the lake when he was home. She had checked Casi was out of town when she made plans to visit wanting to ensure Kyle's undivided attention as she announced her engagement.

"Hello?" She pushed the door and froze. Tarps covered furniture in the living room and dust swirled throughout the home.

"Heads up." She scooted aside as Jake and Riley carried a cabinet past her to the driveway. "Kyle, try to keep the damn things intact. I want to install them in my house to convince Anna it's livable." Jake smoothed his hand over a cracked board.

"Sorry, I got excited about my vision." Kyle assessed the room as he stood in the bare space. His leather tool belt hung low on his hips, accentuating his physique. He wiped a bead of sweat from his brow and grinned as he noticed Lauren. "Hey, what do you think?"

"What the hell are you doing?" Her heart broke as she surveyed Jake dismantling the cabinet she had leaned against when Kyle kissed her for the first time.

"Check this out." Kyle pulled a sheet back from a large antique pine cabinet with intricate porcelain inlay. "This is the hutch I mentioned from the bakery in Bordeaux. Casi secretly bought it and had it shipped with the other things we purchased. I'm tearing out the old kitchen and rebuilding it with this vintage concept. It'll be incredible."

Lauren squeezed her eyes shut, not wanting to witness the destruction. She exhaled through her nose, counting to ten before she spoke. "Awesome." He nodded at the false assurance, barely able to hear her over the music. She stepped over to the stereo and turned it off. "I got engaged." She held out her hand to showcase the ring, wanting to add the excitement about the possibility of a restaurant but remembering to keep it a secret until the family approved it.

Kyle raised an eyebrow. "To whom?" He glanced at the ring, unaware of the similarity to the one he had previously bought.

Lauren cleared her throat in irritation of the idiotic question. "Dalton, obviously."

"Huh, I thought you broke up." Kyle continued to measure a space beside the sink.

"Our relationship was on hold while I completed some work challenges." She seethed at his lack of attention. "I can come back later when you're not busy."

Kyle rose from his knees and grinned. "Sorry, this project has me preoccupied. Congratulations on the engagement. When is the wedding?" He gave her a hug, and she wanted to cling to him.

"October. We haven't announced anything officially, but I wanted to share it with you."

"Good weather in the Fall." He scratched his head and considered the kitchen. "I need to get this done. Jake's wedding is next week, and I can't have it in shambles. I sent you the details, right? My brain has been overloaded, and the invitations were extremely casual, since it's the third time." He smacked Jake on the back.

"Hopefully this one will stick." Jake chuckled.

"Yes, I received your text." Lauren swallowed dryly at the recollection of the informal reminder. "I assume I can bring Dalton?"

"Of course." Kyle grinned. "He's your fiancé now."

"The more the merrier." Jake turned the music back on. "Gail and

Lia are planning everything so tell them in case they have seating charts and organized shit depending on numbers."

❧

Anna threw a balled-up straw wrapper at Casi across the table. "Did you hear anything I said?"

Casi grinned and sipped her coffee. "Not a word."

"Damn it, you're the maid of honor. Why are you not more involved?" Anna feigned annoyance.

"You said to show up and look pretty." Casi saved her document and gave Anna her full attention. "Are there additional requirements?"

Anna flopped back in her chair. "I need emotional support. My family is meeting Jake for the first time at my damn wedding. We tried to arrange dinner, but Charlotte was running a fever. Am I making a huge mistake? Will you hate me if I cancel this whole thing?"

"Yes, you'll break Jake's heart." Casi grabbed her hand. "I suck at party planning, which is why you accepted help from Lia and Gail. The day will be incredible, and Gail will run it like a drill sergeant. You love Jake and you've birthed his kid. Let's face it, you're committed."

"I do love him." Anna slouched. "Will I go insane in his life, though? Living at the lake and family dinners? The boys are cute, but I'm comfortable in my routine with Charlotte."

"After Kyle and I married, I continued to model in LA. You don't have to make significant changes."

"Except your life imploded, and you hit rock bottom while Kyle was almost killed." Anna cocked her head.

"Well, sure if you want to focus on the negative." Casi threw her head back and laughed. "Take it a step at a time. Jake will not rush you to move in. He's immensely happy living across from his brother and it suits my purposes because I'm insanely busy with travel."

"How are the accounts going?" Anna turned the computer to regard the screen. "Damn, you snagged another one in New York?"

"Yup, and it's huge." Casi scrolled through the numbers. "Are you fine handling the local stores by yourself?"

"I love it. This company is a dream to work for and Mary's my idol. I'm afraid my life will become mundane once I get married. The first one was such a disaster."

"You committed to the wrong guy." Casi snapped the computer closed. "Let's get pedicures and wine to celebrate."

"Sounds divine." Anna gathered her belongings. "You're right. My life won't change because I'm someone's wife again. I'll focus on the positive like having my best friend across the street from me."

"Happy hour every night!" Casi promised.

3

THE BEGINNING OF THE END

Kyle regarded Jake, building a frame as he listened to hard rock music and sang the chorus. "You're in a good mood." He gripped the letter tighter as he leaned against the bench saw.

Jake glanced up from his project and analyzed his brother's demeanor. "Did you come to tell me the wedding is off? Don't sugar-coat it; tear it off like a bandage."

"I need to share something with you but it's not about Anna."

"Kyle, get to the point. I don't have all day to guess the millions of things waiting to crush me."

Kyle raised an eyebrow. "Top three?"

"Something happening to you, Casi, or our parents." Jake sucked in air. "Obviously, my kids."

"What about Dingo?"

"Screw the dog. I would be appropriately sad for you, but it wouldn't rock my world." Jake set down his tools and cringed. "Oh God, you don't have cancer, do you? Losing you is at the top of my list."

"We're all healthy." He put his hand on Jake's shoulder. "Except Tara. She's dead. Someone found her unconscious at the pier and alerted the authorities. They transferred her to the morgue and found me as her next of kin through the shelter. They need instructions for what to do with her remains." Kyle exhaled as the finality set in.

Jake turned the screw gun over in his hands and contemplated the information. "My only regret is she was never lucid enough to tell us what the hell went so wrong in her life to abandon us."

"Only me. She always wanted you." Kyle shivered at the thought of how his life would have been altered if the Jensens hadn't adopted them. "I have nothing but resentment for her and thankfulness for the universe delivering us to our real family."

Jake hugged Kyle. "I'm thankful she gave me you. It would have been a very lonely ride on my own."

"Let's have her cremated and buried at the cemetery with our birth father? Her wandering days are over, and she can be settled finally." Kyle smacked Jake on the back. "We can have lunch in Seattle and get this taken care of this afternoon."

"After, can we go to Elmvale and tell Mom and Dad in person? They should hear it from us."

"Good idea. Mom has been prying about what happened between me and Casi and I don't think she's convinced it was a misunderstanding our marriage was over."

"Gee, I wonder who gave her the gory details?"

"Exactly. She thinks I'm putting on a brave face, but I'm concerned she hates Casi now."

Georgia plastered a smile on her face and gripped the counter when her sons walked in the kitchen. "You came for a visit? Is the wedding off?" She glanced at the stack of recipes for the desserts she had been planning. "I haven't bought the ingredients yet."

"Both you and Jake jumped to the same conclusion. Is everyone having doubts?" Kyle kissed her cheek and held up his left hand. "Casi and I are still married and very much in love. Her episode, as you refer to it, was caused by disturbing information about her mother. I overreacted, and unfortunately, Lauren misinterpreted what she witnessed. We had a great time on our trip, and we're not hiding anything."

Peter entered through the back door and his shoulders slumped. "Well, at least this time it ended before the ceremony." He raised an eyebrow. "It's Jake's marriage that imploded, right?"

"My nuptials are still on, although there's still a week to go." Jake grinned. "Kyle and Casi are perfect. Tara bit the dust and we were in Seattle taking care of the details."

"Wonderful news." Georgia covered her mouth. "In regard to the wedding, and Kyle's marriage. I'm sorry to hear about Tara."

Peter surveyed his sons. "Are you boys ok? It's natural to feel upset about her death. She was your biological mother."

"She was nothing to me," Kyle scoffed. "Her only purpose was bringing me into the world to give to you. For the short time she had custody she abused me and throughout the years her contribution has been a soul-sucking leech costing me money and causing me concern for my brother's welfare."

"Don't hold back." Jake squeezed his shoulder. "I agree. I don't remember any of the positive impact of my early years. I believed she was already dead for the last dozen years and discovering she wasn't only brought disgust at her life choices." He felt Kyle's glare. "Yes, her poor judgement has convinced me drugs are bad."

"Was it an overdose?" Peter guessed.

"Most likely. She was considered a transient, so they didn't do an autopsy. We paid to have her cremated and buried near Tommy." Kyle glanced up as Libby came in and glided over to hug them. "I'm unsure if I should continue to send money to the shelter. It was meant for her care, but maybe others benefitted." He set a package down. "These were her personal effects."

"Not much to show for fifty-odd years," Peter observed.

Kyle tore the box open. "I'm sure they confiscated any drugs." He tossed photos on the counter of Tara with Tommy and Jake, and only guitar picks and concert ticket stubs remained.

Libby picked up a photo and shook her head. "Drop these off on your way back and have them buried with her. She stopped living years ago and there is no value in any of this for you boys. As far as the money is concerned, I suggest you donate it to a rehab center instead. Perhaps you can turn around a life before they get to the point of no return."

Ava put her hands to the sides of Jake's face and brought her lips to his. He stood frozen, afraid to tarnish the moment. She kissed him tenderly before stepping back with a smile. "Congratulations."

"Completely unnecessary display of emotion. He gets hitched every other year." Jack winked and shook Jake's hand. "Try to make this one stick. I'm tired of you trying to steal my woman."

"I'll never relinquish the hunt," Jake confirmed.

Ava grasped Georgia's arm in the middle of the living room, turning to point at the newly remodeled kitchen. "This is gorgeous! Did Kyle design it himself? It's stunning with the cabinet as the centerpiece."

"I did." Kyle smiled as he joined them. "It was a huge surprise to open the crate and discover the hutch I lusted after. I couldn't believe Casi could pull off something so monumental."

"I inherited his cast-offs, so my house looks like a rummage sale, which isn't ideal for my new bride." Jake scowled at his brother.

"It was imperative my kitchen was finished for your wedding. Plus, I wanted Casi to know how much I appreciated her generous gift. Patience is not her strong suit, although maybe she's successful in her career because she charges ahead with ideas."

"She could rule the world if she set her mind to it," Mary agreed. "The remodel suits the house beautifully and incorporates your unique personalities."

"I love the vintage touches similar to the farmhouse," Georgia remarked, noting several pieces she had given him. "They never seemed right in the modern kitchen."

Ava smoothed her hand over the countertops. "This makes me want to redo the bar. What do you think, Jack? The restaurant could use a facelift."

"We sell drinks just fine. Your sassy friend would be out of place in such a fancy environment." Jack chuckled.

"I'll tell Roxy." Ava smiled. "Where's Casi?"

"Looking for someone to zip me. This dress was not easy to put on and Anna's finishing her makeup." Casi turned to the side as Ava slid the zipper up. She twirled, letting the floral chiffon flutter about her curvaceous hips and long lean legs.

"You look lovely, Darling." Jack gave her a kiss on the cheek.

"Anna picked it out. I'm her only bridesmaid because she felt it would be too much with her sisters and it wasn't fair to pick a couple. Plus, the pregnant one would be a spectacle at this stage of the game. Kyle is the best man."

"Yet again." Kyle chuckled. He led them to the bar and nodded to the server finishing the setup. "I'll take over."

Jake grinned and extended his hand to Shane. "Glad you could make it..." He stopped when Katie stepped up beside him, eagerly searching the patio. "What the hell?" he mouthed.

Shane winced as Lia rushed toward them. "Perfect timing."

Jake put an arm around Lia's waist, spinning her toward the garden when he noted the tears about to erupt. "This way to the bar."

"Where's Casi?" Katie demanded. "I haven't seen her in ages, and I figured this would be the only place I might catch her."

"I'll have to thank her," Jake mumbled. "She's difficult to find these days. A million work projects are whisking her away."

Shane gazed sorrowfully at Lia and tuned out Katie's incessant nagging. "Jake do you need a hand?" He grabbed the keg, swiftly opening the tap. "These can be a bugger without the proper tools."

"Why is she here?" Jake scowled at the unwanted guest. "Lia expected you as her date."

"I was backing out of the driveway and she jumped in the car. I couldn't even text with a warning." Shane poured a draft. "You know how I feel about Lia. She's not a hookup for me."

"I don't want her getting hurt." Jake glanced at Lia helping Gail with the flowers and figured she was discussing the situation. He noticed a stout red-haired man arrive and smacked Shane on the back. "Find a way to make it up to her. I have to meet my father-in-law."

The man surveyed the patio and directed his gaze to Jake as he approached. "I assume you're the groom?"

"I'm sorry this is the first time we're meeting, Mr. O'Shea." Jake grasped his hand firmly and nodded to the petite woman at his side. "Mrs. O'Shea. I realize custom would dictate I asked for your daughter's hand in marriage, but Anna seems to be in control of her choices, and I wouldn't want to offend her."

Mr. O'Shea omitted a deep guttural laugh. "You know my daughter well."

Jake introduced Austin and Tommy as they scrambled over, pointing to his older children with Gail. "As you can see, we have a tight-knit family. Although unconventional, we pitch in to make it work." He smiled at a woman as she approached with a hand on her large belly. "Hi, Grace. How's the pregnancy?"

"Dreadful." She smiled. "Anna doesn't realize how easy she has it. You're an amazing father."

"Are you keeping the paternity secret?" Mr. O'Shea sighed and regarded the scotch Jake handed him. "I realize I'm old-fashioned."

"Actually, I'll introduce you now." Grace grinned, watching her father's face drop. "Not Jake, although he would have been an ideal candidate. Brian, come meet my family."

Jake chuckled. "Our accountant is your donor?"

"Casi suggested him." Grace hugged Brian and Dylan. "As a bonus, I was also referred to the best hairdresser in town."

Brian blushed as he was quizzed by the family. He felt Lauren's angry glare before she approached. "You fathered a child?" she scoffed.

He straightened his back, remembering how Dylan had coached him not to be intimidated by bossy women. "I've always wanted children, and this was the perfect opportunity for us."

"I get to be an aunt," Dylan asserted.

"I'm pretty sure you'll be an uncle." Brian smiled at him with adoring eyes, radiating the love between them.

"Whatever. My niece will be the best-dressed princess in the neighborhood." Dylan patted Grace's bump. "I'll give Casi a run for her money when it comes to glamor."

"You're having a girl?" Lauren bit the side of her lip.

"She's due in three months. Fiona Lillian." Grace smiled.

"Fifi for short," Dylan announced.

Lauren furrowed her brow. "This is my fiancé, Dalton. His family has a new winery in the valley."

"New to the area. We're the fourth generation." Dalton surveyed the group with distrust.

"Congratulations." Brian gave Lauren an awkward hug.

Lauren shrugged. "You can pass along the news to Lance."

"Sure." Brian smiled at Lia as she joined the group. "Although I believe your sister is quite close with your brother."

"Lance wishes you well." Lia confirmed. "You should consider inviting him. It's time to put the past behind you."

Casi flounced toward them in a semi-sheer floral dress with a tulip hem. "Outrageous," Dylan praised, twirling her around.

"You are breathtaking." Mr. O'Shea gently kissed her cheek. "A vision, as always."

"Thank you. Your daughter is ready for last-minute words of wisdom." Casi smiled warmly at Anna's family, giving Grace a pat on the belly. "When will my new protégé be fully baked?"

"A few more months, but you might have to fight Dylan for her."

Dylan playfully shoved Casi aside. "This one's my plaything. You have the rambunctious boys and the mini ginger."

"Chuckie cheese is like fruitcake." Casi grinned. "Sweet and pretty on the outside, but with bits of evil inside."

Grace howled with laughter. "Our niece is on the spoiled side. Anna needs to reel her in before she becomes a full-blown terror."

"Casi, I've been searching for you." Katie approached with her hand on her hip. "You didn't return my texts."

"Sorry, I've been busy with Anna's wedding." Casi glanced past Shane's wounded expression and noticed Lia hovering. "I didn't realize you would be here today."

"My husband was invited. I assumed I'm included," Katie snipped. "I'm perfectly aware what's going on so let me be clear; this marriage is still in effect, even though you're pretending I don't exist."

"Tough to be on the fringes, isn't it, Katie?" Ava untwisted Casi's strap and whispered, "Focus on Anna. Katie and her drama can wait."

"Georgia." Lauren darted toward her. "Dalton and I are engaged. The wedding will be in the fall."

"Wonderful!" Georgia watched Dalton's eyes glued to Casi's swinging hips beneath her sheer dress. "I'm excited to hear the details."

Mr. O'Shea smiled at Anna perched on the window seat staring at the guests gathering on the patio. "Did you like Jake?" she asked.

"He's extremely handsome." He sat next to her. "He's sincere and I see the love in his eyes for you. You're not making a mistake."

"He's a good man." She smiled at Charlotte, twirling in the garden as her brothers chased her. "It's best for our kids to be together."

He grasped her hand. "Anna, sometimes you have to allow someone else to take control. You've chosen a partner who is loving and kind. Allow him to make decisions and let your guard down."

Anna smiled. "Are you ready to walk me down the aisle?"

He stood and held out his arm. "This time I'll do it without reservations because I know you're in love."

"Where's my brother?" Jake paced the edge of the garden, checking his watch. "Crap, don't tell me Anna backed out, and he's talking her into it."

"No, she's good. He probably got preoccupied with Lauren and plans for her wedding." Casi ducked behind a bush. "Why's Katie here? I didn't want to deal with her issues today."

"I hope her appearance isn't a bad omen." Jake shoved her toward the walkway. "Run, you're in the clear."

Casi raced to the house, taking the steps two at a time. After a quick check of rooms and a nod to Anna, she followed whispers to the garage. She cocked her head and listened.

"I'm not sure what to tell her. I think she's expecting more from me than I'm willing to give. I'm in a difficult position and I'm unclear how to proceed." Kyle's sigh was audible through the door.

"With caution," Libby advised. "Be honest but don't over-commit. It could be an amazing opportunity, but consider your marriage and what might be at risk."

Casi's eyes stung with tears as she tried to decode the conversation. She noted Anna waiting to proceed and rapped at the door. "Kyle? Are you ready?"

He swung the door open, almost colliding with her. "I didn't see you." He cocked his head at her broken expression. "How long have you been there?"

"Long enough."

He offered his aunt a hand to walk up the steps. "Give me a minute to see Libby to her seat." He held a finger up to Jake, frowning at the edge of the patio, as he jogged back inside the house. "The conversation wasn't about you." He tried to recall the order of events and what she may have overheard. "Lauren is asking me to be more involved in her wedding planning than I'm comfortable with. I don't want to cause a rift in our relationship since I realize you don't care for her and I'm testing the boundaries with a friend and former lover."

She smiled. "It will be a comfort to know you're busy when I'm traveling so much."

"You're amazing." He kissed her, swallowing the regret of the slight lie until he could reveal the whole truth.

Gail gave her the thumbs up from the doorway and released Charlotte to toss rose petals down the aisle. The guests cheered her on redirecting her when she wanted to stop at Georgia's chair. Jake held his hand out and she ran to him, dropping the basket on the way. Tommy and Austin were next in line, pushing each other as they fought to hold the pillow with the rings. Casi stepped in and scooted them forward, tucking candy in their tiny hands as an incentive. She smiled at the guests, focusing on Ava and her father and ignoring Lauren's sullen expression. She gave Jake a high-five to a round of laughter. Anna glided on her father's arm, feeling like a fraud in her cocktail length lace dress. She had purposely requested Casi wear something revealing and flirtatious to distract the attention. Her sisters encouraged her with their silent bond, understanding how she despised being on display.

Charlotte grasped her hand and teetered between her parents as the ceremony began. Austin lost interest quickly and ran off to investigate a bug with Tommy on his heels. Gail started to rise, and Jake shook his head indicating it wasn't important to detain the children. Couples held hands and nodded to the sentiments, happy to support the union with the simple vows.

Earl whispered in Libby's ear. "Who's getting married?"

She grasped his hand and smiled, understanding his confusion. "Jake is. It's his third time."

Earl whistled. "Those are all his children?"

"The two older ones as well." Libby pointed.

"Well, as long as Kyle stays with our sweet girl, I guess it doesn't matter who Jake brings into the family."

"Very true."

Jake whispered in Anna's ear while they danced, "Breathe, the hard part is over; enjoy the party with our friends."

She relaxed against his chest. "My family makes me tense." She observed Casi laughing with her own father as they twirled across the dance floor, elegant and skilled in their choreography. "I want you to be close to Charlotte. Don't ever judge her, ok?"

Jake furrowed his brow, unclear where the comment originated until he witnessed the pair. "They're a good example of two people who are imperfect but love without limits. I can promise I'll love my children unconditionally and support whatever road they choose." He smiled and cocked his head toward Olivia, laughing with Kyle as he offered a drink. "She was a handful, but she blossomed this year."

"She's found her niche."

"You don't just get a handsome stud who will keep you satisfied in bed. This deal includes an entire circle of caring people who will never let you down." Jake kissed her tenderly.

"My new tribe."

An upbeat song began, and Dylan secured his place in the middle of the dance floor. "Oh lord, here we go." Jake chuckled as Casi joined him, perfectly mirroring his moves.

Katie pouted on the sidelines, not impressed with the man who proclaimed himself Casi's best friend. The crowd cheered as the dancing intensified and the routine escalated. Like a tornado, Casi scooped up spectators and pulled them to the floor. Kyle slipped between Casi and Dylan with his own display of sexy moves to claim victory.

Casi wrapped her arms around his neck and kissed him deeply, oblivious to anyone around them. "I love you."

Kyle grasped her hips and gazed in her eyes. "I love you too. It's tough to be apart, but don't ever forget how much I need you."

Peter frowned at the pair on the dance floor and turned to Georgia. "We were fed a bunch of malarkey about their marriage being over. Those two are more in love than ever."

Libby smiled. "People view things through their own lenses. You recognize the true nature of their commitment because you see their pure souls." She glanced at Lauren, watching from the sidelines. "She filters out the beauty of the relationship and highlights a tiny flaw, like a speck of dust on a perfect rose."

Georgia grasped her hand and smiled. "Casi brings out the best in Kyle. And Jake. I couldn't bear to lose her."

"Shots!" Shane raised a glass and encouraged others to join.

Jake downed the tequila and held out a hand to Gail to dance the next song. "Thanks for your help with the wedding and the kids. You've been a lifesaver."

"I was thrilled when we first divorced and then incredibly sad. It was hard for me when you were with Lia, yet now, I'm friends with her and Anna. I value the relationship you and I have. I never dreamed we could become so close."

"It's been a hell of a ride. Our marriage was tough because I had a lot of growing up to do. I'm in a good place now and you're still an important part of my life."

Casi giggled with the DJ and whispered in his ear before taking the microphone. "I have a surprise for Jake and Anna." She steadied the glass in her hand.

Kyle winced. "Should I stop her?"

Libby smiled and assessed the crowd, who appeared equally inebriated. "Give her a minute."

Casi adjusted the strap of her dress as it slipped from her shoulder. "Take it off," Dalton cheered.

Libby stopped behind him as she returned from the bar. "You've misjudged your audience. Please keep your teenage antics for your drinking buddies."

Dalton swallowed the remainder of his wine. "Whatever, lady. I know a skank when I see one."

Without hesitation, Libby upended her cocktail over his head. When startled eyes turned toward the commotion, she shrugged. "I guess age has diminished my balance."

"Aunt Libby, are you alright?" Kyle hurried to her side.

"Fine, Darling." She held a middle finger to Dalton in the pretense of sweeping her hair behind her shoulder.

Casi continued to speak without noticing Dalton storm in the house, followed by Lauren. "I've been preoccupied during most of the wedding planning. I couldn't be happier to have my best friend moving in across the street, but I'm also aware of the chaos our tribe will bring to Anna's perfect world." She hesitated momentarily, feeling Katie's glare. "I figured you two could use a little break before settling into our ritual and you didn't plan a honeymoon since we've only been back a short time from Europe. Anna, you've frequented most of the hotels in Seattle." The crowd roared with laughter and

Anna looked aghast while her father chuckled. "I don't mean with men..."

"Have another drink, Monkey, you're doing great!" Jake applauded at the edge of the stage.

"Bite me." Casi sipped her cocktail.

"Not tonight, I have a new wife to take care of. I'll pencil you in for next Tuesday." Jake grinned, and Shane howled in delight of the witty comeback.

Mary chuckled and nudged Ava to rescue the floundering speech. "Anna, since you've lived in Seattle for some time, Casi wanted to choose a new environment you haven't had a chance to explore. As a gift, she has made reservations at the Empress Hotel in Victoria for a romantic weekend." Ava slid her arm around Casi's waist.

Casi smiled meekly. "Thank you. I was circling the drain."

"Perhaps the wrong choice of words." Ava smiled and led her offstage. "Coffee?"

"Nope, I'm going to ride this wave." She slipped to the dance floor, to Kyle's waiting embrace.

Anna wrapped her arms around Casi and joined in their dance. "Other than calling me a whore in front of my family, I appreciate the amazing gift and the thought behind it."

Casi giggled. "My delivery was flawed by alcohol."

Lauren put a hand on Kyle's arm to get his attention as he danced in the crowd. "Hey, we're taking off."

Kyle glanced at his watch. "So soon? The party is just getting started, and we planned a bonfire later." He winked and shook his hips. "Maybe even skinny-dipping."

Lauren smiled. "I'm sure you'll have fun. I have to work tomorrow." She eyed Dalton at the door with his arms crossed over his chest. "We'll get together soon and talk?"

"Sounds good." Kyle chuckled as Shane body-checked him and insisted he take another shot.

"Are you ready?" Katie pursed her lips and tried to get Shane's attention. "I told my mom we'd pick up the kids before midnight."

Shane gyrated on the dance floor, pretending not to hear her. Casi laughed and waved her over. "Katie come dance!"

"No, I'm tired and I think you have enough best friends to hang out with." Katie put a hand on her hip and tapped her foot. "Shane!"

"Give him a damn break," Jake said. "Everyone's having a great time. If you must get back to your kids one of us will take him home in the morning."

"Sure, his girlfriend can drop him off." Katie stormed away.

Ava grabbed her arm. "Calm the down before you get in the car. You're not a teenager anymore and your children depend on you to come home alive."

"Back off, bitch." Katie wrenched her arm away.

Ava leaned closer. "You've downed enough cocktails to put you well over the limit."

"Casi is more wasted than I am."

"She's at home dancing and having fun, not spiraling into a depressed state." Ava narrowed her eyes. "She also didn't do lines of coke in the garden, thinking no one noticed."

Katie's face flushed with rage. "Get off me, whore!"

"You can't hurt me with your juvenile antics." Ava shrugged. "I won't force you to stay since you'll attempt to ruin the party. Jack and I will drop you off and you can leave the car for Shane to take in the morning. It's worth wasting my time to ensure you get home safely. Your mother doesn't deserve more heartbreak over your bad choices." Ava turned to Jack as he approached. "I've offered to give Katie a lift. She's not able to drive. It shouldn't take long to get through the border at this time of night."

Jack assessed the scene and understood it was not out of kindness the arrangement was being made. "Sure, fine."

Kyle observed the heated conversation and turned to Casi. "How much pressure is Katie putting on you to deal with her drama?"

Pain registered in her hazel eyes. "It never ends. My mom harassed me all my life, and now Katie has taken her place."

"Let's keep our needy friends on the sidelines."

"Are you referring to Lauren as well?"

"Yes. She pushes the boundaries of our friendship. We're pulled in too many directions to assist our friends."

"It won't be easier with Anna across the street," she whispered. "Another kid invading our space as well."

"It might be tough. My workload and your career are not simplifying things. Let's focus on one challenge at a time."

"The parents and party poopers are gone." Casi grinned and slipped the straps from her shoulders. "Skinny-dipping!" She ran down the dock and tossed her dress aside as Kyle stripped and chased her.

"Cannonball!" Shane tore off his clothes and led the charge to the lake, grabbing a bottle of tequila on the way.

Anna cradled her head in her hands as she slumped at the counter. "I haven't been hungover in years. I thought I had mastered balancing my drinks, but last night did a number on me."

"We shouldn't have mixed our alcohol." Casi winced.

"It was pretty wild." Jake surveyed the living room. "A responsible adult took charge, right?"

"Ava drove Katie home and Mom has the kids." Kyle yawned and started another pot of coffee.

Gail shuffled to the kitchen with one eye open. "I'll pick them up in Elmvale. I need caffeine. I haven't partied like that since college." She noticed the grin on Jake's face. "Don't worry, I'll take good care of your children while you go on your trip."

"I'm not concerned," he stated.

Anna lifted her head. "Can we postpone the romantic weekend thing? I feel like I might vomit and the idea of being on a ferry is frightening." She grasped Casi's hand. "I appreciate the gift and I'll reimburse you for canceling."

"It won't be a problem to reschedule." Casi smiled. "When we got married, I hit the ground running and my world turned upside down. I should have made my husband a priority."

"Part of the problem was we acted like marriage wouldn't change us. After a rocky start, I believe we're happier than we ever imagined possible." Kyle turned to Casi to confirm.

"Super happy!" Casi gave him a thumbs up.

Anna smiled. "Can we do the trip with the four of us? We're busy with work and it would be nice to get away and spend a weekend shopping and going out to eat. Maybe in the fall?"

"We could do it for my birthday," Casi agreed.

"Perfect, book it. We know I'm terrible at remembering important dates and it would be good to know it's taken care of." Kyle circled the date on the calendar.

Casi halted with the cream hovered above her cup. "We wouldn't want you to stress about my birthday when you have so much to prepare for Lauren's wedding. I'll be sure to plan everything to minimize the burden on you."

"You purposely misinterpreted my comment." Kyle kissed her on the forehead. "My world revolves around you and we'll have a fantastic time celebrating in Victoria."

"Cool, I'm in." Shane reached over Gail for the coffeepot. "I like being part of this group, you're so much fun! Katie put a damper on things last night, but after she bailed it was awesome. I won't let her know about Victoria, so she can't crash it." He smiled at Lia. "A whole weekend together."

4

———

PRESSURE POINT

*C*asi checked her messages after landing at the Vancouver airport. It was typical to receive dramatic rants ranging from neurotic to accusatory from Katie, but the urgent wording of Dawn's text was cause for alarm. She glanced at the time and realized it would be impossible to keep the date with Kyle and stop to see her friends. "Hey, I just landed." She hesitated to wait for Kyle to tell her about his day, to assess his mood. "Maybe you and Jake could go without me since Anna is stuck in a meeting?" She spoke cautiously, not wanting to throw her friend under the bus but aware there wouldn't be a meeting since Mary was in Austria.

"Do you have more exciting plans?" Kyle tried to keep the annoyance from his voice, although it had become routine for her to cancel at the last minute.

Casi swung her laptop bag over her shoulder. "Dawn asked if I had time to meet for a drink and it seemed convenient since I'm already in Vancouver."

"Will Katie be there?" He assumed she purposely left her out of the proposal to minimize the impact.

"Most likely." She exhaled. "It would be nice to see Dawn. With her work schedule and family stuff, we rarely make plans."

"It sounds like you've already made your choice, and this is a gratuitous call to inform me I'm on my own, again." Kyle stared at the lake and swirled the scotch over the ice in his glass.

"Ugh, now you're making me feel bad." Casi listened to the sound of the water lapping against the dock and longed to be home.

"I miss you and I'm acting needy. Have fun with Dawn and I'll invite Jake to the movies. It's more of an action flick, anyway." Kyle downed his drink and rubbed Dingo's ear.

"Will you bring me popcorn?"

"Extra butter. Will you be home tonight?"

"I'll be waiting in the bedroom for you when you return from your evening out." She smiled in anticipation.

Casi strolled in Dawn's kitchen. "Are you sure you don't want to go out? I'm willing to try somewhere other than Swiss Chalet."

"Help yourself to a drink." Dawn caught her eye as Casi slumped after noticing Katie sobbing at the kitchen table.

Casi reeled in her anger at canceling plans with Kyle to participate in another pity party for Katie. She sorted through the bottles on the counter and poured herself a gin and tonic. "Can we order a pizza? I'm starving."

Katie lifted her head. "All you ever want to do is eat! You have no concept how difficult it's for me to stay thin." She surveyed Casi's slender frame in a silk blouse and charcoal fitted skirt. "You should watch your weight too. I've noticed you're getting chunky since you no longer model."

Dawn cringed. "There are snacks in the cupboard."

Casi rolled her eyes and grabbed several bags before sitting at the table. "I'm unclear why you asked me to come over."

"Are you too busy with your amazing career to take time with your friends? Or is your incredibly hot husband demanding you come home to be with him?" Katie mocked.

"Why do you constantly criticize me?" Casi tore open a bag of chips. "You remind me of my mother."

Katie burst into tears again, and Dawn interpreted. "She's upset about Lia and Shane."

"Why? You said you hated him. What does it matter if he dates someone else? You've been clear about sleeping with other men. He spends most of his time in Seattle and takes care of your expenses. What more could you possibly want?" Casi regarded the empty bag. "Why are these so small?"

Dawn giggled. "They're for the kid's lunches. We can order take-out. Maybe a salad for Katie?"

"I'll eat pizza. What does it matter? Shane liked me better when I was fat anyway," Katie sobbed.

Casi placed the order and sighed. "What's really going on?"

Katie shrugged. "After you left me here and took off to LA, I struggled to find out where I belonged."

"I was a terrible friend." Casi directed her glance to Dawn, who mirrored her annoyance at the accusations.

"I hung out at dive bars in my early twenties." Katie settled back in her chair to set the stage for her audience. "I ran into Shane one night when I could barely stand. He was sweet and gave me a ride home. He didn't even try anything, but I invited him to stay over. It was nice to sleep beside someone I could trust."

"Shane's a good guy," Dawn agreed.

"We began hanging out, and it was casual. I would party until I hit a wall and then he would take me home. After a few nights we started fooling around." She turned to the sound of the doorbell and waited for Casi to pay for the pizza before she continued. "I couldn't believe when I got pregnant." She averted her eyes. "It wasn't the first time except for knowing who the father was. He wanted to get married when he found out. My parents love him." Katie shivered. "They say he straightened me out and gave me a purpose in life. You're missing out, Casi. You have no clue what it's like to love someone beyond yourself. This career talk and wild sex is because you're hollow inside."

Casi tossed her pizza aside and wiped her hands. "I don't have children because I don't want them. I had my tubes tied after an ovarian cyst burst, so it's impossible to get pregnant. I have many people I love more than myself beginning with my husband. Why can't you accept I've taken a different path than you? I absolutely love my life now."

Dawn gave her a sympathetic smile. "Life isn't meant to be lived one way, Katie. Casi has blossomed in her career, and I've never seen her so in love. Plus, she's an incredible aunt. She has more than enough to fulfill her." She pursed her lips. "Look, you're jealous of what Casi has, but you make no effort to improve your situation." She shook her head when Katie glared at her. "People assume I'm passive and avoid confrontation, but your assessment is unfair. I also have three kids, Katie, and I worked my ass off to get a nursing degree. I went to school at night and Joey worked extra shifts to help pay tuition. This isn't our dream home, but it's sufficient for our family."

"I didn't criticize your life, Dawn. I know you and Joey sacrifice to provide for your family." Katie eyed Casi. "She was a model and now lives in a gorgeous home on a lake with her super handsome husband. The career thing is a joke really because your friend gave you the job."

Casi's eyes flashed with rage. "A joke? I have a business degree, plus numerous certificates in marketing and promotion. Yes, a career was created for me, but Ava and Mary pushed me to get an education and learn every aspect of the business before I got the opportunity."

Dawn grasped Casi's hand. "Exactly my point. We work hard to achieve our goals. Nothing was handed to either of us. Honestly, Katie, you've been given the easiest path. You're lamenting about what happened years ago rather than focusing on where you want to be today. If you don't like your life, change it."

"If you love Shane, tell him. You pushed him away." Casi regarded her discarded food and sighed. "Honestly, I think you want him back because he's interested in someone else."

Katie lunged forward. "Our relationship happened, and everything revolved around the kids. I got fat by the time the third one was born, and he was content to settle into our routine. I felt like I was missing out, especially when I saw your modeling pictures. I made it my mission to get in shape."

"Great, so now you can stop comparing yourself to me." Casi glanced at the time on her phone and calculated how late she would be if she left in the next few minutes.

Katie slid another piece of pizza on her plate. "Shane introduced our girls to Lia. He told them she was his friend's wife, but I know they spent a week at the lake. I didn't consider what it would be like if he fell in love with someone. He's totally happy. I've checked his phone records and credit cards. He spends hours talking to her and sends her flowers. I came to Jake's wedding because I wanted to see them together. She's head over heels in love with him!"

"She cares about him." Casi turned to face her. "She's my good friend. If you aren't splitting up with Shane, tell him to end it with her. She's sweet and doesn't deserve to be strung along."

"I don't know what I want." Katie cried in her hands. "Why can't someone love me?"

Kyle switched on the light as he entered the darkened living room. Dingo glanced up from his bed and wagged his tail while Jezebel opened one eye to determine which human entered her domain. "Yup, just me. The only one who lives here anymore." Kyle sighed and set the tub of popcorn on the counter, then reached for a beer from the fridge. He twisted the top off and snapped it across the room to the trash. It ricocheted off the wall and plunked on the floor. He shook his head and picked it up to throw away. "I can't get anything right these days." He turned on the TV and settled in a chair glancing at his watch wondering if he should be concerned at Casi's extreme lateness or take it in stride since it had become an increasing habit. After checking his phone and reading several texts explaining Katie's latest drama, he tossed it on the pillow beside the cat and flipped through the channels to a documentary on snow geese.

Casi slipped her shoes off at the door and crept to the sofa. She slid her arms around Kyle's shoulders and kissed his neck. "Have you been waiting long?"

He gazed up at her beautiful hazel eyes and his anger evaporated. "Only about an hour. Share the juicy details of your girl's night."

She smoothed her skirt up and straddled his lap. "First, I love you and appreciate everything you do for me."

"A lot of man-bashing tonight?"

"Only from Katie. Dawn and Joey are great. I had to explain once again how I'm not an empty vessel because I don't have children. Do you think I'm getting pudgy?" She eyed the popcorn bucket glistening with butter.

"Random segue." Kyle gripped her hips. "You're perfect. Slightly curvier than when we first met, which makes me very happy."

"You're not trying to appease me? It's been five years and I'm much older now."

"Five amazing years and you're much wiser. The first time I kissed you my brain exploded. I feel exactly the same way today." He brought his mouth to hers. "I love every inch of your body and worship your wacky spirit. You're my entire world." She smiled and slithered out of her clothes as she raced to the bedroom. "By the way, the view from the back is just as hot as it was the day I returned your wine glasses and you answered the door in panties." He grinned at the memory and cocked his head when she came back in leggings and a t-shirt. "Actually, I enjoy it even more. I know the pleasure your beautiful body holds for me and I anticipate each freckle like a roadmap to the world's most incredible destination."

She turned the stereo to a country station and held out her hands. "Dance with me. I want to wrap my arms around you and feel your heart next to mine."

"I like the way this evening is ending." He sang the words of the love song as they swayed, and she cuddled against him.

She raised her eyes, glistening with concern. "If things get rocky, can we revisit this moment and remember how perfect it is?"

He furrowed his brow. "I would like to believe your prediction is foolish, but I've witnessed how the universe likes to mess with us."

5

———

REMEMBRANCE

"Holy Toledo! Are we moving?" Casi skirted around boxes, staggered across the floor.

Kyle glanced up from the piles he was arranging on the dining room table. "Nicole is finalizing the memorial, and she asked me for pictures from our childhood. I brought over everything we had at the farmhouse, but it's proving to be a difficult project."

Casi picked up a picture of a young Kyle missing teeth with his arm around the shoulders of a slim boy, also dentally challenged. "Grady?" She smiled at the bright faces in the photo.

"Yes, but this tribute is for all the kids. We want to highlight the ones who died, but many were injured or lost someone. I'm not sure which pictures to include."

"If I was building a campaign, I would provide a foundation for the story to honor the friendships you formed from a young age." She began reorganizing the piles to make a point.

Kyle reclaimed a photo from her hand. "This isn't a campaign. Please don't take this the wrong way, but I feel strongly about doing it myself. It's crucial to include everyone and not use pictures where you think I look cute."

"You believe I'm not objective?" She crossed her arms. "My work projects are professional and polished. I'm not playing at having a career. I comprehend how to build a storyboard."

Kyle sighed as he surveyed the images. "You love me, and I realize you're attempting to help organize what you perceive as a disaster, but I don't feel you have a concept of the great loss to our community after the accident. We have one opportunity to do this evening properly and dedicate the plaque at the river in a meaningful and sensitive manner."

"Don't come crying to me when it fails." She turned on her heel and stomped to the bedroom to change.

"Completely unkind," he muttered.

She poured a glass of wine and witnessed his steady concentration, then filled another glass and brought it to him. "Can you talk while you sort? I would love to hear the stories behind the photos and get to know your childhood friends."

He reached for the wine and gave her a kiss. "I would be happy to share, and it'll help me choose which ones to use."

Moonlight filtered through the trees, casting a warm glow on the faces of the enormous group growing restless on the grass at the makeshift memorial site. Whispers and moans penetrated the crisp August night while Kyle and Nicole fiddled with a laptop and projector set up on a folding table. The leg wobbled as Kyle adjusted the cord and photos fluttered to the ground.

"Go help him." Jake shoved Casi. "You're a master at technology and the only one who can rescue him gracefully."

"He didn't want my assistance, and the issue seems to extend well beyond an equipment malfunction." She regarded her nail polish.

Finally, the projector came to life and a sideways image appeared on the smooth slate rock face. Kyle shook his head and introduced the group shot and identified the children. The next photo was upside down and the crowd groaned while Nicole fast forwarded through multitudes of blurry images. Gary glanced over his shoulder at Casi and winked, and she grasped the handle of her laptop bag. Quietly, she stood and smoothed the skirt of her cotton floral dress and padded to Kyle and Nicole, who were furiously discussing how to rectify the disaster. He glanced up and blushed. "It seemed fine on the laptop. I don't understand why it's not coming through properly. We planned music, but the speaker emits a deafening high frequency tone."

"Perhaps the lighting and screen surface are affecting the images? Would you like me to adjust the lens?" Casi smiled.

"If it's clear, we can say who the kids are. We weren't able to add the titles like I had hoped." His shoulders slumped. "I should have asked you for help earlier, but when I realized I couldn't pull it off, it was right before your business trip and it didn't seem fair to bother you."

"I had my laptop in the car if you want to try it."

Kyle nodded and extracted his flash drive, quickly making space for her to set up. She connected her computer to the projector and a sharp picture of a field of sunflowers brilliant in the mid-afternoon sun appeared on the slate.

"Our farm!" Kyle's mouth dropped. "We didn't include the picture in our presentation."

"No, you didn't." She held a small remote control. "I created something behind your back. Do you trust me?"

"Always." He stepped away and raised his hands in compliance.

"Gary and I wanted to give this memorial the treatment it deserved." She cranked the volume and a collective gasp escaped the crowd as the beautiful song, Seasons in the Sun, filled the rocky landscape and lilted above the water. Images of young children playing and laughing layered over one another in precise formation to draw the eye into the story being told. Tears mingled with chuckles and engaged everyone in the incredible depiction floating above them.

"How did you do this?" Kyle gasped.

"I listened to your voice as we went through the pictures and ascertained which were the most important. I researched the accident and each person individually. Gary and I spent a day talking to people around the town to learn about their personal experiences, and Jake was helpful with details. Gary added the special effects and music I chose."

"This is incredible." He wrapped his arms around her and rested his chin on her shoulder. "You saw into my soul."

Segments highlighting each teenager gave a history of their lives in the country town. The survivors were showcased with smiles in their daily life and featured what they were most proud of. Families of the deceased were included to bring closure to the memory of their loved ones. Grady's section had pictures of him with Kyle, Nicole, and Jake, as kids fading to Nicole with her family. Laughter arose at the photo of Kyle holding the tampon at the Little Mermaid sculpture with a scowl, replaced by sighs at the tender moments of him releasing Grady's ashes. A map was included with stars to indicate each place they visited. An image of Kyle standing in swim trunks gazing out to sea brought a round of applause for his magnificent form. Gasps emitted when a closeup of his tattoo below the jagged scar filled the screen, 'Dare to Dream, Hope, Trust, Seek, and most of all, Love.'

A sea of glistening eyes remained locked to the images serenaded by Maroon 5 singing Memories, chanting the lyrics in unison. Kyle squeezed Casi in his arms and whispered, "This is the perfect song to honor them. Thank you for knowing me better than I understand myself." She smiled and sang the chorus in his ear as she witnessed the emotions dancing in the variegated blues of his eyes.

The final picture was them on the Eiffel tower with the full moon and sky glittering with stars. The ashes glistened in the moonlight, leaving a trail from Kyle's hand toward the heavens.

Casi waited for the image to fade away and the music to silence while she surveyed the tearful spectators. She smiled at Gary and cleared her throat. "I hope everyone enjoyed the presentation. Kyle and Nicole carefully considered which pictures to include."

"Fantastic!" someone yelled as others cheered.

"I want to see it again," a man cried.

"Well, actually you can. We made copies on flash drives for

everyone to take home." She noted a few confused faces. "And we're happy to show you how to use them on your computers." As people shoved forward to gather the coveted prize, Gary squeezed in to help distribute them. They handed boxes to Nicole and Kyle and suggested they fan out to reach the eager crowd.

"I haven't seen my boy in twenty years," a fragile voice broke as the woman gripped Casi's hand. "You brought him back to life." Her eyes watered. "Kyle has always been a special part of this community and we're thrilled he found such a lovely wife. I will cherish this."

A man limped toward Kyle and held out his hand. "Thanks for including me. It was the best time of my life before it ended in tragedy."

Kyle shook his hand. "It was great. How are you getting along now?" He observed his bent frame.

He slid up a pant leg to reveal a prothesis and grimaced. "I'm in pain every single damn day, but I'm alive. How about you? We almost lost you to the devil's hole."

Kyle shifted his eyes to Casi across the park as she held a woman's hand and consoled her. "The trek across Scandinavia brought closure. We're lucky to be alive and I'm blessed with a wonderful life."

Jake smoothed his hand over the cool surface of the granite memorial, dipping a finger in the carved words, recalling the day he got the call his brother had been in an accident.

"Jake Jensen," a rail-thin woman announced.

He turned toward the voice and winced. "Miss. Porter. How are you on this fine evening?"

Her taut cheeks broke into a smile. "I was hoping to see you."

"Did you run out of boys to torment? Or have you found a new hobby? I hope you didn't attend this to track me down, it seems a waste of a perfectly good night."

"My nephew was one of the teens who died in the accident." She put her hand on his arm. "I wanted to apologize to you."

"Why? I wasn't at the river and my brother survived with a few scars. Save your sympathy for the families who lost someone." He turned away, and she tightened her grip.

"I was horrible to you when you were young." Her eyes scanned the scar along his forearm. "I'm sorry for the cruel things I said, especially when I wouldn't let you wait on campus for Kyle."

"I'm an adult now and I don't dwell on unpleasant people from my past." He yanked his arm away, and she stumbled. He caught her elbow and steadied her against a nearby tree. "Are you alright?" He surveyed her ruddy complexion and noted the ravage signs of alcohol abuse. "It's been a tough few decades?"

Tears sprung to her eyes, and she spoke softly. "I've struggled with alcohol since college. I thought I had it under control when I was teaching, but disappointment in my personal life made it difficult to rein in." She touched his cheek. "You were a rowdy boy. Do you remember the day you found the bottle in my desk?"

Jake frowned. "In third grade?"

"I asked you to put the markers away, and you opened the wrong drawer. It happened in front of Principal Jordan and I was put on leave. I pretended to get it together for the next few years, but your presence was a constant reminder of my failures in life. I had been fired the day I yelled at you when you were waiting to pick up Kyle. I had no authority to ask you to leave campus, and I completely unloaded my unhappiness on a teenage boy." She raised her eyes to his. "Your mother gave me a tongue lashing for my behavior and warned me to stay away from your family. I moved to Seattle for a few years, but after Neil died in the accident, I came back to live with my sister. I always regretted how I treated you."

Jake exhaled and scrubbed at the scar. "You crushed me. But it was temporary. I've struggled a bit myself figuring out this adult thing. I'm doing my best to raise five kids to be compassionate and strong."

"Wow, five! I bet you're an amazing father."

Jake smiled. "Thanks for the apology. I thought being a kid was rough, but I've learned age doesn't make it any easier."

"I'm happy to see you doing so well as a grown up. I was never up to the task." She patted his hand and stumbled back to the crowd.

6

ULTIMATUM

*A*nna paced the elegant office, seething at being forced into an awkward situation. The receptionist avoided eye contact after quickly determining the glamorous redhead had nothing more to add to the reason for her visit. It hadn't taken long to locate the man with the help of Casi's super sleuthing skills, but Anna wished she could have been honest about her quest to contact the ghost from her past. It was obvious her story had severe holes for motive, although Casi graciously backed off with the questions when Anna shut down. She felt the letter in her purse, crumpled from tears and an initial meltdown. In her wildest daydreams of contacting her daughter in France, she never suspected it would turn out like this.

"Miss., Mr. Salvatore will see you now."

Anna nodded to the receptionist and entered the expansive office with a prime view of Portland. A well-dressed man smiled as he put the phone down and openly admired her svelte figure. "I'm sorry, I didn't catch your name. You work with the senator?" He extended his hand as he walked toward her masking a slight limp.

Anna crossed her arms over her chest and met him with an icy glare. "A fabrication to get a meeting with you."

A shadow of anger touched his eyes before lifting to expose a veil of lust. "May I ask what your true intentions are? You're extremely well-coiffed for a reporter. You appear savvy enough to be a lawyer, but I don't think I have any pending allegations against me." He chuckled in the revelation of a sorted past.

"I wouldn't be surprised if there are many in the works. My visit involves something urgent arising from a very unsavory event years ago." She withdrew several pages from her purse.

He narrowed his eyes and scanned her face. "Anna O'Shea! Didn't you grow up to be a beauty? You were such a little tomboy."

"I'm surprised you remember my name." She willed herself not to blush as he stepped closer.

"Sure, and your lunatic sister, Grace. She ended my football career when she attacked me with the baseball bat. What's she up to these days?" He sat on the edge of his desk.

"She's an attorney." Anna held out the first paper. "This isn't a social visit and I have no desire to reconnect with you. I'll be blunt since you seem to claim to value that in your political ads." She noticed him draw in a breath at the realization his career could be damaged. "Twenty-plus years ago, you raped me." She held up a hand as he tried to defend himself. "I'm not interested in your bullshit excuse. The encounter left me pregnant, and I gave birth to a daughter. I received a letter stating she needs a kidney due to an inherited disease. I recall your father died of the same thing?"

"It's not proof she's mine." He adjusted the collar of his shirt and Anna noticed the beads of sweat on his brow indicating he was in the habit of dodging accusations.

"A DNA test will prove it."

"Are you looking for money? Do you want your name in the tabloids, outing me for a fling we had when we were teenagers? This is bullshit." His agitation grew, and she wondered if he might have a heart attack from the concern for his reputation.

"You created a human being with a faulty kidney. I would have preferred to offer one of mine rather than contact you but I'm not a match. She has exhausted the database and is running out of time. It's your responsibility to give her the chance to survive." Anna squared her shoulders, pleased her practiced speech had been delivered as planned.

"You want my kidneys?" His eyes bulged.

"Just one. You can keep the other."

"No! I'll deny everything you claim. I'm sure I can dig up dirt."

"Perhaps, but I'm not running for office." Anna gave him a sly smile and handed him a card. "You have thirty days to get tested. If you're not a match, you can remain a useless politician. Keep in mind we'll demand your entire family is screened. Chantal has less than a year to continue dialysis. She can live a full life, which is what you owe her."

Anna stormed in Kyle's house and slammed the refrigerator door closed before Jake could extract a beer. "I've been waiting for you to install the tap in Charlotte's bathroom. How do you expect me to move in when the house isn't finished?"

Jake inhaled deeply. "It's not Charlotte's. It's our second bathroom, primarily used for the children, of which we have three, plus two others we would like to encourage to visit. Use the master if you have an immediate need."

Anna's nostrils flared and Casi nudged her. "Jake has to pick up the boys before Lia heads to work. I'm sure Kyle wouldn't mind fixing the tap. Why don't we walk over, and I can help make a list of what should be done before you move in?" She glanced back at Kyle. "Meet me there in a few minutes."

Anna sighed and squeezed Casi's hand as they crossed the street. "I'm sorry for my bad mood. Everything is pissing me off these days, and I'm anxious about the sale of the condo."

"You're not getting the price you hoped for?"

"I'm giving up my independence."

Casi smiled and smoothed Anna's hair. "They make the decisions and you want to fight back except you realize there is no logical argument."

"He's doing everything to make me happy and I'm suffocating under his care." She shivered. "I met with the man you researched."

"Did you truly want to see how he turned out in life, or was there more to it? I hope you called him out on what he did to you."

"It's complicated." Anna wrinkled her nose at the room in disarray. "He's as slimy now as he ever was. I hope my reunion with him will be temporary and I can put the past behind me."

"Don't feel you need to hide things from me. I'll run him down if you want. I destroyed the last asshole for you."

Anna laughed. "Yes, you did. Let me work a few things out and then I'll give you the sordid details." She checked her watch. "I'm late to pick up Charlotte. Why don't I get dinner on the way back and give you guys a break from cooking?"

"Awesome idea!"

Kyle nodded to Anna as she walked past him to the car. She stopped and reached for his hand. "I'm sorry for being bossy. I have a lot on my plate and these ordinary details are weighing on me. I told Casi I'll pick up dinner. Italian?"

"Sounds great." Kyle pulled her in his arms. "Deal with your shit at work and come to me to organize stuff with the house. Jake must balance many tiny lives, and he doesn't respond well to nagging. I promise I'll get it done quickly." He entered the house and frowned at the cabinets haphazardly set against a wall. Plates were stacked on the floor and boxes partially emptied. "I was so busy making my new kitchen perfect I neglected to realize the state of his house."

"Everyone is always at our place. I understand why Anna's not feeling welcome." Casi gathered laundry strewn about the space.

Kyle shoved a cabinet. "I'll secure these and get the countertop in place. Do you want to clean and organize?"

Casi started her playlist and set her phone on the counter. "Let's do this!" She tidied as she danced, making Kyle laugh as he worked on installing the faucet in the bathroom.

Kyle surveyed the completed tasks. "It's a good start. I wish I had ensured this was completed before I had him help me at my house. I assumed he was working on it at night."

"You get tunnel vision," Casi said nonchalantly.

"Meaning what?"

She wrapped her arms around his neck. "When you're involved in a task, the world could burn and you're oblivious."

"Wow, I'm reading a lot into your statement." He picked her up to sit on the counter and placed his hands on either side of her hips and locked eyes with her. "What or who am I neglecting?"

"Me."

"I think you've been away too much and when you get home, you expect me to drop everything and pay attention to you."

"You can spend time with Lauren and her incessant wedding planning unless I'm around. Then it should be about me."

"Emotionally?" He kissed her collarbone. "Or physically?"

"Both." She shivered as he moved his hands under her dress.

"Let me make amends."

"Are you christening my counter?" Jake asked.

"You already got the kids?" Casi slid from the counter and smoothed her dress in place.

"Yup." Jake surveyed the room as Austin jumped on the sofa. "You got a lot done. I guess when Kyle focuses, he accomplishes more."

"I'm sensing a theme regarding my lack of commitment to you two." Kyle frowned.

"Since Lauren got engaged, you've been her personal assistant. Either you're on the phone discussing seating arrangements, meeting to taste menu selections, or visiting venues. You didn't spend this much time planning your own wedding." Jake looked at Casi and she confirmed with a nod.

Kyle's eyes widened in disbelief. "Have you been discussing this behind my back?"

"His personal observation, but it mirrors mine."

Kyle ran a hand through his hair. "I spent zero time planning our wedding because I only cared about being with the woman I loved. Everything else was immaterial. Although, I must give credit to Sonya for making the day perfect."

"She did a great job. Until she seduced my brother-in-law."

7

——————

TROPHY WIVES

Casi flew through the door, flinging her clothes to the floor as she made her way to the closet. "Two minutes and I'm ready."

Kyle exhaled loudly, scanning her attire. "No."

"Why not?" She glanced at her reflection in the mirror.

"Way too much cleavage and the material leaves nothing to the imagination." He surveyed the hip-hugging attire.

"It's a stupid engagement party. No one will be looking at me." She pulled the dress over her head and shoved it in his arms while she searched for another.

"You could wear a paper bag and be beautiful."

"Excellent, get one from the recycling and we can hit the road."

Kyle chuckled and reached past her to a midnight blue sheath. "This will complement my suit, right?"

"Sure." She slithered into the dress.

"Excellent. Ten seconds and you must be in the car." He smacked her on the behind and strolled outside. He frowned when she appeared. "No jewelry?"

She opened her hand to reveal the diamond and pearl starbursts he had given her for Christmas. "Why are you in such a tizzy about how I look tonight?"

"I don't want to be late. I'm trying to be a supportive friend."

"You're an amazing friend. Too good, honestly."

"I understand you don't care for her although the exact reason eludes me. It seems you're having trouble grasping the significance of this wedding for her and why I, as her friend, want everything to be perfect." He turned with a self-satisfied nod.

"How far is this winery?" She secured her earrings.

"About thirty minutes."

"Perfect! Let's start with why I don't like Lauren."

"I wasn't suggesting we discuss it."

"Never in my life have I been criticized, ridiculed, and taunted by someone as much as I have by her." She held up three fingers.

"You're a victim of bullying?" He rolled his eyes.

"Yes! If she had any other position in my life, I would punch her in the face."

"Seems violent."

"She's like the annoying girl in high school who looks down on the popular girls and sucks up to the teachers. They think she's brilliant, but we know she's a snarky bitch who's overly concerned with ratting on everyone who actually has a life."

"Am I like the teacher in this scenario?"

"Yes, a hot math teacher. Or maybe science."

"And you're the popular girl?"

"Obviously." She swung her hair over her shoulder. "She has made zero effort to engage me in conversation or include me in activities. She weasels her way between us and whines for your attention, which you readily give her because of your past guilt."

Kyle glanced at his watch. "Thankfully we don't have an hour to discuss her faults and my failure as a husband."

She smacked his arm. "My critique was in response to your naïve claim you're unclear why I don't like her. I'm not knocking our relationship."

"You have a lot of friends." He reached over and laced his

fingers through hers. "I realized early on Lauren wouldn't be one of them. I enjoy her company, and our history brings kinship. This is not a threat to our marriage, just like I understand you share things with Alix, which don't interest me. I accept your past with him and trust your claim it has evolved to a unique friendship."

She scooted closer. "Your response is levelheaded and fair. Can I still dislike Dalton, or does he have a redeeming quality?"

Kyle smiled. "He's a douche, feel free to hate him. My only request is for you to keep your face in check and not appear like you want to throw up every time he enters a room."

"I don't like how much he touches me."

"When?" He turned toward her.

"He tries to hug me or put a hand on me when I walk by and says things. Normally I would see it as affection, but he gives me the creeps." She directed her gaze out the window.

"I'll be more attentive and ensure he doesn't come near you. I think he's one of those slick double-talking guys masking low self-worth, but I don't want you to be uncomfortable." He parked and opened the door for her, giving her a hand to step out of the car. "You look lovely."

"Is this his family's winery?" She scanned the sprawling buildings with a backdrop of vineyards.

"They had a place in Napa but relocated here a few years ago."

"Run out of town for being smarmy?"

"Probably." He gave her a kiss.

They walked in the expansive hallway and Casi noted Lauren nervously standing to one side, twisting a string of pearls layered over a simple gray dress. Her face lit up when she saw Kyle and waved them over. After a slight nod to Casi, she launched into a diatribe on the various guests and what to expect from the dinner.

"Where's Lia?" Casi strained to see through the crowd.

"My mother had knee surgery and Lia is helping her with recovery. I'm hoping she'll be feeling better by the wedding." Lauren made direct eye contact with Casi. "I've requested Lia not bring Shane as her date. It's inappropriate given his current situation. I agreed to invite Lance to make her happy."

"Shall we get a cocktail?" Casi scanned the room.

"This is a winemaker's dinner. Each course will be perfectly paired. There is no bar," she stated with emphasis on the last word.

Kyle observed Casi's reaction as if she had been slapped. He put an arm around her shoulders. "I told her this was an engagement party. We assumed there was a social element before."

"Oh, sure." Lauren blushed as a waiter strolled by with a tray. "There's champagne being served with hors d'oeuvres."

"My two favorite things." Casi accepted a flute and resisted the urge to down it quickly, taking small sips as they socialized.

"These are good," Kyle said, enjoying crostini with smoked trout, Creme Fraiche and caviar.

"They use the chardonnay vines for smoking." Lauren caught Kyle's eye as if they were sharing a private joke.

"It's a great location and not far from Seattle," he noted.

Casi observed their interaction. "Will you be moving to the area after you're married?"

"Maybe." Lauren turned to greet guests and left the answer unspecified.

Casi felt a hand caress her back before skimming over her hip. She identified the slightly sweaty touch without turning around and grasped Kyle's arm to get his attention. He turned and smiled at the two men. Dalton gave Casi a wink and introduced his father who had a similar sneer and flaccid skin tone. As more guests entered and mingled, Casi slipped away with the excuse of finding a bathroom.

"I'll show you," the father suggested.

"I'm sure it's clearly marked." Without hesitation, Casi wound through the crowd, colliding with a waiter as she rounded a corner.

"I'm sorry." He steadied the glasses on his tray.

"This is serendipitous." She grabbed the flute before it toppled.

He smiled. "Escaping the party?"

"What a bunch of windbags." She helped herself to another and blanched. "You're not related, are you?"

"Merely an employee who shares your observation. I need this job, so don't quote me."

She directed him to an alcove. "What's the scoop on them?"

"I've only been here a few months, but I've heard they have financial issues. The family lounges around the pool, plays golf, and throws lavish parties, but the grandmother appears to be holding the purse strings. Word is they left Napa after some scandal, but I don't know details." His face paled, and he handed her a fresh glass. "Miss. would you like champagne?"

She ditched her empty on a table discretely and turned with a smile. "Hello, Dalton's father."

"Did you find the bathroom alright?"

"Yes, and then I found refreshments."

"Interesting since it's down the other hallway."

"I got lost on my way back. I was asking for directions."

He grasped her elbow and turned her toward enormous doors. "We are being seated. You can leave your champagne out here since the dinner will be paired with wine."

Casi downed the drink before setting it down with a clink. "Wouldn't want to waste it."

He directed his eyes to her cleavage and smirked. "Trophy wives are exactly the same, sparkling on the exterior and damaged inside. Whatever you and Dalton have going on must be discrete. There are certain expectations for his marriage, and you should know your place." Casi tripped over the words to respond as he forced her in a chair. "Your wife seems to have gotten turned around."

"She is directionally challenged." Kyle smiled.

Casi surveyed the table of chatting guests. The women were overly made up, masking the pain of living in a world of false hope and emotional sacrifice. Lauren was a thorn among the roses, with her subtle prettiness obscured by the masquerade. She fiddled with a napkin before Dalton's stepmother, sporting an enormous diamond ring, corrected her. Lauren glanced up and momentarily locked eyes with Casi, and they shared an intimate moment of feeling out of place.

Several courses were painstakingly presented, each with a monologue of the characteristics of the wine being paired. Casi winced at the ache of her bladder, unable to tolerate additional liquids. Kyle surveyed her discomfort. "What's wrong?"

"I have to go to the bathroom. I lied about using it before."

Kyle raised an eyebrow. "Why?"

"It was a ploy to get away from Dalton's father. Then I found a waiter with champagne and downed a few. After two glasses of water and the wine, I might explode." Casi grimaced.

Kyle hid his grin behind a napkin. "You're a nut! Can you wait until after this course?" Casi nodded and faked interest in the food until the plates were cleared. He smiled and stood, nodding to Lauren when her face registered concern. "We'll be right back. Casi's showing me where the bathroom is."

Lauren nodded and turned back to her conversation while they escaped. "I have no idea," Casi confessed.

"I figured." Kyle searched the area and navigated to an alcove in the front hall. "I'll meet you back here."

Casi sighed with relief as she sat, serenaded by women deep in conversation at the mirrors beyond the stall. "What's he thinking with plain Jane?" one cackled.

"Knowing the Stanfords, there's a calculated motive behind it."

"God, please tell me we won't include her in tennis."

"She appears to be athletic, but she's obviously not one of us and Dalton made it clear she'll be too busy on a project to socialize."

"Speaking of," the woman said, drawing out the words. "Where's Gia's husband tonight? He's usually fun for a quickie."

"Gia said he's on a business trip, which is code for he has a hussy on the side. Her grandmother holds the purse strings for the department stores, so she doesn't have control over how he behaves."

"Live the life. Accept the downside or get a job." They laughed at the atrocity of the statement.

"What's this big announcement? The men were hush-hush about it. I overheard a conversation on investments when they were headed out to play golf."

"Something with Dalton's soon-to-be wife. Maybe how dull she is and they're investing money to give her a boob job."

"On the flip side, did you see the guy who's been around the winery with her? Super-sexy. He's a laborer or something, but I would bend over for him in an instant.

"Abso-fucking-lutely!"

Casi exited the stall and moved to the sink to wash her hands. Unfazed the woman continued, "Etiquette would dictate we invite Lauren to the soiree on Sunday morning, but she seems bright enough to understand her position."

Casi turned to them. "If you spackle on more makeup, your face will crack, which would be unfortunate because people will see your massive internal deficit. By the way, Lauren is too good for you so don't bother inviting her to your insidious events. Also, a soiree can only happen at night, hence the name." She held a middle finger up as she exited and called back, "My super-sexy husband owns his business and wouldn't screw either of you skanks."

"Make some new friends?" Kyle asked, overhearing her talking.

"Actually, I called some bitches out for ridiculing Lauren."

"I'm pleased you didn't join in."

She stopped dead in her tracks. "I have never in my life talked behind another girl's back. Not in high school, and not when I modeled. My issue with Lauren is how she treats me, and it would be counterproductive to team up with these Stepford wives." She jutted her chin forward. "I'm not a trophy wife."

"I'm sorry I inferred you were remotely like these plastic replicas. You're beautiful, smart, and funny. Significant qualities they lack." Kyle kissed her forehead.

"Perfect timing." Lauren smiled as they returned. "This is the squid ink pasta I was telling you about."

Dalton remarked about the flavor profiles of the wine, and Kyle noticed Casi push her glass aside. "You don't like it?"

"I overindulged in the champagne already. I'll fall off my chair if I drink more." Kyle snickered and tasted his pasta, giving Lauren a thoughtful review as she hung on every word.

When the meal finished, Dalton's father stood and delivered a speech about the history of wine in the region and how they relocated specific vines from Napa to thrive in the valley. He droned on about terroir and Casi felt her eyelids getting heavy due to the alcohol and plentiful food. Kyle nudged her, and she forced herself awake, taking a sip of water. "But this dinner was not only to honor tradition and the history of our fine family. We're forging ahead with a unique opportunity to bring a restaurant to the winery. Our new daughter-in-law, Lauren, will be at the forefront of this magnificent undertaking and lead us on a new culinary adventure."

Glasses were clinked and Casi realized this was not news to Kyle. "Where did the food come from if they don't have a restaurant?"

"They've been using a catering service. Tonight's menu was Lauren's creation to introduce a few signature dishes. She's been working for months to make this happen."

Mr. Stanford made the rounds and answered questions before returning to shake Kyle's hand. "Now the announcement has been made, I'll need a bid for the work." Kyle nodded, and he smacked him on the back. "Who are we kidding? Lauren made it clear you're the man for the job, and we can circumvent protocol."

"I'll give you a fair price," Kyle asserted.

"Got to keep the wife happy. God knows they always need something." Mr. Stanford downed a glass of wine.

Kyle looked sheepishly at Casi. "I couldn't tell you. The restaurant hadn't been made public. This was a fundraiser."

Casi glanced around the room of fake smiles and gratuitous handshakes. Lauren gently touched her string of pearls each time she mentioned Kyle's name while she spoke about the project. Casi turned to him. "You bought her the pearls, didn't you?"

"What?" He surveyed Lauren in confusion. "Oh, yes. When we were dating. Not recently."

"Now you'll be working on a building project with her in a remote place for a year or so? Awesome." She grabbed her wineglass from the table and stormed out to the patio.

Kyle followed and wrapped his arms around her as she stood at the railing overlooking the vineyard. He removed the glass from her hand and set it down. "I realize you feel betrayed."

"The perfect word."

"I will be honest. Your career has blown up into something incredible and provided you with amazing challenges. You barely sleep between business trips and most nights you're on your computer catching up on reports. What's lacking..." He turned her chin toward him as he felt a sob escape from her. "Don't cry, this isn't negative."

"You're saying I'm not enough for you anymore."

"I haven't had anything exciting to work on lately. This restaurant will provide the opportunity for me to hone my skills and create something incredible for the community to enjoy."

"Only the asshole elite will eat here."

"Probably true. But it will exist, and it's something I can feel good about. It will also bring in a lot of revenue for our business." He kissed her neck and ran a hand over her hip as he spoke, "Do you understand why this is important to me?"

"Yes," she sighed.

"Our relationship is not lacking," he reiterated. "I bought several pieces of jewelry for Lauren while we were together, the string of pearls, gold earrings, a gold bracelet, and an engagement ring which I never gave her. Every piece I purchased for you was designed specifically to your unique taste. There is nothing generic about our relationship. I have put a great deal of thought and consideration into everything for you."

8

―――――

PHOTO BOMB

asi grabbed a magazine and flung it at Kyle. "Stop pacing!"

He picked it up from the floor and put it back neatly as Jake and Anna came in. "Why aren't you ready? You said to be here by three." Jake checked his watch. "Usually you give her the fake time, not us."

"I told everyone the same time." Kyle smoothed a hand over the front of his suit jacket.

"It's only two. It won't take me long to get dressed." Casi glanced at the clock in the kitchen and twirled a strand of hair as she frowned at a chart on her screen.

"Check your phone. It's past three," Jake said.

She jumped up in alarm. "Why did you get a stupid clock with little sticks instead of normal numbers?"

Kyle resisted questioning the source of stupidity. "It looks good in our new kitchen. Anything else would be too modern."

"Modern keeps me on time. Normally you hound me with reminders." She made a face as she surveyed his attire. "Why are you wearing a hideous tie?"

"It was a gift."

"Not from Casi. She has excellent taste." Anna sat on the sofa and flipped through a magazine.

"Lauren bought it for me to wear today," Kyle sighed.

"Why? You're not in the wedding." Casi zipped up a fuchsia dress with a bold flower accent.

"To be nice. Does it matter?"

"Your choice if you want to wear an ugly tie, but it clashes with my dress and I specifically chose this to be demure." Casi tapped Anna's shoulder to get her opinion.

"The combination is atrocious," Anna agreed.

"I'm wearing it." He smoothed the burgundy and tan silk.

"Oh my God!" Casi stomped back in the bedroom.

"Stay strong, Brother. Don't back down to the women. Who cares if we're late?" Jake opened the fridge and grabbed a beer.

Casi returned in a chiffon merlot-colored dress with a hand on her hip. "Final wardrobe change."

"You look wonderful." Kyle winced as she walked past, and he noticed the open back plunging to her waist. "Are you wearing a bra?"

She turned with a frosty expression. "It's built in."

Kyle glanced at Anna engrossed in a text as Jake casually strolled behind her attempting to view her phone. "Obviously, I'm the only one who cares how you look so I'll come out and say it."

She narrowed her eyes. "I'm not up to the standards of the other trophy wives?" Kyle grasped her shoulders and turned her toward a mirror on the wall. "Crap, I forgot to put on makeup."

He removed a pen from her makeshift bun. "We have a few minutes if you would like to fix your hair."

They entered the winery, echoing with waiters scurrying to finish setting up the grand dining hall. "Nice place," Jake commented.

"Why are we the only ones here?" Anna scanned the room.

Kyle avoided Casi's glare. "I offered to come early and help."

"What a good bridesmaid you are," Casi cheered.

Kyle grasped her hand and led her to the patio. "One evening is what I'm asking for. No drama or theatrics. Let this be Lauren's special event where all eyes are on her."

"What's in it for me?" Casi masked a smile.

"Really?"

"I'm kidding. I'll be on my best behavior and let you be her knight in shining armor." Her eyes wandered to a waiter, and she waved him over. "Hi Armand, is the wine bar open?"

"I recall you like champagne. I'll bring it," he said with a wink.

"I'll sit here and admire the view and not make a peep. Too bad I don't have my laptop; I could get a lot of work done." She settled in a chair overlooking the vineyards as Jake and Anna approached.

Kyle squeezed her shoulder. "Your patience will be rewarded with my undivided attention when we get home."

"You'll be my sex slave?" She caressed his thigh with the toe of her rhinestone stiletto.

"You can get as freaky as you want." He gave her a wink.

The sun began to fade, and a light breeze filtered through the autumn leaves. Guests filled the patio, and Georgia and Peter joined the group. "Where's Kyle?" Peter glanced around.

"Tending to the bride." Casi smiled.

"Once the wedding is over things will go back to normal." Georgia patted her hand.

Casi nudged Anna and frowned as she recognized a man approaching. "What the hell is Grant doing here?"

Anna's back stiffened. "I don't know."

"Hello, Ladies," Grant greeted. "Fancy seeing you here."

"My husband is friends with the bride," Casi stated.

"This is my wife, Gia, the groom's sister." Grant smiled. "Casi and Anna work for Macrae skincare. Their line is in our stores."

Casi remembered the conversation she overheard in the restroom and scowled at Grant. "Nice to meet you, Gia."

The woman stepped forward with a pleasant smile. "It's lovely to meet you as well. I love your products."

Jake stood and held out his hand. "I'm Anna's husband, Jake."

Kyle returned and greeted his parents. "The ceremony is about to begin." He noted an air of tension and glanced between everyone standing in awkward silence.

"This is my husband, Kyle," Casi blurted.

"We've met," Gia said, and Casi's heart dropped at the thought of Kyle knowing the gracious woman with silky chestnut hair. "I'm on the restaurant design committee. What a twist of fate my husband works with your wife and sister-in-law through our department stores."

Kyle's jaw tightened as the name elicited the memory of the man with the jaguar and his hand on his wife's leg. "Odd coincidence." He laced his fingers through Casi's and escorted her to the vineyard.

Casi sat one seat in from the edge of the row and looked up at him as he stood nervously. "Aren't you staying?"

He crouched beside her. "Fran isn't very mobile." He hesitated. "Lauren asked me to walk her down the aisle."

Casi surveyed the groomsmen assembling and rolled her eyes when she noticed their attire. "How convenient your tie matches when this is a belated request." She noted his shocked expression and realized he was naïve to the game. "Go do it."

Jake nudged Casi when Kyle left. "Remember, we're going to the island tomorrow. You'll have his undivided attention."

"And maybe you'll have hers?" Casi noted Anna furiously texting with concern on her face.

"At least Shane will be there, so I'll have someone who cares about me."

"I adore you." Casi laced her fingers through his as the procession began. She smiled at Lia on the arm of a squat, ruddy-cheeked man and spotted Lance making a silly face at her from the crowd. She pondered if Lauren knew any of the bridal party besides her sister, and her annoyance lifted concerning Kyle's recent appointment.

Jake squeezed her hand as Lauren walked by on Kyle's arm. "He's giving her away. It's a good thing."

Casi nodded and held his hand tighter. Kyle hesitated at the altar, unsure where to go once they reached the end. Lauren leaned in and kissed him softly. Dalton stepped forward and shook his hand before he escorted her to the archway. The groomsmen made space and Kyle stepped in line to minimize the disruption, blushing in recognition of the awkward moment. The minister read numerous verses in a monotone, seeming to take hours as the guests shifted in their seats. The vows were about commitment and duty, lacking emotion and passion. Finally, the couple kissed, and the minister confirmed they were married. Kyle hung back as the bridal party returned down the aisle, waiting until the guests dispersed. As Casi stood, he hurried to her side. "I'm sorry."

"Stop apologizing." His desperation melted her armor, and she slipped her hand in his. "Did you remember we're booked to leave for Victoria tomorrow morning?"

Kyle met Jake's warning look and smiled. "I've been looking forward to our trip and spending time with you."

The night proceeded without incident, and Lauren beamed with the realization of her dream wedding unfolding. While Kyle delivered a heartfelt toast, Casi whisked his jacket from his chair feeling a chill across her bare back. She raised her glass in good cheer and smiled with relief the evening was coming to an end. The bulk of an envelope in the jacket pocket caught her attention, and she slipped her hand inside. She identified the writing immediately and willed herself to leave it alone. With a swift movement, she tucked it in her clutch and headed to the restroom. "Don't do it," she chanted silently in the stall. The thickness of the envelope was too intriguing to ignore, and she carefully unstuck the glue on the seal. She reasoned once she had a peek inside and discovered it was only a thank you note, she could reseal it and no one would be the wiser. She withdrew the pages and photos fluttered to the floor. Nausea overcame her as she bent to pick them up and witnessed a nude pictorial of Kyle and Lauren, bordering on graphic. The letter explained the pictures as a fond memory of how wonderful their relationship had been. She understood his hesitation for marriage and wished she hadn't pushed so hard. She considered the last few years to have been healing and helping them both grow. Tears streamed down Casi's face as the final paragraph begged him for another chance to fulfill their destiny and how neither of their marriages should get in the way since their kinship was deeper than any vows they had taken. Her hands shook as she enclosed the photos in the letter and slid it back. She staggered to the sink, mindlessly fixing her makeup.

"Are you ok?" Gia glanced at her. "My husband has been cheating since the day we got married. You get used to it." She winked. "I'm sure he's hit on you."

Casi swiped a smudge of mascara from underneath her eye. "I've avoided his advances. Kyle's not cheating. I'm overly emotional due to exhaustion from traveling." She exhaled. "Everything is fine. I'm happy for Lauren and Dalton."

Gia laughed. "I doubt my brother will be a good husband. I'm thrilled Lauren joined our family. It'll be nice to have a woman with brains involved in our latest project." She smiled. "Your husband speaks with such love and devotion regarding you."

"I'm completely in love with him too." Casi grasped her arm. "You deserve better, Gia."

Gia regarded her in the mirror. "You're right. I do."

Casi kept her hand on her clutch as she returned to the table, afraid the magnitude of the secret it possessed could not be contained. Kyle stood and pulled out her chair. "I wondered where you went."

"Bathroom," she croaked, settling in her seat.

He swung his arm around her and kissed her temple. "The big event is over and now I'm completely yours again."

She leaned against him and transferred the envelope back in his pocket. "The way I like it."

They pulled in the driveway and arranged what time to meet the next morning to catch the ferry. Jake held his hand out for Anna as she stepped from the car, then reached past her to grab Kyle's jacket. He flung it over the hood at his brother. "Catch."

Kyle grasped the sleeve, twisting the material in the air. His eyes widened when papers flew out and scattered on the driveway. Three sets of eyes were directed to the photos while one averted hers in shame. Kyle noted her reaction. "Did you open the letter?"

Jake gathered the photos and shoved them in his brother's hands in disgust. "Why are you carrying these around?"

"I was unaware what was in the envelope." Kyle set his jaw in anger. "I should have suspected my things would be snooped through."

Casi burst into tears and ran toward the house. She tore off her dress and turned on the shower sobbing under the running water. Kyle came in and undressed. He thumbed through the pictures and skimmed over the letter, then tore it to pieces and flushed it down the toilet. He got in the shower and pulled her against him. "I'm furious you don't have boundaries for personal belongings. But I'm more upset you were hurt by the contents. You understand I don't share her feelings and those pictures were taken a long time ago when we were drunk and playing around with her new camera phone. We had a long-term relationship. There's nothing scandalous about it. The letter is a desperate attempt to rekindle something which will never happen. Unlike her, my marriage is sacred."

She relaxed against him and let the last of her tears evaporate. "I tried so hard tonight to be a perfect wife. I didn't expect to find something so intimate."

"A definite downside of pawing through other people's belongings. You're like a kid who sees the blackberries but ignores the thorns." He kissed her tenderly. "I've seen many photos of you bordering on pornographic. It's not easy to look at."

"Mine were staged, and I wasn't with a lover." She raised an eyebrow. "Perhaps we should create our own racy portfolio?"

9
____

TRIP TRAP

asi stretched and wriggled deeper in Kyle's arms as she listened to his rhythmic heartbeat. "What time do we leave?" She yawned and reached for the phone.

"In about two hours. We'll take the passenger ferry, so reservations are not required. Plenty of time to make love again. Shall we crank your playlist? You were pretty wild last night."

Casi fell back against the pillow in a fit of laughter. "These are horrible!" She scrolled through the gallery of photos. "Pitbull betrayed me. I believed I was sexy."

Kyle leaned closer. "You're divine. Maybe erase this one."

"I'm deleting these. I look like an amateur porn star." She turned the screen to show him a picture where she had one eye closed and her mouth at an odd angle.

"It was hot last night." He chuckled at another awkward pose. "Wait, there's a good one. Let's keep some."

"I could transfer them to the computer, then put it on a flash drive in the safe. It'll be fun when we're old to reminisce."

They scrolled through the photos, choosing the best ones and laughing at the crossed eyes and strange expressions in others. She set the phone on the nightstand. "It's downloading. I have to pee." She rolled over him and bolted to the bathroom.

The phone buzzed, and Kyle responded to a text. Casi returned and dove under the covers, madly kissing him and wrapping herself in his arms. Jake stormed in the bedroom. "Last night I had the displeasure of seeing my naked brother with his ex-girlfriend, which gave me nightmares and now you're sending me porn? Why are you targeting me for your twisted erotic fantasies?"

"What are you whining about?" Kyle slid up to the headboard.

Casi leaped from the bed and grabbed Jake's cell from his hand. "Kyle, did you use your phone when I was in the bathroom?"

"I responded to Jake's text." He focused on the clock. "I said an hour. Why are you here?"

"You interrupted my download and sent it to Jake!"

Kyle covered his face and broke into laughter. "Oops, sorry."

"Sorry, my ass. I need therapy now," Jake claimed. "I'll keep the ones of Casi's boobs but delete anything with my brother's dick."

"You're not getting any." Casi handed him his phone and grabbed Kyle's with a warning. "Don't touch!" She cocked her head. "You said you took the ones with Lauren on her phone?"

"Yes, must we revisit this?" Kyle sighed.

"Lance said he saw dirty pictures of you guys on her computer. Are there more?"

"No, only the series you saw. When did he tell you?"

"A while ago, but I forgot about it until I witnessed you in raw glory. Those were copies, which means she still has the original files. I'm not thrilled about it, but it's not my call." Casi shrugged.

Kyle flung the covers to the side. "I'll stop by her condo and ask her to delete them. She leaves for her honeymoon in Italy today, and it should get done right away. I'm uncomfortable with those pictures being around." He kissed Casi on the cheek. "Go with Anna and Jake to the ferry and I'll meet you there."

Kyle strolled the hallway to Lauren's condo, not realizing the argument vibrating through the walls was coming from her unit until he knocked. He drew his knuckles back, hoping the sound hadn't been heard above the yelling. He turned away in relief, considering whether he should lie to Casi and say the photo issue had been handled.

"Kyle?" Lauren called from the doorway.

"Oh, hey." He turned slowly and walked back. "I thought maybe you had already left for the airport."

"We're not going." A sob caught in her throat and he noticed the dark circles under her eyes.

"Are you ill? You planned everything so carefully and I booked the cooking class for you. Can you reschedule?" Kyle winced as he considered whether he could get his deposit refunded.

Lauren dissolved into tears and Dalton shoved beside her. "She doesn't comprehend my family's money is tied up in investments and isn't for us to use for vacations. The wedding cost a fortune and our focus should be on the restaurant. You messed up by making plans with your boyfriend instead of consulting your husband."

"I gave you the money I've been saving. It was more than enough to cover the cost for both of us. You said we could get a discount if we used your family's travel agent."

Dalton's nostrils flared, and he focused on an imaginary scene over her head. "I was required to invest more in our share of the business. You should be thanking me."

Kyle shifted uncomfortably in the doorway. Lauren's crushed demeanor tugged at his heart and he reached out a hand to her. "We're headed over to Victoria for a few days. It's a belated honeymoon for Jake and Anna. Shane and Lia are coming. Do you want to join us?"

"Are you paying for us?" Dalton inspected his manicured nails.

"Sure, it'll be my wedding gift since you're unable to take the class in Tuscany." Kyle forced a smile. "I can wait for you to pack."

"Thank you." Lauren hugged him tightly.

"We're meeting everyone at the terminal." When Dalton left the room, Kyle grasped Lauren's hand. "I came to ask you to delete those photos. I'm not sure what you were thinking giving them to me, but I'm uncomfortable with you keeping the originals."

Lauren shrugged and glanced toward the bedroom. "A last-ditch attempt to get you back. You can't blame a girl for trying."

"My marriage isn't temporary and yours shouldn't be either. I hope you were truthful when you stated your vows. I understand you want the restaurant, but there were other ways to go about it."

❧

Jake checked his watch as he paced the dock. "He's never late." He cast a glance at Casi. "Unless you're involved."

"I'm here on time, aren't I?" She stuck her tongue out.

"Because I brought you." Jake smacked her on the behind and paled when he noticed his brother. "What the hell?"

Kyle spoke before anyone else could. "Their honeymoon plans got canceled, so I invited them to join us. Isn't the intent of this trip to relax and get away together?"

Anna and Casi exchanged glances and Lia started to speak, but Casi squeezed her hand. "Super thoughtful, Kyle."

"She sounds pissed," Kyle whispered to Jake.

"Because you're a complete idiot who can't seem to remember anything important." Jake stormed to the line for the ferry.

Kyle strode ahead and paid the fares before dialing his phone when they boarded, assuming it was best to let Casi's bad temper play out on the ninety-minute ride. He phoned Ava and explained the situation and what he had done to rectify it and hoped she could contact her friend in Italy to cancel the reservation for the culinary tour. "Do you know about any classes on the Island? I'm trying to make this a nice trip for them." He was met with a stunned silence.

Ava exhaled and regained her composure. "Do you remember why you're headed to Victoria?"

"Because we postponed Jake's and Anna's honeymoon. Shane and Lia are here too." He frowned at the icy reception he was receiving.

72

"I'll text you the number of a place in the downtown." She hung up and turned to Jack at the bar. "We're headed to Victoria tonight. I'll make reservations at the Keg."

The ferry docked and Casi raced down the stairs as Kyle pointed across the street. "Where are you hurrying off to? The hotel is right there. Don't you want to check in?"

"Tim Horton's." Casi sped along the busy street, weaving between tourists. The group trudged behind her and she directed them to the comfortable armchairs by the fireplace when they arrived. She placed her order and pushed Kyle's hand away when he tried to pay. "I've got it."

While they waited to pick up the order, Kyle caressed her back and tried to explain. "They were fighting, and Lauren was devastated. It didn't seem like a big deal to invite them. Shane invited himself." He glanced at the sullen group, not mingling. "And she deleted the photos."

"You watched her do it?"

"The computer was in the bedroom. I trust her."

She walked away and sat in a chair close to the fire with her knees pulled to her chest. She broke off pieces of a honey crueler while she focused on the flickering of the flames.

"These are too sweet." Lauren tossed her donut on a napkin.

"Don't eat it then," Anna snapped.

"I like them." Lia grinned at Shane.

"Might be part of the problem." Dalton visually appraised her figure while she attempted to adjust her sweater.

Shane jumped up and stood over him in a dominant stance. "I recommend you keep your mouth shut with those nasty comments or I'll dislocate your jaw." He glanced at Jake, who nodded his approval.

Kyle reached over and smoothed a hair from Casi's flushed cheek. "This girl sure loves donuts."

"I remember Joey driving in a blizzard to get honey crullers because he had to make sure she had them for her birthday. Damn, he was smitten." Shane chuckled and reached in the box.

Casi smiled at the memory, and Kyle noted a hint of sadness penetrating her hazel eyes. His eyes widened as he checked the date on his watch and jumped to his feet. "I fucking forgot your birthday!"

"Finally," Jake cheered. "I didn't know if I could keep it quiet the entire weekend and watch you suffer when you figured it out."

"Why didn't you remind me?" Kyle turned to the group.

"We told you when we chose this weekend. You circled it on the calendar with a snide comment about making life easy." Anna stared him down.

"Not helpful." Kyle flipped her off and turned to Casi. "I'm sorry. I know the date. I got overwhelmed this weekend."

"I don't like to make a big deal of my birthday. I wanted to be with friends and relax. Everything is booked. You weren't required to remember." Casi sipped her coffee.

"Your gift is in Seattle," he lamented.

"You can give it to me when we get back."

"Oh, a new car?" Dalton cocked his head and assessed her. "I picture you in a Mercedes sport convertible."

"He already bought her a new car for their wedding," Lauren mumbled, pulling at a thread on the hem of her shirt.

"And replaced it after she totaled it running down my last husband." Anna laughed and nudged Casi.

Jake cocked his head. "Might be a dilemma for us. Which one would you kill, Casi? Where does your loyalty lie?"

Casi giggled. "You have to work out your own shit. You're both good people and I would be furious if either one of you hurt the other."

Anna stood. "Lauren, I didn't know you were joining us, and I've booked spa appointments. Shall I check if there's room?"

"No, thanks." Lauren glanced through her eyelashes at Kyle.

"You should go so the men can hang out," Dalton pushed.

"The men are headed to a pub which serves beer, and we'll be watching sports." Jake scanned Dalton. "Since this is your honeymoon, you should spend time with your wife." He put an arm around

Anna's waist and gave her a kiss. "Let me pay for the spa. You never let me buy you anything." He secured his credit card in her hand.

She protested, then noted his determination. "Thank you."

They escorted the trio of women to the spa and continued to the hotel with their bags. Shane fiddled with his credit card as they waited in line. Jake leaned over and whispered, "Will charging a hotel be a red flag?"

"I told Katie we're done, but she's refusing to give me a divorce. I'm biding my time and avoiding arguments until her green card comes through." A dark shadow crept across Shane's face.

"I'll put it on mine." Jake stepped up to the counter.

"I'll pay you back," Shane insisted.

The clerk brought up the reservations. "Mrs. Jensen has paid for the two rooms overlooking the harbor. Shall I add the second-floor room to her account?"

"No, we'll pay separately." Kyle nudged his brother over and kept his voice low. "Can we add another room there?"

The clerk regarded the couple behind him, bickering as they waited. "Yes, I think a garden view is appropriate."

Kyle handed the key card to Lauren on the elevator. "We'll meet up for dinner." He held the door open and Shane stepped out, waiting for them to follow.

"Which floor are you on?" Lauren asked.

"Eighth." Kyle glanced away while the doors closed.

Jake chuckled and showed him a text from Shane. "You're only dumping them, right? You want to hang out with me. Please say yes. I really want to go to the pub with you."

Kyle laughed. "He's hilarious. Tell him to meet us in the lobby in twenty minutes."

Kyle smiled at Shane's eager expression when they approached. "Lia said not to push you because you have a unique brother bond. You have lots of friends, so it seems alright to tag along. You do like me, right? Wait, don't tell me if you don't."

Shane looked legitimately afraid of the answer and Jake smacked him on the back. "It's cool if you join us. As a matter of fact, I've been looking forward to hanging out with you."

"Do you boys want to be alone?" Kyle teased and began listing which pubs were nearby.

"Walk faster." Jake shoved them through the door but couldn't avoid Lauren and Dalton pushing toward them on the street. Kyle hurried to a kiosk and came back with pamphlets. "There are tons of things to do here." He fanned out the selection. A bright flyer caught his attention, and he pulled it from the pile. "A boat tour would be great tomorrow, don't you think?"

Shane winced when he noticed the price. "Go ahead. Lia and I can walk around and check out shops."

"Book it. I'll split it with you, Kyle," Jake asserted.

Kyle handed the pamphlets to Lauren. "I recommend Butchart Gardens. We'll meet you back at the hotel around five?" He read a text as they walked and moved to the side to place a call. When Ava answered he said, "At least Jack tried to have my back."

"I'm sorry, I couldn't believe you forgot again," she teased.

"I got caught up in Lauren's wedding."

"Now it's over maybe you can redirect your focus?"

"Definitely. Jack mentioned you're coming to the Island for dinner. Would you mind doing me a favor? I have Casi's present in Seattle and, obviously, I spaced on the date."

"Dad!" Casi bolted toward him when they came to the top level of the restaurant. "How did you know we were here?"

"Kyle arranged it," Ava said with a wink.

"What a great surprise." Casi hugged her.

"I forgot what day it was, but I didn't forget you." Kyle smiled as Ava handed him a package. "Thank you for picking it up. And wrapping it." He grinned at the beautiful floral paper with a bow.

"Ah, the typical small box apology," Dalton said. "Our family keeps Tiffany's in business."

Kyle clenched his jaw. "I chose this gift a while ago."

"A month after we got back from Europe," Jake confirmed.

"You were already planning for my birthday in the summer?" Casi untied the ribbon.

"I was inspired by something on the trip." Kyle smiled.

Casi lifted the lid of the box to reveal a delicate gold watch with diamond accents. "Because I'm never on time?"

"No, because it's more elegant than checking your phone during a meeting or social event. You'll notice it has real numbers instead of little sticks." Kyle's eyes creased with amusement.

"It's gorgeous! I love it."

"The true gift is on the back." He turned it to reveal the inscription, *Life is not measured by the number of breaths we take, but the moments that take our breath away.*

"The sign in the garden in Russia!" Casi's eyes watered.

"I hope to give you a lifetime of moments to take your breath away." Kyle kissed her cheek as he secured the watch on her wrist.

10

PREDATOR

The late October sun filtered through the morning clouds and dispersed into globes of light dancing on the walls. Casi stretched her hands out to create shadows chasing the imaginary creatures. Kyle laced his fingers through hers to move in unison. "Have you enjoyed your trip?" He kissed her collarbone.

"Fantastic. I figured we would go out to eat and walk by the ocean. The spa and boat trip were unexpected treats. The highlight was singing karaoke with Ava at the pub. She's so much fun!"

"You sounded amazing together. I realize you were both a bit tipsy, but I think it was a great suggestion to sing together at her bar once a month."

"I'll definitely follow up." Casi caressed his shoulder. "Thank you for my watch. It's a lovely gift and I'll always cherish it."

"I'm pleased you like it. I'm sorry I screwed up this weekend in the beginning. There was so much going on with the wedding and getting the specs ready for the restaurant. They want me to order materials, but I must ensure the measurements are accurate because we're using reclaimed wood and it's pricey." He sighed. "Lauren has a lot of pressure to finalize the menu, and I hoped a week in Italy would have encouraged her to relax."

"What class were you able to book as a replacement?"

"Ava found an advanced Italian one. They'll even make burrata." Kyle's eyes lit up.

"Pasta?"

"Cheese. You use the mozzarella curd and add cream. You love it. Remember we ordered it at the restaurant in Issaquah?"

"With the salad! Super delicious." Casi licked her lips.

"It's a morning class and then we'll take the ferry this afternoon. Do you want to go to breakfast?" Kyle rolled on top of her.

She wrapped her legs around his waist and smiled. "Right after we make love again."

Kyle nuzzled her neck and caressed her breast as she arched toward him. He frowned at a loud cough at the doorway of the connecting room. "Do you ever knock?"

"Why? I announced I was here as I do at home. It's past ten and checkout time is eleven. Get up and take a shower. I'm hungry and Casi needs her caffeine infusion. You must keep normal lovemaking hours like the rest of us."

"Three-minutes doesn't suit our needs," Kyle teased.

"I lasted four last night." Jake chuckled and pulled open the curtains. There was a knock, and he frowned. "I guess I'm the butler." He opened the door and leaned against the frame. "Confused which way the class is? They have maps at the front desk."

Lauren peered over his shoulder. "Dalton doesn't want to go. He says he has no interest in cooking. I realize it was expensive, and I wasn't sure if you could get a refund?"

Kyle rubbed his face in annoyance. "He couldn't have figured it out two days ago?"

"I understand it's last minute." She shoved past Jake and halted when she saw them entwined in the sheets. "Oh, sorry. I thought you would be up by now."

Casi noted the frustration in Kyle's mannerisms. "Kyle, go with her. I'm happy to spend the day shopping. There's no sense wasting the class, especially when it's something you would enjoy."

Kyle discarded the covers and grabbed Casi's hand, escorting her to the shower. "I'll be ready in fifteen minutes. Meet me in the lobby."

"Tell your husband check out time is eleven. We'll meet him at the ferry." Jake walked in the bathroom and spoke over the roar of the shower. "Anna and I are going to get coffee. You can stop with your girlfriend and we'll pick one up for Casi."

"Bring me a honey crueler!" She giggled as Kyle grabbed her hips and made oinking noises.

Kyle dressed as Casi wrapped herself in a towel and began drying her hair. "Are you one-hundred percent okay with this?" He held her gaze in the mirror.

"One-thousand percent." She held two thumbs up, losing the towel in the process.

"An impossible percentage." He wound the material back around her and tucked it securely between her breasts before giving her a kiss. "I'll see you at the ferry. Jake can take our bag with his. Don't forget your watch."

"Have fun. Bring me samples." She set her phone on the charger and cranked the music while she finished drying her hair. There was a knock, and she quickly answered the door. "Did you forget something?"

"Perfect." Dalton scanned her towel-clad body.

"Why are you here?" She slid behind the door and pushed it to prevent him from entering. He stuck his foot in the room to keep it from closing. "They already left for the cooking class. If you want to make it up to Lauren, you should take a taxi over there and apologize. Kyle put a lot of effort into planning."

"He did it for Lauren. I came to see you."

"I have no interest in talking to you." She glanced at her phone, calculating the distance to grab it.

He kicked the door free from her hand, surprising her with his force. "I'm not here to talk."

"Get out!" She made a dash to the nightstand.

He slammed the door shut and locked it with a menacing smile. "You've been flirting with me since the day we met."

"Everything about you disgusts me." She backed up, grasping the towel with one hand. "Jake will be back soon."

"He went for coffee with Anna. We've got plenty of time." He winked. "And no one can hear you scream over your god-awful music."

"Dalton, this isn't funny," she said as her voice wavered.

He lunged and yanked the towel off as she scratched his neck. "Just as gorgeous as I imagined. What a surprise to discover you're a natural blond. I figured the golden mane was as fake as the rest of you." He twisted her arm behind her back in a swift movement. "Wow, real tits. I've been studying your modeling pictures and the video of you in lingerie is incredible. Love the tattoo, a perfect tramp stamp." He ran a finger over her script along her hip before noticing the one on her ribs, *Kyle Jensen owns my heart.* "Yup, bought and paid for like the rest of you. He was smart to invest in such a fine piece of ass. Why don't you dance for me and show off your confidence?"

"Fuck off!" She tried to release her arm from his grasp, but he dug his fingers in her skin. He shoved her forward over a chair and pinned her wrist behind her shoulder blade, sending a lightening bolt of pain through her body.

"Howl all you want. It makes it more fun. You serve one purpose on this earth and it's my turn to grab a piece." He tugged her hair and ran his tongue over her throat. "You can't break free. I used to wrestle in college, and I've mastered the moves to keep you still." He ran his free hand over her breasts, taunting her with his plans as he held his phone up. "I watched how Kyle touches you, and see you respond. Let's take pictures like the ones Lauren has of her and Kyle." She wrenched her face away and knocked him backward with a blow to his face. "You're a wild one!" He tightened his grip.

"Kyle will kill you!" She realized there was no way to escape his grasp and willed herself to go numb.

"You can't say anything. Lauren's pregnant, and her precious Kyle will step up if I'm out of the picture. Obviously, you're too pretentious to want babies of your own. You're a little slut who has been purchased as pretty arm candy. He buys you cars and expensive jewelry in exchange for your services. We both know he'd rather spend time with Lauren. The difference between you and the painted whores in our family is they know their place. You're still under the illusion you can rise above your position. You emulate Ava, she's an entitled self-involved bitch." He chuckled. "Lost your will to fight? It'll be over soon, and you can go back to pretending you have a perfect life." He slid his hand between her legs and groaned in her ear. "Better watch your diet, it would be a shame to get fat and have Kyle leave."

Jake banged at the door. "Casi! Why do you have the lock on? Come get your coffee and turn down the music."

"Jake!" She screamed and kicked as Dalton slammed her face against the chair.

"Your boyfriend ruins everything. In case you're thinking of telling him, consider the fact Anna is screwing my brother-in-law and poor old Jake will be devastated to discover his third marriage is destroyed by a cheating wife." He shoved her to the ground and stepped over her as he extracted his wallet. He threw a twenty-dollar bill on top of her watch. "I always pay for services rendered," he chided before he slipped through the adjoining door, quietly entering the hallway.

Jake turned at the movement and surveyed him, standing behind him. "What do you want?"

"I was coming to find you guys and see if you wanted to hang out. I was in a bad mood earlier and didn't want to go to the cooking class." He clasped a hand over the scratches on his neck and appeared humble. "I'm trying to make this restaurant happen for Lauren and I should've done a better job explaining why we couldn't go on a real honeymoon. I came to apologize for making it Kyle's problem."

Jake scowled at his performance. "Kyle went to the class with Lauren. Check out time is in twenty minutes. Are you packed?"

"I'll go take care of it." He moved toward the elevator. "Does Shane know? I can stop by his room."

"He knows." Jake frowned as Anna stepped off the elevator, engrossed in a text. "Work again?"

She glanced up. "Yes. We have poor reception in the hotel. I had to stop and send a report to Mary."

Jake used his key to enter his room and walk through to Casi's. "I told you I was getting coffee." He heard the shower running and went to the bathroom. He reached in and turned off the water. "How long have you been in there?" She stepped out and collapsed in his arms, sobbing as her entire frame shook. "Monkey, you should have told him not to go. You can't cheer him on one minute and be distraught the next." She scanned his face in desperation, unable to speak. "What's wrong? I bought you donuts."

"Are you ready?" Anna entered the room sipping her coffee. Casi glared at her over Jake's shoulder and pushed away from him. She stormed to the bedroom and threw on clothes. Anna giggled and handed her a shirt. "Your top is a little fancy for daywear."

Casi grabbed the shirt and slipped it on, swinging her wet hair over her shoulder. She shoved her belongings in her bag. "Let's go."

"Don't you want to put on makeup or dry your hair? We have a few minutes while Jake changes." Anna cocked her head.

Jake glanced down and rolled his eyes. "Damn wet monkey." He retrieved a shirt from his room and came back with their bags.

"I want to go home!" Casi yelled.

Anna and Jake exchanged confused looks. "Don't forget your watch. This was very expensive." He picked up the cash and handed it to her and she burst into tears.

"It's probably for the maid." Anna glanced at the bill Casi threw to the floor.

"Are you supposed to tip?" He read Anna's patronizing look. "Sorry, I don't stay in hotels as much as you do."

"Go to hell." Anna held up her middle finger.

"It wasn't meant as a negative comment." He shook his head and fastened Casi's watch to her wrist, noting she was shaking. "He's sorry about forgetting your birthday, but he bought this a while ago. He loves you."

Casi pushed past him, not accepting the cup Anna held out. "What's with her?" Anna whispered to Jake.

"The moods of women elude me." Jake zipped up the overnight bag and checked the room for belongings.

Shane approached them like an eager puppy when they strolled in the lobby. He reached for their bags and added them to the trolley with his own as he surveyed Casi's sullen demeanor. "Cassidy, you're looking rough. The pub wasn't too wild last night. I've seen you kick back way more drinks in the past. Are you ok?"

"Don't ask," Jake cautioned.

"Where's Kyle?" Shane surveyed the lobby.

Jake hung back and filled them in on the cooking class and how Casi had fallen apart by the time they came back from coffee. Lia observed her erratic behavior, pacing and mumbling to herself. "She never gets upset. Are you sure she's not ill?"

"You try talking to her. She won't even look at Anna," Jake said.

Lia put her hand on Casi's arm and frowned. "Why are you bruised? Did you hurt yourself?" Casi turned with tear-filled eyes, suddenly reflecting terror. Without warning, she raced across the street, almost getting hit by a taxi.

"Casi stop!" Jake darted after her through the traffic. "Damn it," he swore as she hurled herself up the steps of a bus as the doors were closing. He glared as it pulled away and cocked his head when he noticed Dalton waiting on the sidewalk with a scarf wrapped around his neck. He waited for the light to change and walked back across. "Should I find out where the number 72 bus goes?"

"She knows this area. If her goal is to get home, she'll have to come back to the ferry," Anna reasoned.

"I don't understand what you're telling me." Kyle paced frantically back and forth at the terminal. "How could she take off and you didn't follow her if you thought she was distressed?"

"Have you ever tried to run after a bus?" Jake scowled.

"Call a taxi!" Kyle checked his watch again. "How long has she been gone?"

Jake grasped his shoulder. "Six minutes longer than I told you the last time, so over four hours. And no, she's not answering her phone. We can't contact the police because she's not missing. She's a grown woman who decided to take a bus somewhere for the day."

Kyle gripped his side and winced. "I'm not getting on the ferry without her. You guys go home, and I'll wait for her."

"There she is!" Shane pointed to her jogging toward them.

Kyle ran and pulled her in his arms. "Where were you? I've been having a panic attack."

"I'm fine." She shook as she clung to him.

"Are you ok? Did something happen?" He put his hands on the sides of her face and scanned her eyes.

She pressed her head to his shoulder and breathed in his warm scent. "I want to go home."

"Then we must run." He grasped her hand and raced toward the ferry as Jake tried to halt the workers from closing the barrier. When they jumped onboard, she pulled her hand away and kneaded her wrist. "Did I hurt you?" He noted the tender area and was shocked to see a bruise erupting over swollen skin.

"I fell getting on the bus." She tucked her wrist under her arm, refusing to let him investigate further. They assembled at the back railing when a whale was spotted. Kyle came behind Casi and she flinched. "Please don't."

"Casi, what's going on?" He stared at her with concern.

She surveyed the surrounding crowd. "I feel a little sick. Maybe I'm coming down with something."

He felt her forehead. "Do you want to go inside? It's chilly."

"Can we stay out here?" A sob caught in her throat as she fell into his arms. "Hold me, ok?"

"Whatever you need."

The ferry docked, and they disembarked, hesitating at the pier before heading off in separate directions. Shane and Lia said a tearful goodbye, embracing as they planned when they might get together again. Kyle hugged Lauren goodbye, and she thanked him profusely for saving the day, yet again.

Dalton gave Casi a wink and leaned in for a hug. "Thanks for a great time. We'll have to do it again."

Jake intercepted, ramming Dalton after he read the panic on Casi's face. "She's not feeling well. Keep your distance."

"Thank you," Casi murmured, trudging toward the car. The sound of rushing footsteps sent shivers down her spine, and she screamed as a hand grabbed her waist.

Kyle stepped back in alarm. "Casi, it's me. Don't you want to drive home in the truck together?"

"Oh." She nodded and grasped his hand tightly.

Jake shook his head. "Anna are you coming?"

She glanced up from her phone. "Not tonight. I need to pick up Charlotte and I have an early meeting. It's easier if I stay in Seattle."

Jake chewed at his cheek. "Lia, do you want a ride?"

She wiped her tears. "Sure."

When they arrived home, Casi bolted for the shower. Kyle fed the animals and started dinner, contemplating what menu might cheer her spirits. He turned to the sound of gut-wrenching cries and bolted to the bathroom to find her hysterically sobbing under the stream of water. "Casi, what the hell is happening?" He tore off his clothing and wrapped her in his arms, gently rocking her.

"I forgot to send a report to Mary." The excuse was ridiculous, but she needed a moment to recover from her breakdown. "I shouldn't have gone away without ensuring my work was complete."

He smoothed her sodden hair from her face. "You're much too distraught for a forgotten report. Please tell me the truth."

She blinked to break eye contact, unable to deceive his loving sapphire gaze. "It's PMS. The cramps are horrific and it's distorting the range of my emotions."

"What can I do to help? I was about to make pasta, but I can prepare something else. Would you like the pesto chicken? I'll go to the store and buy more rocky road ice cream."

She regained her composure and pushed the events of the day to a recess deep in the back of her mind. "You always make things better."

11

STALEMATE

Jake unloaded the groceries while Casi stared in a pot at the stove, mindlessly stirring. "Might work better with the heat on." He chuckled and switched on the knob.

"I was distracted." She continued to focus on the handmade tiles of the backsplash.

He came over with an elaborately decorated tiny cake and set it beside her with a smile. "A gift for you."

"Why?"

"It usually makes you smile." He glanced at the calendar.

She followed his gaze and shook her head. "Is the skull and cross-bones a reference to my cycle?"

"The weepy part usually lasts a day or two. We've been back from the Island for a few weeks and you're lost in your own world."

"Thank you for the treat." She hugged him tightly.

Anna strode in with Charlotte on her hip and handed her to Jake. "Casi, can I talk to you?"

Casi regarded the pot. "I'm busy."

Anna stormed toward her. "Why are you shutting me out? You've been in a pissy mood since we went away. Mary informed me she's switching accounts for the good of the company." She made air quotes to highlight her point. "You have no right to interfere in my business. Is this something you and your best buddy, Jake, cooked up to keep me home more?"

Casi whirled around and slapped her so hard it left a handprint. "Don't question what I have a right to do!"

Anna staggered back, clutching her cheek as Jake pushed between them. "What's going on?"

"Get out!" Casi threw the wooden spoon at him. "I'm sick of you babying me and hovering around trying to decipher my mood."

Kyle stood frozen at the door, taking in the scene. Jake stomped over and pushed him outside. "I'll help you with the rest of the groceries while this boils over."

Casi charged toward Anna. "You want to talk? Let's discuss why you're fucking Grant and how you're the joke of the town. I'm sorry my first instinct is to protect Jake, but I care about him." She lowered her voice as the men returned. "You betrayed our friendship, and I asked Mary to move you off the Stanford account since our company doesn't trade sex for business." She tossed the pot in the sink. "I'm not making dinner tonight. I have an early meeting in Vancouver to prepare for."

Anna ran through the house in tears and Casi slammed the door to the bedroom behind her. The brothers stared after them and Kyle shrugged. "Pizza?"

"Sounds good." Jake opened the fridge and grabbed two bottles of beer while Kyle placed the order.

❧

Kyle loitered outside the restaurant, shuffling from the entrance to the parking meter as he contemplated what to do. He glanced through the plate-glass window framing Casi with a man he presumed was a client. Her manner was carefree with a professional edge, moving her hand slightly as he reached for the bottle to refill her glass. Kyle noticed she barely ate the food on her plate as she spread the risotto in a deceptive act to fool an onlooker. Her face masked reaction, responding in a practiced flirtatious way to engage the listener but not reveal deep feelings. She smiled as she eased the check from the client's side of the table and slid her card inside. Kyle exhaled in relief at the confirmation of it not appearing to be an illicit affair. He turned away, determined to leave the scene without confronting her.

"Kyle?" Casi grasped his arm. "Why are you here?"

He winced and turned slowly to face her. "I needed to source materials in Surrey for the restaurant job." He fiddled with the zipper on his jacket. "You've barely been home, and we haven't talked about your strange interaction with Anna last night."

"You came to spy?" She crossed her arms over her chest and glanced at the client entering the parking garage. "How often do I need to prove I'm not having an affair? Are you tracking my phone?"

Kyle regarded his boots. "It was a last-minute decision to come and find you. I'm not checking up." He raised his eyes. "Screw it, I'll be honest. Why are you booked at a hotel when you're an hour from home? I assumed it had something to do with Katie, but my imagination got away from me with the magnitude of possibilities."

"Stay with me," Casi blurted. She wiped a tear and noted the confusion on his face. "At the hotel."

He smiled and slipped his hand in hers. They walked silently, each lost in their own thoughts. He considered the parking ticket he would get and decided it was worth the cost to seize the moment of being alone with his wife. "Why are you afraid to come home?" He surveyed the premium suite with a view of the city.

"I needed a night to myself." Casi hung her clothes and gave him a sad smile. "Away from Anna, Jake, and the kids."

"Dingo, Jezebel, and I are still on your good list?" He crossed the room and embraced her.

"Yes." She kissed him and gave in to the rhythm of his familiar touch on her over-sensitized skin.

They fell back on the bed and he kissed her collarbone, caressing her slight frame without voicing his concern. As the lovemaking began, he gazed in her eyes and noted they were void of sentiment. She stared at the ceiling in a trance without noticing when he pulled back. He shook his head and rolled away from her. "You're breaking my fucking heart."

She bolted to the bathroom and forced the shower on without checking the temperature as she sobbed beneath the spray. She shivered in the freezing jets and grounded her emotions. Without a word, she toweled dry and padded back to the bedroom.

Kyle sat in bed watching a documentary with a sullen expression. "It's late. I'll pick up my materials in the morning and be out of your way. There's no point driving through the border twice."

Casi shoved the sheet aside and straddled his lap. She put her hands to the sides of his face and gazed in his eyes. "It's not you. My brain is on overload and it's difficult for me to disconnect. I want to be with you." She rotated her hips and felt him respond.

"I love you, Casi." He caressed her breast and inhaled the scent of her skin. "Don't exclude me from what's going on with you. It doesn't protect me if you're hurting inside."

She smiled. "This is what I need. You're the only one in the world I want to be with."

Anna waited until she noticed Kyle's truck pull out before crossing the street. She walked in the bathroom where Casi was putting on makeup and closed the door. "Please listen to me."

"I don't want to hear it. There is no excuse for what you've done." Casi glared at her in the mirror.

"I'm a horrible person," Anna agreed.

"You shouldn't have married him if you had no intention of being faithful. He may not be perfect, but he is loyal to a fault. I protect him because he's emotionally vulnerable, yet he would give his life to take care of us. Why would you try to break him? Especially with Grant!"

"I freaked out after the wedding. Jake was pressuring me to move, and I felt like the walls were closing in. I had finally regained my independence and then the leash was back on my collar. Grant heard my condo was for sale and came to the open house and brought a bottle of wine. After everyone left, it kind of happened."

"Ultra slutty, but I'll give you a drunken bad judgement pass. Why would you continue it?"

"I received a letter back from the convent. My daughter's name is Chantal and unfortunately the only thing the bastard gave her was a rare kidney disorder. I'm not sure if something was lost in translation from French, but she appears to be cold and exacting." She smiled at Casi's expression. "Fine, she inherited it from me. She's been on dialysis for over a year, and my letter prompted her to ask about our medical histories. She needs a new kidney."

"Ugh, you don't have to give her one of yours, do you? Are you sure it's legit? Maybe it's a scam to sell organs on the black market."

"She sent me her medical files." Anna fiddled with a makeup brush. "I'm not a match. I wanted to leave it there, but she insisted on contacting her birth father. He wasn't aware I got pregnant and I don't want her to know the circumstances."

"Did he agree to get tested?"

"The background information you gave me was helpful for forcing his hand. His results came back positive for a match, but he suffers from a similar disorder to a milder extent. His kidneys are not viable for a transplant."

"Does he have kids? Take one of theirs."

"I suggested it and he flipped out. I've already had more contact with him than I hoped. I passed along the information to Chantal, but I'm feeling pressured to do more."

"How does screwing Grant help?"

Anna wiped a tear. "Chantal's paperwork states the cause of pregnancy as promiscuity. She asked if I even knew who her father was. I visited the convent for closure, but my world is in a tailspin. Having an affair allowed me to step away from a comfortable life at the lake with my adoring husband and sweet daughter."

Casi made a face. "She's kind of a brat."

"I can't bring myself to discipline her. Charlotte is a second chance, and I screwed up from the get-go by marrying the wrong man the first time. I crave order and control. Everything's a mess."

"You state the time and place with Grant. Zero emotional involvement." Casi contemplated the scenario.

"He was convenient, nothing more."

"His wife seems nice."

"She's lovely. Do you think she cares about him?"

"I believe their family calculates their relationships like a chess game. It's not based on love, but what they gain from the partnership. Gia has department stores and Grant fits the bill to expand the business."

"Why do you think Dalton married Lauren?" Anna asked. "I understand she receives a restaurant, but he could have hired a chef."

Casi shivered. "I'm under the impression the family has financial issues. Lauren's stable in the community and has connections. I suspect she may have invested quite a bit of money in the business."

Anna leaned forward and stroked Casi's cheek. "What happened in Victoria? Something damaged you."

Casi burst into tears. "Dalton came to my hotel room."

Anna's eyes went wide. "Did he hurt you?"

"He restrained me while he touched me and made lewd comments. He would have taken it farther, but you guys came back."

"Motherfucker!" She pulled Casi in her arms and hugged her. "I'm so sorry. Did you tell Kyle?"

"I can't. Lauren's pregnant." She let the magnitude of the situation sink in. "It will tear everyone apart. Kyle will be obligated to protect her and take care of the baby. I can't destroy her dream of having a restaurant." She grasped Anna's arm. "Dalton's the one who told me about Grant. He threatened to tell Jake."

"He used my affair to keep you quiet? I'll tell Jake myself."

"Please don't." Casi squeezed her hand. "I want it to go away. I've had unwanted advances in the past. I'm fine."

"You're not." Anna shuddered. "I won't say anything until you tell me it's ok. In the meantime, we will plot to destroy him and get revenge. Did you tell Mary about me?"

"No. I faked a report to show we were wasting resources with in-person meetings within Seattle. I created an online presence to streamline our costs. It was meant to get you out of the field, but the theory is quite brilliant."

Anna grinned. "You're excellent at business. Tell me what to do to make it up to you. I'll quit if you want."

"You're a huge asset to the company. On a personal level, I enjoy having you as my work buddy. Sleeping with a client was tacky, and we must rectify it. I'll show you how to use the program for the reorders, and we can talk to Mary about expanding your territory. I should keep the out-of-state accounts because you have a kid and travel isn't as easy."

Anna scrolled through a website on her phone. "Can I have San Francisco and Portland? The Standfords have stores there, and I'll meet with Gia to make amends. I have an idea to make this work in our favor."

"Let's propose it to Mary at the meeting today."

"I'll come clean. There's no point trying to hide it. She has an ear to the ground, and I suspect she's waiting for me to confess."

"Tell her but not Jake. I want the rest of this disaster behind us. We'll move forward and be stronger for it."

Mary nodded through the presentation and made notes. "Excellent conclusion, Casi. Your numbers and proposal are on point. I agree we can expand our reach with Anna's help." She turned to Anna and raised an eyebrow.

"You know already." Anna shook her head.

"You put the company at risk. As wild as my baby girl is, she doesn't cheat or lie, especially to her husband. You betrayed her and harmed people I care about."

"I'm ashamed of my behavior and promise it was a onetime slip. I was dealing with a lot of emotional baggage and acted like a tramp.

I'll dedicate myself to protecting our reputation and ensure the company isn't affected by my mistake."

Mary surveyed Casi. "Is this why you have been acting strange?"

Casi smiled. "Yes. I was concerned for Jake's feelings."

"Are you sure?" Mary narrowed her eyes. "If I'm giving you too much responsibility let me know. You have years before I retire and hand over the reins. Don't take on more than you can handle."

"I find the tasks empowering. I had personal concerns, but I've resolved them. The expanded territory will be a welcome challenge for both Anna and me." Casi sat back in her chair.

Anna stood when the woman with chestnut brown hair walked in and extended her hand. "Hello, Gia, thank you for agreeing to meet. I don't know if you remember me from Lauren's wedding."

"How could I forget my husband's mistress," Gia mused. "What's the proposal? Give him a divorce so you can run off together. No problem, except he signed a prenup and leaves with nothing."

"I have no interest in your husband any longer. It was a tawdry, meaningless affair which hurt key people in my life. I would reverse it in a second." She cringed. "May I ask how you knew?"

"I noted your interaction at the wedding. He's been cheating for years and he's transparent with his lust. You told him it was over? How did he take it?"

Anna smiled. "I sent a text stating our business would be conducted online going forward. He asked to meet at the hotel, and I responded our relationship would be strictly professional. After twelve texts and numerous unanswered calls, I believe he got the message."

"He's not very bright." Gia giggled.

"He's attractive and a smooth talker."

"Your husband is much more handsome. Should I return the favor and proposition him?" She noted the devastation on Anna's face. "We hurt the ones we love the most. Grant was a calculated move on your part. You are one of our strongest accounts. Did you assume he would give you wider distribution if you complied with his advances? I do realize he initiated it. He's practiced at seduction."

"I take responsibility for my poor choice. It had nothing to do with business. It's what I thought I needed at the time, but I was mistaken." Anna exhaled. "I wanted to apologize to you in person."

"Thanks, but I don't care."

Anna studied her perfectly coiffed appearance. "I've done my research and noted you're the driving force behind the company. Why is Grant the figurehead?"

Gia made direct eye contact. "Women aren't respected in my family. My grandmother and I are very close, and we understand the game. The men have affairs and rule the roost while we keep the businesses running. I'm looking forward to having Lauren on board. I sense she's quite independent."

"Could you be more involved if you wanted to?"

"What are you suggesting?" Gia leaned forward.

"Your grandmother is the sole owner of the stores outside of Washington. I would like to expand our reach but leave Grant out of the loop. Is it possible to get those accounts?" Anna smoothed her hands over the tablecloth.

Gia raised an eyebrow. "Interesting. Would you set up the displays in person, or is this also an online venture?"

"Initially everything would be handled in person. Casi has created an excellent online ordering system, but we're a small company and pride ourselves on service."

"Except the Washington stores since Grant handles those."

"Casi doesn't want to work with him either."

"So instead of literally screwing my husband, we would do it through lost revenue? I like it." Gia grinned. "I visit my grandmother on Sunday. I'll let you know what she thinks."

"Thank you for taking time to listen to me." Anna picked up the menu. "Are you on good terms with your brother?"

"No, I'm sorry. I can't help with any favors you need from him."

"I want nothing from him." Anna kept her voice low. "I'm curious about his past and what he might be hiding."

"You've heard about the lawsuits?" Gia swept her gaze over the restaurant nervously.

"Yes. I'm concerned about Lauren's welfare," Anna lied.

"He practically bankrupted our winery with the payouts to those women." Gia shivered. "His marriage to Lauren was arranged to bring stability to the Stanford name. The concept of the restaurant was to keep the focus away from the scandal in California. I'm on the design committee and the dining room will be spectacular. Kyle is the sweetest man in the world! Now there's a man to seduce."

Anna inhaled quickly. "He's having an affair?"

"God no! He's madly in love with his wife. They're such a gorgeous couple." She smiled. "I think Lauren has a crush on him."

"She definitely does."

12

___

COLD TURKEY

"**A**re you telling me the truth?" Casi lounged on the bed and watched Anna packing a bag.

Anna scrolled through her messages and showed her the feed. "They're inducing her tonight. I promised I would be there."

"Why is she having a baby on Thanksgiving? Your sister has lousy timing."

Anna sat beside her. "I was looking forward to dinner at the farmhouse. Since I've embraced this whole small-town vibe, I've been really happy."

"Your conscience is clear." Casi flopped on her back. "Any more contact with Chantal?"

"Not since I sent her the results. It's weird how much I've thought about her over the years and now we're in contact, I'm sorry to know about her. I guess it was easier to think she had a perfect life with an adoring family." Anna shrugged. "She's very accomplished, but I lack any connection with her."

"Maybe you'll meet her in the future and there will be a bond."

"If she lives with this disease. I'm afraid we were her last hope."

❦

The farmhouse kitchen overflowed with baked goods and smelled of turkey roasting. Casi peeked in several pots on the stove before snatching a chocolate fudge cookie from a colorful tray. "Have you been baking all week?"

Georgia buzzed around the stove, happily seasoning the gravy. "Yes. It's lovely having everyone to dinner. I'm sorry Anna can't make it, but it's important she's there for her sister."

Charlotte launched herself from Jake's arms to Georgia's ample bosom. Without skipping a beat, she rearranged her on her hip and continued cooking. "You're the ultimate mother." Casi smiled at her multitasking skills.

"It was easy in my day. Our purpose was to take care of the children and our husbands. I didn't even have a driver's license until Kyle was three and I needed a way to get to the store. It was simple back then." Georgia surveyed the counters to ensure she was on task.

Casi considered which treat to sample next as she chatted to Georgia about her projects at work. She felt the pressure of a hand slide across her hip and glanced over her shoulder and inhaled the remains of the cookie when she saw Dalton. "Hello, gorgeous. Miss me?"

Georgia dashed to her aid with a glass of water and patted her on the back. "Honey did you choke on a crumb?"

Jake frowned as she gasped for air. "Are you seriously choking?"

Casi waved him away and sipped at the water. "I'm fine."

"Darling, let me help you!" Georgia steadied the bags in Lauren's overfilled arms.

Kyle eyed Dalton standing helplessly and pushed past him. "You couldn't manage one bag?" He turned to Lauren. "Did you cook the entire menu?"

She looked sheepish. "I'm struggling to get the seasoning right. I would value your opinion on this bisque." She held a spoon to his lips.

Dalton displayed a bottle of wine. "Do you have an opener? This needs to breathe. You'll love this cabernet." He directed his gaze to Casi's cleavage.

"I prefer white." She escaped up the stairs. She heard footsteps behind her and quickly closed the bedroom door, shoving the dresser to secure it. The handle jiggled, and she perched on the bed close to tears.

"Casi? Why is the door jammed?" Kyle asked.

She jumped up and moved the piece away. "I needed a few minutes alone."

"From me?" Hurt radiated across his face.

"I didn't realize Lauren and Dalton were coming."

"I need to change my shirt. The bisque was hotter than I anticipated." He frowned at a dribble down his front. "I told you last week. I invited them when I was at the winery receiving the order from the lumber company. Remember the mix up and how they delivered a higher grade than I requested? It cost a fortune!"

"I recall the part about the wood." She twisted her hands together. "Did they take it back?"

"No, it turns out Mr. Stanford switched the requirements without my knowledge. It would have been nice to know since my company is covering the upfront cost."

"Is it standard practice?"

"I place the orders. The price is worked into my bid. He shouldn't have been involved. He blew it off and said I was being cheap, but he has no concept of what the build-out will require."

"Did he give you a deposit?" Casi watched him pull his shirt over his head as she admired his lean physique.

"Not a dime. He's a slick talker who acts like a big shot but isn't in a hurry to pull out his checkbook. Gia told me she would ensure the materials are covered by Christmas." Kyle sorted through his closet and glanced back at Casi. "Are you wearing jeans?"

She directed her eyes to her casual attire. "Should I dress up? I was being lazy."

"It's fine."

She giggled and joined him at the closet, reaching to take a hanger down. "I brought this dress. I planned to help your mom with prep, but if Lauren is here, I'm probably not needed."

He wrapped her in his arms. "Don't hide up here and act dejected. She loves having you cook with her."

She kissed him tenderly. "Can you keep Dalton with you?"

"I'll do my best to entertain him and we can station Jake at the kitchen door." Kyle zipped up her dress when she turned around. "Very pretty, my sunshine girl."

They gathered around the table and Lauren rattled on about what she brought and how she was knee-deep in recipe testing. Casi observed her animated performance and how Kyle smiled with pride and understood she couldn't burst their bubble. She caught Dalton's smirk and held up a middle finger in response as she filled her wine glass. Kyle discussed his ideas for design, incorporating a natural theme and using the grapevines as inspiration. Dalton swirled his cabernet, disinterested in the entire affair. Casi refilled her glass absentmindedly, and Jake put his hand on hers. "Take it easy boozer."

"Back off," she warned, almost overfilling it.

Peter glanced her way, raising an eyebrow as she tipped it to her lips. She ignored him and tuned out most of the conversation while she picked at her meal and lamented the loss of her appetite due to the unexpected guests. The talking stopped abruptly, and she noted everyone with their glasses held up waiting for her to join in. "Oh, we're toasting the restaurant?"

Kyle frowned and eyed her precariously full glass. "Lauren announced she's pregnant."

"Oh cool, congrats," she sang out, spilling her wine.

Georgia dabbed at the spot with a napkin and asked Lauren about the baby and what their plans were.

"It's a girl," Lauren gushed.

"How lovely." Georgia glanced sideways at Casi, curious if her sour mood had to do with the announcement.

Dalton put his hand on Lauren's. "She'll be one busy gal in the upcoming year. A new baby and a restaurant. I'm thankful everyone is on board with helping her realize her dreams." He winked at Casi.

The dishes were cleared, and leftovers crammed in the fridge as the men moved to the living room. Casi kneeled to find containers in a cupboard in the laundry room. "Hey, while you're down there why don't you finish what you started." She turned to face Dalton with his hand on his crotch and an evil grin.

She leaped to her feet. "Don't fucking touch me!"

Everyone responded to the commotion to find Dalton with an armful of plastic containers and Casi sobbing by the back door. "I must have scared her when I offered to help." He shrugged with innocent eyes, scanning the group. "Perhaps the amount of alcohol she consumed is making her delusional."

Kyle slid between them and put an arm around Casi. "Are you alright?" She covered her mouth and clawed at the door as the nausea overcame her and she threw up before she could get out.

Jake shoved Dalton out of the way and closed the door. "Poor drunk monkey." He chuckled and surveyed his brother's soiled clothing. "Need a new shirt?"

Kyle assisted Casi out of her dress. "A shower would be better." He tossed their clothes in the washer and wet a towel to wipe her face. "Let's make a run for the bathroom upstairs."

"I'm sorry." She cried in his arms with disgust at her behavior.

Jake opened the door and alerted Georgia. "Can you give them a second to come through?"

Georgia nodded. "Lauren, please escort your husband downstairs to bring up my canning pot."

"I can carry it." Lauren set down the container she was filling.

"Don't be silly. You're pregnant and should be cautious with heavy items. Dalton, please be a gentleman." She put a hand on her hip and forced him down the stairs with a stern look. She waved Casi and Kyle through the room.

Jake put a hand up as Georgia approached. "Give me a minute to clean up and start the washer. I hope her dress wasn't dry clean."

Kyle started the shower and stepped in with Casi. He noticed the blush in her cheeks and how she avoided eye contact. He smiled tenderly. "Are you sure you're ok?"

"Work has been monumental, and I went overboard with eating the delicious food your mom made. I'm sorry I ruined Thanksgiving."

"You didn't ruin anything. Also, you barely ate. I believe it was the two bottles of wine you drank."

"No, I..." She shrugged. "Probably."

"Your moods have been up and down since October." He winced, and she wondered if he figured it out. "It's Lauren? You're jealous of everything exciting going on for her. You're throwing yourself into work and have no interest in coming out to see the progress on the restaurant." He lifted her chin. "The pregnancy announcement took you off guard. I should have prepared you."

"How long have you known?"

"She told me in Victoria at the class and asked me not to say anything. Dalton wasn't thrilled with the timing. But she's trying to prove she can handle the responsibility of a business and being a mother. I realize it's not something you value, but please give her a break and let her be happy. The last few years have been rough on her."

"You don't think I value motherhood?" She pushed him back. "I completely understand the magnitude and the commitment. I admire women who do it well. I believed we were together in the decision not to have children, or did you honestly feel I wasn't up to the task?"

Kyle put his hands on her shoulders. "I misspoke, and I apologize. It would be more accurate to say we prefer not to be parents but understand others who desire a different path. For the record, you're an amazing aunt and it's an extremely valuable role."

13

RUMORS

*D*ecember rolled in with a crisp wind and a flurry of snowflakes. Casi blew through the front door and noted Kyle slamming his laptop closed with a guilty expression. "Looking at porn?"

"No." He tried to remove a flash drive, but she forcefully stopped him. He sighed when she clicked on the icon and brought up the racy photos they had taken.

"I thought these were in the safe." She scowled at him. "We agreed to keep them private."

"I wanted to see something." He brought his eyes to meet hers. "Your face is different lately." He scanned the cropped, layered bob. "And you got a haircut. Did Dylan style it?"

She glanced at the photo on the screen. She appeared younger, with an expression of pure happiness. A quick check in the mirror confirmed his claim; a hardened expression penetrated her beautiful face and carved lines around her eyes accented by dark circles. "I haven't slept well lately." She fluffed her hair. "I got it cut on a whim at a place in the mall. It requires effort to style which could be a mistake with this weather."

"Was Dylan unavailable?"

"He's in Portland with Grace and the new baby. He's copying my idea for a scrapbook and wants to record the moment she is introduced to her grandparents."

"It explains the unusual style, but what motivated it?" He pointed to the photo. "Where is this girl? Have you murdered her and thrown her body in the lake?" A smile crept to his eyes.

"She's taking a break for the winter." She slid on his lap. "Life overwhelmed her, and she needed to retreat."

"Who's the woman I'm sleeping with and where are her curves? She's no longer interested in being intimate and cries in the night. She frightens me because I don't know how to help her."

She relaxed in his arms. "Kiss her gently. She might require special handling for a little while. She's strong and will return when her soul is rested."

Casi read the text message from Jack as she entered the parking garage. His urgency to meet was cause for concern, although she wished he stated what it was about rather than insist she drive an hour out of her way to come to his restaurant. She drove cautiously through the freshly fallen snow, still not experienced enough with the Washington weather to tempt fate. She fixed her tousled hair in the mirror after she parked. She regretted the recent haircut, although she was proud of the façade she crafted, cool and calm. No foolish girl in residence.

She pushed the heavy glass door open and stepped inside the room bustling with late afternoon business. The aroma of hops and bacon filled the air, and hunger pangs clawed at her stomach. Jack was at the bar chatting with customers. She observed him objectively, handsome and confident with an air of deep satisfaction in his life. The resemblance between them was undeniable, and she hoped she was able to hide a core laced with doubt and insecurity as well as he did. "Hi, Dad." She poured herself a beer with a smile.

He turned and smiled, genuine and filled with love. "Do you want something to eat?"

"No, thanks. I already ate," she lied. "What did you want to talk to me about?"

Jack sighed and surveyed the restaurant. He indicated a quiet corner near the wash station, and she followed. "You know how this business is. Rumors circulate faster than an STD."

"You would know." She winked, and he chuckled.

"Usually I ignore it unless it has to do with our business."

"Are you having problems? I can help with money."

"Thanks, we're doing very well." He put a hand on her shoulder. "There's been talk about you and Dalton."

"What?"

"I stay out of your personal life normally, but I love Kyle and I don't want you making a fool out of him. Whatever issues you're having won't be solved by having an affair."

"You bastard!" She lunged at him and delivered a scorching slap across his face. "How dare you accuse me? I'm nothing like you."

Jack stood in stunned silence as Ava charged over and threw her arms around Casi. She directed her to a service hall and hugged her tightly. "What's going on?"

"He accused me of having an affair with Dalton!"

"He heard rumors and it upset him. I told him we should stay out of it." She brushed hair from Casi's face. "Dad loves you and he wanted to fix whatever is wrong with you and Kyle."

"My marriage is perfect!"

"Then why are you so upset? You never have a problem putting Dad in his place. Why are you hitting him and getting hysterical?"

"I'm not weak like him." Casi cried in her hands.

"What are you hiding? You're thin as a rail and bursting into tears over an unkind comment. What's the truth behind you and Dalton? I understand you don't care for Lauren and are probably jealous of the project she's including Kyle in. Is it because she's pregnant?" She pulled back from her with alarm. "Why are you shaking?"

"I'm not jealous! I don't want a stupid baby."

"Casi, I've known you your entire life. You're spiraling out of control. What caused this?"

"You can't say anything to Dad or Kyle." Casi waited for her to nod. "When we were in Victoria, Kyle went to the cooking class with Lauren because Dalton refused to go. I thought it was Kyle coming back for something, so I opened the door without checking."

Ava grasped the edge of a counter. "What happened?"

"Jake and Anna had gone to get coffee. He pulled off my towel and made lewd comments."

Ava's face hardened to an angry mask. "Did he hurt you?"

"He touched me and took pictures. He twisted my arm and pinned me against a chair. I tried to stop him!"

"I know you would have," Ava soothed.

"Jake came back, and Dalton bolted before things could progress. I can't confide in Kyle because Dalton threatened to reveal Anna's affair with his brother-in-law." She read Ava's questioning expression. "She was, and I told her to stop."

"Jake will get over it. You can't keep this to yourself."

"It will ruin everything for Kyle and the job at the restaurant." She inhaled sharply. "Kyle will step up and help Lauren with the baby if Dalton leaves."

"Dalton should be in jail. It's not your problem if it inconveniences Lauren." Ava considered the scenario. "I understand your concern about Kyle's loyalty. Dalton is bragging about having an affair with you. You think he took pictures? What if they get out?"

Casi blanched. "What should I do?"

"Tell Kyle. I'll research Dalton. I'm sure this isn't his first offense. I'm so sorry. We will make him accountable" She escorted Casi to the door. "Drive carefully."

"What did my loony daughter tell you?" Jack scoffed.

"Why do you always take possession of her? I've been there since the day she was born. She may have your blood, but I'm tired of you acting like I didn't have a significant part in raising her."

Kyle waved to Lauren when he entered the coffee shop. He placed his order and answered texts while he waited. He put a cup in front of her and kissed her on the cheek. "I'm thinking we can focus on the design while we wait for the permits." He noticed her push the drink away. "You can't have coffee when you're pregnant?"

"In moderation." She fumbled with her phone and began to cry.

Kyle reached over and took her hand. "Are you upset about the business? I warned you these things always take longer than expected."

She shook her head. "It's Dalton."

"He changed his mind on letting you run it?" Kyle scoffed, knowing there had been threats made.

Lauren opened her photo gallery. "I found these on his phone and confronted him. He admitted they're having an affair."

Kyle studied the image of Casi nude in Dalton's arms as he kissed her neck and fondled her breast. Her head was turned to the side as if in ecstasy. He scrolled through the next few angrily, then shoved it away. He clenched his jaw. "When are these from?"

"He says it started in Victoria. He ended it once we made the pregnancy public. It explains why she was weird at Thanksgiving."

Thoughts raced through his mind with snippets of information in support of the claim. He leaned back in his chair and glared at her. "Why Dalton? She could have anyone she wants."

"To punish us?" She broke down. "I didn't think she would go this far to hurt me. Why can't I have anything for myself?"

"Will you stay with him?"

"I signed a prenup. I won't only lose the restaurant." She shivered. "I mortgaged my condo to invest in it. Everything I have is in there. He told me if we divorce, I walk away with nothing."

"I cautioned you about letting him make the financial decisions. Why didn't you let Brian handle it?"

"Dalton wouldn't let me! He said we had to use his family's accountant and attorney. I believed him until the mess with the honeymoon. I saved over twenty thousand dollars."

"I imagine his family has practice protecting their assets, which is why he wanted everything in his name."

"Will you divorce Casi? I'm not surprised she cheated. This may not be the first time. She's envious of our relationship."

Kyle bit his lip. "We have a great friendship, Lauren. Casi and I share something much deeper. I won't throw it away for a rumor."

"This is proof! You're being played, Kyle. Dalton also said Anna's having an affair with his brother-in-law."

"Gia's husband?"

"These women are the same as Dalton's circle. They take what they want and don't care who they hurt."

&.

Kyle pulled in the driveway and checked his watch. He noticed Anna's car across the street and headed up the path to the house. She smiled when he walked in. "Hello, is Jake with you?"

"No, he went to pick up the kids." He fiddled with the zipper on his jacket. "I need to talk to you."

"Ok." She poured a glass of wine.

"Are you having an affair with Grant?" he blurted.

She turned and raised her chin in defiance. "Who said I was?"

"Not the question I asked."

"None of your business is the answer."

"Anna, I was clear when you married Jake, I would protect him. He's not your plaything to cheat on and discard when you get bored. If you're not in this marriage for love, take your things and leave."

"Shouldn't this conversation be between me and your brother?"

"Here's a topic of concern; is Casi also having an affair, or are you the only one screwing around?"

Anna's eyes shifted to the door and her face paled. Jake set Tommy down and gave him a car to play with Austin. He shook his head at Anna. "What's the answer?"

"I don't know anything about Casi." Anna blushed.

"Then tell me about yourself," Jake stated.

"It was brief, and it's over."

"Sums up our marriage." Jake walked out the door.

Kyle glared at her. "What's wrong with you women? Why can't you be happy in this life?" He surveyed the boys playing, oblivious to the magnitude of the adult issues. "You're smart enough to know I won't let you take any of his assets, including this house. Start making plans for your future and consult an attorney about custody."

Jake fixed a drink and glanced up when Kyle entered. "I can't say I'm surprised. Who told you?"

"Lauren." Kyle put ice in a glass and filled it with whiskey.

"She knows for sure or is she stirring up shit?"

Kyle cocked his head. "Anna admitted it. Didn't you hear her?"

"Who's the guy?"

"Grant, Dalton's brother-in-law."

"Perfect." Jake refilled his glass. "He kisses your wife, then sleeps with mine. Why did you ask her about Casi?"

Kyle regarded the ice in his glass. "Dalton has nude pictures on his phone of them together."

"Him and Casi?"

"Lauren copied them and showed me. She thinks Casi did it to ruin her dream of having a restaurant."

Casi walked in and set down her purse and laptop bag. She surveyed the brothers. "What's going on?"

Two sets of sapphire eyes glared at her before Jake spoke. "Why do you feel the desire to destroy everything?"

"What are you talking about?"

Jake slammed his glass on the counter and watched it shatter against the granite. He gripped the edge of the bar and tried to control his breathing.

Casi slipped between his arms and caressed his cheek. "Why are you angry with me?"

He grabbed her wrist and yanked it from his face as he spoke through clenched teeth. "You knew Anna was having an affair!"

Casi winced and regarded Kyle's livid expression. "Yes, and I told her to stop. It's been over for a while."

Jake tightened his hold. "Are you also cheating?"

"You're hurting me!" She tried to pry his fingers off.

"Answer the question!" Jake roared.

"It's complicated," she pleaded as the pain radiated up her arm.

"I saw the pictures of you with Dalton. You were with him in Victoria. Admit it." Kyle stormed toward her.

"Yes!" Relief washed over her as Jake released his vice-like grip.

Jake shoved her aside and went to get the broom. She crumpled in a chair and tucked her wrist against her chest, sobbing. Kyle regarded her, and his shoulders slumped. He kneeled before her and his voice broke. "I love you, Casi. I forgive you and we can move on. I don't want our marriage to end." As she cried, he stroked her hair. "Please tell me why you chose Dalton? Was it worth it to hurt Lauren?"

She raised her tearful eyes to meet his. "It wasn't consensual."

Jake stopped sweeping. "What did you say?"

Casi rocked as she spoke. "He came to the room when you left for the class. I opened the door because I thought it was you."

Kyle clenched his jaw. "What did he do?"

"He held me down while he touched me and took those photos. Jake came back before he could proceed. It's not an affair. It happened once, and he's been taunting me ever since."

Jake threw the broom down. "God damn it! It explains why you were bat-shit crazy when I came back. Why didn't you tell me?"

"I couldn't! He threatened to tell you about Anna. He told me Lauren was pregnant and said you would leave me to take care of her."

"No, I wouldn't!" Kyle pulled her in his arms. "My loyalty is always to you." He felt her wince and smoothed a hand over her swollen arm. His eyes widened, and he turned to his brother. "You broke her wrist!"

"No, I couldn't have." Jake squeezed his eyes closed at the realization of what he had done. "I'm so sorry."

"I'm ok," Casi whimpered.

Kyle's eyes filled with rage. "We must go to the hospital." He shoved his brother out of the way. "I trusted you to protect her and you let him harm her and then crush her bones? You're fucking useless!"

Jake staggered back with dazed eyes. He snatched his keys from the counter. "Everything is my fault."

"Where's he going?" Casi jumped as he slammed the door.

"Probably to the bar. I don't care." Kyle stroked her cheek. "Let me help you get changed. You'll need x-rays and a cast."

"It could be a sprain. It's been hurting for a while."

Kyle read her expression and recalled when she pulled away from him on the ferry back to Seattle. "Since Victoria."

14

———

PAY IT FORWARD

Kyle paced the hospital room while they waited for results from the x-rays. After numerous texts buzzing in his pocket, he turned his phone off, not in the mood to hear an apology. Casi insisted on proclaiming she slipped on the ice, and he agreed to simplify the process. The realization he missed the signs of an obvious assault nauseated him. He strolled to Casi and smoothed her hair, kissing her on the forehead and apologizing. She was no longer crying and sat in a daze as she stared at an eye chart.

A doctor entered the room and smiled, and Kyle cocked his head in confusion. "Gabby? Why are you here?"

"I'm an orthopedic surgeon. I recognized your name on the chart and I came to talk to you." She held up the paperwork.

"About what?" Kyle shifted uncomfortably.

"Your wife's wrist. Can you tell me how it happened?"

"I slipped on the ice," Casi said in a monotone.

"You slipped and fell?" Gabby glanced between them.

"It was my fault," he blurted.

Casi grasped his hand. "He warned me not to wear my high-heeled boots in the snow. I figured since they were weather proofed, and I was only going out to the car, I would be fine. When I slipped, he grabbed my wrist, and I felt it pop. He feels responsible." She shrugged to make the lie more believable.

"It explains the nature of the fracture." Gabby brought up the image on the light board. "I have concerns."

"About me?" Kyle swallowed.

"No," Gabby assured him. She pointed to dark lines around jagged white pieces. "Have you had a fracture in the past? Maybe from playing sports?"

"I might have broken it when I was fifteen. I never got it checked and wrapped it in an ace bandage until it stopped hurting." Casi redirected her gaze to the floor. Kyle narrowed his eyes and concluded the trauma was caused by Sonya. "Several years ago, I was in a car accident and it hurt, but it was the least of my injuries, so I didn't bother to have it looked at."

"The bone healed, but not straight. It's misaligned, which made it susceptible to a new fracture." Gabby smiled at Kyle. "Even a slight amount of pressure in the wrong direction was a recipe for disaster. This break was inevitable." She glanced at her chart. "Unfortunately, it requires surgery to ensure it doesn't happen again. We must put in pins to hold the bones in place while they heal to provide stability."

Kyle put an arm around Casi. "What does it involve?"

"I recommend we do the surgery tonight before healing begins. I'll make an incision along here." She indicated the placement on Casi's arm. "We can give her a local or full anesthesia."

"Knock me out," Casi shivered. "I don't want to see it."

"Can I stay with her?" Kyle hugged her tighter.

"Sure, we can have you scrub in." Gabby smiled.

Kyle followed her to the hall and grasped her elbow. "Gabby, I realize you're a doctor, but if you harbor any ill-will toward me, please don't touch her. She's the love of my life and I won't put her at risk."

"Kyle, my shift ended thirty minutes ago. I saw your case and signed on to it because I owe you a huge debt of gratitude." She sighed. "The money I got from my false accusation was put toward medical school. I made your family suffer for something you never did. I have dedicated my career to helping others."

"Thank you." Kyle frowned. "Casi was assaulted. She told me tonight, which is why we're acting strange."

"Have you reported it?"

"This accident happened, and I must ensure she's fine before I proceed. He's a friend of the family, and it happened a few months ago. I don't have details and she's insisting on putting it behind her."

"Did he twist her arm during the attack?"

"Her wrist has been hurting since then. She mentioned he restrained her. My brother came back before it escalated."

"I noticed damage to the ligaments in her arm, which would indicate an intra-skeletal injury. We see it a lot with wrestlers."

"Can you fix it?"

"It will heal in time. After the surgery, I recommend a full cast to ensure she's not straining the muscles. It's not comfortable, but it's effective."

&

Gabby smiled at Kyle propped beside the hospital bed, stroking Casi's arm as he gazed at her. "She'll be asleep for a while. Are you sure you don't want to go home and rest?"

"I want to be here when she wakes up." He patted a tuft of hair from Casi's forehead. "In retrospect, I should have questioned this haircut. There were so many signs pointing to a dark secret, but I backed off and figured she would work through it." He smiled. "She can be intense when she's awake, passionate and full of life."

"I admire how much you love her." Gabby sat in a chair beside him. "You were certainly popular in college, but it didn't seem you cared deeply for the girls you dated."

"I wasn't emotionally invested." He narrowed his eyes. "You wanted to punish me for pursuing casual sex?"

Gabby sighed. "I owe you the truth."

"I would appreciate a clarification. I never understood why you targeted me."

"We had several classes together, and you were friendly and

encouraged me to join your study groups." She placed her hand on his. "I developed a huge crush on you and convinced myself you would be interested in me if I could prove I was more than your smart lab partner. I noticed the women you were attracted to and spent a fortune getting my hair done and buying a dress which didn't suit me. I was never invited to frat parties, but I waited until late at night when I figured everyone was drunk. It didn't take long to find you and I admit I was surprised to see you doing a line of coke."

Kyle blushed. "It ended in college."

Gabby's face clouded with the memory. "You looked up and your gorgeous blue eyes melted my heart when you smiled. When you handed me the straw, I couldn't say no. It was the first time I tried it."

"I'm sorry. I guess I assumed everyone at the party did it."

"I was flattered you included me." She glanced away. "I misread your intentions and amped up my flirting, which I imagine was awkward and pathetic."

"I honestly don't remember. Those parties were a way for me to escape from the pressure of work and school."

"Kayla ridiculed me and said I was a loser for thinking a guy like you would ever want to have sex with me."

"Who's Kayla?"

"Really? The woman you invited back to your room! She was in our biology class and always tried to cheat off me."

He grinned. "In a strange twist of fate, I knew your name because I engaged with you intellectually whereas she was only a pretty woman I spent the night with."

She smiled at his lack of recollection. "I followed you like a stalker. I would like to think it was my inexperience with drugs which diminished my judgement, but I wanted to be the girl in your arms and my anger grew the longer I watched you while I stood in the pouring rain. I was hysterical by the time I got back to my dorm and I repeatedly muttered your name. My roommate assumed you had harmed me and sought help from the crisis center. The next day I realized the lie had escalated, but my sister got involved and they convinced me I wanted to recant because I had feelings for you. I was embarrassed and didn't know how to make it go away. Once they pushed for disciplinary action, I couldn't be silent any longer. I signed a statement I had fabricated the story and I transferred to another college. I was humiliated by the payoff from your attorney, but there was no way to return it. I put it away for medical school and promised myself I would never hurt anyone again."

"I wish you had told me back then."

"I finished school, got married, and started a family." Gabby bit her lip. "A few years ago, my daughter was infatuated with a boy in her class and it reminded me of my behavior. I noted how he interacted with her at the swim meet and knew he didn't feel the same way, but I couldn't convince her. I searched for you on Facebook because I was curious to see what you were up to." She nudged him. "You're even more handsome now. I was pleased you seemed content and thought I would reach out and reconnect. Not as the stalker, but a former classmate. When I saw you at Starbucks, I pushed too hard for you to accept my friend request because I was desperate to prove I had evolved into a sane person. I'm sorry if I came off as a lunatic." She squeezed his hand. "You were polite and sweet even though I noted the hate in your eyes for me."

Kyle chuckled. "I was slightly afraid of you."

"I realize I can't take it back, but please know it was a nightmare I couldn't control at twenty-one. I'm a stable woman now."

"I relate to weird better than you think." Kyle touched Casi's cheek. "I forgive you for your accusation, and I apologize for not recognizing your feelings. You were a great lab partner, and I respected your input." His eyes focused on the bandage around Casi's arm. "You're an incredible surgeon. Thanks for allowing me to be in there."

"You were always interested in biology and are perhaps one of the most intelligent men I know. I was always curious to know what type of woman you would marry."

Kyle frowned. "She's beautiful, but there's a lot more there."

"The first images on Facebook convinced me you married her for her looks. Then I noticed how you lit up and I realized I had finally witnessed the rare occurrence of Kyle Jensen head over heels in love."

Kyle grinned and straightened the sheet as Casi shuddered in her sleep. "She was a swimsuit model in LA. I had recently ended a relationship when the woman pushed for marriage. Casi walked right up and kissed me when I was on a job at her building. She didn't even know my name. I fell for her immediately. Not because of her beauty or charisma, but there was something deeper. Our souls connected in a way I can't explain. She's the one who pursued me until I was so smitten there was no way I would ever recover." His eyes filled with rage. "Lauren and I are still friends and it was her husband who hurt Casi. I'm furious with her and at myself for not understanding what happened. Casi told me she was uncomfortable around him. I didn't listen!"

"You couldn't have known. I'm sure she receives a lot of unwanted attention and you assumed she could handle herself given her past vocation. The extent of her injury convinced me he restrained her in a manner a wrestler would use to overpower an opponent. I'm concerned he's practiced at this type of assault and sadly, I comprehend how attorneys silence victims."

"I won't accept a dime for what he did." Kyle's eyes flashed a deep hatred. "This stops here. I refuse to have another woman victimized."

"Are you still with us?" Gabby noted Casi's eyelids flutter.

"Kyle," Casi croaked.

"I'm right here." He grasped her hand.

"He never left your side," Gabby reported.

"I can't feel my arm." Casi strained to lift her head.

Gabby brought a cup and held the straw for her to drink from. "You're on heavy pain medication. Numbness is normal. I'm giving Kyle a prescription for you to take home. We'll keep you overnight and when the swelling subsides, we'll put a cast on."

Kyle stroked Casi's cheek as her eyes rolled back. "You're pretty high. Do you feel any pain?"

"It's all good," she slurred. Her eyes scanned Gabby's face. "You're the wacko from Facebook! Why are you here?"

"She's a doctor. She's not here to harm you." He grimaced and regarded Gabby. "I'm sorry. I told her about what happened."

Gabby smiled. "We'll start bringing her back down to earth and I'll talk to her when she's stable."

"Thanks for being a real friend tonight. The past is behind us and I'm glad we reconnected."

❧

Gabby returned in the morning and woke him with a gentle touch. "It's time to put the cast on."

Kyle rubbed his eyes, staggering as he stood. "Can she walk there?" He noticed the nurse removing drip lines and a catheter.

"We'll put her in a wheelchair as a precaution. She's still adjusting to the medication." Gabby nodded to the nurse.

"Can you get in the chair, Hon?" the nurse asked.

Casi struggled to sit, and Kyle slid his arms under her in a swift motion to settle her in the seat. He lovingly arranged a blanket on her lap and smoothed her hair. "It won't take long, and I'll stay with you."

Gabby smiled at him. "You are a wonderful husband."

Casi frowned as the layers of the cast were applied almost to her underarm. "Why is it so big? Isn't it just my wrist?"

"We don't want you using your arm until it has a chance to heal." Gabby noted her agitation and scrawled in her notepad. She handed the slip to Kyle. "This will help with anxiety."

Kyle caressed Casi's back. "What limitations will she have?"

"I don't recommend driving or lifting. Give it a month and we can check if the ligaments are healed. Use caution with tasks which strain on the wrist." She touched Casi's hand. "The confinement is necessary for a full recovery. Your arm will be stronger than before, and you won't experience pain long-term. I sense you have overcome a lot in the past and consider this one more annoyance."

Kyle phoned Ava on their way back to the room to give her a summary of the surgery. There was silence on the other end, and he wondered if the connection had been lost. Ava cleared her throat. "How did the break happen?"

"Um, she slipped on the ice, but the issue stems back to when she was fifteen. Do you recall her having an injury?" Kyle doubted it had gone unnoticed.

"She claimed she hurt herself playing field hockey." Ava chuckled. "An obvious lie. I didn't know about the abuse by Sonya, but I had taken Joey aside and questioned him to death. Poor kid, he was adamant she showed up to school with the injury. What's the real story about this surgery? It's an odd coincidence how she told me what happened with Dalton, and suddenly she falls and breaks her wrist. Please be honest."

Kyle sighed and watched Casi being wheeled back to the room with her cast sticking out at an awkward angle. "Can we discuss it later? I should get her home and she's pretty doped up."

"Wait, have you spoken to your mother?" Ava asked.

"I have a million calls to return, but my focus has been on Casi. If she is upset about Jake and Anna, it's not my priority."

"Jake's been arrested."

"Fuck! Drunk driving?"

"Assault." Ava condensed the situation. "He beat up Dalton almost to the point of killing him. Lauren is hysterical."

"How long are they holding Jake for?"

"If Dalton dies, it will be considered manslaughter."

"Dammit, this is the last thing I need. I'll call her later this afternoon. I'm so tired my head is spinning."

"Is everything alright?" Gabby glanced up as he came back.

"I have family stuff to deal with." Kyle faked a smile and began pulling a sweatshirt over Casi's head. He frowned and studied the logistics of dressing her with a cast.

Gabby giggled. "There is a severe learning curve."

Kyle unbuttoned his flannel shirt and caught Casi's disapproving look as she regarded her reflection in the window. "We're going straight home." He patted a clump of wayward hair. "I believe this will be a challenging situation for both of us."

15

DAMAGE CONTROL

*A*nna hurried to answer the knock at the door. "Jake!" Her heart dropped as Mary stood before her. "I was hoping he was home."

"No, and he won't be for a while." Mary surveyed the room in disarray with an open bottle of wine on the counter. She noted Anna's unusually disheveled appearance. "Where's Charlotte?"

Anna tugged her cardigan around her and tucked a loose wisp of copper hair behind an ear. "Gail is taking care of her. I've been sick."

"Remorse can manifest itself with physical illness." Mary directed her to sit at the table. "Your husband is in jail." She grasped Anna's hand. "I wanted you to hear it in person."

Anna's eyes fluttered as the room spun around her. "I don't understand. He left yesterday when he found out about the affair. Casi was adamant about not telling him because she wanted to protect him. Obviously, she was right. She won't return my calls, and neither will Kyle. He pretty much told me to move out." She glanced across the street. "Perhaps they're waiting for me to leave before they come home. Did Jake get arrested for drunk driving?"

"Casi told them about Dalton. Jake put him in the hospital."

"Good!"

"She should have told me what was going on before I heard it through the grapevine. Dalton certainly deserved it. But it presents challenges to ensure Jake doesn't serve a lengthy term."

"I'll pay for an attorney and vouch for his character."

Mary patted her hand. "We'll take it one step at a time."

"Is Kyle there?"

"No, Casi broke her wrist and required surgery." She observed Anna's expression to determine what the true story might be.

"When? She was fine at work, and then she went to see her dad. This doesn't have anything to do with Jake, does it?"

Mary pursed her lips. "It's unusual timing." She turned to the sound of a truck across the street. "They're home." She glanced over at Anna's appearance. "I hired you for your confidence and abilities in business. Get your shit together and rectify your mistakes. We've all taken a walk on the wrong side of the tracks, but we figure out how to cross back without getting hit by the train."

Kyle helped Casi inside as a hand touched his back and he turned to look down at Mary's petite stature. "Why are you here?"

"I go where I'm needed. Today I'll be Casi's caregiver." Mary brushed past him into the house. "Let's set her up on the sofa. The cast appears cumbersome and will require support."

"We're fine on our own." Kyle glared at Anna.

"Anna will catch up with Casi and then go to work in Seattle. I have reports to be completed and we'll set up a system for Casi to work from home for now." Mary directed everyone to the living room.

Kyle crossed his arms over his chest. "I appreciate your offer to help but I haven't had a chance to read through the information on the prescriptions and I don't feel comfortable leaving her here."

Mary raised an eyebrow. "If I could handle her in LA, I sure as hell can watch her at a small-town lake house."

"I'm not questioning your abilities." He shifted his weight. "I haven't slept, and the shit keeps getting piled higher before I can deal with one crisis at a time."

"Which is why I'm here." Mary smiled. "We'll go over the medication and make a plan for the day. I have friends working on the issue with your brother, so we won't waste our energy. We must assume you'll be shorthanded for the holidays."

"Terrible timing." Kyle massaged his temple.

"Yes, but you have Riley and Ava has offered to send a crew from her restaurant with construction experience." She held her hand up as he protested. "They certainly can't replace Jake, but they will handle basic tasks while you expend energy elsewhere."

Kyle pulled her in a hug. "Thank you for always supporting us."

"I don't love randomly, but as Casi knows, my loyalty runs deep. We require friends to lean on at times." Mary eased the bag from his hand. "Let's make a schedule for pain management. What else did they give her?" She read the bottle and cocked her head. "Anti-anxiety?"

"The doctor was concerned the cast might become restrictive, and she wants her to remain calm. We should gauge her discomfort level to administer it as needed." Kyle gave her a sad smile.

"Better to have it on hand." Mary glanced at Anna sobbing beside Casi on the sofa. "We might want to medicate her."

Kyle kept his voice low. "I'm royally pissed off."

"Understandable, but in fairness, the issues stemmed from what happened to Casi, not what Anna did." She stepped in front of him. "Or was Jake involved with the broken wrist?"

Kyle surveyed Casi in a daze and Anna with tearful eyes waiting to hear the answer. "Jake grabbed her, and the pressure broke her bones. The doctor explained she had an old injury, I'm guessing from Sonya, and it never healed properly." He clenched his jaw. "We suspect Dalton twisted her arm and damaged the ligaments, which also created an unstable wrist. I'm beyond furious with Jake, but he only caused the final trauma."

"Jake didn't grab me," Casi slurred. "I put my hands in his. He didn't realize he tightened his grip."

Kyle shrugged. "It's still his fault."

Casi burst into tears. "Stop blaming him!"

"We know Jake would never intentionally harm you. I'm sure he is sick with worry." Mary smiled at Kyle as Casi relaxed in her arms.

"Take a shower and go to work. Anna will bring home dinner." She noted the distrust in his eyes. "Nothing will be decided about their marriage until Jake returns."

Kyle barely got in the door before Amy flew in his arms. "I heard Jake's in jail! You don't have to share details. We love you guys and stand behind you no matter what."

"Thank you." Kyle slipped from her grasp and held her at arm's length. "He beat up someone who hurt Casi." He paused and decided to fabricate slightly. "She needed surgery on her wrist and she's not a happy camper. We're working out the details of his release and hope to have him home soon."

Riley clenched his jaw as he gripped a screw gun tighter. "I can help you finish the job if the guy is still standing."

"He's in the hospital, which is a good place for him since I'm sure there will be a line of people seeking revenge. Casi is at home safe." He caught his breath. "Ava is sending a crew to help us with assembly. Riley, I'll need you to step up as a foreman."

"I appreciate the opportunity to extend my skills." Riley grinned with pride at his temporary title change.

"In the new year, you'll have completed your apprenticeship. We've been pleased with your performance and would like to bring you on as a full-time employee. We can discuss compensation when Jake gets back." Kyle swallowed as an emptiness overwhelmed him. He lost himself in paperwork and scheduling work orders between checking his phone for updates on Casi. An invoice caught his eye, and he grimaced, recalling the expensive materials sitting at a job site he was most likely fired from. He contemplated phoning Lauren but determined it would be opening a can of worms with endless problems and explanations. He surveyed his neat piles of completed tasks and picked up his phone.

"Kyle! Where have you been?" Georgia sobbed.

"Casi had surgery on her wrist and we stayed in the hospital overnight." He paused while she asked a multitude of questions. "I'm not sure if we'll come for Christmas. Honestly, I'm trying to get caught up at work and with Jake gone it puts a lot of pressure on me." He held the phone away as she burst into tears. "I understand your concerns. Mary is helping us figure things out."

"Have you spoken to Lauren? She's very upset."

"Please stop pressuring me to take on more than I can handle!" When she was silent, he regretted his tone. "I'm sorry if I'm short with you. I haven't slept, and the stress keeps mounting." He looked up as four men entered the building with their hands in their pockets. "Mom, I need to go. I'll update you as soon as I have news."

He greeted the crew and gave them a tour of the workshop as they followed him around in silence. "Do you speak English?"

"I do, and I can translate. They're used to Miss. Ava speaking Spanish to them, but they know enough to get by," one said as the rest nodded to show they understood.

"Excellent. We need help to build frames. Riley will oversee the work and I'll do the final check. Can anyone drive a truck for deliveries?"

One man raised his hand and Kyle smiled at him. "Perfect. We'll coordinate our schedules and try to have everything done a few days before Christmas. Were wages discussed?"

"Miss. Ava is taking care of it. She said come and work."

"Fine, I'll make arrangements with her." Kyle raised an eyebrow as they immediately scurried throughout the workshop and began sweeping and cleaning while they waited for job instructions. "Ava sent us an experienced team." He turned to Riley, hovering at his side. "Did you have a question?"

Riley blushed. "I realize this isn't a good time, but it may be the only opportunity to speak with you."

Kyle grimaced and waited for him to give notice. "It's best to come out and say it."

"Um, ok. Amy doesn't have a dad." He paled and quickly added, "I'm not suggesting you're old enough to be her father!"

"I'm confused."

"I want to ask her to marry me at Christmas and I know how much she respects you. Even though we're young, I love her and will do everything to make her happy." Riley wrung his hands.

"Are you asking for my blessing?" Kyle grinned.

"Yes, I wanted to ask you and Jake."

"I'll speak for both of us." Kyle put his hand on Riley's shoulder. "We're thrilled you're ready to commit to Amy and support your union. Let us know when it's official, and we'll take you out to dinner to celebrate."

❧

Kyle arrived home and surveyed the women huddled together in the living room. He cradled Charlotte in his arms and brought her to Anna. "Did you forget something today?"

Anna blanched. "Oh, my God! I got caught up at work and then I was anxious to bring the reports to Casi."

He tried to hand the child to her, but she clung to him. "Did you at least remember dinner?"

Ava stood. "Kyle, why don't you relax while I call in an order?"

Kyle slumped. "I want to make sure Casi eats. She shouldn't have medication on an empty stomach."

"I had ice cream." Casi gave him a thumb's up from the sofa.

Kyle kissed her on the top of the head. "How are you feeling?"

"Tired, which is dumb because I slept most of the day." She shifted her eyes to the door when someone knocked. "Dawn and Katie. They wanted to visit, but I didn't realize they would get here so late."

Ava answered the door and gave Dawn a hug. "We were about to order Chinese. Any special requests?"

"I'm easy." Dawn smiled brightly and shifted her gaze to Casi. "Holy Moly, your cast is huge!" She plopped beside her on the sofa and gave advice on bathing and pain control. "I brought supplies to help." She produced an overstuffed bag.

Katie glared at Lia while she pretended to busy herself with tying

Austin's shoe. "I would have brought the girls if I had known it was appropriate to bring children. Dawn claimed Casi was in too much pain to entertain."

"These children live here." Kyle extracted his wallet.

Katie rolled her eyes. "Really? I've heard Lia has a sweet little cottage with flower baskets and lace curtains. I believe it was my daughter who told me."

Ava put her hand on Kyle's as he took out bills and refused to take the money. "Dawn, can you show Kyle how to wrap the cast for the shower? I appreciate you taking time to come and help."

"No problem. I'm happy to use my nursing skills to assist a friend." Dawn smiled at Kyle. "I can get the knot out of your shoulder if you sit down for a minute."

"I'm fine." Kyle winced. "Maybe, if someone can take this child. I can't seem to peel her off." Ava held out her arms and Charlotte launched herself forward. "Perfect, go to your grandma."

Ava cuddled Charlotte. "A welcome title."

Katie frowned. "You shouldn't confuse her."

Dawn motioned for Kyle to sit. "My children address my friends as auntie or uncle. It's a sign of respect. I think it's lovely."

"I agree." Lia squared her shoulders. "Jake and I consider Ava and Jack to be grandparents to our boys, which is nice because they're limited on my side."

Kyle turned to Ava and groaned as Dawn released the stiffness in his shoulder. "Thanks for sending the crew today. They were invaluable. Please let me know what I owe."

Ava shook her head. "I have a deal with Jose to help his family find work. He has been incredibly kind to me over the years, and I'm assisting them with citizenship. Extending their marketable skills will help them gain employment."

"I'll happily give references." Kyle glanced at Casi deep in conversation with Katie and smiled at Dawn. "Thank you, I appreciate your help. You're an expert at pain relief."

"No problem. Next time I'll do it with your shirt off." Dawn giggled and squeezed next to Casi to ease her neck ache.

Kyle directed Ava to the kitchen out of ear shot. "How long have you known about Dalton?"

"She told me the other day. He's been showing pictures of them together, and Jack was upset to hear a rumor they were having an affair. When he asked her about it, she became livid and slapped him." Kyle gasped, and she nodded. "I promised not to say anything but advised her to tell you. After you informed me about her surgery, I told him the truth. You can imagine how hysterical he was."

Kyle chewed his lip. "Did Mary tell you about Jake?"

"She was adamant the injury was an accident. I understand you're in a quandary about how to feel. I told Jack she fell. With your brother in jail, I don't feel it's the proper time to cast doubt on his character." She regarded her stepdaughter. "We failed to protect her when she was a child, and we know firsthand how good she is at hiding her pain under her sunny disposition."

16

———

PRISON BREAK

"Why can't I come?" Casi observed Kyle transfer cash from the safe to his jacket pocket.

"I'll pay the bail and pick him up. Please wait here until we get back and let me deal with this." Kyle pushed past her.

"As if I have a choice! I can't drive with this stupid thing on my arm. I feel like I'm under house arrest."

"Well, Jake is in a real jail until I can get him released!" He kneaded his temple in frustration. "I'm asking you to be patient for a few hours." He wrapped his arms around her. "I understand you miss him. Everything will be back to normal soon." He turned and shook his head as Charlotte launched herself from Anna's arms. "Stop imprinting on me." He kissed her balled up fist and put a hand on Anna's shoulder. "Once everything is sorted out, I'll ensure he talks to you."

He turned the radio to a country station while he drove and tried to ease the tightness in his shoulders. Mary had designated herself as the primary contact to avoid the multitude of requests for updates. He assumed she mentioned his fragile mental state to ensure they abided by the terms. He was curious what the conversation with Lauren had been but couldn't work up the energy to care. He parked

131

and turned his collar up to protect himself from the downpour as he charged inside the building. After what seemed like an eternity, he was summoned to pay the bail. He was directed to drive to the back of the facility where Jake would pick up his belongings and be released. Kyle exhaled and rehearsed what he planned to say to his brother, understanding he might not be in the best mindset. He switched his windshield wipers on high and peered out the window while he waited. He checked his watch and compared it to the time on the radio and wondered if he had misheard the directions. He spotted a guard taking a smoke break and jogged over to him. "How much longer do you think it will be before Jake Jensen is released?"

The guard scanned his clipboard and shook his head. "He signed out over an hour ago." He tapped the signature on the sheet.

"Where did he go?" Kyle searched the yard and roadway.

"Once they're free, we don't monitor them."

❧

Kyle held up his hand when Anna and Casi raced toward him. "There's been a glitch."

Anna glanced behind him and scanned the driveway. "Is this some kind of stupid joke?"

Casi glared at him. "You didn't want to pay the bail? Was it more than Mary told you?" She dissolved into tears, knocking her chin with her cast and swearing as Kyle directed her to the sofa.

"I paid. By the time I arrived at the gate, he had already signed himself out." He touched her chin where a red mark appeared.

"Why did you take so long? He probably thought you weren't coming. We have to find him!" Casi grasped Anna's hand in solidarity.

"I went directly there. He's not a toddler who can't find his mommy. He knew what he was doing. This is how he reacts to a stressful situation." When Anna started to speak, he shook his head. "I know my brother better than anyone! Stop blaming me for his childish behavior. He's acting out, and it's not my responsibility to take care of him!" He stomped to his computer and Casi scurried after him. He wrapped his arms around her as she eased on his lap. "I don't know what to do," he confessed.

Casi smiled. "Pretend it's me. Track his credit card charges. It'll give us a location. Someone must have picked him up. I assume there are cameras everywhere?"

"Yes, and Mary is checking. He has a debit card and credit cards. I'm not sure how much cash, but typically a couple hundred bucks." He read her expression and nodded. "I'll let him give us a lead and then I'll freeze the cards to prevent him from being able to go too far."

"He'll call you when he runs out of money." She noticed his clenched jaw. "What's your prediction?"

"It depends on his state of mind. If he's pissed at me or Anna, he'll take time to decompress and come back like nothing happened."

"What else would he be thinking?"

Kyle smoothed his hand over her arm. "I questioned his loyalty and ability to protect you. My greatest concern is I broke him, and he'll go off the rails." He rested his head on her shoulder.

Kyle slammed the phone down and stormed to the bedroom. "I talked to Mary. He was picked up in a silver Honda. Guess who owns it? Amber! He must have called her when he heard he was being released. He had it arranged."

"Do you think he's staying with her? She lives in Elmvale." Casi tugged at her leggings to straighten the twisted waistband.

Kyle smoothed the elastic for her. "I'll get her address from my mom." He glanced back at her hesitating by the doorway. "Do you want to come with me?"

"I would." She directed her gaze to her feet. "Can you help me put on shoes? I can't do laces."

Kyle smiled tenderly. "Let's go with boots since it's snowing. I'll give you one of my jackets to fit over the cast."

She grinned and held up a woolen shawl. "Ava brought me this. It's super warm and I can wrap it around my shoulders."

Kyle drove up the pothole ridden driveway to the property on the edge of town. The trailer appeared new, but the yard was littered with garbage bags, tires, and broken car parts. "This is literally trailer trash. I can't believe this is how she lives."

"No silver Honda," Casi noted.

Kyle knocked on the broken screen door. After a few minutes, he put his ear to the metal. "The TV is on." He announced himself and pushed the door open. Two children sat on a grubby couch, eating cookies, and watching cartoons. "Is your mom here?"

"She's gone," a soft voice reported from the hallway.

Kyle turned toward him. "Did you see who she was with? Did she tell you where she was going or when she would be back?" He scanned the dishes piled in the sink and laundry strewn across the floor.

The young man stepped out of the shadows, peering from the hood of his sweatshirt. "She was with a guy who looks like you."

"My brother," Kyle confirmed.

"She said they were going out of town and left us money for food." He fiddled with the drawstring on his sweatshirt.

"How old are you?" Casi tilted her head to see his face.

"Nineteen. I can take care of them. Don't contact the police." He slunk back to the safety of the hall.

"It's a big responsibility taking care of kids. Do you need help until she gets back?" Casi stepped toward him. "What's your name?"

"Chase." He tugged at his sleeve. "My sister stole most of the money before she left with her boyfriend."

Kyle noticed a framed photo and smiled. "This is from high school. I can't believe she has it on display."

"Yup, you and my mom, with one of the kids who died. I went to the memorial."

"Grady." Kyle ran a finger over the photo.

"Did you do these drawings?" Casi approached a gallery of pencil sketches decorating the walls.

"I like to draw." Chase followed behind her. "This one is my mom." He pointed to a sketch resembling Amber in a softer light.

Casi smiled and considered it was probably how he viewed his mother. "It's lovely. You did an excellent job." She turned back to the living room. "We can help you tidy while we wait for her to return."

Kyle caught her nod. "I have a truck. Why don't we clear the trash outside and take it to the dump? We can stop at the grocery store on the way back." He switched off the TV, getting little reaction from the children. "Can you guys help my wife clean the inside of the house? It'll be a nice surprise when your mother comes home." They nodded obediently and walked to Casi for direction.

Chase pulled a box from under a table. "Maybe we can decorate for Christmas when we're done? It's my mom's favorite holiday."

"Sure, we can pick up a tree after we buy the groceries." Kyle noted the young man's face light up and he whispered to Casi, "What kind of mother leaves her children a week before Christmas?"

"One who runs off with a man who has gone off the rails."

Kyle squeezed his eyes shut. "There's no other explanation. I guess it's time to start checking hospitals and morgues."

"We're trying to help," Peter stated.

Kyle clenched his jaw. "Reminding me how I've failed my brother isn't helping me find him!"

Casi eased the phone from his hand. "Peter, we're following a few leads and we'll let you know when we hear anything." She listened for a moment and responded to his question. "Yes, Georgia should focus on baking for the Christmas baskets at the church. We have things covered here and I'm sure he'll turn up soon." She hung up and opened her laptop, pecking at the keys with her left hand as if it were her first time typing.

When she shared her frustration, Kyle snapped, "I'm sorry your ability to dominate social media has been interfered with." He poured a glass of scotch and tuned out the suggestions from Lia, Gail, and Anna as they hovered nearby. Charlotte clung to him and Tommy tried to get his attention, tripping Dingo in the process. As the dog somersaulted across the floor, Kyle stopped and bellowed, "The crisis center is closed! Take your fucking kids and go home. You're not helping me, and if Jake has any sense left, he'll stay clear of this clusterfuck. Why do you think he left in the first place?"

Gail calmly picked up Tommy and soothed him. "Jake's acting out, but he'll be back. He would never leave you, Kyle."

"When? I've cut his credit cards and he must be out of cash. How long can you survive on the streets in the freezing weather? Maybe he can pimp out Amber for a few bucks." He glared at Casi as she focused on her computer screen, intent on a series of pictures. "Don't post anything about this on Facebook!"

"Cool your jets." She smirked at his reaction. "I found him!"

"Where?" Kyle hurried to her side.

She pointed to an image enlarged on the screen, clearly showing a shirtless Jake in the background. "His cascade tattoos."

He studied the picture. "Absolutely. Where's this party?"

"Puyallup." Casi stumbled with the pronunciation. "This is two days ago. Let me see if I can get more information."

Kyle pulled a chair over and rested his chin on her shoulder. "I'm sorry I've been a jerk. I should have known you could locate him."

She turned and gave him a kiss. "I tracked you down when you wanted nothing more to do with me."

"Thank God you don't give up. I take back every negative thing I said about your snooping. Years of practice have paid off."

Casi laughed. "Please retain this moment for the future when you suggest I'm like a fat kid eating blueberries."

"I never said fat, and the scenario involved blackberries. I suspect the meaning of the analogy was lost on you." A message icon popped up. "Who is sending this information?"

"Crystal from the tattoo place. They invited him to a rave."

"I hope he didn't get a random tattoo while he was high." Kyle chewed on his cheek. "Why would they post pictures like this on Facebook?" He frowned at the nudity and graphic nature.

"Instagram. There's no moral filter in your twenties, which has worked in our favor. Should we drive over there and check the neighborhoods for Amber's car?"

Kyle stood and kissed the top of her head. "You'll stay here." When she protested, he put a hand on her shoulder. "Casi, no. Look at the picture and who he's with. He's hit rock bottom and slumming. I can't take you there." Anna cried in her hands as Lia hugged her. "It'll take me about an hour to get there. I'll call when I locate him." He surveyed the group of women and gave them a sad smile. "Stay here for now, but it's important to bring him home to an empty house. He'll need a few days to detox, I imagine."

Several hours later, Kyle spotted the Honda parked outside a seedy motel. He sat in the truck and assessed which room they might be in. After watching drug deals and several hookers picking up Johns, he spotted Jake staggering along the concrete path. He was shirtless and barefoot, struggling to light a cigarette as he drank from a bottle. Kyle shadowed him to the room and waited for him to step over the threshold before he pounced. Kyle grabbed him by the arm and shoved him against the wall. "Time to come home."

"Took you long enough to find me." Jake chuckled.

"Perhaps I didn't want to." Kyle shoved him inside.

"Whatever." Jake shrugged and tipped the bottle to his lips.

Kyle snatched the whiskey and threw it against the wall, shattering it in a shower of glass and liquid. Amber stumbled out of the bathroom in panties and a tank top, blinking at the commotion. Her face fell when she noted the intruder. "Party's over. Why don't you head home to your children and try being a mother since it's almost Christmas?" Kyle sighed as she began to cry. "Thanks for being here for my brother, but he also has a family."

"No, I don't," Jake slurred.

"Do you want me to leave you here?" Kyle grabbed his brother's arm and checked for track marks. "How far did you go to end it this time?" Jake pushed him away, knocking himself off balance and falling to his knees. He struggled to get up, and Kyle reached out a hand. Jake grasped it, giving a sly smile as he went through the motions of their secret handshake.

Jake pulled himself upright with Kyle's assistance and frowned at his bare chest. "I lost my shirt."

Kyle unzipped his jacket and put it around Jake's shoulders. "How about your boots?" Jake shrugged, and Kyle walked to the truck and came back with an extra pair. He narrowed his eyes at Jake's bare arm. "Where's your watch?"

Jake cast his eyes to the floor. "I don't know."

Kyle regarded Amber shivering in her tank top and unbuttoned his flannel shirt and handed it to her. "You two are a mess. Do you have enough gas to get home?" Amber glanced away. "Follow me." He directed his brother to the truck and shoved him inside. He texted Casi asking her to relay Jake was fine and to please clear the house.

"Should I make dinner?" she asked.

Kyle surveyed Jake twitching in the seat beside him. "Order take-out. He'll most likely shower and pass out."

"How's Casi?" Jake mumbled.

"She had surgery to stabilize her wrist, and she has a cast almost to her shoulder." Jake covered his face and sobbed, and Kyle reached over and rubbed his back. "It wasn't your fault. She had a previous injury which made her bones delicate, and Dalton damaged the ligament in her arm. She wants you to come home."

"Take me to Elmvale. I need to detox, and our parents have seen it many times before."

"You can stay at my house and we'll get things sorted out."

Jake leaned back in the seat, slumping toward Kyle as he fell into a deep slumber. When they turned off the freeway for the gas station, Kyle eased him to the side. He jumped out and indicated for Amber to stay in her car while he filled her tank. After checking the oil and fluids, he knocked on her window. "You need new tires." She nodded, and he leaned closer. "You have great kids, at least the three I met. They only want to be with you for Christmas."

Amber wiped tears. "I picked up Jake and when he wanted to take off, I couldn't resist the opportunity to run away from my life."

Kyle squeezed her arm. "It's not too late to change things and improve your situation."

Jake slept the remainder of the way, and Kyle shook him awake when they pulled in the driveway. "I can't face her." Jake panicked.

"Have something to eat," Kyle insisted, and Jake stumbled behind him into the house, keeping his eyes glued to the floor. Kyle shook his head when Casi approached. "Let him shower first."

She backed off and waited until she heard the water running, then stormed in the bathroom. "This is bullshit! Jake look at me." When he turned his back, she yanked the door open and grabbed his arm.

"Casi, don't get your cast wet," Kyle cautioned.

Jake eyed her arm and sadness penetrated his deep blue eyes as they welled with tears. She put a hand to his cheek. "It's not your fault. This is nothing compared to worrying about you for the past ten days! You told me I had to face my problems when shit happens, but you run off? Why can't you trust us to take care of you?"

"I let you down." His face crumpled.

"I didn't tell either of you what happened." She turned to Kyle. "You were willing to stay married to me even if I cheated on you?"

"I love you." Kyle shrugged. "I can't give up on us."

"Then forgive yourself for not knowing. I hid the truth to protect both of you. I doubted the strength of our marriage, and I let Dalton fill my head with stupid ideas. Thank you for punishing him, Jake. And Kyle, thanks for standing by me regardless of the rumors." She wiped her eyes. "I ordered Chinese."

"Are we missing a few pot stickers?" Kyle smiled at her tenderly.

"Not this time." Casi grinned. "I couldn't open the carton."

"I'll help you when he's done."

Jake looked over his shoulder as Kyle slid on the counter. "I can shower alone. It's not possible to harm myself in here."

"I wouldn't put it past you. Your behavior has rekindled a lot of bad memories. I most likely need therapy."

"I'm glad you found me. I wasn't sure what to do if you gave up." He stumbled out of the shower. "Did you bring me pajamas?"

"You expect me to do everything." Kyle noted the fatigue etching deep lines in his brother's face. "I'll lend you mine."

"You're a good baby brother." Jake held on to the counter as a coughing fit raged through his body.

Kyle eyed him suspiciously. "How long have you been sick?"

"A few days. I don't think I'm contagious anymore."

"It doesn't sound good." Kyle searched through the cabinet and eyed his brother. "You get straight cough medicine. No codeine."

"You spoil my fun." He sat at the table watching Casi struggle with the containers. "Is this my penance to witness the display?" He snapped open a can of coke and set it in front of her.

"It's not easy being disabled." Casi stabbed the noodles with a fork, sending them flying to the floor.

Kyle pushed the dog back. "No Dingo. Spicy." He noted his brother slumped over his plate with shaking hands. "Eat, Jake."

After a few bites, Jake shoved his plate away. "I can't swallow."

"You need water." Kyle filled a glass and stood by Jake's chair, instinctively rubbing his back when the coughing ensued. "Take small sips." Jake leaned against his brother while he finished the glass. "Smoking probably didn't help."

"Probably not." Jake staggered to the sofa to collapse in a heap. Kyle brought a pillow and blanket while Jezebel curled up in his arms. He looked up and managed a smile. "Thanks for bringing me home."

17

———

COLD FRONT

Kyle awoke with a start in the night. He eased himself from the warmth of the bed and padded to the living room. The moonlight highlighted Jake's crumpled body, restlessly twitching on the sofa. Kyle crept below his brother and sat with his knees pulled to his chest, listening to the erratic snoring and labored breathing piercing the silence of the room. "Didn't trust me to stay put?" Jake coughed.

Kyle reached over and smoothed his blanket. "I had a nightmare you left and all I could see were footprints in the snow."

Jake clutched his brother's shoulder. "I'm not going anywhere."

Kyle grabbed an afghan from the armchair and wrapped it around himself as Dingo curled up beside him. "You should have let me take care of Dalton. She's my wife."

"It was a gut reaction. Although, it was better for me to do it."

"You don't think I could handle jail?"

"You would probably make friends and be elected president by the end of the week." Jake contemplated the snow-covered lake through the sliding glass doors. "The first reason is you're needed more in this life than I am. You could hire someone to replace me in the business and I trust you to take care of my kids."

"Bullshit."

Jake touched Kyle's chin and turned his face toward him. "I went to Lauren's with the intent of beating Dalton to a pulp, but I knew when to stop. You appeared calm, but I suspect you would've killed him if you had the chance without considering the repercussions. I couldn't let you throw your life away and damage Casi in the process."

Kyle considered his brother's words and chuckled as Casi slid between them and stretched out like a cat. "She's sound asleep."

Jake rolled his eyes and tucked an arm around her waist to prevent her from slipping to the floor. "This is ridiculous." He rested his head on the pillow and immediately fell asleep to the rhythmic breathing and warmth of the woman beside him.

Kyle leaned his head against her hip and submitted to the exhaustion. "Goodnight deranged family."

❦

"Why are you sleeping in here?" Anna surveyed the impromptu camp-out in the living room.

Casi woke with a start and cried out as she clawed at the cast. "Take this off! It's suffocating me."

"You can breathe. Your arm fell asleep." Kyle elevated her arm. He nodded to Anna, and she ran to get the bottle of pills.

Jake recoiled. "What did I do?"

"It wasn't you. If the cast isn't properly supported, it puts too much weight on her arm." Kyle placed a pill on Casi's tongue and held the glass of water for her to sip.

"Daddy!" Austin climbed over Kyle and vaulted to his father while Tommy scrambled to intervene.

Charlotte regarded him with distrust and clung to Kyle. "Up."

Kyle frowned and tucked her under his arm while he caressed Casi's cheek and waited for the medication to ease her pain. Austin mimicked his soothing tone, stroking Casi's hair to comfort her while she relaxed in Kyle's arms.

Jake scanned the label of the bottle. "Heavy duty."

"Not for you." Kyle moved it away.

"I need something to take the edge off." Jake collapsed on the sofa in a coughing fit and gripped his ribs as he writhed in pain. Kyle opened the medication and bit a pill in half before popping it in his brother's mouth. "Today only."

Anna dropped to her knees and stroked Jake's hair. "I'm sorry."

Austin patted his chest. "Ok, Daddy."

Kyle noted Lia hovering in the kitchen nervously. "Can you make a pot of coffee? I think we would benefit from caffeine."

"Pancakes." Casi opened one eye.

Kyle kissed her tenderly. "Whatever you want." He turned on the TV and cringed at a festive commercial. "Did we miss Christmas?"

"It's tomorrow." Lia smiled. "I bought presents for the boys. And I got a bit carried away shopping for Charlotte since it's fun to buy for a girl. I didn't decorate because..." She burst into tears.

Kyle embraced her. "None of us were in the mood. Why don't we surprise Mom and bring her favorite son home as a gift?"

"I'm sure it's what she wished for." Jake glanced at Lia. "Do you have plans with your family?"

"My mom went to Palm Springs to visit her sister. She thinks the heat will help her knee. Lauren isn't talking to me." Lia shrugged.

"She blames you because I hurt her husband?" Jake assessed.

"I chewed her out for bringing Dalton into our circle. I was pretty unkind." She grimaced. "I told her she was desperate to get married and chose a pervert who is manipulative and sneaky. She's not used to me fighting back, but she's said so many mean things about my relationship with Shane and I'm sick of it."

"I'm sorry I didn't shop for gifts." Jake scanned the room and his eyes welled. "I suck at life."

"Everyone is here because they love you. We don't want gifts. We need you." Kyle turned his face away and Jake grasped his hand.

"We'll have an old-fashioned Christmas with tobogganing, hot chocolate, and singing by the fireplace." Anna smiled at Lia. "Thank you for thinking of Charlotte. I couldn't get it together." She eyed

Jake. "Lia and I can take the guest room. The boys can stay with you and Charlotte has appointed Kyle as her new plaything."

"You can have her." Kyle tried to release her to no avail. "If I had wanted a child, I would've chosen a boy. This little girl is emotional and needy and completely the opposite of my preference."

Casi curled her lip. "She's a pain in the ass."

"She's so cute though." Jake patted the baby on the head.

She shoved his hand away. "No!"

Anna shrugged. "I'm sorry but without you in the house she's turned into a terror."

"Well, Kyle needs to straighten her out before we regain possession, or she might have to live over here." Jake smirked.

Georgia threw open the front door and was halfway down the steps by the time they tumbled out of the cars. "Jake!"

"I'm sorry, Mom." He hugged her tightly and stifled a cough.

Georgia sobbed as they walked toward the house and froze as Lauren appeared on the porch with a frosty expression. Kyle instinctively held an arm across Casi. "Why are you here?"

"If you returned my phone calls, I would have explained." Lauren glared at Kyle. "You turned my life upside down and disappeared without the courtesy of ensuring I was even alright."

"I'm not responsible for the nefarious actions of your husband!" Kyle stormed toward her. "He got what he deserved."

Peter gripped the porch railing. "Did it bring you comfort to hospitalize the man your wife was having an affair with? You're desperate to hold on to a woman who plays you like a fiddle and you coerce your brother to defend your honor? A man takes care of his own business." His gaze drifted to Casi's cast. "Another ploy for sympathy?"

Kyle bolted up the steps toward his father. "I don't know what lies you've been told, but the mere fact you would rely on rumors indicates exactly what you think of me as your son."

"Rumor? I saw the pictures!" Peter flushed with rage.

Kyle's nostrils flared, and he turned to Lauren with his hand extended. "Give me your phone!"

Lauren narrowed her eyes and slid it from her pocket. "They've seen the photos. There's no denying what happened."

Kyle opened the gallery and enlarged the first photo. His heart sank, and tears sprung to his eyes. "Look at her face! She's terrified." He forced his father to observe the image before turning it to the group. "How did we miss this?"

Anna embraced Casi. "You saw what you were instructed to. It was meant to mislead you."

Peter staggered back. "I don't understand." He searched their faces wildly. "What about the baby?"

Kyle noted Lauren rubbing her stomach as Georgia soothed her. "What have you told them?"

"She's the liar!" Lauren gestured to Casi. "She wants to control you and punished me for having any part of you."

Georgia fought tears. "We've known about the sperm donor request from the beginning. I assume it was the catalyst for the rift between you two before Europe." She pursed her lips as she regarded Casi. "I was led to believe you had come to an agreement when Lauren married, but why couldn't you allow her to have a happy life and not ruin it with jealousy?"

Jake stormed toward his brother. He grabbed his arm and glared at his parents. "Let's go. We don't belong to this family. We've created our own."

Kyle nodded sadly. "I had a vasectomy a year ago, Lauren. When I denied your request, I meant it." He surveyed the photo on the phone in his hand and slammed the screen against the railing before throwing it at her feet. "Your husband assaulted Casi. She's the only one who is innocent in this whole thing."

"What a wonderful Christmas present to walk away from your family and disrespect us," Peter snapped.

Libby stepped in front of Kyle, preventing his escape as she whispered in his ear.

"I can't do it. I'm barely holding on," he said.

"Let him go," Peter spat.

Libby turned to him and smiled. "We can't reset the past, Peter, but we can redirect our future. Half truths and coverups only delay the inevitable." She gave Kyle a squeeze. "Running won't solve anything."

Kyle sighed and regarded Casi. "I won't leave her here."

Libby held her hand out to Austin. "Come with Auntie, love bug. Grandma baked wonderful treats for you."

Austin twisted his mouth as he stood on tippy toe, unsure how to proceed. Kyle nodded to him. "Go inside. We'll be back in a bit." He directed Jake and Casi toward the truck and turned to Lia and Anna. "We need to take care of something. Can you settle the children and get them lunch?" He regarded his watch.

Anna crunched on the shattered pieces of the phone as she walked up the steps. She extracted the memory card from the wreckage. "Evidence of what your husband did. Until we decide how to proceed, I'm taking possession of it." she slipped it in her pocket and picked up Charlotte. "Lia, you should share a room with your sister. It's safer for her if I reside down the hall."

Libby squeezed Georgia's hand as they entered the house. "Kyle is hurt. Give him space to decompress."

Georgia flushed under Peter's scalding glare. "I believed what I was told. There was so much mystery surrounding them these last few months, and I've barely spoken to Ava..."

"I realize you're threatened by my new friendship with her. Nothing sinister is going on. She has not been avoiding you, but she didn't want to come between you and your sons. This claim of paternity was false to gain your sympathy." Libby clucked her tongue at Peter. "Make amends soon, my darling brother. Don't let the wound fester."

"Where are we going?" Casi peered out the window.

Kyle drove a few miles and pulled over. "Libby insisted we cut down a Christmas tree. It's the last thing I feel like doing, but she said we can't abandon tradition."

"What's the point?" Jake sighed.

Kyle stared at the rows of evergreens. "Nothing seems important. I'll do this for Libby and then I think we should leave."

Jake nudged Casi. "What do you want to do?"

Tears streamed down her face. "Everyone hates me. Dalton destroyed everything!"

Kyle jerked his head toward her. "You're right. It's not about the tree. It's an olive branch to fix things with Mom and Dad."

They pulled up to find Anna, Georgia, and Lia on the porch with the children. "The tree is a perfect size." Georgia smiled.

Anna motioned for Casi to join them as the group began launching snowballs. Austin threw one on his foot and Tommy knocked himself down with his first effort.

Charlotte ran to Kyle and clung to his leg. "Don't hit the kid." He swooped her in his arms and turned away from the attack.

Casi sent a wobbly missile down Charlotte's back, making her scream. "Oops." She grinned with satisfaction.

Jake kneeled and prepared for a counter-fire, tossing ammunition to his brother. Kyle caught it with one hand and nailed Anna on the forehead. She laughed and dusted the snow off, returning fire with skill and precision.

"I'm holding your daughter!" Kyle exclaimed.

"A little snow won't hurt her." Anna laughed.

"I believe we have a traitor among us." Jake frowned at Casi.

"I'm unarmed this year." Cast giggled.

Libby smiled with satisfaction. "Peter, they've made the first move to repair the damage. Get off your high horse and apologize."

Peter blanched. "I'm numb with the reality of what happened. Georgia was convinced Lauren was telling the truth. I normally stay out of these gossip-fests, but my sons have been distant."

Libby looped her arm through his. "You adore Casi and it's understandable you perceived a fatal betrayal. Imagine how Kyle felt?"

18

UNVEILED TRUTH

*A*nna placed her palm on Jake's chest and kept her voice low. "I've put my things in your room since the unexpected guest moved in."

He grasped her hand. "I'm sick. You might catch it."

Her eyes welled with tears. "I don't mind."

He surveyed the children wrestling and chatter about the best position for the tree. "I'm unsure what to say. I wish you had given me an ounce of this concern before you cheated. Is the affair over?"

"Yes, for weeks now."

"I caution you not to attempt to repair something you're not in for the long run. I won't forgive you a second time. This is the first marriage I've entered in willingly and it's disappointing we barely made it a few months."

"I stumbled at the starting gate." She raised her eyes to his. "I shut down when issues arose, and I didn't deal with things properly."

"I wasn't aware we had problems."

"Outside of our relationship. My daughter contacted me from France and she's ill. I tracked down her father to find out if he was a match for the kidney she needs."

"Why didn't you tell me?"

"I only told Casi enough to locate him."

"No secret past is safe from her snooping." Jake smiled and watched Casi hanging ornaments with the boys. "Please include me in future dealings. I don't want you to be alone with him."

Peter approached with his hands in his pockets and kept his eyes directed to the floor. "Libby wants you to join her at the cottage."

Jake rolled his eyes. "For a lecture on my behavior?"

"It's best if the four of you go." He nodded to Kyle at the tree gathering the ornaments Casi dropped.

Georgia brought a plate of cookies. "Take these with you."

Kyle steadied Casi as she tripped on a log. "It would have been easier for them to come to us."

"Maybe Libby doesn't want Lauren involved?" Casi eyed the cookies. "Did she make gingersnaps?"

Jake made oinking noises and gripped her elbow to help her up the steps. Earl answered the door with a broad grin. "You came for a visit? Sit by the fire and warm yourselves." He directed them to the living area furnished with eclectic bright floral chairs and an overstuffed ottoman. He hesitated as he considered the number of people and seats. Casi scooted on the hearth with Kyle, and he relaxed after the issue was solved.

Libby smiled from her desk by the window. "Let me save my documents and I'll join you. Earl, can you put the kettle on?"

"I've got it." Jake filled the pot and set it on the stove.

Anna surveyed the woven tapestries, photos, and décor. "This cottage is gorgeous. It seems simple on the outside, but it's like something out of a magazine in here."

"Treasures from my travels." Libby unwrapped the plate of cookies and set it on the coffee table. "Earl didn't have a lot of belongings he wanted to move here so he gave me free rein."

Earl chuckled. "I have no interest in my old life."

Casi smoothed a hand over a colorful throw. "Did Georgia make this? It feels like the alpaca wool."

"Isn't she talented? My brother did well to marry such an amazing woman. One of the perks of farm life is being close to them." Libby poured the water in the teapot and brought it to the living room. "When I lived in Europe, I photographed lovely cottages and bunga- lows and sent them to Peter. He said my taste was ridiculous. We both understood it was a way to keep in touch and the photos were a conversation starter. Eventually he built me this place, so perhaps the seed of creativity was planted after all."

"Is it difficult to adjust to living here after traveling the world?" Anna relaxed in a wingback chair.

Libby glanced at her computer. "It's a quiet place to write, and I'm comfortable here. I've spent many years having brilliant experiences. It was time to come home."

"Why is Mom upset about Ava?" Kyle sighed.

Libby smiled. "Ava and I bonded over our shared travels and experiences. Your mother felt left out and assumed we were keeping secrets, like why you two fought." She eyed Kyle's jagged scar.

Kyle shook his head. "Casi was upset, and I acted like a jackass. We sorted everything out."

"With my help." Jake grinned.

"I understand, Darling. You're like your father. You both process things logically and want to please everyone. Jake reacts immediately, which isn't always for the best. As brothers though, you're a perfect pair." She shifted her eyes to Casi. "Peter's upset about his reaction when you arrived. You must understand he has been fed negative information. Georgia is loyal to her sons and felt deceived."

"How long has Lauren been here?" Kyle asked.

Libby poured the tea and handed out cups. "About a week." She turned to Anna and Casi. "I was a midwife and Earl was a combat medic, so Georgia asked us to come to the house and assess whether there were legitimate concerns with the pregnancy since Lauren refused to go to the doctor on her own."

"Is there a problem?" Kyle fidgeted on the hearth, and Casi read the concern in his expression.

"The stress of the situation was causing premature labor. She needs to rest until the baby is viable. Georgia had no choice but to allow her to stay. Your parents have been sick with worry over this one." She slapped Jake's hand, and he grinned at her. "Why did you do it, Darling? What's the real story? Don't feed me bullshit. I'm old but not fragile."

Casi stumbled through the story while Libby asked questions as if she were an editor fixing plot holes. Casi reflected on the details, understanding the importance of words which had been omitted. She regarded the fire. "Ultimately, it was what he said, more than how he touched me, I can't erase." She turned to Kyle and noted the tears in his eyes. "At no point did I welcome his advances."

Anna wiped her eyes and exhaled. She laced her fingers through Jake's and felt the tension in his grip. "Casi, I'm sorry for my part. He used my affair to blackmail you and I was too distracted to notice how unsettled you were when we returned."

Libby refilled the teacups. "The first step in healing is to release what is bottled up inside. Trauma doesn't only harm the victim, but our loved ones too. Kyle needed to hear your story, not someone else's version or a watered-down account. Your experience and how it made you feel." She smiled at Jake. "I understand your reaction now."

Kyle crossed his arms. "He should have let me do it."

Libby shook her head. "You couldn't have."

Kyle jumped to his feet. "I'm as strong as him! I don't go around threatening people, but I can take care of my own family."

Earl chuckled. "You sound like your father."

"He does. Sit down, Sweetie. I wasn't suggesting you couldn't handle a pip squeak like Dalton!" Libby relaxed in her chair. "Obviously, your wife's injury was your primary concern. I imagine you were levelheaded and focused on ensuring she received the best care." Kyle frowned. "An admirable quality for a husband. Unlike your brother, who goes off half-cocked. You had a responsibility to behave as a mature adult. It was your brother's job to be the enforcer." She regarded the couples. "You're evenly matched. The dreamer and the intellect. The dominant dragonfly and the wild man." She laughed at their reactions. "Earl and I were always meant to be together as well."

"Why didn't you marry years ago?" Casi glanced between them.

"This is the story you came to hear." Libby smiled and patted Earl's hand, and he nodded. "It started long ago, when we were kids. My first series was based on our love story. Earl and Peter were best friends from kindergarten. I tagged along because my other brothers were older and off doing their own thing. We had lost two of them by the time we were in our teens."

"One to smallpox and one in the river?" Casi recalled.

"My mother struggled with depression after another died in combat. Losing three sons was too much to bear, and it became my job to care for her. Earl insisted we would get married when we were old enough, and it seemed like a lovely idea. When I was nineteen, Mother died, and Earl proposed properly. I was a virgin." She winked at Jake as he shook his head. "I obeyed the rules of my generation and we planned a June wedding when Earl and Peter would be released from the army." She stared at the fire. "My father became ill and because my older brother was married, it fell on me to be the caregiver, again."

"I thought Dad did it," Kyle interrupted.

"This is when my life took a turn." She sipped her tea. "A week before the wedding, I was shopping for my honeymoon attire. We weren't going far, just to Banff for a weekend. Money was tight. Earl had a job lined up with a plumber and we planned to start a family, so I did a little writing for the newspaper in the meantime."

"Wow, your life did take a turn," Casi assessed.

Kyle frowned. "Small town life was too boring, so you ran off to travel the world."

"While I was waiting for the bus on Main Street, the Lennon brothers grabbed me and had their wicked way." She pursed her lips and noted the devastation in Anna's tearful eyes. "Men can be evil! They said it was my wedding gift to ensure I had experience for Earl." Her eyes narrowed. "I picked up my filthy bags from the gutter and went straight home. My father was never easy to deal with and when I watched him gasping with his oxygen tank as he sat in front of the television, I knew I would kill myself if I stayed." She slid her hand in Earl's. "The night Peter and Earl were due home, I paid the Lennon farm a visit. They had a meth lab in their barn, and I doused the whole thing with gasoline and lit it on fire." She sat back with satisfaction.

"Good!" Casi and Anna said in unison.

"There was speculation about what happened because the brothers bragged about their conquest. I met Earl and Peter at the train station in Seattle and told them what I had done. They were livid I hadn't waited for them to handle it. Peter agreed to take over the responsibilities at the farmhouse, and we fabricated a story about how I ran away days earlier and called the wedding off." She smiled at Earl. "We made love in the back of the pickup truck for the first time. I abandoned my ideas of marriage, babies, and a white picket fence life and reinvented myself. My dreams became grand and cosmopolitan. I promised I would come home one day, and we would have a cottage by the river and live happily ever after."

Anna burst into tears. "Such a heartbreaking love story."

"We both endured hardships and unique experiences. When the time was right, I came back."

Earl leaned over and kissed her. "Like you promised."

"The Lennons are like cockroaches, and although I killed the older three, the younger one survived and bred a whole new line of filth. Marsha didn't belong with them."

Jake grinned. "You stole her away."

"When Kyle revealed what was going on, I convinced her to leave. She finished school in France and college in England before going on a safari with me in Africa. She's a diplomat in Turkey. She speaks very fondly of you boys. We keep in touch and I give her updates on your lives." She giggled. "I edit some of Jake's mishaps."

"I appreciate it." Jake chuckled.

Libby noted Earl lost in thought as he smiled with satisfaction. She handed him a gingersnap and his face lit up. "It's a blessing his dementia hasn't destroyed our future, but it has altered his perception of the past. It's a filter keeping the bad memories out."

"Have I been your watchdog through the years?" Kyle considered the multitude of prompts to check up on Earl.

"I needed someone I could trust. You're loyal to the bone and gave me unbiased information." Kyle looked crestfallen by her words. "I love you as my own blood. You're my closest ally. Don't think for a minute I permitted you to marry a girl I hadn't thoroughly vetted."

"I only met you last year!" Casi cocked her head.

"When Kyle told me he wanted to propose, I researched you and was astounded by your beauty. I was concerned you were all fluff and no substance, but I wasn't impressed with Lauren as a mate."

"Why didn't you come to our wedding?" Casi asked.

"I had malaria. They wouldn't let me leave the country." Libby sat beside her. "He was adamant about his feelings, and I had never seen him so smitten. Once I met you, I understood; you are his true love. It's as rare as a perfect diamond and just as precious. Cherish it and rejoice in the knowledge it will last forever, no matter what obstacles you must overcome."

"Are you preparing me for disaster?" Casi cringed.

Libby grasped Kyle's hand. "I don't care for Lauren, but her world collapsed, and she needs a friend she can trust to help her find the light. You make solid decisions despite the chaos."

"Unlike your brother." Jake kicked his knee.

"Very true." Libby turned to Casi. "I realize you were hurt by her and it would feel good for the moment to break her friendship with your husband, but it won't benefit anyone long term."

"I don't interfere with his choices," Casi mumbled.

"He reads your emotions like a blind man reading brail. Your words are meaningless against the rhythm of your heart."

Casi smiled. "What a beautiful assessment."

"I've known this man since he was a baby. In fact, would you like to know a secret?" Libby winked.

Kyle chuckled. "You've hit the jackpot to gain her affection."

"The queen of secrets and spying," Jake added.

"These two were not adopted randomly." She paused for dramatic effect. "I found them first. I was working at a crisis center in Seattle, helping a teenager get her child back. We had gone to the foster home, and I saw you there. Kyle was scrawny with huge blue eyes. He was so beautiful with a vibrant soul bursting through his meager frame. I toyed with the idea of adopting you myself and traveling the world with my tiny sidekick. Then I met Jake! What a wild little devil. I loved him instantly but realized you had to stay together and needed a real family and a stable home."

"You told Dad to get us?" Jake questioned.

"Raising a child is a monumental task. It would have been unfair to sway them to children who came with so much baggage. I had met Tara, and I realized she wouldn't let Jake go easily. You boys had been through hell and deserved a family who could love you. Georgia was stoic about not being a mother, but she was a natural for it. Such a kind heart. I knew she would be perfect. She was convinced she wanted a girl, but I suggested they go to the home and meet the children. As soon as she spotted Kyle, she fell in love and there was no convincing her otherwise. When Dad discovered Jake, he couldn't resist the challenge." She threw her head back and laughed. "What a hoot watching them deal with you two the first few months. It was like a feral cat circus."

"You never considered having children?" Casi asked.

"Too much work and responsibility." She waved her hand. "I was better suited to be an aunt. I lived life on my terms and had precious boys to smother with love. It takes more than a mother to raise a child properly. Aunts don't get a Hallmark holiday, but our position holds immense value."

"I have three children," Earl announced. "Two sons who don't give me the time of day and a daughter who passed early on. They never felt like mine." He grinned brightly. "I prefer these boys and this beautiful girl who touches my heart with her pure love. This is the family I cherish."

Georgia rubbed Jake's back as he sprawled over the kitchen table, coughing and gasping for air. "You must see a doctor."

"Did you give any consideration to how your health affects others when you were running about town acting like a hoodlum?" Peter wrung his hands as he surveyed them.

Kyle suppressed a laugh and checked the time. "I'll take him to the clinic. Come on beatnik."

Peter embraced Jake, and he rested his forehead against his father's shoulder. "You're burning up. Please see a doctor. I couldn't bear it if anything happened to you."

When they realized the clinic closed early for Christmas eve, they drove to the drugstore. Jake bolted for the door as a coughing fit racked his body. "Wait here, I can do this on my own."

Kyle read through emails on his phone until a commotion inside the store caught his attention. He hurried inside and pushed through the spectators. "What's wrong?"

The young female clerk snapped her gum as she cut through the plastic. "His credit card doesn't work."

"He lost his wallet, and I temporarily froze the account. It was unnecessary to destroy it." Kyle glared at her and picked up the carton of medication, tossing it back on the counter. "You can keep your overpriced merchandise. We won't be doing business with someone who treats customers this way." He swiftly directed Jake to the truck and shoved him inside. "We'll go to Seattle. You need a proper diagnosis and most likely an STD test."

"You're a self-righteous asshole. You love having this control over me. How great did it feel to take away my credit cards and know I would have to come crawling back to you to handle things? I hate you." Jake tried to continue but broke down in a coughing jag, lurching forward to clear his lungs.

Kyle spoke calmly. "I don't enjoy this. I froze the cards to prevent you from running up balances. It's not about control. Did you recognize the checker?"

"I don't know her," Jake sputtered.

"She's Amber's daughter. I'm certain she knows who you are."

Jake rolled his eyes. "Amber says she's a useless brat."

"Her older son is a sweet kid. He seems familiar to me." Kyle contemplated where he recognized the teenager from.

"He hovered in the background. I didn't pay attention to him."

Kyle squeezed Jake's shoulder. "Imagine how it feels to be a kid of a woman who runs off with a random guy?"

Jake winced. "I never considered her children. I figured Amber was a sure bet to come get me and go find a party."

"At least she's predictable."

"Don't judge her. Life has been difficult raising those kids on her own." Jake stared out the window.

"She came from the same place we did. She made one bad choice after another and it's reflected in her life."

"You're a generous person, but you pick and choose who deserves your kindness."

"You think I should do more for Amber? She's a girl I dated in high school. Why would I waste my time?" Kyle shook his head. "My wife already gets less attention than she should. I'm overwhelmed with the prospect of assisting Lauren get out of the mess she created. Anna is barely holding on and your daughter thinks I'm her father. Lia's in a difficult relationship and her new lover is our friend, so our advice is biased. Your well-being has been my primary concern. Despite the chaos swirling around in my head the monumental fact is how I epically failed Casi. She's been a basket case for months." He cringed. "I can't erase the image of her face in those pictures!"

Jake squeezed his eyes shut. "I keep replaying the sensation of snapping her wrist like spaghetti. I felt the pop but didn't realize I broke it! She smiled at me through the pain."

Kyle set the bag with prescriptions on the table. "Your son should live another day. Bronchitis is the diagnosis, and he's on antibiotics." He surveyed Lauren at the kitchen table, rubbing her stomach. "Everyone has been exposed but only the ones with close contact run the risk of contracting it."

"Should we test Casi?" Georgia grinned as she watched her daughter-in-law snuggle in Jake's arms with the iPad between them.

Kyle smiled at them. "Luckily, she was already on antibiotics after the surgery so her immune system can probably handle it." He glanced back at Lauren. "Let me know if you get a sore throat or develop a cough."

She nodded and regarded her swollen belly. "I need a new phone. My contacts and photos were in there."

Kyle winced. "I'll buy you one. Did you save the memory card?"

"Anna has it." Lauren glared at her across the room.

"I'm keeping it as evidence to put your husband in jail." Anna slammed the refrigerator door and poured a glass of orange juice. "Can Jake have this with his pills?"

"Yes, no grapefruit." Kyle read through the instructions. "Casi, how do we remove photos from a memory card and put them somewhere safe?"

"Do a data transfer." She giggled at the screen as the colorful candies exploded. She looked up and realized what images he was referring to. "Oh, I can walk you through it if you get my laptop." She bristled. "Actually, let's use Lauren's computer so we can save her information to her drive."

"No, remove the photos of you and leave everything else alone." Lauren jumped to her feet.

Kyle looked between the two women with hate in their eyes. "What am I missing?"

"I'll bet you one million dollars your trust is misplaced," Casi declared with a hand on her hip.

"Don't bet what you can't afford to lose," Jake chuckled.

"I won't lose." Casi stepped forward. "Get your computer."

Lauren jutted out her chin as tears slid down her cheeks. "You're determined to take everything from me!"

"Some things aren't yours anymore!" Casi bellowed.

The room fell silent and Kyle cocked his head at the discourse. "Lauren, please tell me you erased those pictures as promised."

Lauren stormed from the room and lumbered up the stairs. She returned with her laptop and set it in front of Casi. "Delete everything. I have nothing left to lose. You win."

Casi shook her head. "They don't belong to me either. Kyle needs to make the decision. As far as the images of me are concerned, I don't want them kept. I won't go to court with this. When Dalton comes out of the hospital, he needs to stay away from me, or I swear to God I will finish him."

"Erase your pictures and any with me." Kyle glanced at Lauren and whispered to Casi, "Any naked ones."

19

———

CHRISTMAS PRESENCE

"Merry Christmas!" Casi launched herself from the bottom step into Jack's arms, almost knocking him over.

He chuckled and embraced her. "Why didn't you tell me the truth about Dalton? I'm mortified I believed the rumor."

"I'm sorry I slapped you." She blushed and kissed him on the cheek. "You took me off guard and I overreacted."

Jack narrowed his eyes at Jake. "Ava explained. Apparently, I'm supposed to let you sort it out regardless of my personal feelings."

Jake shrugged. "You can hit me if it'll make you feel better."

"I have mixed emotions about the protection of my daughter and who should be responsible." Jack glanced at Kyle.

"No one here was at fault and I want this to be the last discussion about it." Casi swept past them to the living room and plunked on the sofa against Charlotte's protest. "Beat it, Chuckie," Casi said in a raspy voice, poking the child in the ribs.

"No!" Anna cringed. "I detest the nickname."

"Chuckie," Austin and Tommy mimicked, encouraged by Casi as the room broke into laughter.

Kyle suppressed a smile and gathered the sobbing child in his arms. "Are they bullying you?"

Jack grinned at Casi. "I'm glad you're in good spirits. Let us know what you require help with."

"Buttons and laces." Casi bopped Austin on the head. "But I've trained my minion to do most of the fiddly stuff. Although, he sucks at tying shoes."

"He's three," Jake frowned.

"It's a big world out there. Keep up or fall behind," she warned, upending her coffee as she struggled with her left-hand positioning.

"The same applies to you." Jake sprung to his feet and helped her stand, leading her to the kitchen to blot her sweatshirt.

He poured a fresh coffee and added cream. She observed his shaking hand. "Are you having trouble coming down?"

"I hit it hard this time. Regrettably age hasn't improved my recovery. I used to spring back quicker."

"Meth?" she questioned.

"Almost, but I pictured Kyle's pathetic face when he was twelve and he found me in the barn." His face crumpled with remorse.

She caressed his cheek. "Thanks for what you did to Dalton and not allowing it to be Kyle. This fracture is nothing compared to the thought of losing either of you."

"I'm so sorry," he pleaded.

"Stop apologizing. I'll be stronger than ever with these titanium parts. This cast is a pain in the ass, but the doctor said it's best I had the surgery at my age because it'll heal faster. Hey, guess what? Kyle's lunatic stalker, Gabby, is my doctor!"

"He told me." Jake chuckled. "He researched her and ensured she's the best in her field. Her care for you is a sort of penance for her lies." He studied her humming while she picked at a cinnamon roll. "Your ability to bounce back is unbelievable." He kissed her on the forehead. "Any sage advice for an addict?"

"Hydration, vitamins, and a special concoction Alix created. I'll text him for the recipe. He'll also advise meditation and yoga. You're not an addict, just a wayward party-boy."

Jake added brandy to his cup and gave her a wink. "To take the edge off." He leaned against the counter. "If I can make it through the holidays I'll get back on track in the new year."

❧

Kyle hesitated in the doorway of the guest room and surveyed Lauren partially reclined on the bed while she attempted to balance her laptop on her stomach. When it slid off suddenly, he bolted forward and caught it before it tumbled to the floor. "Thanks. It's hard to get comfortable with this big belly."

"You're definitely showing," he chuckled. "Can I talk to you?"

"Sure." She shoved papers over to provide a place to sit.

"Several things are bothering me. I'm coming to you as a friend, not to lecture you about things beyond your control."

"I realize I made some bad choices."

"Who hasn't? Especially in this house. The most important thing to address is the pictures of Casi. Did Dalton keep a flash drive or are they only in the gallery on his phone? I want them destroyed. We're not going to court. He has no right to have images of her in the nude."

Lauren rolled her eyes. "Really? Anyone can search the internet and find millions of her posing in next to nothing. What does it matter?"

"He forced himself on her! Why can't you comprehend how wrong it is? Did you see the anguish in her face?"

"I was distracted by my husband's hand on her perfect breast!"

"I witnessed my wife in agony. She was required to pose suggestively as a model. It was an image, not the woman I know."

"Oh, the difference is she got paid. Let me get my checkbook."

"Go to hell!" Kyle jumped to his feet. "It's time for you to leave. Your husband should be getting released from the hospital soon and you must be anxious to reunite with him."

"Kyle, wait!" She clutched her stomach and sucked in air as a cramp tore through her abdomen.

"Don't bait me with imaginary pain."

She exhaled and dabbed at her forehead with the back of her hand. "I almost lost the baby from the stress of what Jake did. I came here to relax and I'm off work until she's born."

Kyle eyed her suspiciously. "You're staying here until March?"

"My mom will be back from Palm Springs next week and I'm moving in with her for a while. I must sell the condo." She patted the bed. "I promise I'll go through everything of Dalton's and ensure there are no other copies. What else did you want to talk about?"

Kyle sighed. "How much did you invest in the restaurant?"

"My entire savings, including what I set aside for a honeymoon. I mortgaged the condo and withdrew money from my 401K."

"You made a serious mistake."

"Dalton said it was temporary and promised to replace it when the money from his trust fund was available."

"I'm pretty sure he lied." He narrowed his eyes. "Speaking of lies, why did you tell my parents I was the father of your baby?"

"I suggested the possibility." Her cheeks burned with embarrassment. "I made a mistake marrying Dalton. I wanted to erase it and pretend you were the father of the child growing inside me.

He frowned at faint bruises exposed under her sleeve as she kneaded her side. "Did he hit you?"

Her lip trembled as she spoke, "He changed after we married. He has a terrible temper when things aren't going his way."

"God damn it." Kyle pulled her in his arms.

She wiped a tear and rested her head on his shoulder. "Dalton was excited about the restaurant. I had seen my dreams float by too many times to pass it up. I got pregnant the first time I tried, and I thought everything would be perfect. I can't lose her, Kyle. She's all I have."

Kyle kissed her forehead. "I'll help you get things straightened out. I have a lot of money invested in materials I may never recoup either. Dalton sure screwed all of us over." He furrowed his brow when he heard raised voices. "What's going on?" he demanded as he sprinted toward the argument.

"It's not fucking difficult! Why are you so stupid?" Casi slapped

Austin's tiny fingers while he tried to release the row of buttons. "Fucking do it, you idiot!"

"I try, CeCe," Austin cried with tears streaming down his cheeks.

"You're useless!" she rebutted, twisting away.

Kyle shoved the sobbing child aside and surveyed the issue. "Why are you wearing pants with so many buttons?" He noted the minuscule row along her hip, preventing the release.

"I have to pee! I can't deal with your backwards fashion critique." Casi clawed at the fabric.

"Hold still." Kyle struggled to undo a button.

"Hurry!" Her eyes filled with panic.

Kyle pulled out his pocketknife and sliced the blade over the string of buttons to release the seam. He walked her backward to the bathroom and yanked the material down. "Did we make it?"

"Barely," she exhaled.

"Perhaps a poor choice of outfit in your condition?"

She fingered the frayed material and nodded. "I'm tired of wearing yoga pants. Anna helped me put them on this morning, but I didn't anticipate how difficult they would be to remove."

Kyle smiled and smoothed her hair as he slid the damaged pants off her legs. "I'll get you something more comfortable."

Jake and Anna giggled as they returned from a blustery walk in the pasture with rosy cheeks. As they unwound themselves from scarves and jackets, Jake turned to spot Austin crumpled in a sobbing heap in a corner of the hallway. "Hey, Buddy, what's wrong?" He crouched and rubbed his back. "Are you hurt?"

"CeCe say I stupid," he wailed, filling in how he failed to help her and embellishing how Kyle threw him out of the way with dramatic flair and extended tears.

Jake cuddled him in his arms, kissing his damp cheek as he stomped up the stairs. Kyle crossed the hallway clutching a pair of leggings and Jake cut him off, kicking the door to the bathroom open. "I understand you're overwhelmed with your injury, but step aside from your pity party and stop lashing out at my kid. I've been lenient with letting you tease them, and I rarely intervene. Grow the fuck up and remember your harsh words can crush a little guy.”

Casi burst into tears and Kyle pushed him away with a glare. “This isn’t the time to offer your superior parenting advice.”

“There are more people in this world than you, Casi. Your needs don’t always come first, even though my brother caters to your tantrums at the expense of the well-being of my children.”

Kyle stormed toward him, inches from his face, glaring at Austin peeking at him from under Jake’s collar. “There’s the magic word. YOUR kids. Your responsibility not ours. You accept our help to care for them and pay their bills but jump on Casi when she makes a mistake. As usual, you weren’t here and are relying on the account of a toddler for what the situation was. If you’re so worried about their mental health, stop letting them run wild with zero discipline. They’re working the system, using us to their benefit to get what they want.”

“I take care of my kids,” Jake asserted.

“Really? You’ve been gone for over an hour and Lia is nowhere to be found. Did you feed them lunch, or did you assume someone else did? It’s safe to conclude your daughter was glued to me since I’m the only one who seems to be able to deal with her.” He leaned forward with sapphire eyes on fire. “You bolted and left them without a second thought. Don’t lecture us on their fragile psyche.”

Jake reeled back from the verbal attack as Kyle led Casi across the hall to the bedroom and slammed the door. He turned and met Anna’s shocked expression, both left speechless.

Kyle sat Casi on the bed and sighed. He kissed the top of her head. “This has been a horrible holiday break. I’m ready for the new year.” Tears streamed down her cheeks and she opened her mouth, anticipating the next step. He placed a pill on her tongue and held the glass to her lips, massaging her jaw to encourage her to swallow. “Relax and don’t fight it.” She reclined on the bed and he pulled a blanket over her. “I’ll wake you for dinner.”

He walked silently down the stairs and entered the living room. Jake held out a glass of whiskey and he accepted it with a nod. “I’m sorry," Jake began but Kyle turned away and picked up the remote for the TV, setting it on a documentary and slumped on the sofa. Charlotte immediately scrambled on his lap, pumping her legs to encourage him to rock her. He swung an arm around her waist and jostled her against his chest, sipping his drink and leaning back with a sigh.

Peter came behind him and squeezed his shoulder. "We love Casi. Our failure to support you is due to our own inadequacies and lack of confidence to fix this wretched situation."

Kyle exhaled. "I'm spinning in circles to do damage control."

"You're the strongest man I know..." Peter's voice broke. "I'm eternally sorry for how I behaved."

Kyle shifted his gaze to his father and smiled. "It's Jake's fault. His meltdown destroyed our armor and we imploded."

Jake chuckled and held up his glass. "Cheers."

Several hours later, Kyle checked his watch and slid Charlotte on his hip. She giggled as they bounded up the stairs and he smiled at her joy. He hesitated outside the bedroom door, hearing a muffled conversation inside.

"Alix, I'm going insane. This cast is huge, and I want to tear it off with my teeth, but I'm afraid to witness what's hidden beneath. It's like one of those horror movies where an alien has taken over a person's body. No one else can see it but the evil is growing, eventually exploding and killing everyone." Casi punctuated the conversation with sobs, choking from the emotional outburst.

Kyle pushed the door open and sat on the bed, stroking her back while she finished talking. When she hung up, he waited a few minutes. "Should I be concerned about your mental state?"

"Yes," she cried. "This medication is making me crazy. I hate everyone, and my anxiety is off the charts."

"I'll talk to Gabby about an alternative. I realize you don't like being medicated, but the pain will get to a point of being unmanageable without it." Kyle wiped her tears with his handkerchief.

"I would rather deal with the pain."

"You have no idea how intense it will become," Kyle exhaled. "Come eat dinner."

"I'm nauseous."

"One of the side effects. Eating will help. Mom made pot roast because she knows how much you like it."

Kyle studied Casi as she slept fitfully, untwisting the sheets threatening to imprison her. He frowned at her bones protruding from her frail frame, taking the opportunity to scan her nude form. Her sunken stomach stretched between her hips, revealing the truth about her refusal to eat. He caressed her rib, smoothing his hand toward her breast, gauging her weight loss. A sudden violent blow crashed over his face, sending him reeling backward as Casi sat up with a howl. "Stop!" She searched the room in a panic, unsure of her surroundings.

"Calm down!" Kyle leaped to his feet, clutching his nose to stem the flow of blood as she tore at the sheets wildly, screaming and crying.

"What's going on?" Jake raced in the room and surveyed the chaos, pulling his brother back from the flailing woman. "Did she hit you?"

"By mistake. She's still asleep." Kyle assisted Casi to her feet. "Wake up. You're fine. It was my hand on you."

Casi blinked and looked at him with glazed eyes as Georgia clamored in. "Kyle, apply ice to keep the swelling down."

Jake followed his brother down the stairs and grabbed a bag of peas from the freezer. "She needs to see a doctor. She's gone psycho."

"What's this ruckus about?" Peter yawned and tightened the belt on his robe. "You're going to have a shiner. Is your nose broken?"

Jake ran a finger over the cartilage against Kyle's protest. "Nope, cut and bruised."

Casi pushed between them and slid in Kyle's lap as she wound her arm around his neck, resting her cast awkwardly to the side. "I'm sorry! You scared me."

Jake glared at Casi. "You can sleep on the sofa or take the spare bed in the room with Lauren. Kyle hasn't slept in days."

"Where's Lia?" Georgia cocked her head.

Jake cringed when he realized he highlighted her absence. "She left for a few days with Shane."

"This wasn't the best time for a getaway." Kyle stood and scooped Casi in his arms with an exhausted yawn. "Let's try this again."

Lauren hunched over the kitchen table while Georgia rubbed her back. "Are you sure they're not contractions?"

"It's a sharp pain in the side." Lauren blew short breaths and wiped a tear. "I'm spotting."

Georgia motioned Kyle over. "You must take her to the clinic. We shouldn't wait. Libby said blood could lead to an infection."

Kyle retrieved her jacket and assisted her as she grasped the table for support. "Casi's taking a nap. Make sure she eats something when she gets up and let her know I'll be back soon."

He paced the hallway at the clinic, checking his watch incessantly. After two hours he called Georgia. "Lauren was dehydrated, and they have her on a drip line. The baby is fine, but it might take another hour. How's everything there? Did Casi eat?"

Georgia glanced over at the ensuing argument in the living room between Casi and Jake and kept her tone light. "She had a little bite," she lied. "We're managing. Make sure Lauren is alright before you head home. There's no hurry."

"I'll buy you a new one!" Jake tossed the cracked iPad on the table and grabbed Charlotte away from the path of Casi's swinging cast.

"It's not about the money! Your brat kid destroyed my iPad, and it's the only thing I have with a touch screen." Casi clasped her hands to her face in despair, knocking herself backward when the cast thumped her cheek. She clawed at it in a craze, plucking the gauze from the opening. "I want this off!"

"Stop acting like a lunatic." Jake grasped Casi's hand and Charlotte twisted from his grip, screeching at the top of her lungs.

"Shut up!" Casi doubled over and clamped her hands over her ears, again hitting herself with the cast. "I can't handle this!"

"Darling, calm down." Georgia dashed to her side. "Charlotte's feeling out of sorts without Kyle and it won't help to yell at her."

"I hate her!" Casi collapsed in a heap. "I want to go home. I need Kyle. Why is everyone taking him away?"

Jake raised an eyebrow and twirled a finger by his temple to demonstrate his analysis of the situation. Casi jabbed at her phone and it slipped from her grasp, bringing on a renewed tantrum. Earl kneeled beside her and patted her back. "It's ok, Sunshine. You'll be better soon. Do you want me to get Libby? She's terrific in a crisis."

"I want my dad." Casi scrolled through the contacts with one finger and pressed the button before handing it to Earl.

He held the phone gingerly to his ear. "Hi, um, Dad. This is Earl. I think we've met. Your daughter needs you. She's a little unhappy. No, not hurt," he assured him. "Just sad."

Georgia tried to intercept, but Earl hung up and continued to soothe Casi as she cried in his lap. "She needs her daddy."

"Or medication," Jake mumbled.

Earl frowned at him. "This girl is suffering from trauma."

"She's not in the war, Earl," Jake assured him.

"There are battles outside of the military." Earl gazed at Casi and smoothed her hair. "Someone hurt her."

Jack and Ava arrived within twenty minutes. He gasped when he noted Casi in a heap. "Honey, what happened?"

"She's being dramatic. Kyle's with Lauren at the hospital and she had a meltdown." Jake gave up on containing Charlotte and released her to run screaming through the house.

Ava frowned at the noise and shook her head. "I'm sure this is overwhelming for Casi when she's not feeling well." Casi clung to her father, rocking in his arms as she conveyed her distorted mental state.

Kyle returned with Lauren and settled her in a chair before noticing his in-laws. He glanced at the turmoil, stricken with panic when he noticed Casi on the floor. "Did she fall?" He bolted toward her and Ava put a hand to his chest to prevent him from coming closer.

"She's overwrought. This is not a proper environment while she is healing. We'll take her home with us." She nodded to Jack, and he swung Casi in his arms.

"Christ, she's as light as a feather. Has anyone bothered to feed her?" Jack glared at Kyle.

Kyle sidestepped Charlotte as she charged toward him. "I'll take care of my wife. I was only gone for a few hours."

Ava shook her head and frowned at Lauren. "This is too much for her. You have your hands full."

"Her mood is because of the medication," Kyle snapped.

"I'm not taking it!" Casi screamed. "I've been spitting it out after you give it to me. I'm barely in pain, but my brain is fucked up!"

"Casi," Kyle exhaled. "I realized what you were doing, so I've been crushing it and putting it in your coffee or food. I medicate you every four hours. You're not in pain because the medicine is working. Your mental state is a side effect."

"Kyle!" Ava gasped. "You've crossed a line. You had no right to betray her trust and dose her against her will. It's obvious you're not in a solid state of mind to make proper decisions about her care." She gathered Casi's purse and phone, eyeing the shattered iPad and realizing the catalyst for the meltdown. "We'll contact you when she's feeling better. Give her space."

"Wait." Kyle grasped Ava's sleeve. "Take her since you feel you can do a better job, but I have one request."

"Yes?" Ava opened the door.

"Tonight, when she wakes up screaming and writhing from the pain and you realize there's nothing you can do to stop it, call me. You have no idea what she's going through and how it will tear your heart out when you can't help her."

Ava surveyed his cut and bruised face and nodded. "We'll be fine. Get some rest."

"Maybe it's for the best," Georgia offered after they left. "Casi needs peace and she certainly can't get any with these children raging through the house."

Kyle surveyed the scene. "Ava's right, my priorities are misplaced." He bounded up the stairs and slammed his bedroom door.

He returned a few minutes later with a packed bag and Jake cut him off at the front door. "Where are you going?"

"I have an errand and then I'm driving to Bellingham, so I can be close by when they call." Kyle shoved him to the side.

"I doubt Ava will give in," Jake assessed.

"She will when Casi implodes."

"Are you sure you're not hungry?" Jack slid a plate in front of Casi and held up a piece of bacon.

"I want to take a shower and go to sleep," Casi mumbled. "Do you have a bag I can use?" She struggled to tuck the over-sized garbage bag securely around the cast, wincing as water trickled inside the moment she stepped in the shower.

"Do you want a flannel nightgown?" Ava noted her shivering.

"Yes, I'm freezing. Why is your house so cold?"

Ava regarded the thermostat and turned it up a few notches before helping Casi to bed. She touched her forehead and frowned. "You're flushed. Should I remove some of these blankets?"

"No, I can't get warm." Casi shuddered. "The pills must be wearing off. My temperature fluctuates these days."

"Call me if you need anything." Ava kissed her cheek.

"Why is it so hot? Did you turn the heater up?" Jack asked when Ava returned to the kitchen.

"Your daughter is ice cold with a burning fever. Maybe we should have asked Kyle about what to expect."

"He's the one who medicated her and caused this problem." Jack grinned. "She's our daughter and we can handle this. It shouldn't be worse than a hangover, right? I believe we've dealt with those many times through the years."

"True and we had a lot of experience with Sonya's drug abuse." They went to bed secure in the knowledge they had a handle on what to expect and anticipated a late morning with a refreshed daughter thanking them for intervening. They were awakened after midnight to blood-curdling screams vibrating through the bungalow as they leaped out of bed to rush to her aid. "What's the matter, Honey?" Ava gasped as she witnessed Casi writhing in agony.

"She's burning up!" Jack extracted Casi from the blankets.

Ava winced at the mottled skin of her fingers peeking out from the cast and traced the source to the knotted material, cutting off the flow of blood. Casi wailed when she attempted to release the pressure, pushing her away. "I'm going to throw up!"

Jack whisked her in his arms and bolted for the bathroom, cringing when he couldn't deliver her in time. He locked eyes with Ava, who suppressed a laugh. "I told you it would be like in high school after she's been at a wild party."

Ava crouched beside her as Jack balanced her against the bowl of the toilet. She smoothed her hair while she retched up the non-existent contents of her stomach, spitting up bile and heaving her small frame. "Get her water."

"Should we take her to the hospital?" Jack returned with a glass of water after he changed his pajamas.

"Hopefully this is the worst of it," Ava forecasted. An hour later the howling intensified and Casi shivered in pain from a strangled arm. "Phone Kyle and let him know we're taking her to the hospital. He's her husband and we can't make this decision without him."

Kyle fidgeted in his truck, clasping the phone to his chest and checking the time and volume repeatedly. When it buzzed with an incoming call, he bolted upright. "I'll be right there," he announced before Jack could speak. Within minutes, he knocked on the door.

"You were quick." Jack answered the door with a weary smile.

"I was in my truck around the corner." Kyle rushed toward the soul-crushing screams and kneeled at Casi's side.

"I can't handle this!" Casi flailed on the linoleum.

"We should take her to the hospital," Jack reiterated.

Kyle investigated the twisted material. "Can I cut this?"

"Sure, I couldn't unknot it." Ava regarded the streaks of vomit down the front.

Kyle extracted his pocketknife and drew it through the bunched-up fabric, releasing the murderous grip. He peeled it from her skin and ripped open a paper bag. "I have a different prescription. Gabby said this one won't alter your mind like the other one. It has a mild sedative to help take the edge off." He placed the tablet on her tongue and held a cup to her lips. "Look at me," he encouraged, massaging her jaw as her eyes rolled back. "About fifteen minutes and the pain will be gone. We'll talk about alternatives in the morning, but you can't function in this state." He surveyed the frayed cast and fingered the damp edges. "Did she shower?"

"I gave her a bag." Ava glanced at it scrunched on the counter.

Kyle felt Casi's forehead and kissed her cheek. "Can you hand it to me? I must get her cleaned up and try to cool her down." He set his phone on the counter and queued up a playlist, singing the words to keep Casi's attention on him as he covered her cast.

Ava smiled as she watched him and noticed the title of the list, 'Songs for my Sunshine girl.' "You created it for her?"

"Music helps her focus and calms her down. I put this together at the hospital while I was waiting for her to wake up. It's not my kind of music, but she loves it." Kyle adjusted the temperature of the water and stripped out of his clothing before propping Casi under the stream.

"I'm sorry I doubted your ability to care for her." Ava sighed.

"This whole situation is screwed up. Neither of us has slept properly in weeks. I didn't anticipate her reaction to the medication would be so extreme." He noted Ava gathering towels, and he moved the shower curtain aside. "I'll clean up after I get her settled."

"I've been cleaning this bathroom for twenty years and believe me, she's not the first one to puke in here." She brought fresh towels and stripped the bed linens, then turned down the heat to a reasonable level. When she returned to the bathroom, she heard laughter and the tension she hadn't realized was in her chest suddenly lightened.

"I look like a punk rocker!" Casi giggled hysterically.

"I'm unsure how to style this haircut," Kyle chuckled, wielding a blow dryer and brush as she sat on the counter. He turned and held it out to Ava. "I think I require assistance."

Ava smiled at Casi's tousled look. "It needs to go under not up."

"It was bad timing to get a haircut," Casi assessed.

Jack leaned in the doorway. "New meds kicking in?"

Casi grinned. "A perfectly mellow high."

"Shall I fetch another nightie?" Ava followed them to the bedroom and turned the covers back.

"It's best not to wear anything." Kyle grinned as he dropped his towel. "She moves a lot in her sleep lately." He propped a pillow under her cast, ensuring it was level with her body before sliding behind her and arranging the covers neatly on top. "This keeps her locked in place."

❧

Kyle awoke to an empty bed and bolted upright. He heard a harmonious conversation sprinkled with laughter. Sunlight radiated throughout the room, bathing it in a soft glow and easing his worried mind. He located his clothing, assessing the missing piece, and smiled as he padded to the kitchen. He kissed Casi on the top of her head, smoothing his hand over his flannel shirt. "Comfy?"

"Very." She hugged herself.

Ava handed him a cup of coffee and kissed him on the cheek.

"Jack and I would like to apologize for yesterday. We thought we had the parenting thing dialed in, but we completely failed."

"You did great. These are unusual circumstances, and each day has presented unique challenges." He touched his bruised face and turned to Casi. "Guess what we're doing today?"

"Cutting this ridiculous thing off so I can breathe?"

Kyle smiled. "I'm not sure how your arm relates to your lungs, but it's time to dispose of your weapon and downsize to a regular cast. I scheduled an appointment for this afternoon. Gabby said it's been enough time to rest your tendons, and it's crucial not to lose mobility."

"Hallelujah!" Casi smiled. "Did you tell her I was a danger to you?"

"I may have noted my status as a victim." Kyle leaned in and kissed her before pushing a plate closer. "Eat."

20

UNSTABLE

Casi sat on the exam table, swinging her legs and humming to herself. Kyle embraced her and breathed in the scent of her hair. "Careful, don't mess my do," she teased, breaking into a bubbly laugh.

He parted her uneven bangs with his ring finger and gazed in her eyes. "How did I miss it?" She cocked her head in confusion and he clarified. "You've been acting out of character since your birthday and I attributed it to me spending too much time with Lauren or your work ramping up for the holidays. I ignored every sign indicating something terrible had happened to you. Once everything was revealed, we had to deal with the surgery and Jake's bender. I should have called the doctor right away when you complained about the pain medication." She glanced away with a slight blush. "You've told me everything? Please don't hide things and expect me to guess. I'm dealing with too much on barely any sleep." He nodded as Gabby entered the room. "You didn't need to come. I appreciate you being available on the phone already."

Gabby smiled. "I wanted to check on things in person. The reaction to the pain medication is unprecedented, and I felt it was prudent to run additional tests."

"I'm fine." Casi frowned. "Once this cast is off, my mood will get back to normal."

Gabby peered at frayed the edges of the cast. "There appears to be a rash. Kyle says you've been nauseous. You seem to have dropped weight, which isn't healthy. There's not a chance you're pregnant?"

Casi burst into tears and Kyle rubbed her back. "She had a tubal ligation a few years ago." He winked at Gabby. "And I had a vasectomy, so the odds are zero for conception."

Gabby smoothed a hand over Casi's knee. "What else is going on? Do you want to speak to a psychologist?"

"I'm not crazy!" Casi pulled away from her.

"Her mother was unstable. Although most of it was due to drug addiction, is there a possibility it's inherited?" He felt the heat of Casi's glare and grasped her hand. "Let's not pretend it didn't exist. If there are tests, we'll take care of it now. Medication can help." Casi grabbed her purse and jumped from the table, catching the strap on a chair which sent the contents flying. She dropped to her knees, frantically gathering her belongings. Kyle spotted the pill bottle before she could grab it. "What the hell is this?"

Gabby winced. "Diet pills? Who prescribed those? It's not in your medical chart. I suspect it may be the source of the reaction." She walked to the computer and typed in the drugs to cross reference.

Kyle seethed as he bent and threw the remainder of Casi's items back in her purse. "Are there long-term side effects?"

"It might be causing the rash." She indicated for Casi to sit and nodded to the technician to begin cutting. Her eyes widened as he pulled the gauze away and revealed swollen blue and red patches stemming from the incision. "Did you poke anything inside your cast?"

Casi wiped a tear. "It was on fire. I had to make it stop."

"What did you use?"

"One of Georgia's knitting needles."

Kyle covered his face in disbelief. "Fuck, Casi!"

Gabby investigated the wound. "I'll give you an antibiotic cream to help heal it and we'll keep it wrapped with a dressing covered by a splint." She directed her gaze to Kyle. "It can only be removed to change the bandage and then it goes back on. Make an appointment for next week to have a new cast. She'll need the stability."

Kyle rubbed Casi's back. "Why are you shaking?"

Casi strained to speak, and Gabby riffled through a drawer to find a stethoscope. "Has she been having trouble breathing?"

"She claimed the cast was suffocating her." Kyle watched as Casi's eyes rolled back. "What's happening?"

"Recline her. She's having a seizure!" Gabby forced her back and pulled her legs on the table as she began to flail.

"What should I do?" Kyle put his hands to the sides of Casi's face to hold her steady.

Gabby inserted a needle in Casi's arm and barked directions while the technician and Kyle obeyed. "We were lucky this happened here. It could have been deadly if she was driving or if she had been alone." She caressed Casi's shoulder as the spasm subsided. "I'll have a cardiologist give her an exam."

"Run every test imaginable. If there's damage, I want it treated immediately." Kyle rocked Casi in his arms.

"We'll run a CT scan to help determine signs of mental illness. From what you've told me about her personality, I doubt she inherited anything, and her mood swings are a result of the drug interaction. What do you think the motivation was for taking diet pills?"

Kyle's eyes clouded. "Modeling was a rough career, but she normally has a positive body image. I'm worried the assault messed with her brain."

"There can be a lot of hidden triggers." Gabby made notes on the computer. "Shall we have her speak with a therapist after we run the physical tests?"

Kyle gazed at Casi as her eyes cleared. "Sweetheart, I need you to be ok. It's killing me to see you suffer."

Casi winced. "I need help."

Jake braced himself as he strolled down the hallway and spotted his brother slumped in a chair. He smacked him on the back, hiding his fear. "Any news from the doctor?"

Kyle exhaled. "Thanks for coming. I'm waiting for the test results while she's with a therapist. They wouldn't let me go in there."

"I'm sure she's telling them what a horrible husband you are." Jake noted the pain in his eyes. "I'm kidding. This is good for her to converse with a neutral party."

"You refused to seek help." Kyle narrowed his eyes.

"Sure, but I'm a rebel with anxiety issues." Jake grinned. "Casi is a bright, sweet girl with the disposition of sunshine and bubbles. Medication dampens her spirit and mixing in diet drugs was a deadly combination. Lia confessed Katie offered her some, and it made her batty as hell. Did you know she hit Austin?" Kyle looked aghast. "I know! My sweet ex-wife admitted to beating the shit out of him for spilling his cereal. When she realized how irrational it was, she told Shane and he asked me to take the kids for a week to ensure she was back to normal."

"When did it happen?"

"In the summer. Lia was too ashamed to tell anyone. Gail and I took Austin to a child therapist to check if he was damaged, but she determined he'd forgotten about it."

"I'm sorry for Casi's outburst. Those pills made her insane."

"I realized later my reaction didn't help given the household our poor girl grew up in. I basically inferred she was Sonya." Jake shrugged.

"Maybe drugs affected Sonya's temper and caused some of her issues. The brain is a complex organ."

Gabby smiled as she walked toward them. "Hi, Jake."

He stood and shook her hand. "Nice to see you. Thanks for taking care of Casi."

"No problem. Even though this isn't my specialty, I offered to bring you the results." She noted Kyle's agitation. "All good news! The seizure was caused by a interaction between the medications, spiked by the infection in her arm, which entered her blood stream. We caught it in time and there should be no long-term damage. I've prescribed antibiotics. Keep her on the new prescription I gave you for pain management. Under no circumstances should she take the diet pills. Did you know they were sourced in Canada?"

"I'm not surprised. She has friends there. I was concerned about her weight loss, but she lied and said it was from the medication." Kyle leaned back in his chair.

"Women are complicated. Keep being a wonderful husband, and you'll get past this." She handed him the paperwork and nodded to a nurse paging her. "Keep in touch and let me know how she's doing."

Jake watched her walk away. "I have to tell you something."

"No, I can't handle any more shit." Kyle turned to him. "I thought I was losing her. I'm trying to appear calm, but I'm a disaster."

Jake sighed. "I'm dumping this on you now before you recover. I did something in college which had severe ramifications for you."

"I only had the issue with Gabby, and we've completely moved past it. She's been amazing through this entire cluster-fuck."

"I was the cause of the problem and it involves Amber."

"This is probably a good time to tell me since I'm numb and might be slow to react." He frowned at his brother.

"Let me finish the story before you hit me," Jake pleaded. "Amber came a few times to see me at college. I brought her to a party or two, but it was obvious how young she was, so I began making out with her in my room."

"I'm glad she found it more exciting than the romantic stuff I did." Kyle rolled his eyes.

"One night I passed out, and she wandered off to a party by herself a few doors down. We were high, and she was pretty out of it."

Kyle covered his face. "This had better not end how I suspect."

"It does." Jake cringed. "She got passed around like a party favor, oblivious to what was happening."

Kyle socked him in the jaw. "You knew better!"

"Damn, I see your numbness wore off. Gabby's sister, Stella, was in my year. She ran a crisis group, and they found Amber naked and unconscious in one of the bathrooms. She couldn't remember what happened, but someone recalled her being with me. When Amber sobered up, she insisted she was alright, and no assaults had taken place. I drove her back to town and told her to stay away from the college. I was disciplined for bringing an underage girl on campus, and I lost my credits for the semester."

"Which is why you fell behind," Kyle reasoned.

"And why Stella had it out for you. She was determined to prove the college culture took advantage of women and you were the perfect target. She coerced Gabby into reporting you and twisted the details. I honestly had forgotten about what happened with Amber until you told me about the accusation against you."

"Did you ever check on Amber?"

"The summer when I came home, I asked her to come over so we could talk about it. I wanted to confess everything to you, but you caught us before I had a chance."

"You wanted to confess after you had sex one more time?"

"It made sense in my twenty-year-old brain. When she found out she was pregnant, I assumed it had been from some random guy."

"It was probably you given your history of knocking women up."

"Most likely." Jake shrugged. "You wouldn't hear me out and there was no point bringing it up. I figured it would only give the Jensens a bad name if it was mentioned during your inquisition."

"Very thoughtful of you. Why tell me now? Cleansing your soul?" He jumped up when he noticed Casi at the end of the hallway.

"I'm afraid to know how much of my behavior influenced Amber to live her life the way she does." Jake sighed. "Janie called this morning to check up on me. She regretted the way she treated me in the past and wishes she could go back in time. She still has the engagement ring I gave her and she wondered how our lives would have turned out if we stayed together."

"I thought you threw the ring in the river?"

"I did, but she fished it out. I told her I had her initials in my cascade tattoo and in spite of the heartache, I'm glad we had a rela-tionship." He sighed. "The conversation magnified the dumb shit I did to everyone." He squeezed Kyle's hand. "Do you forgive me for hurting Casi?"

"Yes, and please forgive me for the horrible things I said. You're not useless, and I was terrified when you went on your bender. I depend on you to be my partner in business and life."

Jake hugged him. "I feel the same way."

Casi glanced between them. "Worried about my mental state, so you called in reinforcements?"

Jake grinned. "I had to save my brother from having a breakdown after you scared the shit out of him."

"Your medical tests were perfect. No damage." Kyle hesitated. "Did things go well with the therapist?"

"She was nice. It was good to talk to someone about what happened and how I was processing it." Casi embraced him. "But I prefer to share my personal thoughts with you. The consensus seems to be my manic state was caused by a drug interaction and lack of sleep. She lectured me about the pitfalls of diet pills and suggested I enroll in exercise classes to ease my anxiety."

"I'm happy to go with you." Kyle smiled.

"Can we stop on the way home and buy hiking shoes without laces?" She shuddered. "I'm mortified at how I treated Austin."

Jake grasped her arm. "He's fine. I overreacted. You've been an amazing aunt and I should have perceived your brain was off kilter."

"Let's go out to dinner with only the three of us. Will Anna mind?" Kyle turned to Jake.

"She dropped me off on her way to visit her sister." Jake's eyes filled with tears and he swiped them with the back of his hand. "When you called me, I was terrified I was coming here for bad news."

Kyle pulled him into a hug. "It scared the crap out of me."

Casi giggled and squeezed between them. "I can't leave you guys yet. I love you too much."

They lounged at the table overlooking the Puget Sound, sipping coffee with Bailey's and whipped cream. Casi studied Kyle's demeanor, relaxed at first glance but with a current of tension pulsing below. "We must return to reality at some point." She smiled at him.

He exhaled. "Today was the pinnacle of the stress I've felt about your injury. My heart hurts."

"It was intense. I had no clue how well you controlled the pain or monitored each detail such as pillow height and what angle my arm was at. I was terrified when you weren't there last night and suddenly you appeared and fixed everything."

"I was waiting in my truck. I couldn't let you suffer even to prove my point." Kyle squeezed her hand.

"I appreciate your thoughtfulness."

He twisted his spoon, observing a trickle of coffee beading along the edge, dipping it in his cup before it dripped on the tablecloth. "When you finally relaxed in my arms and drifted off to sleep, it was the first moment I felt we might see the light at the end of the tunnel. Hearing you laugh this morning brought me back to life. Your seizure shattered me. Were you aware what was happening?"

"I was stressed about you discovering the pills and I felt my blood pressure rising. My vision blurred, and everything was muffled. Suddenly I was in your arms and I had no idea how much time passed." She shuddered at the recollection.

"It felt like an eternity. When you received the pictures of your mom I reacted badly, and I regret not saying or doing the right things. I promised myself to be patient in the future and not push you. When you told me about the assault, I had zero time to process it before we were forced to focus on the surgery. Now I must factor in Jake, Lauren, and even this dumb kid who worships me."

"It's tough to be a hero." Jake winked at him.

Kyle's eyes crinkled with a smile. "Casi, are you ok? It's truly my only concern. If you need time away or feel like you want to talk to a therapist again, I'll arrange it. You're off work for a few more weeks, and we can go out of town, maybe somewhere warm." He winced as he glanced at her cast. "Maybe a beach would be a bad idea."

She laced her fingers through his. "The relief of you knowing the truth was worth the shit-storm after. The diet pills made me feel in control, yet I didn't realize how anxious they made me. I'm sorry I risked my health, and your mental well-being, by doing something idiotic."

Kyle studied her face. "The pills were from Canada, so I'm convinced Katie is involved. I also cannot grasp why you felt the desire to lose weight."

Casi blushed and surveyed the brothers. "You'll be disappointed by what I did."

"Jake confessed to letting Amber get assaulted at a college party so I doubt your revelation will rock my world." Kyle sat back and crossed his arms over his chest.

Casi glanced out at the waves cresting in the distance. "When we get back to Elmvale, go see Amber. It's important for you to apologize and she should set the record straight on some other stuff." She pursed her lips. "Katie has a hookup with a pharmacist in Canada. A guy she's sleeping with."

"I knew this involved her." Kyle's eyes narrowed.

"I can't blame Katie because I'm an adult and it was ultimately my choice. She was distraught about money and I figured if she could get a side income, Shane would be freed up to spend time with Lia. It's a difficult situation, and I'm aware you warned me to stay out of it. She gave me samples of the diet pills and I handed them out to models I know in LA. The feedback was great, and I realized there was a demand. Around August I began picking up the pills in Vancouver and repackaging them in my sample boxes for the business. I transferred them back once I got to LA so they couldn't be traced."

"You put your company at risk." Kyle clenched his jaw.

"At first it was a fun experiment to see how many I could get through the border. Nadia was my contact in LA who distributed them."

"The Russian woman who gave you the drugs you overdosed on?" Kyle's eyes sparked with rage. "Did you consider the women who were taking them? What if one of them got sick or addicted?"

Casi shivered. "The drug is safe. I shouldn't have mixed it with the other medications."

Kyle grasped her hand. "No prescription is safe without a doctor's consent. You have no clue what drugs, legal or otherwise, those girls were using." Casi blushed and he squeezed her hand. "When and why did you start taking them?"

"After Victoria. I decided to try them and see what they offered. I liked the energy they gave me and the sense of control I had over food. Alix caught on to what I was doing and pointed out I made zero profit and handed all proceeds to Katie, but I was the one jeopardizing my career. When I broke my wrist, my business trips were rescheduled for the new year. I figured it would be a good opportunity to end distribution. Dawn only knew a bit of what was going on and cautioned me to get out of any dealings with Katie. I'm aware what can happen now, and I won't do it again."

"Are you done with being a drug mule?"

"I messaged Katie and said the market dried up and my friends were on a new diet craze."

Kyle exhaled. "I love you more than life itself. If anything happens to you it will kill me. I understand your desire to take on challenges and battles, but you have to use your brilliance to propel yourself forward rather than getting sucked into hairbrained ideas."

"I love you. I'm sorry for everything I put you through."

"Why can't you comprehend your figure is perfect? You never needed diet aids or energy boosting shit. If you can love all of us with our imperfections, why can't you do the same for yourself? Your mother could never appreciate how incredible you are because she was blind with jealousy. Look at the people in your life who adore you. We know you best." Jake reached across the table and grasped her hand.

"Thank you. After the new year, I want to go back to work. It's good for me to be busy rather than sit around and play Candy Crush." She frowned. "I need a new iPad."

Jake nodded. "I said I would pay for it."

"You're broke for a while," Kyle chuckled. "I'll buy it."

"I can afford it." Casi threw her head back and laughed. "Isn't it cool I have enough money now to buy a computer on a whim? Things have changed so much in a few years!"

"There's my sunshine girl." Kyle gazed at her with immense love. He signaled for the bill and pulled out his credit card as he checked his watch. "We have a couple hours until the mall closes."

Jake sighed. "I can't believe I lost my watch."

Kyle shook his head. "Do you have any idea where?"

"If I knew, it wouldn't be lost," Jake sulked.

"Did you pawn it or trade it for drugs?" Casi eyed him. "My mom would have."

"I don't recall giving it away willingly. I woke up at the motel and I didn't have it anymore. Amber was no help." Jake regarded his empty wrist. "This is an all-time low."

"Don't give up just yet." Casi patted his hand.

"Super-sleuth is on it?" Jake cheered.

21

REBORN

"**B**illy Bob!" Casi twisted to see up the stairwell when they arrived at the farmhouse.

Austin hesitated on the landing with his bottom lip jutted out. His curiosity got the best of him as he surveyed Casi's new cast. He slithered down the stairs, accentuating his damaged feelings. "Hi."

Casi grabbed him as he came eye level and hugged him tightly. "I'm sorry I yelled and called you names. I love you my little nugget, but my brain was broken."

Austin stroked her hair and attempted to see inside her head through her ear. "Owie?"

Casi glanced at Kyle. "I took pills and they made me mean. I promise I'll never take them again."

"Ok." Austin hugged her tightly. "I love you, CeCe."

She kissed him noisily and made him laugh before she released him to run back to play with Tommy, who regarded the scene from the landing. She blew him kisses, and he fell back in a fit of giggles.

"Happy Holidays." Kyle held up a bottle of whiskey.

"The new tires weren't enough?" Amber blushed. "I was saving to get them with my next few paychecks."

"I figured you had other expenses. They're from Jake to say thank you for keeping him alive." Kyle grinned and pushed his brother inside the trailer.

"I'm very thoughtful," Jake agreed.

"Is this a welfare visit to ensure I haven't let the house return to shambles?" Amber glanced around the room.

"Your kids were helpful, except the older girl," Kyle said.

"She's a bitch. She quit the drugstore and headed to Vegas. I wished her the best of luck." Amber surveyed the colorful decorations and a haphazardly decorated tree. "Chase lost his job at the grocery store because he missed too much work to care for the little ones. He doesn't trust my eldest daughter to be alone with them. He was trying to save for art college, but it'll have to wait. He's in his room sulking." She lit a cigarette and passed the pack to Jake with the lighter.

"No thanks. I'm at the tail end of bronchitis." Jake resisted the urge to punctuate the sentence with a cough.

"Sorry, does the smoke bother you?" Amber waved it away.

"He's fine." Kyle poured three drinks in the glasses she set out and sipped his slowly, nodding to his brother.

"I told Kyle about what happened at the college when you came to visit me," Jake blurted.

Confusion registered in the lines of Amber's face as she tried to recall what he was referring to. "Oh, the party?" She shrugged. "I don't remember, and I have no desire to try. What good would it do?"

"Did I mess up your life?" Jake cringed.

Amber threw her head back and laughed. "More like I screwed up yours!" She grinned and held up a finger. "First, I damaged your relationship with your brother, thank God, only temporarily. Next, I told Jenna Porter about our fling and she told her sister, Janie. I know it ended your engagement to her, and it was a messed-up thing to do."

"I deserved it."

"We made stupid choices. I was determined to raise my kid and be a good mom. I got it half right." She leaned closer and whispered, "I should've only had Chase. He's the best thing in my life. We would've been better off."

"Why did you have more?" Kyle probed.

"Haley was a mistake. I met her father at the bar, and he was a one-night stand with lasting consequences. I begged her to finish high school and warned her it was necessary to have a basic education. She quit at sixteen and said there was no point if you ended up in a trailer with snot-nosed kids like I did." She regarded the two younger children watching TV. "They kind of came along and I barely remember the encounters." She took a puff of her cigarette and blew the smoke out slowly. "High school was the highlight of my life."

"Casi said you needed to tell me something." Kyle tugged at his shirt sleeve. "I'm not the father of your kid, am I?"

"All four of them. Pay up, buddy." She twisted a streaked blonde strand of hair. "Did she say what it was about?"

Kyle shrugged. "No, she said you should set the record straight."

Amber glanced at the photos neatly arranged on the shelf, noting they had been dusted and organized. "Did she come here with you and tidy the house?"

"Yes, she cleaned inside while I cleared the trash and went to the grocery store." Kyle refilled their glasses.

Amber nodded. "Chase, come here for a minute, please."

"You were kidding, right?" Kyle panicked, assessing the age of the young man hovering before him.

Amber slid her son's hoodie back and caressed his cheek. "It would have been a long pregnancy. You did know the father though."

Kyle squinted at the angelic face with pale blue eyes and a sprinkle of freckles over his nose. Tears sprung to his eyes as he made the connection. "Grady!"

"What the hell?" Jake gasped. "How did we not notice?"

Chase shifted, uncomfortable with the sudden attention. "Who's Grady?"

Amber grasped a photo from the shelf and handed it to him. "A boy we went to high school with. He was Kyle's best friend. Sadly, he died in a boating accident the summer we graduated."

"And you were pregnant with me?"

"Go get your sketchbook." When he left, she said, "I slept with Grady at the graduation bonfire down by the river. I was so damn thrilled I had completed high school." She smiled and winked at Kyle. "I know you're the one who put the detailed study guide in my locker. There's no way I would have passed finals without it."

Kyle smiled. "I didn't want you to fail. You struggled with math and it would have been unkind to allow you to be held back while the rest of us moved on."

"You and I had reached an understanding and basically passed each other in the hallways. Grady told me he was honestly happy we had broken up because we spent too much time together before. He talked about the epic journey you were planning after summer and how excited he was. I liked hanging out with him because he was one of the few people who didn't treat me like a jerk for hurting you. One night we were drinking under the bleachers and he revealed he was nervous about traveling to Europe as a virgin, especially since you weren't. I told him if I graduated, I would help him out."

"He was adamant about me sharing my study guide." Kyle chuckled. "He insisted it was the honorable thing to do."

"Glad it paid off for him," Jake remarked.

"I hoped to get it on with you after the party but when they made the announcement about Europe, you raced off in a huff." Amber shoved Jake's knee with the toe of her shoe.

"He blindsided me." Jake punched his brother on the arm. "It probably wouldn't have been a good idea. Kyle was still bitter about what happened between us and I assumed the trip was his way of telling me to go fuck myself."

"It really wasn't," Kyle insisted. "I explained I wanted to do something different for a year. It was never about you."

"Your life revolves around me," Jake teased. "I disappeared for one week and you couldn't handle it."

"Ten days. You're absolutely correct."

Amber smiled at the good-natured teasing. "When I found out I was pregnant, I hoped it was a boy. I always admired your relationship and wished I had a brother. My sisters and I never got along."

"You seem close with Chase," Kyle noted.

"I am. I found out I was pregnant the morning of the end of the summer party. I contemplated whether to tell Grady. He was excited about the trip and I figured you would be irate if I screwed you over."

"I would've been pissed. Grady would have been a basket case and it would have ruined the trip." Kyle downed his drink.

"I figured I would wait until you returned and see how things went. I understood there was a good chance I would be raising the kid myself because it wasn't fair to saddle Grady with the responsibility after a one-night hook-up." Amber lit another cigarette.

"He would have done the right thing," Kyle insisted.

"What kind of life would we have had?" She waved her hand around the trailer. "Grady didn't come from better circumstances. Maybe if I had been married, my family would be happier, but it was still a teenage pregnancy. My mother claimed I screwed up my life the day I cheated on you."

"Did she know it was with me?" Jake asked.

"Of course! My stupid sister made sure to tell everyone what an idiot I was. She always had a crush on Kyle." Amber sighed. "When the boat capsized, I ran to your farm and told your parents. I stayed with your mom and tried to keep her occupied because she was worried sick. I told her about the baby, but not who the father was. She asked if it was Jake's. I assured her it was someone else, and I questioned whether I should keep it. She said a child was a blessing. She knitted me blankets and sweaters and came by weekly to ensure I had food in the house. My parents kicked me out, but she helped me find an apartment I could afford. I assume she was disappointed when I spiraled downward, but she never judged me, and every Christmas she still has a basket from the church with my name."

"Has she seen Chase?" Kyle asked.

"Sure, he helps her at the church every week."

"She knows whose son he is." Kyle smiled at Chase when he returned. "I'm happy to help with your tuition."

"Thank you." Chase handed him the book. "But your wife came by with a red-haired lady and said she had big plans for me. I'm not sure what she means, but she took pictures of my drawings."

Kyle furrowed his brow, curious when the meeting had taken place. He thumbed through the elaborate sketches as his eyes watered. "You have your father's talent."

Chase pulled a chair over. "Can you tell me more about him?"

"You never discussed this before?" Kyle glanced at Amber. "Does Nicole know?"

Amber regarded her drink. "After the accident, the whole town was in mourning. Other than my family, no one reacted to my pregnancy. Your mom was the only person who visited me after he was born. Nicole moved away and when she returned, she had a rich husband. It would look like a scam to introduce her to a secret nephew."

"Who's Nicole?" Chase asked.

"Your dad's sister." Kyle found a photo on his phone.

"I know her. She's kind of weird," Chase mumbled.

"Why?" Kyle asked.

"Sometimes when I'm stocking shelves, she stares at me. I've asked if she needs help, but she starts crying and wanders off. It's happened a few times."

"You look a lot like your dad. Did my wife mention when this big thing was happening?"

"No." Chase blushed deeply. "I googled her though and saw her modeling pictures. She's super-hot."

"Casi," Kyle called when they got home.

She grinned as she bounded down the stairs. "So?"

He grasped her shoulders. "When did you figure it out?"

"I suspected as soon as I met him. I only had pictures from the memorial slide show to go on but when I saw his drawings, I calculated the timeline and guessed who the dad was."

"Who have you told?"

"No one. I wanted you to know first."

"What's this surprise? Please don't jump ahead and introduce him to Nicole without preparing her. I wish you had discussed this with me before you planned anything."

She scowled and slipped out from his grip. "Fine."

He grabbed her hand. "I realize you get excited about things, like planning the memorial, or even taking care of the ashes. This is a living person though, and we must tread carefully."

"I won't take the wind out of your sails."

"This revelation is a shock. I need time to absorb things."

"Kyle, when you head home, can you please stop by Lauren's and ensure she has everything she needs?" Georgia asked as she entered the hallway. She glanced at Casi's defeated manner. "I'm sorry, did I interrupt?"

"No, we're good. I'll pack and be ready to leave soon. I can go with Anna to make things easier." Casi turned toward the stairs.

Kyle embraced her. "We'll leave tomorrow. Go ahead with your plans. I'm sure it will be incredible and thoughtful, as always. What can I do to help you get ready?"

"I have a few last-minute details to work out. Can you invite Nicole, Amber, and Chase around teatime?"

Kyle turned to Georgia as Casi ran up the stairs. "What's wrong?" He frowned at her anxious manner as she hovered near the doorway to the kitchen. "I'm sorry, did you want us to leave today?"

"I don't want you to go," she whispered. "Can you stay through the weekend?"

"You must be overwhelmed with us here."

Georgia glanced toward the living room. "Can you come downstairs and help me with something?"

He held the door to the basement, following her down the stairs. She strode to the far end of the room and reached behind a canning crock to extract a pack of cigarettes. "Don't judge me."

"We all have our vices," Kyle chuckled. "I've always known about your secret stash and why you stroll through the garden on your way back to the kitchen."

"I realize it wasn't secret, but it was a habit I formed early in our marriage. Dad pretended not to know, and I ignored his trove of dirty magazines in the barn."

"We found those too." Kyle sat on the worn leather sofa beside her. "You don't have to pretend to like Casi. I realize she's challenging and maybe not who you hoped for as a daughter-in-law. I'm sure you would have preferred I married Lauren. I'm sorry you're disappointed to find out I didn't father her child."

Georgia broke down in tears, coughing from the smoke. She grasped his hand. "The truth is I knew about Lauren's request for you to be a sperm donor and I thought it was preposterous! I felt it would be a betrayal to Casi, but Dad insisted I stay out of it. When we didn't hear more, I was relieved." She shivered. "Lauren came to visit when you were in Europe. She said she witnessed a devastating fight between you and Casi and how you called it quits on your marriage. She alluded to the fact you would reunite with her and hinted to a pregnancy. I was so distraught." She glared at the wall. "Ava had become fast friends with Libby, which didn't surprise me since they're both dynamic women."

Kyle grasped her hand. "Ava adores you. Finding common interests with Libby wouldn't detract from your friendship."

"They left me out of the loop. When I fretted about your marriage, Libby assured me Ava had gone to Austria to intervene." She scowled. "We were relocated to Victoria on a sudden vacation to ensure we were in the dark about everything!"

"Casi had been sent a journal by her mother with disturbing information. Ava came to unravel lies." He grinned. "Sonya grew up in a cult! Ask her to tell you about Mary."

"Another powerful woman." Georgia wiped a tear. "It's obvious they don't need a silly housewife like me in their circle."

"I guarantee you have misread their feelings."

"I love Casi like my own daughter. I adore everything about her, especially how feisty she is." She snuffed the cigarette in a tin can. "Lauren showed up here the day after Jake put Dalton in the hospital. She was frantic and showed us those damned pictures without a thought for how your father would react seeing your wife displayed in such a way! She told us about Anna, too. You wouldn't answer your phone and Jake was in jail. Lauren was suffering from cramps and I tried to take care of her the best I could. How was I to know she was telling us lies? She was secretive about the paternity and suggested the affair may have been Casi's way of punishing you two."

"I had a vasectomy because I never want Casi to think I would entertain the idea. She had been supportive of whatever choice I made, but I honestly don't want kids and certainly not with anyone other than my wife."

"Libby warned me. She said something wasn't right with Lauren's story. She refused to look at the pictures, and Earl was unsettled by the accusations. He said Casi was too in love with you to cheat, and Libby agreed. She believed something sinister was going on and Dad claimed her writer's brain was in overdrive."

"Sounds like Dad."

She tried to light another cigarette as her hand trembled with emotion. Kyle assisted with a smile. She inhaled and held the smoke for a moment before exhaling and waving it away. "I was convinced Jake was dead. I went into a trance. I wouldn't let myself feel anything because I knew it would be the end of me. I went on autopilot and cared for Lauren, cleaned the house, and cooked. I made Dad take the baked goods to the church, so I wouldn't eat them, and I couldn't face the questions. He told them I was sick, but they had heard the rumors."

"About Jake going off the rails?"

She nodded. "And then you showed up, and he was alive!"

"Barely," Kyle sighed.

"I wanted to rejoice, and I didn't care about anything he had done. I couldn't look those women in the eyes after the trouble they caused. Jake loves Casi dearly, and I feared he had risked his life to punish a man she had an affair with." She winced. "When the truth came out, and you pointed out her expression in the photo, I wanted to throw up. Jake's reaction suddenly made sense!"

"Casi was trying to calm him when he found out about Anna. She soothed him by putting her hands in his. I asked her if she had been with Dalton and he didn't realize he broke her wrist. It was my fault. She screamed for him to stop and said he was hurting her. I needed to hear the answer and didn't intervene." He scrubbed his palm across his face. "When she said it wasn't consensual, he lost it and I went numb."

"We reacted badly. We should have trusted Casi. I welcomed a predator into our home, and I have been caring for his wife and unborn child like they were part of this family!"

"We can't blame Lauren."

"She lied to us!"

"Then why have you been encouraging me to take care of her?"

"Because I don't want to do it anymore. Even her sister is annoyed with her. Take her home and her own mother can step in."

"I keep replaying all the obvious signs, like how she behaved at Thanksgiving. I hate how she suffered alone. When Jack retrieved Casi, I realized she had been left to fend for herself. I was medicating her to ease her pain, but it worked to my advantage. The pills knocked her out, and she was safe. I could deal with my wretched brother, his kids, and Lauren, and remain emotionally detached. Casi was taking diet pills without my knowledge. She had a seizure at the hospital, and I thought I might lose her." He turned to Georgia with tear-filled eyes. "It shattered my heart in a million pieces."

"Oh, Honey! I'm so sorry." Georgia grasped his hand. "Our sweet Casi. I'm sick with guilt about how I've neglected her needs." She tapped out the cigarette. "I mended her trousers. Make sure to take them home with you. Those are the tiniest buttons! Austin never could have undone them, poor baby."

"Hey, I talked to Amber about her son. She told us how good you've been to her. Did you always know?"

"The damn girl was so in love with your brother. I saw it the first time they met, and I prepared myself for a broken heart." She patted

Kyle's hand. "I suspected something was going on the summer you broke up and I was happy it ended. You were very popular and didn't need to waste time with a girl who betrayed you. Nicole was sweet, and I was pleased you moved on quickly. The day of the accident, Amber came to tell us, and she stayed with me while Dad went to help. She told me about the pregnancy, and I wasn't surprised. It was the typical road for a small-town girl with little potential after high school."

"You thought Jake might be the father?"

"I hoped he wasn't! She assured me it was someone else. When you were in the hospital, she did lovely things like bring flowers or homemade cookies. When you left for college, I looked forward to her visits and seeing how the pregnancy was progressing. I enjoyed knitting for the baby and encouraged her to come to church, so she would have community support. We even threw her a baby shower. I was disappointed when she had another child. I knew it wouldn't end well. When Chase was about five, they were here visiting, and he was playing in the garden and it struck me. He was the spitting image of Grady! She acknowledged it was true, but asked me not to tell anyone, especially you. She didn't want to burden you with the knowledge because she suspected you would try to support him financially."

"I wanted to help with college, but Chase said Casi has something lined up."

"What is our sneaky girl planning?"

"Do you want to bake cookies and we can invite Nicole over to find out?" Kyle grinned. "I can help you."

Georgia's face lit up. "Can you give me an hour?"

22

OPPORTUNITY KNOCKS

"Those are for the guests." Georgia playfully smacked Jake's hand as he snatched a cookie.

"Quality control." He kissed her on the cheek and grabbed another. He surveyed his mother humming while she bustled around the kitchen preparing an elaborate spread of cookies, cakes, and tea. "Do you still love me after what I did?"

"I will always love you and I know you didn't mean to hurt Casi." She noted the pain in his eyes. "Thank you for punishing Dalton before Kyle got to him." She shuddered. "He would have killed him."

The doorbell rang, and she shooed him to answer while she finished glazing the fruit tarts. He escorted Nicole to the living room and made small talk while Kyle helped Casi set up her computer. "Is this something additional about the memorial?" Nicole glanced at the table laden with treats.

Kyle smiled. "I found out something recently."

"About Grady?" Nicole turned to greet Amber as Chase fumbled behind her. She did a double-take and gasped. "No!"

Amber started to cry. "I couldn't tell you before."

Nicole pulled Chase in her arms. "How old are you?"

"Nineteen." He stood stiffly.

Nicole stepped back and caressed the side of his face. "I've seen you at the grocery store. It was like spotting a ghost."

"Why did you cry?" Chase cringed.

"It broke my heart. The resemblance is uncanny."

"He draws like Grady. He's very talented." Kyle handed her the sketchbook they brought.

Nicole smiled and patted the seat beside her on the sofa. "Tell me about yourself." Chase fidgeted while he talked uncomfortably, and Nicole hugged him. "You're as shy and sweet as Grady. I can't believe you raised him alone. You should have told me."

Amber smiled at Georgia. "I've always had a guardian angel."

"What are your plans for college? I want to pay for it. Whatever you need." Nicole grabbed her purse.

"This is where Casi takes over." Kyle grinned.

"Oh God, is this another presentation? Your pent-up aggression at being off work is about to be unleashed in a three-hour documentary on life?" Jake sprawled in a chair.

Casi flipped him off and Georgia patted her on the hip. "Let her do her thing without interruption."

"It's not a presentation," Casi clarified. "The intro is for Chase to introduce him to someone. Please hold comments to the end."

The video began with a colorful display of artwork. Massive installations featured in galleries and chaotic work spray-painted on walls. "I recognize Alix's artwork!" Kyle sat forward.

"Shh," Casi warned. A biography began on Alix's career, showing him with celebrities and accepting awards. Casi giggled at several pictures of herself beside him, then gave Kyle a wink as he feigned disgust. "I dated him, and we've remained great friends," she informed Chase. She watched as his eyes lit up, taking in the images and relating to the artistic journey. "Do you like his work?"

"He's incredible," Chase exhaled. "Can I meet him?"

Casi smiled and advanced the video. "Hey, Chase." Alix grinned into the camera. "I've heard about you and I've seen your work. You're seriously talented, dude!"

Chase grinned widely. "It's like he's talking right to me."

Amber smiled at him and Georgia grasped her hand, anticipating what might happen next. "I'm all about my art, man. College is awesome and I'm sure you'll learn a lot, but a skill like this has to be felt." Alix pounded his chest with his fist. "It's in your soul. If you want to peel back the layers and expose what's truly in your heart, I have an incredible opportunity for you. It won't be easy, but it'll be an epic journey, dude."

"I want to do it," Chase said without hesitation.

"Wait to see what it's about first," Amber cautioned.

Casi closed the laptop. "Alix is offering to take you on as an apprentice. It's a rare privilege to work in his studio with him. You'll get a place to stay and a little spending money." She glanced at Kyle. "You can still do night classes to get your degree because a formal education is important."

"Wow." Amber leaned back. "So, he would go to LA?"

"Yes, Alix's studio is in West Hollywood." Casi surveyed the room, unsure what the consensus was. "I understand if it's not what you want, Chase. Don't feel pressured to make a decision."

Chase looked at Amber with longing. "I really want to do it, Mom. I can come back and visit you."

"I'll be fine." Amber glanced at Georgia, who nodded. "You should follow your dreams. There's no life for you here."

"Chase, your dad would have given anything for a chance to see what was out there and explore his talent. We're willing to cover any costs to get you set up." Kyle smiled. "And your mom could take a vacation as an excuse to visit you."

Nicole wiped tears. "I absolutely agree. Don't let this chance pass you by." She gave Casi a wink. "I might come for a visit and meet this sexy artist myself."

"I guess you're moving to LA!" Amber squeezed his hand.

"I was hoping he would say yes, and I assumed it would be an ideal time for you to only have the younger ones at home since Haley moved out." Casi caught her breath as she noted Kyle's skeptical look. "Um, she mentioned something about a job in Vegas."

Anna nodded. "Yup, the other day when we went to see Chase."

Amber laughed. "You bribed her to go because you knew he wouldn't leave if she was around."

Casi smiled. "I contacted a friend who owns a nightclub. He'll give her a job and it pays more than the strip club."

"She works at the drugstore." Kyle chuckled. "Oh."

Amber rolled her eyes. "She thinks I don't know, but no one comes home with a stack of singles after a night out."

"She must not be very good if they pay her in dollar bills," Jake teased, getting smacked on the arm by Georgia.

"My life will be much easier." Amber smiled at Chase. "Are you ready for a big adventure?"

"When do I leave?" Chase beamed.

"I have an upcoming business meeting in LA, and I was thinking I could take you with me and introduce you to Alix," Casi said.

"Do you want me to come?" Kyle scanned her hesitation. "Only because you still have the cast and it might be difficult for you to manage traveling and setting up for your meeting."

She avoided Lauren's pained expression. "If you can get away, it would be fantastic for you to be part of Chase's journey."

"Jake can take care of himself and he owes me time at work." Kyle smiled at Chase. "This is an amazing connection for you."

"It's not wise to leave me unattended," Jake cautioned.

"I'll keep you in line." Anna narrowed her eyes at Lauren's attempt to gain Kyle's attention. "As a matter of fact, it would be good for you two to get away. Take a few extra days and I'll help out wherever I'm needed."

Kyle remade the bed, glancing up at Casi as she entered the bedroom. "Is Haley really in Vegas or did you dump her body in the river? A word of caution, it could float up come Spring."

"My story was true. Mostly."

"But you'll tell me since we no longer keep secrets?"

"When I met Chase, I had a hunch who his father was." She sat on the bed and toppled his carefully folded pile of clothes. "Obviously, it wasn't the proper time to investigate."

"Sure, missing brother trumps snooping every time." He straightened the fallen items and transferred them to his suitcase.

"I asked Anna to drive me over to Amber's place. She was at work and we could hear Chase and Haley fighting about her stealing his paycheck to buy drugs." She giggled. "You should have seen Anna's face at the trailer. I think she used an entire bottle of sanitizer."

"I can imagine her disdain."

"The minute we walked in Haley was in my face, questioning who I was and what business I had with her brother."

"Big mistake," Kyle predicted.

"I talked to Chase in private while Anna set her straight."

"I would've loved to witness it."

"I was fairly certain he was Grady's son, and since he had a gentle soul, I decided to help him regardless of the truth. I ascertained he couldn't leave with the situation at home."

Kyle sat beside her. "Anna helped you hide the body?"

"No bodies. And not to be catty, but the girl has lumps in all the wrong places. She would never make it as a stripper in Vegas. The cream of the crop works there unless you're off the main strip making peanuts. It was easy to find out she had a police record and after a few phone calls I offered her a deal she couldn't refuse."

"Do you think she'll stay?"

"She literally can't refuse," she reiterated with a grin. "She had twenty minutes to pack her shit, and I had a car pick her up and deliver her to the airport. The club owner made her sign a two-year contract and if she violates it, her ass is thrown in jail. Her driver's license is suspended, and she doesn't have a passport, so her options are limited. I predict she'll enjoy the stability and a steady paycheck. Who knows? She might turn her life around. In the meantime, Chase and Amber get a break and the little kids get more attention."

"What if she sucks at the job? Will this jeopardize your relationship with your friend?"

"He'll keep her in line. He's bought a lot of art from Alix, and he's not someone you cross. I was straight forward with him about who she is and what my end-goal was."

"What did it cost you?"

"An appearance by Alix at his next event. I'll need to attend as well." She gave him a kiss. "But you can come as my date."

"Alix agreed? He's doing a lot for Amber's family already."

"He's super-stoked about having Chase as an apprentice."

"His words, I assume?" Kyle flopped back on the bed.

"Yes. He'll act haughty and aloof at the event, but the media attention will be great for his career. He might bring Chase and introduce him as his protégé if things work out."

"You've had a lot of time on your hands to plan this."

"I'm going insane, not working. I needed the release. I get high from the endorphins when I'm busy."

He poked her in the ribs. "You're a work addict."

She glanced back at him and smiled. "Want to make out?"

"Is it time to cash in on some of my rain checks?"

"The forecast predicts a thunderstorm!" She straddled him in a swift motion and attempted to pull her top off. "Damn it!"

Kyle chuckled and eased the sleeve over her cast. "Easy storm trooper. You still have limitations."

Georgia approached Casi in the hallway as they were preparing to leave. "May I speak to you privately?"

Casi nodded and followed her to the kitchen. "I'm sorry for my outburst at Austin. I messed up Thanksgiving and now I ruined Christmas. I promise the boys are safe with me. The stupid diet pills made me crazy and I was a whiney brat about my cast."

Georgia laughed. "When Jake was about six, we were at the grocery store and he was impossible! I put items in the cart, and he chucked them out. He screamed and carried on like a wild animal." She clucked her tongue. "I had a complete meltdown. I yanked him from the shopping cart and bellowed at him, smacking him on the bottom as I dragged him to the car. I threw him in the backseat and drove to the plumbing shop to leave him with Peter." She squeezed her eyes shut. "Do you know the worst part?"

"Peter chastised you?" Casi suggested.

"No, he was extremely understanding. He calmly asked where Kyle was, and I realized I had forgotten him at the store. I was too embarrassed to go back, so Peter went to retrieve him while Earl cared for Jake. It was one of the worst days of my life, and when I learned to ask for help." She brushed Casi's hair from her cheek. "I was taking pills the doctor prescribed, mother's little helper, he called them. Basically, I was coked up during the day to accomplish my insane amount of responsibilities and too wired at night to sleep."

Casi smiled. "I can relate."

"I must apologize for my reaction to the rumors. I adore you and it broke my heart to imagine you had deceived Kyle. I allowed my jealousy of Ava's and Libby's friendship to interfere with my good sense and I mistreated you." She cringed. "Thinking back to Thanksgiving, I should have known there was an issue with Dalton. I'm devastated you were left alone to deal with your trauma."

"I'm fine now." Casi embraced her. "I should have come to you. I was overwhelmed with emotions and I tried to protect Kyle and Jake. I failed at everything. Also, your friendship is important to Ava. Although she has a lot in common with Libby, she relates to you differently."

"I spoke to her this morning and she assured me I was being foolish." Georgia laughed. "We're having drinks this evening to catch up properly. She told me Mary is her sister!"

Peter shuffled toward them. "Before you leave, I need to get something off my chest."

"Don't make it sound ominous," Georgia warned.

"When I first met you, I was convinced you were a beautiful woman who seduced my son to fall in love with her." He smiled when Casi grimaced. "I learned I misjudged you within hours. After the catastrophe in LA, I was thrilled you had faced monumental challenges so early in your marriage. It proved you both had what it takes to commit to a true partnership and weather any storm. These last few years I've witnessed the effect you have on people, bringing out the magic in them. Jake has evolved into the best version of himself and you've encouraged him to thrive. Kyle has never been happier. Your devotion helped him move on from past sorrow and live his life to the fullest. Your love is endless, and you have a heart of gold. Please forgive me for ever suspecting otherwise. I was a fool to ignore what I already knew to be the truth."

Casi blinked back tears. "The only thing worse than Dalton's creepy touch was hurting those I love. I'm sorry your family was hit in the crossfire. I cherish all of you and Kyle is the love of my life."

"You are a crucial member of our family." He kissed her cheek. "We will never fail you again."

23

DEADLY CHOICES

*J*ake surveyed Anna pacing the room with Charlotte on her hip. The toddler was dressed in an expensive plaid dress with a velvet collar. Navy tights and patent leather shoes completed the privileged baby ensemble, highlighted by a bow clipped in her strawberry blond hair. "Is there a reason our daughter is not permitted to play or eat until your guest arrives?" He checked his watch.

Anna sighed. "I want her to stay clean. This will be a brief interaction, and I'm overwhelmed by the emotional aspect of it."

"I imagine meeting your first daughter is daunting." Jake put an arm around her shoulders as a black Mercedes pulled in the driveway.

A slender woman arrived and greeted them formally, kissing them on both cheeks. She smiled at Charlotte and sat on the sofa with her hands folded in her lap. Anna offered a plate of lemon poppyseed madeleines and poured tea as Chantal glanced around the room through the fringe of her dark hair, resting her gaze on Anna. "I didn't picture you with red hair."

Anna smoothed a hand over Charlotte's lighter version. "I always assumed you inherited it."

"Perhaps I resemble my father?"

"Yes, you do." Anna kept the disgust from her voice. "I'm sorry he also gave you a kidney disorder. You received the medical records?"

Chantal removed a stack of paperwork from her bag and placed it on the sofa. "I'm a software engineer. I'm telling you this to preface why I can't give up on a cure without extensive research. I understand you're not a match and my birth father's kidneys are compromised." Her eyes shifted to Charlotte. "Would you consider testing her?"

"Absolutely not!" Jake jumped to his feet. "Ask the rapist's children. They're older and can pay for the sins of their father."

"Jake!" Anna glared at him.

Chantal nodded. "I was curious about my beginning. Given your age, I suspected it may not have been consensual."

"I never intended for you to know." Anna fought back tears.

"I appreciate you contacting him." Chantal sipped her tea.

Jake caressed Anna's shoulder. "I'm sorry for my outburst. I won't allow Charlotte to be tested and I'll never give consent for her to donate a kidney at her age." He felt Anna shiver under his touch. "Our friend told us your birth father has four children in their late teens. I feel they would be a more viable option."

"He won't give permission to have me speak to them." Anna shook her head.

"If he didn't require consent to create a life, why should we be concerned with his opinion?" Jake raised an eyebrow.

Anna noted Chantal's silent, desperate look. "I believe you have brought up a valid point. When Casi returns from her business trip, I'll ask her to find out their names and addresses."

"Today is the best day of my life." Casi proudly displayed a pewter silk blouse on a padded hanger.

"It's cool how a new shirt dictates your mood," Jake teased.

"Not new, neglected. Today it'll get the star treatment it deserves." Casi smoothed a hand over the material.

"It's gorgeous. I'm glad you'll be able to wear it again. I would have stolen it if it fit me." Anna admired the blouse.

"The color would be fabulous on you," Casi agreed. "This impediment will not be missed."

Kyle paused at the coffeemaker, dissecting the conversation. "You get the cast removed today?"

"Duh, that's why I'm excited," Casi said.

"What time?" He sipped his coffee cautiously.

"Ten. We can leave for Seattle from the wood shop and have an early lunch after." She furrowed her brow. "Why are you looking nauseous? You said to make an appointment. There can't be anything urgent at work." Before he could reply, she wagged a finger at him. "Lauren! You double-booked yourself and now you're sweating about which woman to choose."

"I suggest the super-hot one who could kill you in your sleep." Jake nudged his brother.

"I'm not conflicted," Kyle said slowly. "I agreed to go to Lauren's ultrasound, and it happens to be at the same time. Technically, I did commit to her first."

"You're a moron." Jake glanced at Anna, who nodded in agreement. "For the record, I would pick you before any of my exes."

"Go to her appointment. Seeing her blurry baby is more important than me not being handicapped any longer." Casi sulked.

"Proceed with caution." Jake noted Kyle preparing a rebuttal.

"Casi, I want to be with you but there are concerns about the size of the baby and she's been having contractions. They must check the fluid and weight." Kyle handed her a cup of coffee.

"Hot liquids. Brilliant." Jake grinned at Anna.

"Sounds like you had a lengthy conversation. Your support will be invaluable. My procedure is simple, and I'll take myself to lunch to celebrate." She grabbed her shirt and turned toward the bedroom.

"My morning is free." Anna smiled. "I'll go with Lauren. I'm sure my experience as a woman supersedes your dedicated friendship. Feel free to pass along the extensive research you have done on her pregnancy ailments."

Kyle quickly surveyed the heat level in the room and gave her a taut smile. "I appreciate you stepping up. Thank you for making it possible for me to escort Casi instead."

"You don't have to go, Anna," Casi mumbled.

"It's an excellent solution." Kyle fumbled with his phone.

"No need to text her. When I was pregnant, I was so focused on the baby it wouldn't have mattered who came with me," Anna stated.

"She's dealing with a lot." Kyle rubbed his temple.

"Yes, my marriage was a picnic," Anna snapped.

"Which is why you're the best choice so you and Lauren can talk about ignorant husbands." Jake transferred the coffee to travel mugs and handed them out. "Am I taking my truck or driving with you guys to the wood shop, where you'll abandon me?"

"I can drive my own car after the cast is off." Casi slid the keys from the hook with a smile.

"It's been six weeks and your arm may be weak." Kyle gently grasped the keys from her palm.

"I didn't forget how to drive. Why would strength be an issue?" Casi frowned as they walked to the car.

"It's snowing." Kyle blinked the snowflakes away. "There are hills in Seattle which could be slippery."

"I only need my feet."

"Can you clarify the pluralization?"

"One on the gas and one on the brake in case the car slips."

"Perfectly logical." Jake chuckled.

"We can drive your car and Jake can pick me up after lunch so you can meet Mary." Kyle held the door for her. "Can we agree on holding off on extended outings until we've considered your mobility?"

"We can negotiate over cocktails." Casi threw her head back and laughed when he halted in his tracks. "Totally kidding."

Jake kissed Casi on the cheek. "Send me those addresses. I want this taken care of before Anna reconsiders cutting into my precious child to scrounge for spare parts."

"Remember, the blade cannot hurt you." Kyle caressed Casi's back as she sat on the exam table. "It'll be easier than the last time. Especially if you don't have a seizure."

She read the pain in his eyes. "I haven't taken any pills."

"Has Katie accepted it?"

"I agreed to talk with her next week, but I'm standing firm."

Kyle kissed her forehead. "Please don't let her sway you."

"What are your plans when you're released from cast jail?" the nurse asked, distracting her from the vibration of the saw.

"Cocktails, being able to type, feeding myself, and making my husband happy." She blushed deeply as the room broke out in laughter. "Oh, I didn't mean sexually! Although I guess it should be on the list."

Kyle chuckled. "It'll be nice not to be smacked in the face while you sleep." He kissed her cheek and whispered, "I've missed your right hand and the magic it possesses."

The doctor swabbed her arm with antiseptic and began removing the stitches. "There is a little redness and swelling which will go away in a few days. Soak in a hot bath and don't rush into your old activities. Squeeze," he directed, making her clench a fist.

Tears sprung to Casi's eyes as she attempted and failed. "Is it still broken?"

"The muscles are weak from lack of use. You'll have a full range of motion after a few weeks of physical therapy."

She slumped on the table, regarding her arm with disgust. "I thought once the cast came off, I would be as good as new. What was the point of the stupid surgery?"

Kyle cringed at the accusation in her tone. "The bones were shattered and wouldn't have mended. The surgery was not elective."

The doctor patted Casi's knee. "You're obviously an active woman and it can be disconcerting to have limitations. Physical therapy is an important step in the process."

Casi burst into tears and Kyle hugged her to his chest. "She was in a car accident a few years ago, which broke her pelvis. It was a long road to get up and walking again. And it's not easy for her to be held back. She's used to being independent and her patience is wearing thin after so many weeks of confinement."

The doctor nodded. "She's lucky to have a supportive husband. It can be tough to undergo traumatic events alone."

Kyle's temple throbbed as he glanced at the clock with guilt, realizing the disappointment Lauren was experiencing. "I can imagine."

They strolled to the parking garage and Casi slipped her newly freed hand in his firm grip. "Thank you for being with me. I do understand it was a difficult choice."

Kyle stopped and stepped in front of her. "It wasn't a choice between you and Lauren. You're my wife and my top priority. I don't like to let my friends down when I've committed to something. Anna's solution was perfect." He escorted her in the restaurant with a smile. The maître di led them to a table by the window, and a waiter filled their water glasses.

"Did you make reservations?" Casi regarded the dining room bustling with business.

"I called this morning." He pointed to an elaborately carved piece dominating the restaurant. "I built the entire back bar. The owner has made a point to reserve a table without question ever since."

"Have you brought Lauren here?" Casi held his gaze.

"Yes." Kyle fiddled with his napkin.

"Then the food must be great. She has a superior palate and I'm excited to try something new." Casi picked up the menu and perused the choices. "Pasta maybe."

"Fake happiness? I struggle with how to read your emotions."

"It's real. One of my new year's goals is to be less of a bitch about Lauren. She has enough crap to deal with and I've been blessed with an incredible husband."

Kyle grinned at her. "Thanks for trying. I'm blessed to have you too. Do you think pasta might be a challenge with your wrist?"

"Let's give it a try." Casi smiled at the waiter.

Kyle regarded the surf outside the window and contemplated

how to explain the situation to Lauren. His phone had buzzed incessantly for the last half an hour, and he didn't need to check to know it was her. A crash of cutlery brought his attention back to the table, and he smiled as Casi wiped Alfredo sauce from her shirt. "Maybe the pasta was too difficult for a freedom meal?"

"I'm glad I didn't change yet." She stuffed the napkin beside the plate. "I'll take this home and eat it in private."

"You barely touched it," Kyle lamented. "Order a sandwich or something easier to eat."

"No, let's go. I'm sure you want to check in with Lauren and I'm anxious to see Mary and work on the campaign."

He reached over and laced his fingers through hers. "I'm not in a hurry. How about dessert? I know you've mastered ice cream."

She giggled. "I guess I could manage."

"I'll text Jake and tell him we'll be done in a half an hour." He frowned at the multitude of messages on his phone.

They chatted over dessert and coffee before Casi went to the restroom to change. She returned with a smile and sat beside Kyle. "Can you take my food with you? Tell Jake not to eat it."

"I'll hide it in the back of the fridge. Are you sure you want to drive? It may be difficult to manage if your arm is not strong enough."

"I could have driven with the cast, but you were adamant about not letting me."

"I was concerned for your safety. It's not responsible to operate a vehicle when you can't have two hands on the wheel. How would you have put on the windshield wipers or put the car in reverse? Not to mention you were heavily medicated in the beginning."

Casi clasped her hands together and spoke carefully. "I understand your hesitation. I'm a grown woman who can make decisions for herself. Although your care and commitment to my wellness is appreciated, please back off a bit."

Kyle read the determination in her face. "Understood."

"How's gimpy?" Jake asked when Kyle got in the truck.

"Depressed about her lack of mobility and taking it out on me."

"You still made the right choice to go with her. She would have been crankier to hear the news if she was alone." Jake turned up the heater as they waited for Casi to leave the restaurant.

"I didn't know what day she made the appointment. I wouldn't choose Lauren over Casi and I don't appreciate you suggesting I would."

"Perhaps Casi isn't the only one with displaced anger?"

Kyle slumped in the seat and exhaled. "I'm walking on eggshells. Either I'm not attentive enough or I'm overbearing. I shouldn't tell her what to do, but then everyone accuses me of not protecting her. How do I ensure her safety if she won't let me?"

They watched Casi walk toward the car, slipping on the ice in her high heels. Kyle tensed, and Jake put a hand on his shoulder. "She'll be alright. You've told her not to wear those shoes in winter. If she falls on her ass, maybe she'll listen."

"She should clean the windshield." Kyle shook his head when she activated the wipers, scraping across the ice. "Defroster first."

"Do you want me to follow her?" Jake surveyed her exit.

"No, if she spots the truck it'll make her angry. I won't be responsible for distracting her while she's driving." He turned his attention to his phone, scrolling through the messages.

"Anna said everything's fine. Lauren's on bedrest, but she's at her mom's house."

"Great, Fran is probably using her as a nurse. I don't think she understands the complications with the pregnancy."

"I asked Lia to check on her. Fran can use a cane to get around and, like Casi, they're mature women who can take care of themselves." Jake pulled onto the on-ramp for the freeway.

"Wrong direction." Kyle frowned at his brother.

"We need to make a stop in Portland."

"Almost three hours! Fine, I have another side trip on the way." He clenched his jaw as they rounded the bend an hour later and drove around work trucks. "Son-of-a-bitch."

Kyle bolted from the truck and stormed inside the shell of the restaurant, shutting down the power at the box. Work stopped, and the foreman scowled. "Who the hell are you?"

"I'm the guy who paid for these materials and was never reimbursed," Kyle stated.

"Not my fault if you were fired from the job."

"I was scammed." Kyle surveyed the work in progress.

"It's our job now." He pushed past him to turn the power on.

"Have you been paid?"

"A deposit and the rest upon completion."

"What about materials?"

"They were already here. The guy keeps changing his mind about what he wants. This reclaimed wood is not our specialty."

Kyle grabbed the blueprints. "These changes aren't in compliance."

"Not my problem."

Kyle turned to Jake. "Load up the truck. Don't bother with the junk wood, but I want the cherry, reclaimed pine, and trim pieces."

Jake nodded and flexed as a worker tried to block access. The man backed down quickly. "I just work here."

"Excellent, carry these to my truck," Jake instructed.

"We're not getting in the middle of this fight," the foreman concluded. "When the police arrive, you can explain it to them."

Kyle extracted an invoice from his wallet and held it in front of the man's face. "I'm taking what's mine. You can continue to work for a criminal, but you're not doing it on my dime." He turned to gather supplies. "I would have expected solidarity from a fellow tradesman."

The foreman surveyed the truck emblazoned with the Jensen Brothers logo and nodded. "You've paid for more than what will fit in your truck." He motioned to a nearby flatbed. "We'll drop off the remainder. I live in Everett, so it's on the way. Load it up, boys. We're still getting paid for the day whether we can work or not." He handed Kyle a business card. "Keep us in mind if you hear of jobs in the area. I have a feeling we won't be here long."

Kyle nodded. "I'll be happy to give you referrals."

"What's our plan?" Jake chuckled as they drove away.

"Not sure yet, but the slimy fucker doesn't get to use them and expect me to pay. I already contacted the supplier when I realized the job would fall through. They can't take them back and I was stupid enough to pay for them out of pocket."

"Since when does our company finance the job?"

"I'm sorry. I got caught up in the idea of the restaurant and how much money we would make in the long run. I missed the red flags such as them wanting to run it through the accounting department after the new year. I ordered the materials in October, but they kept changing the start date. I should've known it was a scam. I'll take the hit for it personally."

"Our company, our problem," Jake asserted. "The profit would have been shared so this setback will be too."

"It's high-end materials."

"We'll use them, eventually."

Amy raised an eyebrow when they pulled in and began unloading the truck. "Is there a job on the docket I haven't listed yet?"

"Cancel the Stanford job," Kyle replied. "Don't answer any calls from them either. We'll let the attorney handle it from here."

"What about Lauren's new restaurant?" Amy asked.

Kyle paused, unsure how much to tell her. "Her marriage might be imploding, which would also end her involvement in a restaurant."

"Oh, how sad." Amy regarded her engagement ring. "She came by an hour ago and I said you were with Casi."

Kyle surveyed her demeanor. "Your marriage will be happy, Amy. Riley is a great guy and you love each other. Lauren misjudged Dalton and his family, which creates complications."

"And you chose well with Casi," she said sweetly.

"I did. Hopefully, my brother finally got it right the third time around." Kyle smacked him on the back.

Jake held up a middle finger. "It's a work in progress."

Kyle checked his watch. "You can head home, Amy. Jake and I wasted a lot of time taking care of errands."

After the supplies were neatly stored in a far recess of the wood shop, they checked the dockets and reviewed the schedule. Kyle assembled a file in anticipation of an upcoming legal battle. He closed the door to the office and phoned Lauren, listening to her list of complaints as he sorted his files. "Everything is fine?" He hoped he had come to the proper conclusion.

"Not really. I'm stuck in this house with my mother and Lia is useless. I was looking forward to seeing you today and talking more about what I should do with the condo."

"But the baby is healthy, which is a relief," he reiterated. "Let Brian handle the financial end of things." He switched on the speaker, realizing the conversation would not be brief. He straightened the office, ignoring an incoming call which he anticipated would be coming from the Standfords. He tried to interrupt her to give her a heads up about the restaurant situation, but she continued to rant about her mother and how hard it was to be pregnant and alone. Jake shoved the door open and Kyle held up a hand, pointing to the phone. "Uh, huh, I can imagine the difficulty."

Jake stormed to the desk. "Hey Lauren, Kyle has to go. His wife has been in a car accident and she's desperate to talk to him. Bye now."

Kyle's face paled. "Are you lying to get her off the phone?"

"Nope." Jake walked toward the door. "Call your wife."

Kyle dialed with trembling fingers. He heard her sobbing and eased on to the edge of the desk for support while he waited for her to calm down. "Are you ok? What happened?"

"Don't be mad."

"I promise I'm not upset." His chest squeezed and his vision blurred momentarily.

"Can you come get me?"

He grabbed Jake's arm and shoved him toward the door. "Where are you?"

"At Mary's."

"Thank God!" He caught his breath. "I was waiting for you to tell me which hospital."

"I'm not hurt." She hesitated. "The car skidded on the ice and the heel of my shoe got stuck under the pedal. My wrist wasn't strong enough to hold on to the wheel. I was only a few blocks from Mary's house when it happened, so I walked back."

He noted an odd tone in her voice. "What are you leaving out?"

"My shoes are destroyed."

"No surprise. They were a terrible choice, but I feel there's something more." He put the call on the speaker in the truck.

"I was on the phone." She broke into tears. "I got in a fight with Katie when I told her about the thing. Jake texted you would be late, so I had dinner with Dylan, which was more successful than lunch. He harassed me about my hair and insisted we go to his salon when we were done. It looks a lot better! Did you put my pasta in the fridge?"

"Jake ate it." Kyle chuckled. "We had errands to run, and he smelled it under the seat."

"It was delicious." Jake made chomping noises.

"I had chicken wings. Guess what happened?" She sighed.

"You spilled on your new blouse," Kyle concluded.

"Yup. Right down the front. Two shirts soiled in one day. Isn't it zany? Mary offered to take them to the dry cleaners for me and gave me a sweatshirt to wear."

"Hey, turn." Kyle pointed down a side street.

"Why?" Casi turned around.

"Not you. Jake. I see your car. It might not be too bad."

"I couldn't back it out." Casi launched into a theatrical description of how it had jumped over the curb of its own volition, and she barely made it out alive.

Jake rolled his eyes. "Take it off speaker. I'm getting a headache."

"We'll see you in a few minutes." Kyle hung up and frowned at the caller id on his phone. "Why's Shane contacting me?"

"Katie probably gave him an earful about Casi." Jake hooked the chain to her bumper and glanced up as Kyle's face dropped. "What's up?"

"Katie's dead."

24

CHAIN OF EVENTS

Jake rushed over as Kyle fell to his knees. "What happened?"

"Car accident." Kyle inhaled sharply and turned to him with tears in his eyes. "They saw on her phone she was texting Casi."

Jake squeezed his eyes shut. "Were the kids with her?"

"Yes. They're alive and he'll give us an update on their injuries. It could have been Casi!" Kyle rocked back on his heels.

"But it wasn't. Give me two minutes to yank her vehicle out and we'll go get her." Jake jumped in his truck.

"You heard her voice, right? I didn't imagine the conversation?"

"I heard every whiney note." Jake inched forward and Casi's car slid free of the snowbank. He scrambled out and detached the chain before peering in the driver's seat. "No blood. The airbag didn't deploy. You weren't talking to a ghost. Get in and follow me. Do not call her! Your voice will tip her off."

Casi flung the door open and greeted them enthusiastically. Kyle locked her in an embrace. "Why are you shaking? Is my car totaled?" She regarded their somber expressions.

Kyle put his hands to the sides of her face. "Are you sure you're fine? You didn't hit your head?" He raised an eyebrow. "Your hair looks fantastic. Dylan is a miracle worker."

Mary surveyed them and frowned. "Is the wreck worse than she assumed? She's been in good spirits."

"The car is fine." Jake nodded to Kyle, and he led Casi to the sofa as they settled on either side of her.

"I got a call from Shane." Kyle laced his fingers through hers.

Casi drew in a sharp breath. "He's pissed because the kids were in the car. Did they hear what I said? I was belligerent, and he hates when I swear around them. Katie kept arguing and bringing up stuff from the past. I hung up because I was pissed at how she was making me feel." She reached over to the coffee table and grabbed her phone. "I don't usually text when I drive, but she bombarded me with vicious messages. I tried to reply, but I misjudged the curve."

Kyle scrolled through the thread of messages and winced when he read the last text. "You know what, CASSIDY? You can go fu..."

"I assume she used all caps to remind me where I came from. I'm unsure why she didn't finish. Maybe the kids interrupted her."

"Shane called because Katie was in an accident." Kyle tightened his grip. "She died."

"You're lying!" Casi jumped to her feet. "This is a cruel way to convey the severe consequences of distracted driving!"

Kyle wrapped her in his arms. "I'm telling you the truth. He wanted you to hear it from us not on social media."

Casi sobbed on his shoulder, muttering incoherently in disbelief. "It's my fault." She raised her tear-stained face to him. "I should've gone to Vancouver like I promised and talked to her in person. It was a lame-ass thing to handle it on the phone."

Kyle brushed strands of hair from her cheek. "I must confess something. The other day I called Katie from your phone."

"Why?" Casi blinked through her tears.

"I basically threatened her." Kyle cringed and ignored Jake's hand motion to stop. "I felt you were on shaky ground with recovering from the assault and your injury. I perceived a lot of the negativity came from her and I viewed it as counterproductive." He wrung his hands. "I'm going to tell you everything."

"Ok." Casi slumped beside him.

"Jake and I went to a hockey game with Shane and Joey last week. They asked how you were doing, and I shared my concerns. They both warned me to keep you away from Katie. Joey was especially adamant and said Dawn didn't think you understood Katie would not let up until she got her way. Shane was stressed about her dark mood and ended things with Lia to focus on raising his kids. He was contemplating moving in with Katie's parents to keep them safe. I told her if she ever involved you in any of her dealings again, I would alert the authorities and have her children taken away."

Casi's eyes went wide. "She loves those kids!"

"It seemed like the only way to get through to her. Apparently, she didn't believe me since she called you anyway." Kyle held her gaze. "I'm sorry, but I couldn't sit back and wait for something terrible to happen to you."

Casi stared into space and evaluated his words before turning to Mary. "Last month I had a seizure at the hospital when they were removing my cast. It was probably caused by a drug interaction because I mixed prescription diet pills with the pain medication."

Kyle quickly added. "She didn't know I was still giving it to her in food. I crushed it because I wanted to minimize her pain and she refused to take it."

Mary frowned. "Casi, why in the world would you take a diet aid? You're too thin as it is!"

"I talked to a therapist, and we concluded it was more about feeling in control. I transported the prescription across the border from Canada to LA using our packaging. It was removed before distribution, but I realize the tremendous risk. I understand if you fire me."

Mary caressed her arm. "I've told you this company will be yours one day. It was a stupid thing to do, but you had to realize it yourself. What was the point of jeopardizing your career?"

"There was no point." Casi let the tears flow down her cheeks. "I didn't make any money. I thought I was helping Katie, but it evolved into a nightmare." She turned to Kyle. "I wish you had told me, but I understand why you don't trust me."

"I'm paranoid about failing to protect you!" Kyle clasped a hand to his chest. "My heart can't handle losing you."

Jake leaned forward. "Casi, it's tragic, but it's not your fault. Or Kyle's. Katie made ridiculous choices and depended on everyone else to clean up after her. You say she adored her kids? She should've been focused on them while she was driving and not getting into a fight with you. Shane loves them too, and she had no right to put them in harm's way. He's at the hospital praying they survive." He shifted his gaze to Kyle. "I talked to Shane on our way over here. They suspect the cause of death was a stroke, which in turn caused the accident. I'm willing to bet those diet pills had something to do with it." He squeezed Casi's hand. "It may sound callous, but thank God you're crying over Katie's death rather than us being devastated by yours."

Anna raced in the house. "Where's Jake?" She settled Charlotte on the carpet and dumped toys in her lap.

"He stopped by Lia's." Kyle assisted Casi with her jacket and led her to the sofa. "Do you want a glass of wine?"

Casi remained silent and kneaded her hands. Anna assessed her demeanor and noted the absence of the pewter blouse. "Did things not go well at the doctor's office?"

Kyle sighed. "We found out Katie was in a car accident and died late this afternoon. Casi is overwrought."

"It's my fault," she murmured.

Anna flew to her side. "I'm sure it's not."

"Katie was texting her at the time, so she feels responsible. Jake spoke to Shane, and it appears there may have been an underlying cause such as a stroke. They won't know until after the autopsy." Kyle ran a hand through his chestnut hair. "Jake went to talk to Lia."

"Of course." Anna hugged Casi tightly. "What can I do to help?"

"Would you mind checking in with Mary to see what business needs to be handled this week?" Kyle glanced at the calendar and noted several trips highlighted in yellow.

"I can travel." Casi put her head on Anna's shoulder.

Kyle shook his head as he paced. "No. I'm sorry, but it's not a good idea for you to be away." She glared at him and he held a hand up. "Deal with this first. There will be a funeral in a few days, and you cannot miss it. It's important for you to talk to your friends and we need to support Shane and his children."

"I don't want to." Casi burst into tears.

Kyle kneeled before her and grasped her hands. "You've handled so much, especially in the last few months. There's a light at the end of the tunnel. I promise."

"It's probably a train." Casi half-laughed and wiped tears. "Can I have a pain pill?"

"Are you hurting?" He smoothed a hand around her neck. "Sometimes symptoms arise after an accident."

"I just don't want to feel anything."

"What accident?" Anna cocked her head.

"She drove into a snowbank this afternoon while she was texting. A random chain of events." He sighed and walked to the bedroom and came back holding a bottle. "How about a half dose? It'll help you sleep." He cut the pill and poured a glass of water.

Casi swallowed the medication and rested her head against the back of the sofa while Kyle turned on a documentary to soothe her. Jake came home and nodded to Anna. "You heard?"

"Yes, it's horrible. How's Lia?" Anna strolled to the counter.

"Upset. She's in a difficult position. She wants to comfort Shane and be there for his girls, but she's basically the mistress. She was worried about Casi." His eyes drifted to the prescription bottle.

Anna grasped his hand. "I understand other things have taken precedence today, but we must talk about what happened in Portland."

Jake shrugged. "We drove there and requested the Salvatore clan get tested to see if they're a match. If my daughter is considered a viable option, why wouldn't his children be fair game?"

"He said you threatened him."

"I strongly urged him to comply." Jake raised an eyebrow. "Why does he have your phone number?"

"Email. I had to be in contact for Chantal's sake. Mary suggested I use my business email and document every encounter. Unfortunately, I now also have his claim you bullied him."

"What a fucking wuss. One of his kids is over eighteen. Technically, we can contact him without his father's consent. It's not a crime to ask them to be tested, and we can eliminate those who are not a match."

"Did you threaten him with violence?" Anna winced.

"I simply stated it would be in his best interest to take the easy route." He grinned and got a beer from the fridge, twisting the cap off. "I would love to punch him in his self-righteous face, but ultimately I would allow cyber-spy to crush him." He surveyed Kyle, stroking Casi's hair as she relaxed in his arms.

"Thank you." Anna kissed him tenderly. "I appreciate your help and although I would love for you to destroy him, I must remain calm."

"When this is over, I might creep up on him in a dark alley."

"Sounds like a good plan." She smiled. "I'll see you at the house later. Don't stay up too late."

"Are you concerned for my welfare?"

"Always. I'm learning to express myself better." Anna bid them goodnight and picked up Charlotte.

Kyle carried Casi to the bedroom and helped her undress before settling her in bed. He kissed her on the forehead. "I'll be back in a few minutes." She snuggled in the covers, blissfully medicated. He returned to the kitchen and eyed Jake near the prescription bottle. "Not for you."

"I'm good with this." He held up his beer. He observed Kyle's labored breathing. "Are you ok?"

"I can't get ahead of this train wreck. It keeps piling up like one of those multi-car crashes in winter. You can see the inevitable collision, but you're unable to move out of the way. It's in slow motion and played on a continuous loop." He exhaled and locked eyes with Jake. "We finally put Sonya to rest, and now this? How do I help her get over it? When you went off the rails the one good thing was knowing Tara was dead and couldn't lure you into her drug den."

"I went to the pier. I sat on a bench in the rain and thought about what I would have done if she came up to me." He shrugged. "It's good she's dead." He reached for the pills and pushed Kyle's hand away when he tried to stop him. "Take the other half. I'll stay over tonight and ensure you two are safe. I doubt you've slept properly in weeks. You should be celebrating your wife's freedom from cast prison, but enjoy being numb tonight instead."

Kyle popped the pill in his mouth and swallowed a swig of his brother's beer. "Wake us if there's a fire."

Kyle appeared at the bedroom door and surveyed Anna packing a suitcase. "I need your help."

She smiled. "Sure, I have time before I leave for the airport. This is my first trip back east for the company and it's been a challenge to assess what the weather may be."

"Cold." Kyle grinned and led her across the street. "We may get a lot of rain, but at least the snow is minimal. Thanks for taking the meeting for Casi. It's been a struggle to convince her to attend the funeral." He pointed to Casi staring into the closet without moving.

Anna slid beside her. "Are you wondering what to wear?"

Casi's lip trembled. "I don't want to go!"

"I know, but you must. Everyone is sad about what happened, and it'll be good for you to talk with your friends." Anna sorted through dresses. "Charcoal will be suitable. You're too young to be clad in black." She slipped the dress from the hanger and handed it to Kyle before sourcing appropriate accessories. "Maybe your black boots? They're stylish but good for the weather in Vancouver."

"I love those boots." Casi stood still with a blank expression.

"They're gorgeous. The detail is stunning." Anna grasped Casi's hand and brought her to the bedroom, helping her dress as they talked about fashion and the latest trends.

"Don't wear heels in New York." Casi shivered. "I fell on my ass when I slipped on one of those manhole cover things. Everyone sped past, oblivious to me sprawled on the ground."

"When did you fall?" Kyle asked.

"Last year. It wasn't a big deal. Models are trained to bounce back up. It's inevitable with the outfits they dress you in. Thankfully, I never bit it on the runway, but I've had my share of tumbles during shoots." Casi regarded her image in the mirror. "I want this day behind me. It's not right to be attending a funeral for a woman who was barely thirty-five."

❦

Casi stopped in her tracks as they entered the church overflowing with people. Kyle gripped her hand tighter and encouraged her to walk forward. "Look, there's Joey and Dawn."

Dawn broke down as they approached and pulled Casi in her arms. "This is so sad! I can't even wrap my head around it."

Joey shuddered. "We've known Katie since kindergarten, and now we're attending her funeral. What the fuck?"

"How are the kids?" Jake held his hand out to Shane.

Shane pulled him into a hug. "One broken arm and a few cuts and bruises. They haven't grasped their mom is not coming back." He kept his voice low. "A while ago, Katie went on a bender and was gone for weeks. They think she's away even though they were in the car with her." He sighed. "After Katie had the girls, she settled into a happy mood for the first time. When she got on a weight loss kick, the discontent crept back. Three years ago, she had gastric bypass surgery and lost over a hundred pounds. Things fell apart between us. Suddenly I was a pathetic fat guy who couldn't do anything right, and she monitored everything the girls ate." He exhaled. "She had a stroke. Thirty-five years old and a blood clot fried her brain. The assumed cause was an interaction between drugs."

Casi's knees buckled. "The diet pills?"

Shane grasped her elbow as Kyle steadied her. "Mixed with cocaine. Too much stimulation weakened her arteries." He regarded Lia. "We've had our green cards for months, but I couldn't move them to Seattle because Katie required too much medical care. After the gastric bypass she got a tummy tuck and boob lift, which was covered. She wasn't happy, so I paid for more surgeries in the States. There was always something else she needed." He looked up as a woman with a cane made her way over. "Mum, let me help you."

"Darling, I'm fine. I have to get used to this thing." She smiled warmly. "Cassidy, you're even more beautiful than you were as a girl. Ava told me how happy you are."

Casi sobbed as the woman hugged her. "I'm sorry."

"Our poor Katie was a lost soul. She was thrilled to reconnect with you and her friends were the most important thing in her life aside from the girls. We sensed we would lose her at a young age. Shane has been a blessing." She smiled. "You must be Lia? We've heard a lot about you from Shane and the girls." Lia blushed, unsure what to say. "We understood the marriage was to keep Katie insured. No money or procedure would lift her spirits for long." She shivered and patted Lia's hand. "You've been good for Shane. He deserves someone who cares about him."

Ava and Jack approached, and he kissed Casi on the cheek before offering an arm to assist Katie's mother to her seat for the ceremony. "How are you doing, Sweetie?" Ava embraced Casi. "Your dress is perfect for the occasion."

"Anna picked it out." She relaxed in Ava's arms. "I didn't realize you were close with Katie's mother."

"Since grade school." Ava smiled. "I attended most of your events and was on the PTA. It was an odd situation, but your mother wasn't interested, and it was important to your dad to have the family represented. Of course, these days the men are equally involved."

"There are so many things I'll have to learn about how to raise these kids." Shane's face radiated pain as he observed his mother-in-law struggling to sit with Jack's assistance. "She has cancer. Katie depended on her too much to help with the kids, but she's been unable in the last few months. The doctors say she won't be here much longer." He clenched his jaw. "God damned Katie couldn't even let her mother die without dealing with this shit first."

The ceremony proceeded with comforting words and hymns. A slideshow of Katie's life played, carefully choreographed to highlight her happy moments. Casi watched herself evolve from a pig-tailed second grader to a smiling teenager, always in the middle of the trio as they wound their arms around each other. Dawn laced her fingers through hers and gave her a sad smile.

"When's mummy coming back?" a tiny voice asked, evoking tears and silent sobbing.

"She lives in heaven now," Shane explained as three sets of eyes gazed at him in confusion. He redirected their attention to the pictures of themselves as babies, and they clapped and enjoyed the show.

Jake slid closer and casually swung an arm over Shane's shoulders. "You have us to lean on."

"Can you guys stay over? I want to do a bonfire at the beach." Shane regarded Casi, clinging to Dawn as they cried. "We should say a proper goodbye with only our group."

25

KICK START

*C*asi exited the bedroom clad in minuscule spandex shorts and a cross-back bra top. Jake surveyed her attire. "Nope, go change."

"I'm late for my kickboxing class." She searched through papers on the counter to find her keys.

"Kyle has your car." Jake waited until she finished looking under the pillows on the sofa.

"Why? I'm in a hurry. I bought a series of three and you can't miss the first one or they cancel your membership without a refund."

He scanned her outfit. "They'll make an exception for you." He turned back to the stove. "You should be thankful he's getting the paint repaired after your snowbank incident. Perhaps the auto-body place could sell you a series of repairs. With the fender damage after you hit Kyle's truck when you tore out of here before our European trip, a bulk discount would be handy."

"Hysterical." She rolled her eyes. "Give me a ride."

"I'm feeding my children." He held his middle finger to her.

"It's ten minutes away. They won't starve."

"Look at those angelic faces." He grinned as Austin chased

231

Tommy into the bedroom with a howl, then switched the burner off. "Anna, you're in charge. We had three here last time I checked."

Anna strolled over with Charlotte. "The boys are jumping on the bed. I told them to stop, and they pretended not to hear me."

"I'll deal with it when I get back." He gave her a kiss.

"No." Charlotte pushed his face away.

"This attitude needs to change," Jake cautioned.

"You're the one who indulged her and now she bonded to your brother. He makes her obey by treating her like a dog. We may need parenting classes before they require therapy," Anna sighed.

"Bye brat." Casi stuck out her tongue, making Charlotte screech.

"I'm surrounded by insolent children." Jake pushed Casi toward the door. "Put on a jacket. It's still winter."

"I don't need one. The workout will keep me warm."

"You make zero sense."

Casi leaped from the car and sprinted toward the studio, waving as she entered. "Thanks for the ride."

Jake parked and peered inside the class, ensuring she wasn't the only woman to join. He noted the professional appearance of the instructor and was satisfied the class was legitimate. He arrived home to Charlotte screeching and the boys wrestling to command the Google speaker. He witnessed the irritation on Anna's face and unplugged the blaring unit, holding it above their heads. "No screaming inside. We'll sit down like a civilized family and have dinner." He checked his pot on the stove. "Did someone lose a crayon?"

"Mine," Austin yelled, tripping over coloring books on the floor and plunging into the cabinet face first. "Owie."

"No doubt." Jake picked him up to inspect the damage.

"No," Charlotte screamed, smacking Tommy in the face with a dinosaur and grabbing the ball from him.

"Why didn't I use a condom?" Jake turned to Anna.

"I'm happy you're experiencing firsthand what I went through this summer. It's outrageous, isn't it?"

"Maybe Lia needs to take the boys more."

"Charlotte is spoiled, and she must understand her brothers are a full-time part of our family."

Kyle walked through the door and the toddler glued herself to his leg. "Why is my house a wreck?" He swung her in his arms.

"We have concluded we have too many children. We're deciding which ones to sell. I voted for Casi." Jake grinned.

"Funny," Kyle said. "Where is she?"

"Sold to the highest bidder." Jake attempted to remove the melted crayon from the pot.

"Disgusting. Throw it out." Kyle frowned.

"One less thing to get spilled. Pick up your wife from her kick-boxing class in thirty minutes."

"I'm not sure if her wrist is fully healed enough for a class."

"I believe they use their feet, as the title suggests." Jake opened the oven. "Meatloaf with mashed potatoes and peas. The gravy was intended to mask the vegetables, but some people objected to a little wax with their meal."

"Make more and you can wait to serve it until I get home with Casi." Kyle winked and picked up his keys.

"Maybe we should buy our own house so these people will stop telling us what to do," Jake suggested.

"I saw a nice one across the street. Let's check it out after dinner," Anna teased.

"Great idea. We'll leave the children here and sneak over there. We could have sex in the kitchen." Jake grabbed her backside.

"Beep beep." Tommy cut between them with his toy tractor.

Jake smiled down at him, not bothered by the interruption. Without warning, Charlotte kicked Tommy in the face, leaving him howling with a bloody lip. "What the hell? She's a demon child. Do you think it's the red hair?"

Anna winced. "I believe she's jealous of the attention the boys get from everyone, especially Casi."

Jake cradled Tommy in his arms and soothed him. "It's ok, Buddy. I think we've decided which one to sell. She's pretty cute, we could make a bundle."

Anna wrangled the screaming child. "I would prefer not to give up any of our brood."

Jake blanched, noting her slumped shoulders, and wished he hadn't joked about adoption. "I was kidding."

"I know." Anna leaned out of the way of Charlotte's swinging arms as she tried to wiggle free.

"We discussed having them together in daycare. Let's start checking out places and see if it helps to have more of a routine."

Kyle strolled in the studio and stood at the window watching the final minutes of the class. He smiled at Casi's attire, enjoying her long, lean figure and taut muscles as she spun and kicked at the bag. The instructor gathered the class and demonstrated basic moves, then had them break into pairs and practice. Casi stood rigid with a blank stare and the instructor put his hand on her shoulder, talking softly while she nodded. Kyle tried to ascertain what the conversation was about, noting the agitation in her stance. He shifted his eyes to the groups of students going through the motions of what appeared to be self-defense moves. His heart wrenched when the instructor positioned himself behind Casi and she fought with all her might to take him down. Her form was impeccable, and she managed to slip from his grasp each time, delivering a blow to his groin or throat without hesitation. She glanced up and locked eyes with Kyle, freezing in place. The instructor dismissed the class after giving them the agenda for the next lesson.

Kyle entered and nodded to the man as he collected the mats. "She's pretty feisty, isn't she?" he joked. Casi burst into tears and he stopped in his tracks. "What did I say?"

"The classes can bring back trauma for some of my students," the instructor said, handing her a bottle of water.

Casi glared at Kyle. "Say it!"

"Great workout?" He glanced around the room for clues.

"You've been lurking around for months, making your sly comments and looking at me funny."

"I seriously have no idea what you're talking about."

She turned to the instructor. "He blames me. If I didn't want the creep to touch me, I would've fought him off."

"I don't," Kyle said with a slight hesitation.

"Assault is difficult. It harms more than the victim," the instructor said. "If you have questions about what happened, it would be healthy to talk it over. Unspoken words can leave deep wounds."

Kyle surveyed his well-built frame and fit physique. "Dalton is half the size of this guy and you wriggled away with ease. I realize you weren't expecting him to come to the hotel room, and he threw you off guard because you only wore a towel. To be totally honest, I'm curious how he was able to take pictures while restraining you and freely running his hands over your body. Were you too shaken by his words? Did he drug you? Something in this story doesn't add up."

Casi sobbed in her hands and the instructor soothed her. "Hey, I realize this hurts, but it's better to let it out. Run through the scenario in your head and help your husband understand."

She twisted her hands together and recalled Dalton's manner and how he challenged her. His words were vile and being nude hadn't helped, but she had faced superior combatants in the past. She frowned, realizing Kyle's concerns had also been plaguing her. The loss of control was the one factor she couldn't explain. The throb of her bones reminded her of a key element. She guided the instructor to the side and kept her voice low. He clarified details, painting a picture of the situation.

He brought a chair over and wedged it against the wall, glancing at Casi. She nodded, and he proceeded, turning back to Kyle and extending his hand. "No hard feelings? I'm a crisis counselor at the rec center on weeknights."

"We're good." Kyle grasped his hand. In a swift motion his arm was twisted behind his back and he was pinned to the chair, knocking the wind out of him.

"Try to fight me off. You outweigh her by at least fifty pounds. This should be easy," he hissed. He shoved his hips against Kyle's ensuring he couldn't slip out from under his hold. Kyle wrenched his shoulder forward, gasping from the sharp pain. He tried to get a leg free to kick at the assailant, but the pressure on his hips trapped him.

Casi cried and hugged herself, rocking in distress as the attack became too real. "Stop!"

"Let me get a picture," the instructor said, demonstrating the freedom of his left hand. He pulled back and released his hold. "An advanced wrestling technique. It's difficult to master but highly effective if the opponent is caught unaware."

Kyle rubbed his wrist. "Thanks for the demonstration. I appreciate the lesson." He stormed out without another word.

Casi trailed behind him and slipped in the passenger seat in silence. He fired up the engine, peeling out of the driveway with disgust. Halfway home, he skidded to a stop on the shoulder. "I'm sorry I reacted poorly. It felt like a cruel joke to be unable to break free."

"I didn't do it to embarrass you. I wanted you to understand and not doubt I tried to make him stop."

"So you're taking self-defense classes?"

"I was sober, strong, and angry, but I couldn't stop him!"

"You can't prevent a virus. He's a fucking little germ who weaseled his way into our lives. He targeted you from the beginning. I was never upset with you. I hated myself for not noticing what he was doing. The fact you couldn't fight him off scared me because I didn't know why, which meant I couldn't protect you in the future. I've always feared men trying to harm you, but you're confident and self-assured, and I felt ridiculous voicing my concern." He shrugged off his jacket. "Why didn't Jake insist you wear a coat? It's freezing out."

Casi slipped on his warm jacket and moved closer to him. "For the first time in my life, I was scared. If Jake hadn't come back, I'm certain he would have raped me." She choked on a sob. "Suddenly I'm afraid of everything! I picture him lurking behind bushes, and then I leap to the image of Katie's last moments and wonder what it's like to have your brain explode. I'm anxious and the kids are making me insane."

Kyle squeezed her hand. "She probably didn't experience pain. The clot would have killed her instantly."

"And the angels came to lead her to heaven like in the hymn they sang at her funeral." She wiped a tear.

"Absolutely." He embraced her. "Let's make time to do the trail a few times a week with Dingo. It would be good for us to be alone, and hiking has always calmed you. I think it's time we make ourselves the priority. Would it help if I get a restraining order on Dalton?"

"I have a better idea. Have you gone over to Lauren's?"

"Fran's giving her a bad time about moving stuff in." He hesitated and looked her in the eyes. "I told her she could store her furniture at the shop. She needs to get the condo sold."

"There's plenty of room. I can put a tracker on his phone and set up an alert if he's in our area. He would have no idea it's there."

"How do we do it? I don't want you near him."

"Explain you want to check his phone for pictures. Call me and I'll guide you through it."

"I love your super-spy persona." His gaze shifted over her attire. "Your outfit is incredibly sexy. Maybe you shouldn't wear it to the gym."

"I won't hide my body because a man can't monitor his response." She smiled at him.

"What about your husband?"

"He can look all he wants because he knows he can put his hands on me anytime." She wriggled out of his jacket and pulled her shirt over her head with a smile. "As a matter of fact, we should make love now before we return to the chaos of our house. I hope you don't mind, I'm a little sweaty."

Kyle ran his tongue over her collar bone. "Not an issue. I like it when you're extra salty."

Casi slouched in her seat and watched as the girls clad in kilts giggled across the road. She double-checked the photos on her phone and eased the car forward to follow as they scrambled on the bus. After running a red light and making an illegal U-turn, she parked outside the mall and grabbed her purse. It was easy to keep up with the teenagers, stopping every few minutes to take selfies and flirt with boys. When the girl with long brown hair separated from the group to try on a ridiculously over-priced pair of ripped jeans, Casi made her move. "Those are darling on you."

"Thanks." The girl smiled with appreciation as she scanned the stylish woman with a knock-out figure. "Do they make me look fat?"

"Not at all. They suit you." Casi pretended to sort through tops she would never buy as she eyed the group returning to their friend. "Hey, aren't you Joe Salvatore's daughter? I'm sure I saw a picture of you on his desk when I was helping him with the campaign."

"Yes, he's my dad. I'm Alyssa."

"Casi." She held up a blue shirt. "I'm a model scout and I'm recruiting teenagers for an editorial." She glanced at the girls approaching. "No offense, but your friends aren't the right type. You would be perfect though. Can I give you my card?"

"Really?" The girl eagerly read the name. "Macrae skincare."

"They are expanding their line to feature teens who exemplify beauty and adventure for the younger clientele. The products are amazing." Casi smiled with perfect white teeth.

"You're so pretty."

"I was a model, and it can be tough on your skin."

"You look like a model." Alyssa eyed her svelte figure. "My dad would never let me do it. He's really strict."

"Alyssa, let's go," a girl called as she scrolled through her phone.

Casi opened her wallet and produced her driver's license in a last-ditch effort to separate Alyssa from her friends. "This is who I am. Can you talk to me for about twenty minutes? I can give you a drive home and you'll arrive faster than if you take the bus."

Alyssa wrapped an arm around herself and glanced at the identification. "Can we stay here at the mall? You seem nice, but I'm not supposed to go places with strangers."

"It's a good rule. We can talk at the food court."

"Hey guys, I'm going to hang out for a while longer. I'll see you at school tomorrow." Alyssa gave them a wave and went to change.

"Are you buying the jeans?" Casi noted the disappointment as Alyssa put them back on the rack.

"My dad doesn't let me wear trendy things. I like to try them on and pretend I'm a normal kid. It's dumb."

"It's a fun thing to do."

"You can wear what you want though, because you're like twenty-five," Alyssa assessed.

"Thirty-four." Casi smiled. "How old are you?"

"Fifteen. I have two older brothers and a younger one. I'm the only girl." Alyssa's eyes lit up when Casi stopped at the cinnamon roll kiosk. "Can we get one?"

"Absolutely." Casi placed her order and paid. She directed her to a table far away from other patrons. "I'm not a scout. I'm a marketing rep for Macrae and I was a model. I haven't met your father, but he does know my best friend from when she was your age." She noted the girl processing the information. "He hurt her."

"Like how?" Alyssa paused mid-bite.

"He raped her." Casi let the shock wash over her. "It's an absolute fact and we're not trying to harm your family. The issue is my friend got pregnant and gave the baby up for adoption. The girl is in her twenties now and has a kidney disorder."

"My dad has the same thing." Alyssa blanched. "Oh my God!"

"She needs help. Your dad can't be a donor because of his condition. We're desperate to find a match. Would you consider being tested?" Alyssa twisted her hands and Casi noted several cuts along her wrists. She smoothed a finger over the scars. "Are you alright at home? If you don't feel safe, I can help you."

"I'm super stressed. My parents fight constantly. Last week my mom accused him of sleeping with an intern." She shuddered. "I don't want to believe you but too many things make me think it's true. He's so strict with me. I can't even go to a dance. He says boys have hormones they can't control."

"The good ones rein it in and there are plenty of them out there.

I'm sure he's concerned a boy might act like he did when he was young. He needs to be accountable because his daughter will die without a kidney."

"She's my sister." She gazed at a group of teenage girls teasing boys at another table. "I want to help her. What can I do?"

"You need parental consent. Will your mother sign for you?"

"Not without my dad's permission."

Casi grasped her hand. "You seem like a sweet girl. I appreciate you considering this. Have you been checked to ensure you don't carry the gene? We can do the initial blood test for a match before we do a tissue test and cross-matching. If you're a candidate, I'll come with you to talk to your dad with some of my friends."

"I donate for the blood drive at my school next week. Can they take a sample?"

"Is it open to the public?"

"Yes." Alyssa wrote down the information and slid it across the table. "I've always wondered if I could do more in life than become a debutant and follow in the footsteps of my family."

"I believe you're destined to do great things." Casi smiled. "With your family's connections, you could make a difference for a lot of women. I love how you're unafraid to take a bold step. When I stopped being a model it was scary to try something new, but my life evolved into an incredible adventure and now I have deep and rewarding relationships."

26

BROKEN HEARTS

yle approached Ava and gave her a hug. "I'm aware your sudden remodel is a pity job."

"We've been wanting to fix up the place for years. When Casi mentioned you had a reserve of reclaimed wood, it seemed ideal."

He ran his hand over the tattered laminate cabinets. "I won't charge you for labor. I appreciate your help with the inventory already. Dalton royally screwed us over."

Ava set a laptop on the counter. "This is what I had in mind. Is it possible? I love how you remodeled your kitchen and it would be incredible to have a feature piece in here. I've been searching for a back-bar to create the wow factor."

Kyle grinned at the expansive notes and pictures. "You have been considering this for a while. You won't find something big enough. An antique hutch will be dwarfed by the size of the room."

"Make sense." Ava gazed at the photos with regret.

"I'll build you a more spectacular one. After the initial tear-out, we'll improvise to ensure the place remains functional. Jake will build the frames at the shop and we can install them in a matter of days. The finishing work takes longer, but I'll work around your schedule."

"This is so exciting! When can we get started?"

"I'll take measurements now and we'll go over your must-have features. I'll draw up the specs and we can begin this weekend." Kyle put an arm around her shoulders. "You deserve a magnificent bar to reflect the hard work you've put in."

❧

"I can't believe you're forcing me to work on a Sunday." Jake hauled his toolbox from the truck.

"You should be thrilled to escape the mad-house." Kyle shook his head. "How do you live with those kids on a daily basis?"

"I stash them at your house and run back across the street."

"It appears like it. Anna seems content, so I'm happy to help."

"I've come to realize what a handful the kids are and how I basically dropped them in her lap. It's brought us closer as we work on a solution to tame the zoo creatures. Gail offered to take them a few days, but they overwhelm her townhouse and I can't afford to replace her salary from the office she works at. She loves the kids and insists on babysitting for free but it's not fair."

"Having a reserve of wives has certainly played in your favor." Kyle chuckled.

"Good morning." Ava smiled as she carried a tray of steaming lattes. "Roxie came to help, so let her know what you need."

"I was promised hot shirtless men instead of money." Roxie assessed the brothers. "I hope this requires a lot of bending."

"We'll do our best to entertain you," Jake grinned.

Ava signaled to a group of men. "I organized the crew you had at the wood shop." She turned and relayed instructions, and the men nodded and began unloading the truck.

"I'm adding you speaking in Spanish to my fantasy." Jake gave her a wink as he fastened his tool belt. He noted Kyle's grin. "No, the workers are not in it."

"Just checking." Kyle slapped him on the backside and Roxie howled and whistled.

They began the demolition and an assembly line was set up to carry the debris to the parking lot and toss it in a dumpster. Ava came to check on progress and Kyle smiled. "Thanks for the additional labor. We'll get this done in a quarter of the time I allotted."

"I felt it best to expedite the process. The Standfords put out word your company is using stolen materials and anyone who accepts a bid from you is committing a felony."

"Assholes," Kyle swore. "I have the invoices. They didn't contribute one cent. I imagine investors are breathing down their necks to get repaid since the restaurant isn't happening."

"But it is," Ava asserted. "I've heard there's a grand opening next month. They brought in a hack construction company after the other crew walked off. It's nowhere near as elegant as the original plans, but they're financing a celebrity chef from Napa."

Kyle narrowed his eyes. "They bled Lauren dry and used her insight to create a professional kitchen with the promise she would run it. I designed the dining room and left them with the specs and blueprints and never got paid. Fucking scammers! I wonder if Lauren has heard about this?"

Ava grasped his arm. "I have to caution you to proceed carefully. Lauren gives you an edited version where she is the victim."

"I appreciate the advice, but Lauren and I have been friends for a long time, and I won't walk away when her life is crumbling. You have no idea how Dalton treated her."

"True, but Casi's well-being is paramount to me, always."

Kyle put his arm around her as she turned to walk away. "I'm sorry. I've been on edge since everything happened and I'm lashing out at the wrong people. Casi is taking self-defense classes, and she had the instructor restrain me in the same manner Dalton had done to her. The point was to demonstrate how she couldn't get away because she perceived I doubted her story. I've been left with a hole in my heart knowing I blamed her for any part of it."

Lauren walked carefully to her car, straining under the weight of the pregnancy. She shifted the bags in her arms, searching for the keys. "Need a hand?"

She turned abruptly to the sound of the voice, losing her grip on a grocery bag. "Why are you here?"

Dalton regarded the torn paper spewing its contents but didn't offer to pick it up. "Your boyfriend is ignoring my calls. You had better insist he contact me to make retribution for the materials he stole."

"He paid for them. Your family is a bunch of thieves."

"My lawyer is putting together a case against Jake for what he did to me. His brother and their whore wives will also be included in the lawsuit." He stepped closer. "You don't fuck with the Standfords. Remember, the kid is mine. Don't think for one minute I'll allow you to ride off into the sunset. I have the due date marked on my calendar. A few more weeks until my heir arrives."

Lauren wiped a tear. "You'll never know her. You've stolen everything else from me already."

"The grand opening of the restaurant is next month. I hope you can make it. Bring my daughter, we can introduce her to the investors."

"Happy Valentine's Day." The barista added hearts to the foam of the latte with a smile.

"Oh, right, thanks." Casi glanced up from her phone. She strolled to Anna's table. "Do you know what day it is?"

Anna peered up from her laptop. "Yup, and this year we're doing it right. I've made reservations at a fancy steakhouse in Fairhaven and booked a night in a luxurious room. We'll drop the children at the farmhouse on our way. Selfishly, the plan doesn't only free us up for the weekend, but it shows our in-laws how much of an effort I'm expending to make amends. Making my marriage a priority has been invigorating. I'm seeing a whole different side to Jake. I don't think I've ever laughed with anyone as much as I do with him. We've lowered our defenses and we've let each other in." She turned with a smile. "Do you know what Jake did? He texted me to meet him at the bleachers of his old high school. When I arrived, he was wearing his letterman jacket and had set out a blanket and a picnic lunch." She sighed at the memory. "We kissed and he asked my permission to make love. He said his gift was to recreate my first time."

"How romantic!"

"It was sweet." Anna smiled. "He gave me something no money could buy and proved how well he knows me."

"You're glowing," Casi giggled. "I'm thrilled you guys patched things up. Jake has been so happy lately."

Anna surveyed her demeanor. "He's still your best buddy. Our relationship won't change his devotion to you."

"I'm genuinely pleased. I'm moody because everyone is celebrating, and Kyle hasn't even responded to my text."

"I thought you didn't care about Valentine's Day."

"I don't normally, and I honestly forgot, again. I wish I had been on top of things this year. We could use some romance. Kyle is preoccupied with the job at my Dad's bar, and every spare minute is spent with Lauren. I heard the Standfords are finishing the restaurant, so Kyle has been extra vigilant about protecting Lauren's feelings."

"Send him a sexy text. Kyle's a Rockstar, but he's ignorant at decoding your emotions. Spell it out for him. You've pushed him away and it's time to bring your stallion back to the barn."

"You're right. I've never held back in the past. I don't know where this insecurity comes from."

"Someone stole your confidence. Reclaim it and be the uninhibited woman your husband adores."

"Did you already buy lingerie for tonight?"

Anna checked her watch. "Let's squeeze in a shopping trip after our meeting." She noted a cloud cross Casi's face. "Did he answer?"

Casi held the phone up with a response about what he wanted to do for dinner. "I don't care. Pizza?"

"Lame. Plan B. A romantic evening at home. He's obviously forgotten, so he'll feel bad when he realizes. He'll be extra amorous."

"I feel like I'm never alone with him anymore. We're an old married couple going about our daily routine."

"Take it from me, ordinary is under appreciated." Anna surveyed Casi's face brighten as she read a message. "Did he clue in?"

"Nope, but Chantal has a match! Your assailant's fifteen-year-old daughter. We sent her blood to the lab last week."

"Fifteen? She's too young." Anna slumped in her seat. "Did Joe give permission? Jake said he refused."

"I tracked her down and had a girl talk with her. She had a blood drive at her school, and I stole her sample." Casi grinned. "Keep in mind your age when he assaulted you and then you had a baby. A kidney seems minor in comparison."

Casi tucked the bag with the lingerie in her purse and texted Kyle. "What time will you be home? I'll start dinner." She had decided against takeout, figuring the time spent cooking would be a relaxing way to begin the evening. Reservations would be impossible, and a crowded restaurant seemed overwhelming.

As she contemplated what to cook, her phone buzzed with a reply. "I'll be late. Lauren's in labor and I'm at the hospital with her."

"Motherfucker!" she fumed. She gripped her phone and resisted throwing it across the parking lot. A neon sign caught her eye, and she stormed toward the venue. "Whiskey on the rocks." She slid on a bar stool and glared at the TV.

"Happy V-D," a man slurred.

"Fuck off," she snapped, making the bartender laugh.

After her second drink the bartender glanced at her ring finger. "Husband issues?"

"He's at the hospital helping his friend who is in labor. How romantic, huh?"

"Bad timing, to say the least. He's not the father, is he?"

"He's acting like it." She glanced at her watch. "How long does it take to push out a kid?"

"I have no idea. Another drink?"

"No, two's my limit, especially when I'm pissed off." She left a generous tip and walked back to her car, shrugging off the gentle snowflakes falling on her shoulders. She blinked up at the star-studded sky and sighed. Harboring frustration toward Kyle for being a good friend was ridiculous. He had been patient while she worked through her emotions, and she needed to take the high road when it came to Lauren's immeasurable problems. She headed to the hospital and inquired where the labor and delivery floor was, cringing at the cheerful balloons and flowers on display. Plastering a smile on her face, she peeked inside the room. She froze in place unable to speak at the sweet scene before her. Kyle cradled the infant in a soft pink blanket, obviously knit by Georgia's skillful hands. Lauren beamed at the pair and held the baby's tiny hand. They engaged in joyful conversation, the quintessential couple with their new child.

The clang of wheels brought her back to earth, and she jerked her arm away as she collided with the cart. "Sorry, Miss.," the orderly said, leaning over to pick up an object. "I think you dropped this."

She received the gold and diamond watch as tears streamed down her cheeks. The band had caught on the edge of the cart, breaking the clasp. She backed away from the room and staggered to the nurse's station. "Do you have an envelope?"

"Sure, Honey," a robust woman in kitten-print scrubs answered.

Casi shoved the watch inside and sealed it. She scrawled a message on the front and handed it to the nurse. "Can you please give this to the man in room 109? There's no hurry."

The nurse nodded, intrigued by the dramatic exit. "Cheating husband?" another nurse suggested getting a round of nods.

Kyle kissed Lauren on the cheek as he handed her the baby. "I should get going. Let me know when they release you and I'll pick you up. Do you need anything?"

She rocked the child in her arms. "Would you mind getting the car seat from my Mom's? This was so sudden; I didn't think to grab it."

"Sure, no problem." He strolled to the corridor.

"Sir," the nurse called. "Someone left this for you."

Kyle reached for the envelope, surprised by the delivery. He recognized the handwriting and furrowed his brow at the message, "I don't know if it can be fixed." He tore open the paper and grabbed the broken watch. "When did she give this to you?"

The nurse gave him an angry stare. "About an hour ago. She seemed upset."

"Goddamn it. Why didn't you give it to me right away?"

"I'm not the mailman and she said there was no rush."

Kyle stormed out of the hospital, dialing Casi's number as he rushed to his truck. When she didn't answer, he left a message, then followed up with a text. He pulled in the driveway, not surprised she wasn't there. After a quick sweep of the house, he noted nothing was missing to indicate she had left him permanently. Dingo whined, and Kyle stopped to give him a pat on the head as he filled his bowl with kibble. "I made a mess of things this time," he told the dog.

The restaurant in Bellingham was overflowing with couples celebrating, and Kyle winced when he noticed the sign. "Of course, it couldn't be a normal day."

Ava greeted him and glanced back at the dining room. "I didn't know you guys were coming tonight. Give me a minute to set up another table. Or do you want to eat at the bar?" She noted Kyle's pain-stricken expression. "What happened?"

"I screwed up big time." His shoulders slumped as he surveyed the sparks of romance in the room. "Lauren went into labor and I stayed with her through the delivery. I didn't give it a second thought, but I guess Casi came by the hospital. I'm unclear what she saw, but she's taken off and left me this." He produced the watch with the note.

"It's a knife through the heart! How could you?"

"It didn't seem like a betrayal! I don't know why she's angry, but if she needs time alone, I must know she's safe. She won't answer my calls, but she might if she thinks it's you."

Ava glared at him and withdrew her phone. "Hi Sweetie. Yes, he's here. Thanks for answering. We wanted to make sure you're ok. No, of course you're not. He's an asshole." A smiled touched her lips as Kyle frowned and she walked behind the bar out of earshot and continued the conversation while he strained to hear. She came back with a glass and filled it with scotch. "She's in LA. Give her space and don't call, she won't answer."

Kyle sipped the drink. "Did she mention if she's coming home?"

"You really don't understand how you shattered her?"

"I'm clueless. What should I do?" Kyle shoved the glass away.

"Your heart will guide you to do the right thing." She took a sip of the scotch. "True love can weather any storm if both partners are committed to moving forward." She smiled. "Even when Jack has pulled some monumental shit, I felt our love was worth fighting for."

"I didn't cheat." He regarded Casi's broken watch. "Physically. I betrayed her trust and hurt her by being insensitive to a deep insecurity."

Ava grasped his hand. "You're catching on. She doesn't want children, but she's paranoid you might change your mind."

"How can I prove she's the only one who matters to me?"

"You've bought her lovely gifts. What she needs is a grand gesture. Stop being logical and consider things from her perspective."

"Think like a lunatic?" He caught a glimmer in Ava's eye and pulled out his phone. He scrolled through Alix's feed on Facebook with images of his artwork embedded with hype about an upcoming installation. He pondered the secrecy and understood Alix's game to garner attention. "Vegas! Casi's going with him on Sunday to introduce Chase as his protégé. I was supposed to go with her, and I forgot again."

Ava smiled. "What will you do?"

"I have one day to put a plan into action. I'll get her watch fixed and book a flight to Vegas." He leaned over the bar and kissed her on the cheek. "Don't tell her I'm coming. I want to surprise her."

"Go get her, Cowboy."

27

BELIEVE IN LOVE

"Good morning, party girl," Alix teased as Casi entered the galley kitchen clad in panties and one of his t-shirts.

Casi searched the small counter in despair. "Don't you have a coffeemaker?"

"Babe, I don't make coffee. There's kombucha in the fridge."

"I need caffeine." She sank in a chair at the table. She felt the scorch of a glare and lifted her gaze to Chase's accusing eyes. "Nothing happened. I'm taking a break from my life for a weekend."

Chase cast his glance to the floor, shifting in his seat and sniffling back tears. "I thought you and Kyle were the perfect couple. That's the kind of love I wanted to have when I'm older."

Alix chuckled at the sting of the word 'older' on Casi's face. She regained her composure and absorbed the sentiment for it's intended value. "Kyle did something asinine, and I needed a moment to recover. I'm not sleeping with Alix. I'm taking a breather from my husband's constant apologies and excuses," she said, rubbing her arm briskly.

"Kyle's awesome. Maybe you misinterpreted what he did. He's so kind to everyone and really helped my Mom out a lot. Most people treat her like trailer trash," Chase mumbled.

251

Alix laced his fingers through hers. "Babe, for what it's worth, I think he was helping out a friend." He slid his hand over her scar. "Stop rubbing it. You'll make it worse."

"He was there for her during an insanely intimate moment." She ran a finger up her scar. "I hate this thing. It's a constant reminder."

"They've had sex in the past, so he's seen all she has to offer already. He's not into kids and it's not his. He was probably relieved the baby was alright after what you said she was suffering from. It could have been brutal." Alix squeezed her hand. "Cherish your love."

"Would you be there with me if I gave birth?"

"Fuck no! I would vomit if I saw a gooey blob squeeze out. Babe, you know I love you, but I can't handle gross stuff. I couldn't have sex with a woman who was all stretched out and shit."

Casi smiled at his candor. "Perhaps I overreacted."

"Definitely punish him for being insensitive to your needs. Hang out with us in Vegas. It'll be epic! Guess what we have planned for this morning?"

Chase beamed. "I'm getting my first tattoo!"

"Shower and you can borrow clothes from me for today. We can shop later for the installation. You'll need a radical dress." Alix kissed the top of her head. "We'll stop for coffee on the way."

Kyle scrolled through Alix's Facebook feed as he searched through the casinos. "Why can't you name the damn thing?" He cursed at the clever riddles turning the event into a scavenger hunt. An image on the enormous monitor on the strip caught his eye. "Got you!" He wove through the crowds toward the monumental casino tucked away from popular destinations. The throngs of partygoers pushed toward the stage of the glamorous new resort, sparkling like a diamond amongst rhinestones. Kyle caught his breath as he noticed Casi at the side of the room, graceful and poised in a sliver of magenta silk wrapped around her curvaceous figure. He smiled at her confidence as she floated beside Alix, shoulders squared and unashamed of her beauty. He longed to feel her in his arms, and his heart skipped a beat, knowing it wouldn't be much longer.

Alix raised a hand, and the crowd went wild. He squinted at the lights, emitting a sultry glare to whip his fans to a frenzy. Chase hesitated at his side, slender in tight jeans and a graphic t-shirt topped with a leather jacket. Casi kept a hand on his arm, propelling him forward and ensuring he appeared calm. A spectator's eye would be drawn to the alluring woman and assume she was arm candy for a celebrity. Kyle watched her tenderly guiding Chase and understood she may have taken off for LA in a rage against him, but she came to Vegas with compassion for the fledgling artist. The announcement was made, and Chase raised a hand to wave at his new admirers while his sketches were flashed on a giant screen briefly to pique interest. Gasps and a round of applause followed the presentation, and Kyle clapped for the tech-savvy woman who produced the show.

Champagne was served, and Kyle stalked his prey as his pulse raced. Casi glanced behind her, sensing she was being followed. Kyle read the concern in her hazel eyes and quickly slipped an arm around her waist. "It's only your adoring husband."

"Don't you have daddy-duty?" Her voice was clipped with a raw edge of hurt dripping through.

"I prefer to be child-free. My wife is all I need." Kyle breathed in her scent and touched his lips to her throat.

She sipped her champagne. "Did Ava tell you where I was?"

"She told me to let my heart guide me. I trolled Alix on Facebook and figured out the location. You should be proud of my novice snooping skills."

"It hurt seeing you holding a newborn. You looked like a family." A sob caught in her throat and she lifted her chin to appear poised.

"I'm sorry. She had a close call last week after a run-in with Dalton. The baby's heartbeat was irregular. She went into labor early and it was difficult." He placed his fingers to Casi's cheek and turned her face to look at him. "Lauren went into cardiac arrest during delivery. It was traumatic, and the baby wasn't breathing. What you saw was the happiness from not losing them. She's my friend, not my family." Casi nodded, and he could see she was struggling not to cry. He caressed her hip and smoothed his hand over her wrist, stopping suddenly when she winced. "You got a tattoo?" He regarded the delicate script above the scar, *Believe in Love.*

"I went with Chase and I had a sudden urge to turn this hideous reminder into something positive. I needed a prompt to cherish everything beautiful in the world and remember to not lose hope."

"In me?" Kyle gazed at her with piercing blue eyes.

"In your intent."

"My motive is pure, but my delivery is often flawed."

"I ran because I needed to get my emotions under control."

Kyle slipped her watch from his pocket and fastened it on her wrist. "The answer to your question is yes, everything can be fixed. I understood your message as a cryptic account of our marriage, but it can be repaired, time and time again. We won't break, although sometimes we must bend to accommodate the crap getting piled on us. I love you always and forever."

Casi settled into his embrace. "I was always coming back."

"Sure, you have a meeting tomorrow." Kyle's eyes crinkled with laughter. "I promise I'm finished helping Lauren. The baby is here, and she can figure it out." He gazed at her with love. "When I was in Seattle getting your watch repaired, I realized I forced you into my world without considering what sacrifices were required by you."

Panic flashed in her eyes. "I'm honestly happy!"

"I know." He kissed her. "You've made wonderful friends and turned our house into a home. You've excelled at a career and blossomed into a woman I absolutely adore and respect. I love our life, although I would like you home more." He smiled. "I was terrified when I got your note, but I reasoned you needed space to work through your emotions. I'm sorry I hurt you. It was completely unintentional."

"My previous life in LA was shallow. I'm more fulfilled than I have ever been, and I've found a tremendous purpose. My relationships are deep and fulfilling, and I'm close to my childhood friends. I couldn't ask for more." She turned and smiled at Chase meeting fans. "I have new challenges and goals to achieve constantly."

"What tattoo did Chase get?"

"A dragon. He created a sketch of the one on Grady's arm. It was meaningful to him to have a connection to his father."

Kyle's jaw dropped. "Were you there with him?"

"Yes, he was nervous, so I held his hand."

He tapped the end of her nose with his index finger. "That's more monumental to me than witnessing a birth."

"Really?" Casi surveyed Chase standing awkwardly nearby and considered how it felt for Kyle to experience his lost friend reborn. "Perhaps I didn't think of it from your perspective."

Kyle put his forehead to hers. "Can we accept we were both a bit thoughtless in our mission to help others?"

"It's a fair assessment." She motioned for Chase to join them. "Kyle wants to see your tattoo."

Chase blushed and slipped his jacket off, turning to reveal the image. "I like how it came out."

Kyle's eyes watered as he surveyed the dragon brought back to life on the replica of his lost friend. "It's perfect. It suits you. Thanks for taking the opportunity to live your life to the fullest. I'm proud of you."

"You're the first guy who has been supportive of my dreams. Thanks for believing in me. I bet my dad would be happy you're such an amazing friend, even after he's gone."

Alix came to direct Chase to prospective clients. "Hey, Kyle. Glad you were here for the big announcement." He grinned. "I had faith you would figure out where your heart was."

"You didn't make it easy." Kyle smiled and turned to Casi as they left. "Can we go back to your hotel? I'm desperate to connect with you and drown out this chaos." He cringed as another firecracker boomed.

"We're booked on the midnight flight back to LA. When do you return to Washington?"

"First thing in the morning." He glanced at Alix, signing autographs. "There's no point in being in Vegas without you. I guess I'll get a shuttle to the airport and see if I can catch an earlier flight."

"Can we make a date for tomorrow night? The two of us with a romantic evening in front of the fireplace. No restaurants or hotels and fur babies only."

"Consider it booked."

Kyle smiled as Casi entered the house. "Wine?"

"Thank you." She pursed her lips. "Before our romantic evening begins, can we get a few issues dealt with?"

"Ok, what did you want to talk about?" Kyle grasped the counter and hoped the evening wasn't ruined.

Casi sniffed the air. "Crispy pork with cherry glaze?"

"Roasted potatoes and a salad. Dessert is a surprise."

"I'm totally looking forward to eating it." She smiled and set her glass on the counter. "Come talk with me while I shower. I don't want to make a big deal out of stuff, but I feel it's better to address it."

"Good advice from Ava."

"She understands complicated relationships."

"Our marriage is not difficult."

"I was referring to Lauren being intertwined in ours. Although it was a different dynamic, Ava had to deal with my mother's meddling."

"I agree." He stripped down and stepped in behind her.

"No sex until after dinner. I want to take our time and lounge in front of the fireplace. Did you lock the door?"

"Phones are turned off and annoying parties have been alerted tonight is reserved for my lover." He wriggled his eyebrows.

"Well done. First, are you the kid's godfather?"

"Her name is Madison. I've declined the request because I take the role seriously and I already have three. A couple would be a better choice and I suggested Lia and Shane, which is a little awkward for now, but he could step in later."

"Did your mom make the blanket for her? Lauren must be pleased to have her darling baby wrapped in a special gift."

"Mom felt pressured to knit her a blanket since she has always given a new baby one, including Chase. Madison looks like every other infant, except for Jake's new batch of kids. He has unusually good-looking children right from the get-go."

"It's the blue eyes. They make them look like perfect little dolls," Casi pondered. "Do you love her?"

"No! I never did. My feelings didn't change because I witnessed her giving birth."

"I meant the baby, Madison."

"I have no connection to her. The birth was brutal, and I'm sure it hurt like hell. It was horrible to watch Lauren in so much pain and not be able to do anything." He wrung his hands. "My mind was on you and how I'm thrilled you didn't want children because I couldn't have handled witnessing you being tortured."

"There are a few things I didn't tell you about Dalton." Casi inhaled sharply. "Maybe I blocked it out, but I realized in LA it's been in the back of my mind. Compounded with something Katie said, I sense it might be like a grain of sand creating a blister."

"Tiny yet creates significant damage." Kyle smoothed her hair back from her face and kissed her cheek. "Tell me."

"First, he said I was too vain to want kids because they would ruin my body. And if I got fat, you would leave me."

Kyle caressed her stomach. "You have an immeasurable reservoir for love. From all the broken people you help to better themselves, to the children we have brought into our home. Your figure is gorgeous, and I love every inch. My fear isn't you becoming blemished. Your self-confidence is sexy and we both keep in shape to be healthy. I'm more concerned about everyone making you feel unworthy for a valid choice we made together."

"Thank you for saying that." She swallowed. "When Jake knocked on the door, Dalton pushed me to the ground and purposely stepped over me to throw a twenty on top of my watch. He said it was for services rendered."

"Fucking asshole!"

"I told Katie, and she laughed. She said I should have kept the money and bought something with it instead of leaving it at the hotel. Jake thought it was mine, and Anna assumed it was for the maid. Every time I see a twenty, it reminds me of how he made me feel."

Kyle slid his hand behind her neck and gazed in her eyes. "He's the kind of guy who buys a Lamborghini to get noticed. He has no idea of the power beneath the shiny exterior and the sheer joy of driving an immaculate machine. He noticed your beauty but can't appreciate how it runs to your core. You can't be purchased or controlled, and his words are meaningless. He's a void in the universe and a waste of space. You were right to leave the money behind. Katie didn't comprehend the evil in the currency, but then I honestly don't believe she knew you. Your friendship never evolved into a mature relationship and she played ridiculous games to get your attention."

"Do you see me?" She brushed her lips to his.

"I worship every cell in your body." He grasped her hands above her head. "I don't make love to you, but with you." He turned his head to the sound of the front door opening. "I swear I locked it."

Jake entered the bathroom with Anna and slid on the counter. "No lock is beyond my control." He handed them towels and grabbed Casi's arm as she reached to take it. "When did you get a tattoo?"

"In LA." She shrugged.

"What about the rules?" He glared at her in the mirror. "You should always be able to cover it and take a responsible party with you."

Kyle grinned and held out his left arm to show identical script above his own scar, *Always and Forever.*

"I love it!" Casi leveled her arm to his. "When did you go?"

"When I got back this morning. I spent the night at the airport in Vegas thinking about a way to prove my commitment to you. This seemed appropriate."

Jake scowled. "Now I'm the only one with a stupid scar and no script. What kind of band of fools is this?"

Casi smiled and picked up her phone. "Chase got this."

"It's identical to Grady's." Kyle exhaled.

"It's awesome," Jake agreed. "What an incredible tribute. One life ended at eighteen and another journey is beginning." He glanced at Kyle, who had tears in his eyes. "Grady would be so proud of how you're taking care of his kid and guiding him. There's a reason he inherited his dad's artistic talent. The world needs dreamers. Kyle should have been there. It was his friend."

"He was busy attending a birth." Casi rolled her eyes.

"Personally, I would rather have witnessed the tattoo instead of a baby who wasn't even mine being born." He glared at Kyle. "Your first tattoo where I wasn't by your side. I'm crushed."

Kyle winced. "I'm sorry."

Anna patted Jake's hand. "Consider it a punishment for the hell you put your brother through." She smiled at his devastated expression. "But you're back, and we're moving forward."

Jake sighed. "She has concerns about Lauren's kid."

Kyle's shoulders slumped. "Is the baby not alright?"

"She's fine other than looking alarmingly like Dalton." Anna shivered. "Lauren was not thrilled I was sent as the pickup wagon."

"Too bad." Kyle toweled off. "You remembered the car seat?"

"I understand what's required to take an infant home," Anna scoffed. "She gave me the death glare when I arrived and insisted on waiting for you. I stated she would be there a long time because you had plans with your wife."

"I haven't read her texts," Kyle admitted.

"There was something suspicious about her hesitation to leave. She refused to fill out the paperwork entirely."

Kyle shrugged. "It took Jake almost ten days to label his kid. Maybe she's not committed yet?"

"I don't think it's the child's name causing an issue. I would be willing to bet she listed you as the father." Anna pointed a finger at him.

"She can't! Wouldn't I be required to sign something?"

"I didn't sign anything for Charlotte." Jake frowned. "Am I not on her birth certificate?"

"You signed." Anna grinned. "For a delivery at the wood shop. Kyle was conveniently out of the office."

"You corrupted my sweet Amy?" Jake gasped.

"Why would you sign for something you didn't read?" Kyle smacked his arm.

Jake shrugged. "These women are cagey. They probably used real boxes as decoys."

"But you should check to ensure the order is correct." Kyle frowned at him. "It's not possible to fool me."

"Be prepared. She has ten days to file the certificate. She might even come right out and tell you it's in the best interest of the child. I'm not sure what the ramifications are with custody if Dalton isn't listed," Anna pondered.

Kyle glanced at Casi's reflection in the mirror and noted the devastation. He pulled her toward him protectively. "Casi and I are out of town for the next week and a half. Starting now, which is a nice way of telling you to go home."

28

RETRIBUTION

Casi opened one eye as a strand of hair repeatedly tickled her cheek. "Go away." Jake laughed and sat back on his heels with a grin as three children tumbled on the makeshift bed by the fireplace.

Kyle stretched. "Ouch, this seemed comfortable last night, but now I wish we had relocated to our mattress."

Casi cuddled the boys and crossed her eyes at Charlotte when the toddler pushed her away from Kyle as he struggled to sit upright. Jake grasped his hand and assisted him. "Getting old, brother."

"Just stiff." Kyle rubbed his eyes.

Jake heaved a large package with tattered wrapping paper on top of Casi. "Mom sent this for you. I tried my best to keep the critters out of it."

Casi launched herself into a cross-legged sitting position to the amazement of Kyle. "How are you so flexible in the morning?" He smiled as she tore through the paper to discover a soft blanket rich with color and design.

"Mine." Charlotte tugged at the afghan.

"Fuck off, it is not." Casi shoved her back in Kyle's lap.

Jake frowned. "Maybe we could explore alternate methods of disciplining the kids? Perhaps without curse words?"

"They'll learn them at school. I'm preparing them for life." Casi picked up the note to read aloud. "Dear Casi." She turned the paper to Charlotte. "Do you see your name here? I didn't think so."

Jake rolled his eyes. "Like she can read."

Casi raised an eyebrow and pointed to the letters as Austin stumbled through a rough rendition of the first line. "I have been working on this for almost a year." He looked at her for approval.

Jake's jaw dropped. "When did you teach him?"

"You don't teach reading. Since he was a teeny nugget, I've read books to him and he follows along. They pick it up naturally." She smiled at Kyle. "Chuckie cheese is falling behind because you give her what she wants rather than developing her intellect."

Kyle hugged Charlotte. "Austin is almost four."

Casi tapped Tommy on the cheek. "Your turn."

He contorted his mouth, and she helped him with the first few words. "The blanket represents." She glanced up. "Obviously, those are too big for him."

"Love. Sun. Happy." Tommy pointed.

Jake smiled. "Wow, little guy! I'm impressed. Maybe your aunt is teaching you positive things."

"Are you kidding me?" Anna scowled. "I'm paying for an elite preschool and my daughter doesn't recognize a letter?"

"I'm sure she has the curse words down." Jake poked Charlotte in the belly.

"No." She pushed her bottom lip out.

"Mine and no are all she knows at three years old." Anna sighed. "We must revisit this daycare issue. I'm investing a fortune and her brothers are light years ahead."

"I doubt they inherited it from Lia, so it must be environmental." Kyle grinned and dodged his brother's slap.

Casi held the blanket up to appreciate the intricate design as Kyle finished reading the note. "I wanted to incorporate the things I think of when I see you. Love. Sunshine. Happiness. Your protege shortened a few words." He patted Tommy on the head. "A baby blanket welcomes a child into the world, but this afghan is a testament of how important you are in our family. I had hoped to have it ready for Christmas, but my loser son fucked up my life."

"You improvised," Jake scoffed.

"I read between the lines." Kyle grasped an edge of the afghan to see the entire picture. "It's incredible. Our mother is talented."

Casi smiled. "I love it."

Jake patted Anna on the shoulder. "Maybe you'll get one next year if you continue to show your devotion to me."

Anna laughed. "I'm thrilled they didn't toss me to the curb. Your dad actually hugged me the other day."

"He can be harsh. Family is important to him." Jake surveyed the children sprawled on the blankets. "Any more news about Chantal?"

Anna nodded. "We found a match. The creep's fifteen-year-old daughter, Alyssa. She's willing, but we need her parent's permission."

"Fifteen?" Jake cringed. "What if she gets the disease? It's a huge risk to only have one kidney."

"She didn't inherit it." Casi eyed Kyle. "Gabby pulled strings to do cross-matching and tissue tests without parental consent."

Kyle cringed. "You made her risk her career? She's apologized and gone out of her way to help you. We can't demand more."

"It wasn't for us. Alyssa asked her to do it. She explained the situation and said she wanted to ensure she was a match before approaching her father. The tests are non-invasive." Casi took Jake's hand. "We also tested Charlotte."

Jake's eyes sparked with rage. "And?"

"She's not a match," Anna said.

Jake clasped his hands to his face. "Good."

"Chantal is flying in next week to meet Alyssa. It's crucial to convince her parents to allow her to do it by then. The procedure can be done here since the donor is American." Anna sighed. "I've offered to take care of any costs not covered by insurance."

"It could be substantial." Kyle put his arm around Anna's shoulders. "Her birth father can cover half. There's a responsibility attached to bringing a child into this world."

"He didn't know." Anna plucked at the fringe on the blanket.

"He planted the seed," Kyle said. "I've taken on the responsibility for children who aren't my own, including Lauren's, because it's the right thing to do."

❦

"Turn on channel five," Casi insisted as she raced in the living room with Anna.

"The game is on." Jake sipped his beer.

"I don't care. Alyssa texted me about a news conference at six o'clock. Your dumb jocks will still be trying to catch each other in ten minutes. Nothing earth shattering will have occurred." Casi glared at him with a hand on her hip as she tapped her foot.

Kyle wrangled the remote from his brother to switch the channel while Casi reclined in his arms and eyed Jake. "We would like a glass of wine."

"You women are demanding." Jake smacked her on the knee and went to fill her request. "Another beer?"

"Sure." Kyle set his empty on the table as a breaking news report flashed on the screen. "Who's Joe Salvatore."

Jake handed out glasses. "The rapist?"

"Please don't call him that." Anna shuddered. "It's Alyssa's father. He's running for office. I wonder why it's breaking news?"

"Another government scumbag is hardly newsworthy." Jake settled on the sofa beside Anna.

The man on the screen stared at the camera with intense brown eyes. "I'm withdrawing as a candidate." Flashes of light and a multitude of questions were directed at him, and he held up a hand as the cameraman pulled back to show his family at his side. Alyssa peeked through her thick dark bangs at the crowd before glancing up with flushed cheeks.

Casi leaned forward. "It's like she wants to make sure we're watching. I wonder if she told her father?"

"Recently I was confronted with something from my past I hoped would never come to light. I had honestly put if behind me and lived my life with deep faith and commitment to my constituents. What I've realized is you cannot run from wrongdoing and secrets will always haunt you." He looked directly ahead. "Twenty-four years ago, I raped a fifteen-year-old girl." The crowd gasped while questions and accusations were yelled. He waited for silence. "I must provide history, not as an excuse, but I cannot continue to live in denial. I attended an elite catholic high school. Although the education was superior, it was governed by priests who preyed on young men. I was abused for several years at the hands of father Dunnigan." Again, the spectators gasped.

Casi turned to Anna and raised an eyebrow. "Disgusting little priest. Did you know?"

Anna shrugged. "I heard rumors."

Joe continued with his cheeks aflame. "I was humiliated and confused by what had happened. Several other boys also shared their feelings, and we made a pact to prove our experience had not affected our manhood." He cringed and appeared to be about to vomit. "I targeted a girl from a private school to be my conquest. I had seen her at sporting events and knew her family to be upstanding, which convinced me she wouldn't report an assault. In my juvenile mind, I saw my behavior as justified for what had happened to me." He gazed at Alyssa with adoration. He pinched the bridge of his nose to stem the flow of tears. "I can't imagine what I put her through."

Jake hugged Anna tightly. "I'm glad he has a daughter."

"I'm not confessing this today to ask for understanding, and I realize I'm not worthy of forgiveness." Joe wiped his eyes with the back of his hand. "I met with the woman from my past and discovered I had fathered a daughter. I did not want to be accountable and asked her not to contact me further. As some people know, I suffer from a rare kidney disorder. Sadly, I have passed this on to several of my children, including my twenty-four-year-old daughter. Alyssa has insisted she will donate a kidney to save her sister, and I do not have a say in the matter." He squeezed her hand and smiled at her tenderly. "When I witnessed how brave she was at fifteen, I understood what a coward I was. I'm truly sorry for the act I committed and the lies I told to cover it. I understand my victim has a fulfilling life and I won't interfere in it other than to apologize publicly. I want to assure you I never touched another woman without consent, and I should have dealt with the abuse I suffered rather than let other boys continue to be assaulted. Today I'm bringing formal charges against Father Dunnigan, and I hope other men will step forward. We'll focus our energy in loving support of our daughter in her upcoming surgery. As my family heals from this, please give us privacy." He turned away from the camera as the press pushed forward and hounded him with questions.

Casi grabbed her phone and texted. "Alyssa, we're so proud of you! Thank you for being an amazing woman."

"Are you ok?" Jake caressed Anna's back.

"I thought I was over it, but suddenly I have a sense of relief to hear his apology. I guess I needed him to acknowledge he was wrong, and I wasn't in any way responsible." Anna turned to Casi. "Thanks for not giving up on this. You pushed me to bring closure and as painful as it was for Joe, I believe he'll be better off." She glanced at her phone and gasped at the message from Chantal. "You have given me life a second time. I love you."

"Are you happy with the result?" Kyle surveyed the bar dominating the dining room.

"I love it! We've revamped the menu to celebrate." Ava poured him a beer. "Seventy percent of our business comes from the bar. We're bringing in live music on Thursday nights and Casi is handling the marketing."

"Nice work. You can barely notice the stolen materials." Dalton sauntered toward them.

Kyle turned and narrowed his eyes. "You're not welcome here or anywhere around my family."

"Easy boy," Dalton mocked. "I brought papers for you to sign. Lauren said you were here. Do you know she tried to leave my name off the birth certificate? I wonder who she would've put instead."

"I have no idea. Your child is not my issue. And I'm not signing anything without my attorney present."

"I'm dropping the suit against your brother for assault and releasing your company from liability for the damage caused when you forcefully removed materials from my property."

"You don't have a case on either claim."

"It's a mutually beneficial agreement. I stay out of your way and you stay out of mine." Dalton surveyed the liquor selection. "Do you have decent wine?"

"I've tasted wines from your vineyard. I wouldn't serve it on two-dollar Tuesday." Ava poured him a glass of cabernet. "This is on the house. Drink it and go away."

Dalton wrinkled his nose. "Lacks depth."

"The same has been said about you." Jack approached and glanced over Kyle's shoulder to read the contract.

"He wants me to relinquish any claim to his fancy new restaurant. I guess your lawyer spotted the glaring holes in your family's fraudulent endeavor." He slid the papers toward Jack.

"This is bullshit." Jack noted the signature. "Why would Lauren sign this? She forfeits rights to the recipes she created and is barred from duplicating them in any form, including sharing them."

Dalton surveyed the lively dining room. "Lauren has a talent in the kitchen. It could be a disadvantage if she openly shared the menus which were created exclusively for our restaurant."

"What's in it for her?" Kyle asked.

Dalton shrugged. "I won't sue her for custody. I maintain my rights as a father, but she gets the kid eighty percent of the time. She signed a pre-nup, so it's the best I can do for her."

"You stole her money." Kyle fumed.

"She invested it, and sometimes those things don't pan out."

"What do you want from me?" Kyle asked.

Dalton's lip curled into a sneer. "You don't pursue me for the issue with Casi. You have no proof it wasn't mutually agreeable, but I don't need my name dragged through the mud by a bunch of rednecks."

Jack clenched the bar and frowned when Kyle replied, "Fine, I want every picture you have of her. We wouldn't want those tarnishing your good name."

Dalton set his phone on the bar. "I only have the originals. Lauren made a copy, but I'm not swift when it comes to technology."

Kyle opened the gallery, deleting the pictures featuring Casi. A quick scan proved Dalton's claim he didn't have a backup. "Give me a minute." He walked to the side and called Casi with his own phone. He followed her directions, forwarding the contacts, texts, and emails to her cloud account, then cleared the history after setting up a tracker.

"Sign here." Dalton snatched a pen from Ava's apron.

"You're a free man." Kyle scrawled his signature at the bottom. "This process must be old hat for you although there is usually a large payout to ensure the women you assault don't talk."

Dalton grabbed the pages and shoved them in his jacket pocket. "I guess you get what you pay for and in Casi's case I didn't get much."

Kyle smiled. "I have no rights over Casi. She can pursue whatever case she wants. It's her body you violated. My signature means nothing."

Dalton paled. "She'll do what you tell her to do."

"She's not one of your pathetic trophy wives. She has a mind of her own." Kyle glanced at the script on his wrist. "But our marriage is sacred." He swung at Dalton, knocking him to the ground and pouncing on him in a flurry of fists and rage.

"Jack, you have to stop him!" Ava panicked.

Jack stood still. "In a minute."

Ava signaled for a busboy and kept her voice low. Jack slowly made his way to Kyle and held his arm. "Don't kill him."

Kyle grabbed the contract and shoved a bill in Dalton's bloody mouth. "Payment for services rendered."

Ava liberated a bottle of whiskey and a funnel from the bar and nodded to the men who had assembled. They dragged Dalton to his feet and escorted him out a side door. "Stay here," she cautioned as Jack attempted to follow. "Make sure Kyle is alright."

"Sure, I'll get ice for his knuckles," Jack chuckled. He observed a crew cleaning the floor in an eerily efficient manner as he wrapped ice in a towel and handed it to Kyle. "I'm concerned my wife might be involved in an underground gang."

Kyle nodded. "You had better watch your step. She appears to be the leader."

Jack put a hand on his shoulder. "I realize no matter what your brother delivered, sometimes you must get your own hands dirty to release the pain in your heart." He tapped the new script on his wrist. "What does hers say?"

Kyle smiled. "Believe in Love."

29

CONVICTION

"I'm sorry, Mr. Salvatore is not meeting with anyone today. His schedule is fully booked." The secretary didn't bother to look up as she continued to pack her desk.

"Please tell him Anna O'Shea is here to see him."

The secretary sighed and went to deliver the message. She came back with a questioning expression. "He's available now."

Anna nodded and strolled to the office. She glanced at the moving boxes and general disorder of the room. "You're really throwing in the towel? I would have thought you would gain new supporters with your candor."

Joe smiled with an air of exhaustion. "I'm done with politics." He poured two glasses of scotch and handed her one. "I've been living at the bottom of a bottle for years now to escape my past, and my marriage. I married for the political connections and because it's what good catholic boys do. Too early for you?"

Anna brought the glass to her lips. "My first marriage was socially motivated. I was miserable. I love my second husband and even though so many signs highlighted a disaster, I've never been happier. We have a three-year-old daughter." She finished her drink and set the glass down. "I wanted to express appreciation for what you're doing to support Alyssa and help Chantal. I understand your confession wasn't easy and took courage knowing you were destroying your career."

Joe sat on the edge of his desk and refilled his glass. He held the bottle up, and she shook her head. "I wish I could take it back. I was a mixed-up kid, and I never considered the ramifications of my actions. It's not an excuse, but I was told forcing myself on you was merely a rite of passage." He exhaled loudly. "My daughter is the same age you were. I've kept her in a virtual prison for fear some boy would mistreat her." He downed his scotch. "Do you want to know the worst part? I sent my sons to the same high school where I was abused. I didn't protect them." He shrugged. "My wife is leaving me, and the older boys won't speak to me. The younger one is confused by the whole circus." He regarded his empty glass. "I've reached my limit."

Anna directed her gaze to the bottle and read further into his despair. "You can't give up. This is a low point in your career, but it will get better."

"I've disappointed everyone. At best, I have another twenty years before my disease makes me a burden. I'm glad my confession gave you closure, but you know what they did with Father Dunnigan? Moved him to another parish and swept the scandal under the rug. My high school friends have abandoned me and claim they were never abused. What's the point? My family is better off without me."

Anna grabbed the bottle and threw it in the trash. "To hell with them! Alyssa needs you to be there for the surgery. Twenty years? You can walk her down the aisle, see her children born, or help her recover from heartbreak. You aren't a joke to her. You're her father and even with your flaws, you're her hero. Girls love their dads, no matter what. She is the only one who matters."

Joe hung his head and let the tears flow down his cheeks. "I'm sorry for what I did to you. I had no right to touch you."

"No, you didn't." Anna moved to the desk beside him. "Your apology meant a lot. It has allowed me to put the memory to rest." Her eyes filled with tears. "I never understood why you did it. I always wondered what I conveyed to deserve your attention."

He put his hand on hers. "You did nothing wrong. You've grown into a beautiful woman. I'm sorry if I ruined your childhood."

Anna smiled. "The sex was horrible. And painful. I didn't trust men for a while, and I prefer to be in control. But I've had mostly good relationships and I'm confident in who I am. I'm able to separate what happened from the wonderful things in my life." She stood and gave him a hug. "I'll be at Chantal's surgery with my husband. I didn't want our meeting at the hospital to be awkward, and it was important for me to speak with you in private. I wish you well in your future endeavors."

"Anna O'Shea, you're one hell of a woman."

❧

Kyle walked in Fran's kitchen and tossed paperwork on the table. "Why would you sign a legal document without a lawyer?"

Lauren noted the blood-splattered pages. "What did you do?"

"We had a chat." Kyle sat with a shrug.

"He threatened to take Madison. I had nothing else to offer."

"You've made horrible choices since you met this guy. Were you blinded by your feelings for me, revenge against Casi, or desperation to have a baby?"

Lauren sucked in air at his biting words. "The more I tried to achieve my goals, the further away they seemed. Dalton presented the best options and suddenly everything fell in place. I overlooked the warning signs because I didn't want to fail at one more thing."

"These documents are proof the Standfords are scrambling. They're grasping at straws to hide their sins. Believe me, it's all crashing down." He smoothed a finger over the baby's arm. "They don't want her. She's a pawn to get what they value and shut everyone up. You are her mother."

"Hello Kyle, I didn't hear you come in." Fran limped to a chair as he jumped up to help her. "That was Lia on the phone. She said there was an incident involving Dalton last night."

Kyle covered his ravaged knuckles. "Where at?"

"Apparently, he attended a card game in Renton. One of those off the grid things." She clucked her tongue. "The police suspect he couldn't pay when he lost."

"Huh, Renton? Does he gamble a lot?" Kyle asked.

"Yes, one of his many faults," Lauren scoffed. "I think he owed a lot of people money. I'm not surprised his name was mud."

"Is he dead?" Kyle raised an eyebrow.

"Good gracious, no, badly shaken. He can't recall what happened. Lia claimed he was so drunk he was practically in a coma."

Kyle smiled at the recollection of Ava grabbing the bottle of whiskey and assembling her staff. "I guess he got what he deserved. How did Lia hear about it?"

"It happened outside one of the hangers on Boeing property. Shane discovered him in a ditch this morning."

Kyle tried not to laugh at the ludicrous situation. He had underestimated Ava's ability for revenge and was astonished by her careful construction in a heated moment. Relying on a past ally such as Shane was a calculated move. He lacked a connection to the Standfords and was loyal to Casi. He estimated Lia was used for her naïve relating of facts to populate the story. He smiled and reached for his phone as it rang. "Are you serious?" Kyle listened intently and indicated for Lauren to put on the news channel.

A pretty reporter with a fake scowl stood on the steps of a courthouse. "On the heels of Mr. Salvatore's shocking confession, it appears we have another scandal erupting." She turned seductively toward a flurry of activity behind her.

"Dalton?" Lauren leaned closer to the retro television to peer at the image of a man being led up the steps in handcuffs.

"Several women have come forward to claim they were victims of the Standford family. The accusations range from sexual assault to money laundering." The reporter paused to gaze flirtatiously at the camera while doing her best to appear angry without highlighting the lines around her eyes. "After Dalton Standford was arrested this morning, the family's attorney issued a statement warning women to obey the gag orders they signed."

"In other words, those conniving bastards already paid them to keep their mouths shut." Kyle reached over and grasped Lauren's hand. "This isn't necessarily good for you. Any hopes of recouping money you invested pretty much went up in smoke with Dalton's arrest."

Lauren gazed at the child in her arms. "As always, Casi benefits."

"What do you mean?"

"Dalton will serve time for assault and she doesn't have to testify." She raised her tear-filled eyes to his. "She's savvy with technology and I'm sure she had a hand in revealing this scandal."

Kyle leaned forward. "Perhaps. The question I would like answered is how much did you know?"

"I had heard about payouts to women when we first started dating. There's a certain type who falls victim to men. I figured it didn't concern me because I had brains and talent to create my own opportunities without leeching off the weakness of men."

Kyle sat back in his chair. "And yet you got taken for all you're worth. I guess Casi did benefit from having people who care so much about her. They nailed a predator and ensured no more women were hurt and she leaves with her dignity intact." He stood and walked out of the room without another word.

Fran shook her head when they heard his truck back out of the driveway. "You always push him too far."

30

FALTER

*J*ake surveyed his brother slumped on the sofa, drink in hand, as he watched a documentary on wombats. The stubble on his face indicated he hadn't shaved in days, which mirrored the disorder of the living room. He picked up dishes and began loading the dishwasher. "Do you want to take a shower before the game?"

Kyle sipped his scotch. "I'm not in the mood for sports." He switched the channel to a news report on fires ravaging California while tearful residents recounted their experiences.

"Can't you find something less depressing to watch?" He waited for a response and noted Kyle's glazed eyes before he grabbed his phone and sent a text. He sat beside his brother and made casual conversation about work. "Can you at least go brush your teeth if I have to sit so close to you?"

"I didn't invite you here and there are plenty of seats farther away." He rolled his eyes and sighed. "Fine."

Jake downed the remainder of the scotch while switching the channel to a cartoon. Kyle returned and picked up the empty glass and shuffled to the bar for a refill. "A little early in the day for alcohol."

"Then don't have one." Kyle eased in a recliner. "Why are you here? I thought Gail was sick, and you needed to watch your own kids."

"Anna took them to check out daycares. She feels they should have input, and I believe our consideration should be based on affordability and access. We're spending half the day carting them around to three different places and trying to remember where we left them. Gail offered to take them full-time, but it's not feasible in her townhouse, especially with the workload Reid has this year. He needs a quiet place to study and having young siblings doesn't help."

"Give Gail the little ones and take Reid."

"I actually enjoy my children."

"I don't see why. It seems your time is spent working to provide and cleaning up after them. We haven't been hunting once this year because one of them is always sick or has an issue beyond what your three wives can deal with."

"I understand how your life is much more appealing." Jake waved his hand around the room. "Drunk by noon on Sunday and no requirements to shower or clean the house."

"Outside of work, there's not much to enjoy in my life. Casi has barely been home more than three days this month." He startled as arms laced around his neck and a soft kiss was planted on his cheek.

"I'm home now." Casi slid on his lap and smoothed a hand over his unshaven cheek. "Have you missed me?"

Kyle rested his forehead against hers. "Jake called you?"

"Yup, and now I must return to my disgusting offspring and tend to their incessant neediness. Enjoy your wife." Jake smiled as he left.

"I realize I've been traveling too much. The business has expanded and now we added Asia to our territory," Casi confessed.

"Are you happy?" Kyle brushed his thumb over her bottom lip. "We never have a chance to talk anymore." He regarded the rain dancing on the lake. "I miss having you at home with me. It's incredibly selfish. I'm not sure what to do when you aren't here. I think the weather is affecting me. You know I'm not usually melancholy."

"I'm not happy." Tears slid down Casi's cheeks. "I'm exhausted."

Kyle inhaled sharply. "Is our marriage in jeopardy?"

"Never. In about six months, I'll be thirty-five. I've accomplished more than I could have imagined. I miss being home and the simple life we had in the beginning. I haven't played Candy Crush with Jake in weeks, and he's probably forgotten the tricks to get ahead. I don't even know if my plant is still alive at the wood shop."

"It is." Kyle caressed her back. "I bought another one to keep it company on the windowsill." Jezebel jumped on Casi and kneaded her thigh to prepare a place to sleep while Dingo rested his head on her foot. "They're lonely without you. I'm not much of a companion."

He reached for his drink and Casi intercepted, placing it back on the table. "I haven't worked out in months. I spend evenings at restaurants and bars entertaining clients. Do you know what I had for dinner last night? Tons of bread while I waited for my client. Three glasses of wine. Fried calamari and fettuccine Alfredo with extra parmesan. In the middle of the night, I had to take an Uber to the drugstore to buy antacid." She exhaled deeply. "Then I bought a candy bar and a bag of chips."

"Wow, you went all in."

"We need to make serious changes." She ran a hand over his cheek. "Starting with shaving. This caveman look isn't working for me." She touched the fine lines around his eye. "What else is bothering you?"

"I had a disagreement with Lauren. She's texted to apologize, but I haven't had the desire to hear her out. It seems pointless to revisit the same issue constantly."

"Am I the issue?"

"Partly." Kyle swirled the ice in his glass. "Since the problem with Dalton..." He cringed at his wording.

"I'm fine with the terminology."

"I was naïve to what she knew about his past and overlooked how it could affect you. I've accepted you don't like each other, but your welfare is my priority." He rested his head on her shoulder. "I let you down and I'm having trouble processing my failure."

She kissed his cheek. "My dislike for Lauren overshadowed my instincts about Dalton. I should have been more vocal."

"It's probably best if I terminate my relationship with her." Kyle frowned at his drink. "Fifteen-year-old Macallan."

Casi downed it in one long sip. "Shame to waste it." She kissed him and let him taste the scotch on her lips. "Lauren has been a good friend. I appreciate you defending me, but I sense she needs you now more than ever. Call and tell her we're moving forward. There will be no further discussions about Dalton. She should focus on opening a restaurant on her own. I'm sure there are opportunities if she's resourceful."

"Will you spend the night at home?" He cocked his head. "Where were you when Jake called?"

"At SeaTac. I had an hour layover between my flight from New York to Vancouver." She noted the concern in his eyes. "I'll leave early and make it there for my meeting."

Kyle glanced past her to the calendar. "You were scheduled to stay overnight in Vancouver tomorrow."

"It's Joey's birthday and Dawn planned a party. It's no big deal. I'll come home instead."

"I don't want you to choose between them and me. Go to the party." Kyle rubbed Dingo's ears.

"There's never a choice. You are number one. If you don't mind the drive, I would love for you to join me. It's a fun restaurant we used to go to in high school." She smoothed a finger over his tattoo. "Bring Jake if you like. He needs more adult interaction."

"Thank you for coming home. I didn't realize how much I needed to connect. My world is empty without you."

Kyle grasped Jake's arm when they entered the restaurant. "Hold on a second."

Jake followed Kyle's loving gaze to Casi, laughing with her friends as she ate chicken wings. "Ah, like one of your beloved documentaries; observing the chimpanzee in its natural environment."

"I like when her defenses are down."

"She's her goofy self around you." Jake shoved him forward. "Go get your primate and show her how much you missed her."

"You made it!" Casi's face lit up when she noticed them. "We ordered everything on the menu. Icing!" She wagged a finger at the TV and joined in the shouts of her friends berating the hockey player.

Kyle's eyes widened. "I didn't think you liked sports."

"Hockey isn't a sport." She cheered with the group as they yelled, "It's a National pastime!" They beat their chests while Casi and Dawn belted out a cheer mimicking Queen's, 'We are the Champions.'

Jake surveyed the lively atmosphere with big screen TV's, dart boards, and video games. "Cool place."

Casi downed a beer and extracted a bill from her wallet. "Ok birthday boy, are you ready?"

"Getting a lap dance?" Jake teased.

"Better!" Joey approached a video game with flashing neon lights. "A chance to redeem myself. She used to be a challenge in high school but somehow she perfected her skills and I can barely keep up."

Everyone gathered around as the competition began. "Go Joey." Dawn winked at Casi and gave her a thumbs up.

"Who are you really cheering for?" Kyle nudged Dawn.

Dawn smiled at Casi's sly move as she purposely fell behind. "She'll let him win for his birthday. Don't tell him or he'll be devastated."

Kyle observed Casi's screen and noted she dropped a level while swearing at the scoreboard. "She's pretty tricky."

"I love her like a sister. Secretly, we were always closer. If anything happened to Casi, I'd be devastated, but for Katie, I feel..." She gasped, "relief. I'm a horrible person."

"No, you're not. We understand things differently as adults. Katie didn't fit into your world anymore and brought pain and misery. Her death was a result of her bad choices."

Casi strolled over with her bottom lip jutted out. "I lost."

"I'm sure you tried your best." Kyle pulled her in his arms. "Would you like a drink to lift your spirits?"

Casi laughed while he kissed her neck. "We don't date enough. Isn't this fun?"

"It's awesome." Kyle grasped her hand and led her to the stage.

Casi flipped through the songbook and smiled. "This one."

They each held a mic, and the group gathered around to sing the chorus. Kyle sang the verse of the Florida Georgia Line song, 'Meant to be' and Casi joined in with Bebe Rexha's part. Cheers and clapping ensued to encourage them to continue. Kyle smiled at Casi while the room melted away and only their two hearts existed.

Casi pushed Kyle back on the bed and kissed him passionately while she rubbed against him. She put her palm over his mouth when he began to speak. He joined her in the intimate dance, sensing a desperate desire to connect physically. He studied her face as she climaxed and ensured she reached ultimate pleasure before giving in to his own release. He stroked her cheek when she collapsed beside him in satisfaction. "Squeezing in a session before you hit the road?"

She smiled through her tears. "I'm running on empty. I don't know how much longer I can push myself at this level."

"Scale back on the hours. This isn't healthy." He hovered above her and gently kissed her lips.

"The product line is taking off and it would be stupid to limit the success because I'm too tired to promote it." She yawned. "I require a few hours of sleep, and I'll be fine."

Kyle held her through the night, waking each time she tensed in her sleep. He caressed her back and whispered in her ear when she shuddered and clenched her jaw. He regarded the clock and sighed, wishing he could silence the alarm but aware it would create additional stress if she missed her meeting. He smoothed his hand over her hip, and she stretched. "Is it time?"

"Are you sure you can't postpone your trip?"

She rolled from the bed and ran a hand through her hair. "I must be in Toronto by this evening and there's a weird time difference so I'm taking the first flight."

"The East coast is three hours ahead."

"Sure, but then you need to factor in Canadian time and it's too much math for the morning." Casi fluttered her hand through the air.

"It's a good thing you're insanely beautiful," he laughed.

"Come join me in the shower."

"You're insatiable lately." Kyle tickled her as they rushed to the bathroom in a tangle of limbs.

"When I'm with you is the only time I feel like myself. I have a strange disconnect in my life where I'm standing on the outskirts and watching myself go through the motions of business."

"Should I be concerned for your health? You promise you're eating well and cutting back on drinking?" He surveyed her frail frame and raised an eyebrow.

"No drugs." She smiled meekly. "I'm trying to eat better."

After they showered, Kyle watched her studying her image in the mirror. "You're beautiful, but honestly, you look exhausted."

"I look old." She sighed and tapped her brush on the powder compact. "I'll talk to Mary about reducing my travel schedule. Anna is willing to take more trips, but I don't want to overload Jake with the kids. They need a better daycare situation."

"He drove to Seattle on Thursday to pick up Charlotte, but Anna's sister had her for the weekend. Lia called me in a panic to get the boys because she was late for work." Kyle rested his hand on hers. "Age is not a bad thing, Casi. One day I want to be standing here with you in our nineties. Wrinkles and gray hair are rewards for living a good life. My love isn't limited to your youthful beauty. My feelings run much deeper and they are eternal."

Kyle placed their orders while Casi chatted to Lia, nodding at the lengthy tale of woe involving the difficulties of dating a widower with three children. The young manager interrupted with obvious annoyance, insisting Lia return to the barista station. He frowned at Casi. "You're looking ragged. Life not going well?"

Kyle caught the devastation on Casi's face before she bravely shrugged. "Just busy."

Kyle's fist contacted the pimply jaw of the manager before another word was said, shutting down conversations in the coffee shop as everyone turned to stare. The manager grasped his chin as he writhed in pain. "You're banned from here!"

"Fine." Kyle cupped Casi's elbow and led her quickly to the car. "I'm sorry. I reacted without thinking."

"I guess we're not getting coffee today."

"I'll make some at work." Kyle checked his watch. "Let me drive you to the airport."

"I'll be home in three days. Will you pick me up?"

"I don't mind. I'm concerned about how pale you are."

"What a confidence booster!"

Kyle chuckled and pulled her in his arms. "I love you."

They walked in the wood shop and Jake shook his head. "Thanks for getting us banned from the only place in town with decent coffee."

Kyle grinned. "You heard?"

"I talked to Lia." Jake surveyed Casi. "Are you alright?"

"Jesus! Now you're calling me ugly?" Casi stomped to her office.

"You're a beautiful monkey," Jake called after her. He turned to Kyle. "Are you sure she's not sick?"

"She's been traveling too much. Did Lia get in trouble?"

"He yelled at her and told her we weren't allowed in there anymore. He threatened to call corporate and file a harassment claim."

"He deserved it! He told Casi she looked ragged." He glanced toward the back and lowered his voice. "Should I have stood there and let him ridicule her? I'm sorry if I made things difficult for Lia, but it's not a high-level job."

"I told her to quit."

"Good!"

"She needs the health insurance. Can we add her on ours?"

"You already have a wife on the policy. When is the mourning period over for Shane so they can move forward with their relationship? I'm sure he has good insurance at Boeing."

"I feel it may be inappropriate for me to ask him." Jake grinned. "Let's have Casi do it. It was her friend who died."

"We..." Kyle stopped mid-sentence when a crash vibrated through the building. He raced toward the back and threw himself to the floor. "Casi!"

Jake grabbed his arm as Kyle began to scoop her in his arms. "Don't pick her up. I called an ambulance."

Kyle tore his shirt off and placed it under her head. He reclined beside her and stroked her face as tears welled and he coaxed her to open her eyes.

Jake put his palm to her forehead. "She's burning up."

Casi blinked against the bright light penetrating her eyelids. "Wake up, sweet girl," Ava cooed.

"Kyle!" Casi searched the room, trying to grasp where she was.

"I'm here." Kyle sat beside Ava and slid a hand under Casi's neck. "I was talking to the doctor. Do you remember what happened?"

"No." Casi clawed at the bedcovers and tried to break loose from the wires and tubes preventing her from getting up. "I must get to my meeting. What time is it?"

Mary put a firm hand on her arm to calm her. "You collapsed from exhaustion. Anna has flown to Toronto."

"I'm fine." Casi burst into tears and noted Kyle's broken demeanor. "I didn't take anything. I swear!"

"I know." Kyle straightened the sheet. "You're overworked. You can't continue at this pace."

"Georgia has taken the children for a few days to allow everyone to come up with a better strategy." Mary wiped Casi's tears. "You're my golden girl. You've surpassed every goal we set. Let's breathe for a moment and enjoy our thriving company."

"I have so many ideas swirling around in my head." Casi flopped back on the pillow. "I can't quit."

"Oh, Sweetie, Anna and I need you at the helm. We depend on your wacky brain to put things in motion." She glanced at Kyle. "But work can't be the only thing you're investing your time in."

31

TRAIL OF BROKEN DREAMS

Casi inhaled sharply as she noted the scene with Lauren cradling the baby as she slumped on the sofa in the living room. Kyle glanced up and caught the annoyance etched on her face. "Lauren brought over real estate flyers for possible locations for a restaurant. Blackberry Falls isn't necessarily a high-end destination, but it's close to where she's living, and it could bring in a decent clientele."

"Sounds promising." Casi stormed to the bedroom and stripped out of her business attire. She sensed Kyle behind her and shrugged. "I'm going for a run. I've been feeling good since I've been back to my regular workouts and I want to get in a few miles while it's not raining, since it's pretty rare." She exhaled and turned to face him. "I'm not knocking Washington weather."

"It can be tough this time of year." Kyle smiled and reached out to take her hand. "May I come with you? I could use some exercise."

"What about Lauren?"

"Lia's helping her figure out breastfeeding, which is ironic. I'm hoping Anna will be home soon since she seemed to master it." Kyle slipped on track pants.

"You don't like breasts on display?" Casi threw her shirt open.

"I can look at yours all day." He grinned from where he kneeled to tie his running shoes.

Casi yanked a t-shirt over her head. "Then try to keep up, big boy." She raced through the living room and sidestepped Jake, who held his beer above his head in anticipation of a collision.

"Where are you going? The game's starting, and Shane's coming." Jake frowned as they bolted toward the side door. "Weirdos."

"Dingo, come." Kyle held up a hand as the toddler tried to follow. "Charlotte, stay. Sit." He threw her a candy from a dish and patted her on the head as the dog pranced at his heels.

Lauren balked at the action, and Lia laughed as she grabbed Tommy's hoodie to prevent him from running after Kyle and Casi. "You have no idea how hard it is to wrangle kids once they become mobile."

Jake noted Lia getting scolded by Lauren for her poor advice on mothering and surveyed her crushed demeanor. "Hey, Lia, can you help me get food ready? My brother is busy chasing his lunatic wife." He smiled as Anna walked in. "Speaking of wives, I'm happy to see you."

"Did you miss me?" Anna smiled brightly.

"As always." Jake greeted her with a kiss.

Anna put a hand on Jake's arm. "I was at the hospital. Chantal went into distress, so they had to rush the operation. I didn't have time to contact you."

"Is she alright? I'm sorry you had to be there alone. I would have rearranged my schedule."

"It was a success. Alyssa is already awake and talking. A huge load has been lifted off my shoulders and I can finally breathe." She made direct eye contact. "Joe was there, and it was sweet to see him so distraught. He was alone because his family won't talk to him, but he's standing by Alyssa and signed the consent forms." A smile touched her lips. "I held his hand, and it was the strangest feeling to be sitting in a waiting room, not knowing if the child we created as the result of his assault would survive. I felt pity for his situation and thankful for the life I have. Oh, by the way, a doctor named Gabby came to be with Alyssa and she said she knew Kyle. She was very compassionate."

"She's a friend of Kyle's and performed Casi's surgery." He pulled her in his arms. "You made the right choice to be there for Chantal. Perhaps Alyssa has been Joe's salvation."

❦

"What's wrong, old man? Can't keep up?" Casi jogged backward up the hill, watching Kyle struggling. He glanced through a bush and grabbed his side as he collapsed. "Kyle!" She ran to him. "Is it your hip?"

Kyle pulled her down and rolled on top of her. "Gotcha."

She turned her head away to prevent his lips from meeting hers. "I was devastated."

"I want to show you something." He kissed her gently.

"On the trail? It's kind of mucky." She scrunched her nose at the mounds of dirt embedded with leaves.

Kyle perched on his elbows above her. "If I wanted to make love right here, would you?"

"Anytime and anywhere."

"I figured, which is one of the million reasons I love you." He jumped to his feet and offered her a hand. "There's a property I would like to check out."

"For Lauren?" Casi dusted off her backside and laced her fingers through his as he held a branch for her to enter a side trail.

"She's looking at standard locations for restaurants to lease. This old hotel has been out of business for years. I think it would provide an amazing opportunity for her to invest for greater financial gains."

Casi surveyed the sprawling property in desperate need of repair. "Her money or yours?"

"Mine. She asked to borrow a hundred grand. It would cover the basic equipment and lease for barely a year. She thinks she can turn a profit by then, but I'm doubtful."

Casi squeezed her eyes shut. "What if I say I'm uncomfortable with you lending her so much money?"

He drew his thumb over her bottom lip. "Then I won't do it."

"You'll tell her I'm preventing you?"

"I'll say it's my decision." He led her along the trail. "When we bought the old dairy, everyone told us it was absurd. They said it was too far out of town and required extensive work to bring it to code. I loved every minute working on it and there hasn't been a moment I regretted investing my money in something I could create." His smile stretched across his face as he helped her over the broken boards of a fence. "When we were kids, my grandfather on my mother's side would let us come in his workshop to watch him. He was a boat builder by trade. I was enamored of how he crafted each piece to suit his goal. You never knew what he had in mind until it started to take shape. It was miraculous."

"He taught you the trade?"

"He's the one who inspired me to become a woodworker. Jake had the technical skills, and I could see how the labor transformed his anxiety and helped him cope. My professors urged me to study for a more intellectual career, but I wanted to have my own business and have the ability to create works of art which were useful." He shrugged. "I realize they're only cabinets, but they started out as piles of wood."

"Or tiny acorns." Casi squeezed his hand. "I understand your desire to take on this project. You see dilapidated buildings and imagine a kingdom. You still have the little boy inside who believes in magic."

"Perhaps." He sighed. "I'll be thirty-nine next month. I'm antsy about not moving forward with my achievements."

"I trust your abilities. Can you give me a week to absorb the impact of this on our relationship? It's a shit-ton of money to a former lover whose life is in the toilet. You're a mighty knight, but you're still my prince charming. Has Jake agreed to take on this project?"

"He thinks I'm insane." He kissed her cheek. "A week is more than fair. I'll work on general ideas and run by financials with Brian. I know if you're on board everyone, especially Jake, will cheer us on." He grabbed her hand and wound through the thick overgrowth covering the trail leading to the hotel. His eyes lit up as he surveyed what was once a spectacular building. "Isn't it amazing? I imagine the inside is incredible."

"Let's find out." Casi pushed a broken window frame open.

"You're trespassing!" Kyle clawed at her shoe to prevent entry, but she slipped from his clutches. He peered in the dark void and turned back to Dingo. "Stay here, boy. Bark if someone comes."

"Come save me." Casi called as she strolled through the grand foyer. "This place is fantastic!"

Kyle shimmied through the window and sprinted after her. "If we get arrested, I'm blaming you." He smoothed his hand over the carved wood of an enormous fireplace. "I love this architecture."

Casi observed him touching the intricate details of each piece and understood he was seeing the decrepit structure, how it once was. She snapped pictures of the rooms and added comments from his commentary on what he felt needed to be repaired or reconstructed. Kyle's initial hesitation at trespassing transferred to fascination of the transformation he pictured in his mind. Casi glanced out a window to a run-down house in the meadow. "Is the shack part of the property?"

"It was the caretaker's cottage. Lauren could live there." He carefully placed a foot on the first stair and held out his hand. "It might have dry rot."

After touring the upper floor, Casi had a pictorial of the interior and a rough layout of the property. She smiled at Kyle standing in front of a large stained-glass window shrouded in a kaleidoscope of light. "This place is magical."

He turned and smiled. "Anytime and anywhere?"

Casi laughed. "Do you want to christen your new hotel?"

Kyle placed his hands to her waist and shimmied her t-shirt over her head. "Perhaps if you see things from another angle, you'll be convinced this is an ideal location."

She shivered as he brought his mouth to her breast. "The carpet is filthy." She smiled when his gaze drifted to the worn patterned stair-well. "You're picturing the antique wood floors beneath?"

He grinned and slid her up on the ledge of the railing. "In the meantime, we can make use of this ornate architecture."

❧

Jake grinned as Gail stood above him in her tennis skirt with a seductive smile. "How's the plumbing issue going? Do you need assistance?" She drew the toe of her shoe over the zipper on his jeans.

"I'm a happily married man." He sat up and handed her his tools. "All done. Turn on the tap."

"It works. Are you sure about the sex? Your third wife is in Europe."

"She is." His eyes crinkled with amusement. "Three wives are my limit, so if I can't make this work, I'm throwing in the towel." He stood and dusted off his jeans, regarding Gail with shock as she lit a joint. "What are you doing?"

She giggled and held it to her lips. "I found it in Olivia's room. I was curious to see if I still liked being high."

"Do you think she'll notice it's missing?"

Gail shrugged and lounged on the sofa. "Do you ever wonder if you were meant for more in life?"

"Ah, marijuana philosophy." He settled beside her and put his arm around her shoulders. "Honestly, I'm so busy running in circles to remember where I left the kids, and which wife I'm disappointing, I haven't had time to reflect on my life's purpose." He took a long drag and watched the smoke circle above their heads. "I miss Casi being home. I prefer our simple life with us eating dinner together and hanging out at Kyle's. I don't mind Anna traveling accept it makes our life chaotic. My three young children are in twelve different places at any given time. I worry how it will affect their upbringing."

"No perfectly run Georgia-style home?"

"Kyle and I originated from chaos. Our picture-perfect farm life was ideal. Imagine what would have happened if I wasn't adopted?"

Gail shivered unintentionally. "I doubt it would have been good." She began a meaningful conversation on the roads not taken and fears of growing older without direction in life. He rested his cheek on top of her head, slipping into a deep sleep as her words danced in the fragrant mist of the marijuana.

"Dad!" Olivia shoved Jake's shoulder. "Your phone is ringing like crazy!" She eyed the stub of a joint. "Did you guys raid my room?"

Jake grinned. "It's Mom's house. Contraband is fair game."

Olivia scoffed and tossed the phone in his lap. "Whatever. Check your messages. You're suddenly very popular."

He yawned and slid his arm from behind Gail, shaking off the pins and needles from compression. He frowned at the log of missed calls from Anna and Shane, almost dropping the phone as the screen lit up with an incoming call. "Hey, what's going on?" He blanched and checked his watch. "Sorry. I came to Gail's to repair the kitchen sink, and I lost track of time." He jumped to his feet. "Anna, calm down. They won't sell her because I'm a few minutes late to pick her up." He held the receiver away as her voice escalated. "I'm on my way. I must get this. Shane keeps messaging me." He exhaled with annoyance. "I doubt it's about sports. Remember, I have two other children he's involved with. Fine, bye." He kissed Gail on the cheek as he answered the phone and walked to his truck. He froze and grasped the door handle. "Wait, slow down. Are my sons in danger?" He felt the panic rise in his chest and ended the conversation with a brief reply. His hand shook as he dialed Kyle. "I need your help."

Kyle strolled in the elite daycare and noted the annoyance of the caregiver as she glared at the clock. "I'm here for Charlotte." He smiled as the little girl ran toward him.

"Obviously, since she is the only child left." She rose and jutted her chin out. "Identification?"

"I'm Jake's brother." He sighed and showed his driver's license. "I'm on the list." He picked Charlotte up and kissed her cheek as she snuggled in his arms. "Hey, little peanut. How was school? Did you learn to be bossy like Mommy and your teachers?"

The woman scowled. "There's an extra charge for late pickup."

"Add it to the exorbitant invoice you're already charging us every month," he said over his shoulder as he carried Charlotte to his truck. He buckled her in the car seat and answered the phone. "I've got her and there's no sign of mental anguish." He touched her cheek and listened to Jake's incoherent trail of words. "Hold on. I'll come over and assess what's going on. Don't engage with her. You'll only make it worse." He smiled at Charlotte as he drove. "Your Daddy is a hot mess with these women and kids." He parked in Lia's driveway and glanced at Charlotte, asleep in the car seat. "Stay." He patted her tummy and rolled down a window before walking inside. He halted at the threshold and a flood of distant memories washed over him as he surveyed Lia in a full-blown tantrum, screaming and throwing dishes while Austin raged, and Jake stood in a daze on the sidelines. Tommy sat on the floor coloring with a marker in circles on a discarded pizza box, oblivious to the scene. Kyle's heart dropped when he noted the glazed expression on his face as he focused on the smear of marker digging deeper into the cardboard. He stormed inside and grabbed Tommy in his arms. "Austin, come here!"

"You're not taking my kids!" Lia charged toward him.

Kyle grasped Austin's hand and shoved him toward the door. "They're coming with me until you can get a handle on your anger. I don't know what set you off, but they will not witness this any longer."

Jake shuffled toward him and whispered, "Shane broke up with her. He's overwhelmed with taking care of his girls and juggling the boys. He phoned me because he was concerned." His eyes watered. "She's completely off balance. Apparently, Austin knocked the phone out of her hand when she was talking to Shane and it pushed her over the edge." He regarded his son's tear-stained flushed cheeks highlighted with red welts from being slapped. "Help me."

Kyle exhaled and noted Lia crumpled on the sofa in a heap of sobs. "She's irrational. We can't leave her alone. I'll take the kids home with me. Stay here and see if you can get her to a doctor in the morning. Maybe they can check for menopause. Mom might have insight."

Jake nodded and wiped his eyes with the back of his hand. "Why won't my life get easier? Anna was worried Charlotte was damaged by a late pick up. How will this affect the boys?"

Kyle grasped his hand and gave it a squeeze. "You've lived this. Our parents ended our nightmare and we must protect the boys."

Jake watched him back out of the driveway and turned to Lia. "Go take a hot bath. I'll clean this place up and we can sit calmly and talk." He waited for her to stomp toward the bathroom before leaving a message. "Monkey, I know you're on your way to Tokyo or somewhere way too far away, but I'm desperate to hear your voice." A sob caught in his throat and he leaned against the wall. "I'm completely broken, and the world is spinning out of control."

He was about to slip the phone in his pocket when it buzzed. He smiled at the GIF of a monkey hugging a dog and a text, "Change of plans. Be home tonight. Hang in there. I'll help you get through this."

۞

Casi slipped in the house quietly, setting her bags and laptop by the door. She cast her shoes to the side and padded to the bedroom, smiling as she regarded Kyle with Charlotte asleep on his chest and the boys tucked on either side. She showered before crouching beside Austin perched on the edge of the mattress. She stroked his cheek and noted the scratches along one side. "Hi, chicken nugget. Do you want to cuddle with Auntie?"

Austin's lips curled in a smile and he reached out for her, still in the depths of sleep. "Hiya, tater tot."

She clasped him in her arms and settled beside Kyle, encasing Tommy in a loving embrace between them. She held her phone above the scene and snapped a picture, sending it to Jake. "I'm home. Everyone is fine. Take care of Lia."

Casi stretched and purred as the warm hand rubbed her back in a circular pattern. "Where's Lia?" She peeked at Jake beside her.

He reached over and smoothed Austin's hair. "At work." He read Kyle's intense stare. "I told her to come over after and we can figure out what the best plan is going forward."

Kyle shifted to a sitting position and cuddled Charlotte. "There will be no more discussion. The boys are staying here. I'll build out the room in the office nook and set it up properly for them. Anna should cut back on travel and ensure Charlotte's needs are met. This circus must stop. It's ridiculous to cart these kids around town because you're trying to make everyone happy."

"Lia won't agree. I'm their father and I can take care of them."

"They're my blood, too. Their needs come first." Kyle's nostrils flared. "Last night I had an appointment with Lauren to survey a possible site for a restaurant. It's difficult for her to manage a newborn and figure out a lease on top of everything she has already dealt with. I canceled to help you instead. Your situation is a train wreck with no solution to improve."

Casi's bottom lip trembled. "I knew this would happen!"

Kyle adjusted Charlotte in his arms. "Me stepping in to take care of the kids?"

Casi directed her gaze to the boys cuddled against Kyle as he rocked Charlotte. "You love being a father. It's the ultimate role for you with your insane organization and ability to multitask. You didn't think you wanted kids because of the work involved and unpredictability, but you've discovered these tiny humans adore you." A tear slid down her cheek. "Lauren has become the perfect mate for you, damaged and in need of rescue. You can swoop in and fix her life and become the ideal father for her child."

"You know what I consider perfect? Every second I spend with you." Kyle caressed her cheek. "I've supported you in your career and cheered you on from the sidelines. The truth? I hate it! It breaks my heart to wake up alone and spend all day wondering what you're doing. My ideal life is us drinking coffee together and going for walks while you rattle on about obscure ideas and baffle me with random knowledge." He regarded the children. "I didn't expect to love these guys, you're right. My stance has not changed on fatherhood. As always, my concern is for my brother and how I can help him cope. I cannot stand by and allow these kids to be harmed. Lauren isn't a threat to our relationship. I'll help guide her through this process of rebuilding her life because she's my friend and I feel responsible for not speaking up earlier about Dalton. I don't know what you want from me anymore, but I must protect these children until the other adults in their lives can grow the hell up." He kissed her forehead. "I understand this decision impacts you. You're amazing at making everyone feel good and you've put Lia back together a few times already. I'll do it on my own if necessary, but I won't back down."

Casi blinked away tears. "You're choosing the kids over me?"

"No, I was referring to the care and cost. I prefer you to be my partner in this and everything I do in life."

Casi laced her fingers through his. "Last night I didn't get on the plane to Tokyo because my family needed me here. I'm one hundred percent committed to these children. On the flight back from LA, I had some ideas of how we can make this work. Can you trust me?"

Kyle's expression softened. "If anyone can work miracles, it's you. I'm sure your brain is swirling with concepts beyond what we've considered. Thank you for coming home."

Jake slumped against Casi. "Last night broke me. I witnessed the irrational look on Lia's face and it was like an alien invaded her body." He ran his thumb over Tommy's cheek. "The babysitter suggested we should have him tested for autism. I watched him completely inside himself, drawing circles to escape the chaos. Do you believe there's something wrong with him? Is it my fault?"

Casi caressed Tommy's back. "He shuts down at the babysitter's because it's too much stimulation. He walked earlier than Austin and he chatters away with me and Kyle, plus he's begun to read. He will thrive in the proper environment. It's our responsibility to create it."

32

ORDER FROM CHAOS

"Where's Charlotte?" Anna stormed in the bedroom and pulled the covers off Jake.

He yawned and glanced at the clock. "My brother has taken temporary custody." He swung his legs over the bed. "He's declared he's the best parent for my spawn."

"Bullshit! I apologize for yelling at you the other day. It wasn't the end of the world Charlotte was picked up late." She cast her eyes to her hands. "I'm failing at juggling being a mother and having a career. I thought I could balance it, but I can't control everything."

"Don't worry, I'm completely aware of my shortcomings. Kyle will take over the father role."

"The reason I was pissed wasn't because you were late." She shivered. "In the last month, I've arrived late four times and forgotten her twice. They warned me if it happened again, she would be removed from the program."

Jake pulled her to his chest and chuckled. "You little sneak. You're as bad as I am at this!"

She rested her head on his shoulder. "I guess it's time to give up my career and learn how to be a stay-at-home mom. Do you think Gail could teach me how?"

"Gail excelled because her goal was to be home with her kids. Before you throw in the towel, let's hear what Casi has to say. She's been spinning some creative web of how we can manage better."

"She sent me a bunch of texts with questions. I was concerned I might come back and find out I no longer had a job because it focused on career satisfaction and life goals."

"She's a nut. Who knows what her demented brain is calculating?" He slipped on shoes and held his hand out. "Come see where my children reside now. They'll never want to leave."

They walked across the street to an immaculate house, and Anna did a double take when she noted the curtains strung across the corner of the room. She listened to a gentle voice reading a story. Jake led her to the opening of the makeshift bedroom, and she scanned the colorful cavern decorated with giant stuffed animals, maps, and toys. She watched Kyle reclining on one of the twin beds with the children gathered around while he held a book. "Do you know I've never read to my children?" Jake nudged Anna. "My dad always read to us at night and it was magical. My older kids were usually already in bed by the time I got home from work. With this batch, I'm running around trying to remember where I left them and wondering if someone fed them before I drop them off. Kyle is so much better at this."

Anna's lip trembled as she regarded Charlotte kneeling beside Kyle, eagerly pointing to a character in the book while he explained the story. "She hasn't even noticed I'm here."

Kyle looked up when the story concluded. "Time for breakfast."

The children scrambled off the bed and clamored to the kitchen to set out bright placemats and cutlery. In perfect unison, they sat in a row and waited for bowls to be placed in front of them. Casi entered with a smile and reached over Austin to take a slice of apple. "CeCe, no." He pushed her hand away as she dipped it in the yogurt in his bowl.

"Blech." She made a face. "Unsweetened!"

"It's healthier." Kyle nodded with satisfaction as the children focused on the fruit and yogurt while he added homemade granola.

Casi grabbed cereal from the cupboard, eating it straight from the box. She smiled at Anna. "You're home. How do you like Kyle's quintessential fantasy land for tiny tots?"

"It's fantastic." Anna sighed.

"I may have gone a little overboard on the toys." Kyle glanced toward the corner. "It's deceptive when they label them by age group because I feel it limits their imagination."

Jake shoved his hand in the cereal box. "I'm sure you've done hours of research on the essentials of raising children."

"There are studies proving a regular schedule creates harmony and improves a child's chance of succeeding in school." He noted the pain in Jake's eyes. "I'm not keeping them indefinitely. I wanted to provide a place for them to feel safe and loved."

Jake clapped. "It's incredible. You've done an amazing job. Congratulations, you get the father of the year award."

Kyle handed him a cup of coffee. "Everything will be moved to your house. It didn't make sense to put the boys in an empty room on air mattresses. Bringing them with us to work is convenient, but not ideal in the long run."

"Anna, he's turned our office into a daycare." Jake grinned. "Oh, but no electronic toys because they impede learning."

Kyle rolled his eyes. "There are studies…"

Casi put her hand over his mouth. "Brilliant. Assemble in the living room for my presentation."

"Wait, Kyle must do his little darling's hair." Jake nudged Anna. "He watched a YouTube video on making ponytails and bought her a bunch of hair things."

Kyle shrugged. "It's adorable, and she likes it."

Casi shoved past him to the coffee pot. "I wish I got half as much attention as the little brat gets."

Kyle grabbed her and kissed her neck loudly. "You get all kinds of attention, once the children are safely tucked in."

"You tuck them in?" Anna wailed. "Casi, I'm sorry, but I have to quit my job. Your husband has made her believe in fairytales."

"And warrior princesses." Kyle helped Charlotte off her stool.

Charlotte ran to Casi and threw her arms around her legs, trapping her in an embrace. "Wa Wa pincess."

Casi giggled and patted her on the head. "I've won her over."

Kyle chuckled. "We were reading a book and there was a blonde princess. She was convinced it was Casi, so I embellished the story to make her a valiant warrior and Charlotte was hooked."

"Awesome, now she'll never want to move home." Anna shook her head as she watched Casi rally the children to get dressed.

Kyle eyed the process. "I planned to take them to the zoo later. I hope what you picked out will be suitable."

"You didn't invite me." Casi jutted out her bottom lip.

"You're always working. Free up time for me on the weekends and we can spend it doing whatever you want." He poked her in the ribs as he went to supervise bed making.

Lia arrived with Gail and Lauren, and she handed Casi a box. "I brought you donuts. I know Kyle is strict about the kids having sugar." Tears came to her eyes as she watched the boys following Kyle's directions to straighten the room. "So, this is permanent?"

"Lia..." Jake halted when Shane entered.

Shane froze at the doorway. "Casi told me to come."

Casi frowned at Lauren as she tried to calm Madison. "Kyle, you have an infant to soothe. I can't have a crying baby during my presentation."

"I don't do babies." Kyle shuddered. "They can't reason yet, so my skill set is wasted."

Gail held out her arms to take the baby. She swayed with her until she slipped into a peaceful sleep. "I'm good with kids until they're teenagers, then I'm apparently useless."

Lauren stretched. "I don't think I can have a restaurant until she's in school." A cloud of sadness spread across her face.

"Take a seat. I would like your undivided attention for the next three hours." Casi grinned at Jake as he cringed. "I'm kidding. There will be no commenting until the end, so hold your questions." She directed Kyle to remove a picture from the wall as she set up her laptop with a projector. She pointed to a blanket as the children skipped in. "Silence until I give you your cue."

Casi regarded her audience and swept a hand around the room. "You have donuts and coffee. There's also fruit, which is required by the food police. No questions until the end." Jake whispered to Kyle and Casi threw a grape at him. "Zip it. This presentation impacts your future." She wiggled her fingers. "I hold all the cards."

Kyle frowned. "Why do we need a video on child rearing?"

"The children are a minor part of what needs to be discussed."

"Their well-being is a priority," Kyle asserted.

"This room is full of dysfunctional adults who are overwhelmed by the enormity of life." She swept her hair behind her shoulder. "Luckily, some of us are able to think outside the box."

"I'm not dysfunctional." Kyle sulked.

"Your entire world revolves around your brother's offspring and you've put your dreams on hold." She kissed him. "If you interrupt me again, you'll be cut off from sex for a month."

Jake chuckled. "Like an adult time-out!"

"First thing." Casi smiled and held out her hands to Jake. "Do you love me?" She laced her fingers through his.

"Every crazy molecule." His face clouded. "Do you need a public declaration of my immense guilt for hurting you?" He eyed her wrist under the bulk of the sweater.

"A thank you will do." Casi grinned and slid an object to his arm.

Jake's eyes widened when she latched the clasp. "My watch!"

Kyle's mouth dropped. "You bought him a new one?"

"I tracked his to a pawnshop. I hinted the police were on the trail since it was evidence in a crime. They were happy to part with it for a relatively low price."

"I'll pay whatever it cost." Jake stroked the watch.

"It's my gift to you." She clasped her chest. "As your friendship is to me." Her eyes watered. "Once you accepted me, you've been a truly loyal friend and I cherish you."

Jake pulled her in his arms. "I love you, monkey brains. You create the magic moments making life worth living."

Kyle squeezed her hand. "Thank you. You've solved one more dilemma tearing me apart."

Jake held his arm beside Kyle's. "We match again. The world is spinning in harmony and my heart is healed."

Casi motioned toward the wall. "I would like to revisit the option of putting Lauren's restaurant at the abandoned hotel." She yawned with dramatic flair as the first image appeared with minor repairs and a few generic flowers, and a sign, Lauren's boring restaurant costing Kyle too much money.

"Unkind," Kyle gasped.

"I'm happier to lease the space in town," Lauren pouted.

"Dull and shortsighted. Lance did the preliminary designs. He's incredibly talented." Casi switched to the next image of a beautifully restored building and manicured gardens brimming with color. A new sign hung on the porch, Blackberry Falls Resort. She held her finger to her lips as comments erupted. "Stage one, the restaurant." Polished stainless appliances highlighted a commercial kitchen. Kyle's rendering of the previous dining room at the winery had been altered to fit the new space. "Stage two, this is where it gets exciting." The guest rooms were restored to their former glory with views of the lake and gardens. "Gorgeous, huh?"

"We can't afford it." Kyle crossed his arms over his chest.

"We still have tons of the reclaimed wood," Jake chimed in.

"This is too much work. I only wanted a restaurant." Lauren scowled at the screen. "I can't do any of it now with a child. This is painful to see what could have been."

Casi pointed to the children playing quietly on the blanket. "Even the minions understand the no talking rule. Please wait until after the presentation to comment." She smiled at Anna as she brought up the next set of slides. "A boutique hotel should be a destination, and what draws high end business? A spa." Renderings of a sanctuary overlooking the lake featuring Macrae skincare line appeared.

"You're stealing my hotel for your business?" Kyle narrowed his eyes and avoided Lauren's glare at his proclamation of ownership.

"There's something for everyone." Casi beamed as she advanced the photos to a coffee shop named Lia's. "Georgia is on board to share her baking recipes and is happy to teach you."

"Oh my God!" Lia jumped to her feet and hurried to get a closer look. "Is it really mine? Can I quit my job?"

"None of this is real. It's a fantasy costing way more than any of us could ever afford," Lauren said bitterly.

"I love it." Lia bubbled, not easily deterred from the dream.

Casi snapped her fingers and Austin stood to deliver his line. "I wish there was a place for us kids."

Tommy grinned. "I demand pre-cool."

Casi frowned at Charlotte. "Charkie, get with the program."

Charlotte stood. "I be smart like brothers."

In unison they pulled off their sweaters to reveal colorful t-shirts emblazoned with a logo, Blackberry Falls Preschool.

Anna smiled. "You hit on a nickname I like. Ditch the others."

Casi nodded. "I like her now, so I needed something cuter."

Jake shook his head. "Nice coaching. How does this precocious performance relate to this boring slide show?"

"Funny you should ask." Casi cued the transformation of the caretaker's cottage to a whimsical school. "And we have the perfect person to run it, Gail!"

Kyle clapped. "You've spent a lot of time putting this together and I appreciate your imagination. I'm curious if this is your way of telling me my idea was ridiculous or was it enjoyable to mock me?" He stood and gathered coffee cups. "Come on kids, it's time for the zoo. I think your aunt has had a good laugh at my expense."

Casi cocked her head. "Don't you love the ideas I presented? Imagine how well a business could do with these amenities."

"Sure, but we can't afford any of it. Even the hotel is a preposterous idea. Your feelings are hurt because I've invested so much time in the children. Your point is I'll never expand my dreams because I'm too dull to think outside the box."

"Wow! You completely failed to grasp my point." Casi put a hand on her hip. "You're correct, your plan is insufficient. Lauren's restaurant is too elite for this town, and who would stay at your hotel?"

"I fucking get it," Kyle snapped.

"A preschool isn't only ideal for Jake's spawn. Madison will require care and as Anna discovered, our little town doesn't have a decent place for young children or after school care. The stuck-up place in Seattle is terrible for her development and inconvenient." She shrugged. "The closest spa is in Seattle."

"Residents won't spend money for a fancy resort," Kyle started another pot of coffee.

"We aren't catering to the locals. Our draw is a sanctuary for the city folk and out-of-towners." Casi tapped her toe in annoyance.

Anna bolted upright. "That's why you were asking me those questions? We could bring clients here instead of traipsing the globe! It's the perfect solution and an ideal way to demonstrate the product rather than handing out samples. The cost would easily be absorbed in what we're shelling out for travel."

"Whatever your long-term goal is, we can't afford to build half of what you created. The mortgage alone is out of my comfort zone." Kyle turned suddenly. "Wait, if you had the spa, would you travel less?"

"One of the advantages," Casi said.

"I could mortgage the building." His eyes swept the room. "And the house."

Casi stepped toward him. "You would be willing to risk your assets to have me home more?"

"I would do anything to bring a better balance to our lives." He reached for her hand. "Life is meaningless without you."

"I feel the same, except it's not solely about our dreams." Casi grinned and advanced the slide. "Which is why we have investors. Each person is putting in twenty-thousand dollars and offers a unique skill to make the business a success. Brian estimates the return will be greater than fifty percent over five years, which is incredible."

Kyle read the lists. "Ava?"

"She'll oversee the bar setup and events."

"Bree from the resort on the island? How did you contact her? Why would she want to be part of this?" Kyle's eyes widened.

"She travels the world opening resorts and understands what it takes to make them successful. We have been friends since you locked lips with her at the last job. Anna is quite close with her." Casi grinned.

Anna smiled. "I admire her tenacity. She's the perfect choice."

"Obviously, Anna and I will manage the spa and Mary is also an investor." Casi pointed to the list. "Mildred from LA is a silent partner so her primary role is to promote us in her territory. Your dad and Earl are not contributing money but will oversee the plumbing and Ava's construction team have agreed to be your crew."

"Excellent, we have the backing of the mob and the cartel." Jake chuckled. "Why is my name there? I don't have money to put into this fantasy world."

Anna smiled. "I have a surplus from the sale of my condo I should invest. You own the house we live in and we're partners. You'll be required to do a lot of labor, and it's only fair for you to benefit financially in the end."

Jake elbowed Shane. "You have money to spare?"

Shane regarded his hands. "I had a small life insurance policy on Katie. This seemed like a good opportunity to maximize my investment."

"This could be risky." Kyle frowned at Casi.

"He came to me after Dawn insisted on being involved. No one will contribute what they can't afford to do without for a few years."

"Maybe Casi's insane plan will work and everyone will have a new start?" Kyle cocked his head when he read the next name. "Gabby? Casi, you have over five hundred thousand dollars in investments. How will this get paid back? Even if this place is a huge success, we won't see a return for many years, if at all."

Casi raised an eyebrow and brought up a picture of herself in lingerie in a remote setting. "Do you know how much a company pays for a location shoot? I've offered exclusive use to the top people in the industry. Not only are they fighting to book, DeShawn

Matthews wants to film his next music video before any of the work takes place."

"The rap star who ran you over?" Jake asked.

"His girlfriend did. Since his generous donation to keep youths out of trouble, his music sales have doubled. He's at the top of his game." Another list of names appeared. "Libby is booking a writer's retreat with people from all over the world. Alix will donate paintings for the property and he and Chase will hold an exclusive art auction along with Nadia."

"Your drug dealer?" Kyle grinned.

"She's hit it big in the art world." Casi giggled. "Oh, and Ray Dawson will be filming several episodes of his new show. It would be a fun interaction with a professional chef in his home cooking segment."

"He has a show?" Kyle smiled. "You created it?"

"I talked to friends. He's passionate, and it's been a huge success." Casi smiled. "Now, do you believe in the magic of positivity?"

"I think you're amazing." Kyle kissed her tenderly and turned to survey the room. "Everyone has a role?"

"Including Shane. He'll do the electrical." Casi noted Lia twisting her hands together and nodded to him.

Shane smiled and held Lia's hand tighter. "Things have been crazy for us and I've had to make a lot of tough decisions and you've made many sacrifices. Katie's mom isn't doing well, and it's difficult for her to manage the girls. I can't keep running back and forth between Washington and British Columbia and be a full-time parent."

"I understand," Lia said as tears streaked her cheeks. "I've officially begun menopause, so I'm not easy to be around."

Shane slid from the couch to one knee and held out a sparkling diamond ring. "Marry me. We can figure out the details later, but I want us to be together as a family. The girls helped me pick this, and Katie's mom is the one who told me I was being a fool to end things with you."

"Oh my God!" Lia's hand shook as he slipped the ring on her

finger. "I don't know if we'll fit in the bungalow, but are you saying you're willing to move to Washington permanently?"

"It will be best for the girls and soon you'll have your own coffee shop and it's close to my work." Shane kissed her.

Casi sat next to Lia. "The boys could stay with Jake as their home base and there will be plenty of room for the girls at the bungalow." Lia's eyes brimmed with tears. "They should be settled with their sister. You'll see them every day because your coffee shop is beside the preschool. You'll have quality time with them."

"You considered our needs in the design?" Jake smiled.

"The children will be together during the day. We're a community." Casi pinched the baby's toe. "Including Madison. I also considered the long term when Riley and Amy start a family. She wants to keep working for you guys and this would provide an option."

Lauren wiped a tear. "You're aware I don't have money to invest? Can I pay it over time? I'll be close to the restaurant if I'm living at my mom's so maybe this could happen?"

"Oh, I forgot a slide." Casi jumped up and clicked a key to bring up a beautifully furnished apartment. "Lance designed a space for you in what used to be the master suite. It has two bedrooms and a living area. The kitchen is basic, but you'll be on site to use the amenities of the hotel. With Madison at the daycare, you can dedicate your time to running your restaurant. We have enough cash, so your investment can be time and knowledge."

Lauren clasped a hand to her mouth in disbelief. "You thought of every detail and considered all of us."

"I had a lot of time on my hands after I stopped worrying about you trying to steal my husband. I figured it was a better use of my talents to bring my friends' dreams to life." Casi clicked the remote and a photo of her with Kyle in the windswept hills of Copenhagen filled the screen. "Happy birthday, Kyle. My gift is the project of a lifetime which will hopefully bring us together rather than tearing us apart."

He embraced her tenderly and gazed in her eyes. "This is the best present you could give me. The most incredible part will be having you by my side."

Casi shook her head as she surveyed Kyle with the large group gathered around the dining room table. They were in a heated discussion about the agenda for the resort while they half-heartedly worked on a puzzle. "Do we have extra time for games? Our offer was accepted almost a month ago and we haven't begun work yet." She eyed them individually to get their attention.

"Permits take time." Kyle hovered above the puzzle with a piece, trying several locations. "Mom brought over games for the kids and this was in the box. We were never able to complete it in the past, and the lid was lost years ago. We're taking a guess what the picture is. We became involved while we figured out the best timeline to proceed. Hey, what do you think of using my friend Nick as a coffee distributor? I thought it might be nice to use a local source rather than a corporation." He blushed. "Unless you wanted to stick with a big name."

"I love it. He's well-known in Elmvale, and we should support small businesses. I concocted the big picture, but your ideas and advice are valuable." Casi tossed a stack of index cards on the table with a pen and picked up a handful of pieces. "List each task. Don't organize it, just verbalize." She finished the edge of the sky as she spoke.

They began speaking at once, and Georgia jotted the various jobs on the cards. "Wait, one at a time!"

Peter scoffed. "It would be asinine to frame the kitchen cabinets before the plumbing is done."

"The electrical needs to be in place before we install the coffee machine." Shane regarded Lia. "I know you're excited, but there are millions of tasks to be completed before you officially open."

Jake frowned. "We might want to check the foundation before any interior build out is done."

Casi giggled as they went back and forth with claims of which jobs were the most important. She snapped the last piece in place and held out her hand. "May I have the index cards?"

Kyle's eyes widened. "You finished the puzzle!"

"Impossible." Peter scanned the finished landscape.

Jake smacked her bottom. "You're a genius at random things."

"If the preschool is functional, we have a safe place for the children while the parents are working." The group nodded, and Casi placed the card to the right. "Coffee shop next? It'll bring local interest and serve the employees." Lia beamed as they agreed it was the proper order.

"Consider the multitude of tasks within each space. You don't throw paint on and call it done." Peter rolled his eyes.

"Not my problem." Casi smiled. "You tradespeople can create subcategories on each card and figure it out for yourselves. We don't speak your language." She continued through the list, adjusting as suggestions were made. She smiled at Anna. "Our spa is the last priority."

"Although, if it means you being home more, we can move it up." Kyle grasped her hand.

"I've started a marketing campaign and notified my clients. We'll build excitement for the Fall. I'll work from the wood shop and spend time at the resort helping with planning. I can handle the bookings for the shoots and future reservations when I'm not traveling." She leaned forward and kissed his forehead. "Perhaps you could come with me to Asia? I can reduce it to annual trips once the resort is open. You mentioned you would like to visit Japan."

Kyle smiled. "As always, you've created the perfect solution. I would love to go with you."

"In the meantime, Casi and I will visit spas to assess what services are most beneficial to our resort." Anna nudged her.

"Count us in." Ava swung an arm around Georgia's shoulders. "We would be thrilled to help you compile market research."

33

MODEL REMODEL

Jake opened the door and yawned as he surveyed his brother laden with a mountain of toys. "Sorry, no room here."

Kyle shoved past him and dumped the load. "You've had possession of the boys for weeks and I'm returning my house to our glorious kid-free zone."

"You still read to them every night and your little princess won't let anyone touch her precious hair." Jake followed him across the street.

"Good, are we finally evicting our boarders?" Casi smiled.

"Yes, I'll maintain my awesome uncle duties such as story time and specialized hairstyling, but the real father can take over cleaning, feeding, and general zookeeper activities." Kyle grinned.

Casi regarded her watch. "Do you guys have a spare hour later this afternoon? I'm meeting Anna for covert spa tours and lunch in Seattle and it would be great if you could meet us after."

Kyle considered the multitude of tasks waiting for him and smiled. "We would love to."

Casi wrapped her arms around him and whispered a location in his ear. "I'll see you in a few hours."

❧

Jake paused when he noticed the sign. "Why are we here?"

"Casi requested our presence." Kyle opened the door and peered inside the dimly lit room.

"She calls, and you jump," Jake chuckled.

"Yup. She's moved mountains to bring everyone's dreams to fruition. I'll do anything to ensure her happiness." Kyle waved to Casi and noted Anna reclining in the chair. "Welcome to the wild side."

Jake smoothed a hand over the pale, supple skin of Anna's exposed hip. "What tattoo are you getting?"

Anna smiled. "A dragonfly. I wanted to do something bold to symbolize putting my past behind me." She grasped Jake's hand as the artist began. "It's only for my husband to see."

Casi smiled and put her palm to Jake's chest. "Sit." She covered his eyes. "Don't peek until it's done."

Jake gritted his teeth as the needle pierced his skin. "I can feel I'm getting script above my scar."

"It's important to tie up loose ends. Your feelings were hurt because you didn't match your best friends." Casi smiled at Kyle. "Now we're back together as a trio." She placed her forearm above Jake's and brought Kyle's underneath as she read the new sentence; Believe in Love, Magical Moments in Time, Always and Forever.

Jake focused on their arms linked and his eyes welled. "Thank you, Monkey Moonshine." He leaned forward and kissed her as the artist twisted to finish his design.

Casi whispered, "We've had a lot of reality checks and must believe there is still magic in the world."

Jake nodded and regarded Anna. "Before we leave, I need to complete my cascade. This time I want to spell out the full name of the woman I love because she deserves more than an initial."

❧

"This is not happening!" Casi bellowed.

Kyle set down his tools and rounded the corner to the foyer. "Is there a problem?" He glared at the group fussing around Casi.

"Sorry, did we disturb you?" Casi sighed. "They want to take the shoot in a direction I'm not comfortable with."

"We want her to be part of it," the director explained.

"This isn't who I am anymore." She waved her hand to the scantily clad models. "I've left that life behind."

Kyle smiled and held his arms open, capturing her in an embrace. "I completely understand. As much as I want to keep you all to myself, do you feel it might be beneficial to resurrect my fierce girl?"

"Because of Dalton?" she whispered.

Kyle caressed her cheek. "You can outshine any girl. I fear he damaged your confidence and part of your mission to prove yourself in the business world is to bury your past. The sweet, sexy girl had tremendous value, she just needed to grow up a bit."

Casi regarded the models lounging on the stairs. "I'm not as thin as I was five years ago."

"Which is a good thing." Kyle swept her hair behind her shoulder. "You've blossomed into a beautiful woman who embodies grace, intelligence, and passion. Go strut your stuff."

Casi exhaled and nodded to the director. "Fine, I'll do it." A grin spread across her face. "My husband will join me."

"No, I'm not part of the deal!" Kyle blanched.

"Oh, how delicious," an assistant purred as she swiftly attempted to rid Kyle of his t-shirt.

"Take one for the team, brother." Jake smacked him on the back as Shane cheered beside him.

After an hour of prep and coaxing, Casi made her way to the set and posed awkwardly as she tugged at the sparse lace. "I can't do this."

Dylan pushed Kyle forward. "Focus on the prize. He's the only one watching." He smiled at the crew. "The rest of us are checking out your hot husband."

Kyle squinted at the bright lights as he heard the whirl of a digital camera. "I'm not a model."

"The first time is the hardest." The photographer bounced around him as he angled the camera. "You're super fit."

Kyle looked pained, and Casi giggled as she bounded toward him. "Let's make this fun." The girls clamored to their new prop, winding around his legs and tugging at his jeans as he tried not to lose his balance on the stairs. Casi swept a hand to the side of his face and gazed in his eyes as she rediscovered her edge and posed seductively.

Jake smiled. "There's our girl back in action."

Lauren perused the scene and shook her head. "She's fantastic. The other girls are pretty, but Casi offers something incredibly unique."

Jake nodded. "A ray of sunshine sparkling brighter than any flame. Her lovely exterior is only a vessel to house a miraculous spirit."

"She's always had a unique quality." Shane shoved beside him. "Joey claimed she wasn't from earth, but he was smitten since second grade, so he may have been biased."

"She might have been sent from somewhere divine to rescue this sorry bunch." Jake yawned. "This is dull. I'm ready for this place to open next month so we can focus on a new list of complaints from our women instead of working around these bookings."

"I heard the rapper was insane." Shane mimicked dance moves.

"He paid a bundle to book the place. He wanted a run-down hotel for his video, and we delivered." Jake spun to the vibration of a crash and raced toward the hallway as Kyle tripped down the stairs entangled with the off-kilter models. He grabbed his brother's hand, ensnaring Casi in the rescue before she could tumble to the floor.

Kyle steadied himself and winced. "I almost bowled down the whole crew." He kneaded his side. "My hip gave out when they all leaned on me. I guess I'm getting old."

Jake slowly released his grip, maneuvering through their handshake. "Perhaps you're meant to be a one-woman man."

Casi waved to a pleasant onlooker. "Hey, Ray Dawson."

"You're as beautiful as ever and twice as charming." Ray greeted her with a kiss on the cheek.

Casi gestured to Lauren hovering to the side. "This is the chef you'll be working with today. I believe she is featuring dishes from her new restaurant, which will be open in a few weeks."

Lauren smiled. "Casi, you looked amazing out there. I don't know how you remain so poised. I'm nervous, and I'm fully clothed."

Casi laughed. "Just let your talent shine through."

"Oh, I didn't mean to imply your figure was all you had to offer."

Casi read the blush in Lauren's cheeks. "I have an idea to boost your confidence and get you ready for the camera. Can you get Lia?" She bent her head toward the photographer, indicating the sunlit foyer sending prisms across the stairs. She grabbed Dylan's arm and relayed her plan before beckoning Kyle to join them. He grinned and waved Jake to the group. "Even the older ones?"

"All the women," Casi confirmed.

The men scattered and set out on their mission, returning moments later in a flurry of questions and confusion. Casi smiled and held up a hand. "This won't take long. When I was doing the photoshoot, I realized I'm empowered not only from the challenges I've overcome but by the relationships I've made. I've asked the crew to do one more photo, and I want all the women in it."

Georgia, Ava, and Libby laughed as Mary clucked her tongue. "Don't be silly. I'm sure the mature ladies would prefer to sit this out."

"Everyone," Casi insisted.

With minimal prompting and prodding, the men rallied around the group to ensure no one escaped while the hairstylist and makeup artists fluttered around the women.

"Please tell me we're not wearing lingerie," Ava joked.

"I hope you are." Jake blew her a kiss.

Casi surveyed the scene and whispered with a set designer who rustled through boxes to extract scarves in brilliant jewel tones. As the women assembled on the staircase they were draped, tucked, and fussed with until Casi gave them an approving nod. She turned and smiled at Kyle before smoothing the collar of her raspberry pink blouse and sinking in the middle beside Anna and Lia on a step. She gave Gail a thumbs up and winked at Ava as the camera whirred and lights flashed.

Kyle surveyed the group, laughing and linking arms as they submitted to the fun. He applauded when the shoot concluded, and the men circled around to congratulate them. "Cheers to the beautiful women of the Blackberry Falls Resort." He smiled at Casi as she joined them. "Did the glamorous life lure you back?"

"Not for all the money and fame in the world. I've discovered my niche and prefer to work with intelligent friends." Casi giggled as a model tried to push a door clearly marked pull. "Alix's new girlfriend."

Kyle shook his head. "She suits him."

Lauren grasped Casi's arm and led her to the side. "I was blinded by jealousy and devastation over losing Kyle. I understand what charms everyone, beyond your beauty. You truly are a compassionate and soulful person. I hope one day you'll consider me a friend."

Casi squeezed her hand. "The intent of the photo was to feature significant women who have contributed to this project. It also happens to be the circle of friends who inspire me to climb mountains."

34

TIME AFTER TIME

"Hey, are you busy?" Casi bounded in the kitchen and surveyed the action as Lauren directed the staff through the catering menu. "I asked Lia and Lance to join us in the dining room."

"Sure, did you want to go over the agenda?" Lauren followed her down the corridor. "I can't believe every room is booked."

"The timing of this may be awkward, but I didn't want to wait." Casi directed her to sit beside her siblings and nodded to someone in the hallway, as a stout man appeared with flushed cheeks. "You agreed you wanted me to search for your dad. He lives in Florida but happened to be in Oregon on business this week."

Lance was the first to jump up and rush toward the stately figure. "I recognize you from the one picture I hid away." He embraced him and pulled Lia into the hug as she hovered nearby.

Lauren stood slowly. "It's been almost thirty-five years. Did you forget you had a family?"

He held out a hand to her. "Lauren, you were always my level-headed one. I understand you're getting ready for your big opening, but can we sit for a few minutes and catch up?"

She nodded and sat at a nearby table as Casi disappeared to the foyer to give them privacy. He clasped his hands together. "I won't sugarcoat it, nor will I blame your mother. We had very... different beliefs, and it became impossible for us to continue in our marriage."

"You mean because she's a bitch?" Lance pouted.

"She said you committed the ultimate betrayal. If it's worse than cheating, I don't want to know." Lauren shivered and hoped Casi had done a thorough investigation.

"Do you remember when we went on vacation to Florida? You were quite young." He smiled with the memory and read from their blank faces time had erased him from their minds. "I enjoyed the weather, the beach, and the vibrant lifestyle. I also fell in love with someone I met there."

"So, you did leave us to start a new life." Lauren frowned.

"I considered walking away from the affair, but your mother couldn't cope with it and insisted I move out the moment I told her."

"But you were willing to leave the woman for us?" Lia whispered and tucked a stray hair behind her ear.

"My lover was a man." He waited for the information to sink in. "I always knew I was gay, but this is a small town and I figured I could be happy in a traditional family. When I met Ronaldo, I couldn't hide that part of myself anymore." He smiled at Lance. "I'm sure your mother was devastated when she realized you shared my nature."

"Do I look gay?" Lance turned to Lia.

"I haven't been active in your lives, but my arrangement was I would send child support until each of you turned eighteen. In exchange, I got one letter a year with highlights and pictures of my children. It was a raw deal, but it was the best I could negotiate. At first the writing was full of anger and disapproval, but over time she softened and included successes." He grasped Lauren's hand. "And heartbreaks."

"You know everything?" Lauren gasped.

"The basics, but not the details. Lia has two sons and you have a daughter. Lance is an interior designer who lives in Seattle."

"Did she tell you my husband is an asshole who ended up in jail for multiple counts of assault?" Lauren wept in her hands.

"Ex-husband. Your friend Casi sent me an incredible PowerPoint presentation on the wonderful things happening in your lives. It was like watching a movie where I knew the actors and I longed to reach out." He sighed. "When you each turned eighteen, I pushed to renew contact. Your mother claimed none of you wanted anything to do with me. When Casi contacted me, I suspected I hadn't been told the truth."

"We didn't know anything!" Lia embraced him. "I'm getting married. Will you stay and walk me down the aisle?"

Tears flowed down his cheeks. "You want me to be a part of something so special? I hear your fiancé is a terrific guy."

"I've missed having my father for every significant occasion. I don't care who you love. I need you." Lia wrapped her arms tighter.

Lauren nodded and dabbed a tear. "We all do. Please stay and join us for this monumental day. We've come a long way as a family to work together for a common dream."

❧

Lia bubbled over with excitement as she shared the details of the visit with Casi. "He's extending his stay, so he can spend time with us. Aren't you excited, Lauren? I can't wait for the kids to meet him."

Lauren smiled at her sister's exuberance. "The timing is perfect. I'm ecstatic my life is coming together so beautifully. Thank you for making this happen, Casi. It put a lot of things into perspective. I understand we were my mother's world when everything came crumbling down. She built her life around a man who didn't want her and it was a tough reality check."

Casi cringed. "You aren't suggesting her life is similar to your relationship with Kyle?"

Lauren laughed. "Kyle enriched my life and still does. I was thinking of how Dalton screwed me over and why I don't want Madison to be part of his life." She paled as an attractive brunette entered the kitchen with fashionable flair. "Gia, hi. I didn't expect to see you."

"Kyle said this would be a good time to catch you before the event and give you a few updates." Gia withdrew a large envelope. "I'm hesitant to admit I had knowledge of Dalton's unsavory behavior. The men in my family have their own standards and the string of step-mother's I've had played by the mistress rules. I honestly hoped you would bring a new level of intelligence and class to our clan, and the restaurant was the first thing I've been excited about in years." She glanced at Kyle. "When I heard what he did to Casi, I was disgusted! I'm the one who provided the documentation to the police to support the investigation. My grandmother is refusing to pay for an attorney and said he can rot in prison. I realize Dalton took a tremendous amount from you and unfortunately, I can't repay it. Casi suggested this was an adequate peace offering." She handed the envelope to Lauren. "Twenty thousand dollars in cash. It won't show on our records, which is important because we're being audited by the IRS. Casi wouldn't let me invest in the hotel to avoid any paper trail, but she mentioned you wanted to be an equal contributor. I hope this goes towards making amends."

"This is incredible!" Lauren clutched the package to her chest. She grinned and held it out to Casi. "Can you add me to the investor list? I have a good feeling this place will be very successful."

"Consider it done." Casi motioned Anna to the gathering. "Tell them about Grant."

"Ugh, what a pig!" Gia shuddered. "Apparently his new thing is teenage girls. He was caught loitering around a catholic high school. I ended our sham of a marriage and reclaimed my name and what was left of my wealth. My grandmother decided the men in our family weren't worth saving. We've taken back full ownership of the depart-ment stores." She turned to Anna. "I hope you'll consider still having your products there."

"Absolutely, and now we have a spa to make the experience even more exquisite. We welcome you to book a retreat." Anna winked.

"Definitely on my list." Gia grasped Lauren's hand. "Will you allow me to be an aunt to Madison? I'm moving back to California in a week, but I want to visit her."

"I'm thrilled to have you in her life." Lauren cocked her head. "What's happening to the winery? Will your father and cousins still run it without your grandmother's backing?"

Gia laughed. "Our girl here had a delightful solution. Ava has connections to a family in the market for an olive orchard. It appeared insane, but they came to test the soil and determined the Columbia Valley is ideal. The rock-bottom price was an added incentive."

"Their products are premium quality and diverse. They also make vinegars. I was hoping you would want to use them." Casi transferred a box to the counter and set bottles out.

"I would be happy to meet with the new owner." Lauren surveyed the bright labels on the array of products.

"You've met him." Casi's eyes sparkled. "Matias was working with the construction crew until his paperwork was finalized."

"Oh." Lauren blushed at the recollection of the handsome man who always greeted her with a genuine smile each morning. "It would be wonderful to use local products and support his family's business."

"His family backs the venture, but he's not married." Casi winked. "He's a friend of Ava's and she arranged to have the families from Argentina work at the property. They're highly skilled and super excited about the opportunity."

Lauren smiled. "You have a remarkable way of spinning the universe to benefit everyone."

"The intriguing thing is his family partners with an orchard in Italy. He has offered to host us for an extended tour next year." Casi clapped with excitement. "Another one of your dreams realized!"

35

THE GRAND OPENING OF THE
BLACKBERRY FALLS RESORT

"I have the bar staff pouring champagne as the guests come to the garden. Do you need assistance?" Ava surveyed the spotless kitchen laden with well-organized platters and chafing dishes.

"I haven't slept in three days." Lauren grinned. "And I've never been happier in my life. This restaurant is a dream come true and I can't wait to showcase our menu at the event."

Ava noted the selection of olive oil bottles on display. "Aren't the products terrific? I've been using them for years and I'm thrilled they're coming to the valley."

"With your help." Lauren smiled. "What a brilliant idea to suggest an olive orchard. I never realized they could grow here."

"The variety they cultivate does well in this climate, if the winters don't drop severely in temperature. The crew from Argentina are fantastic at farming and know the tricks to make things thrive."

"You ensured a lot of people had jobs. That's admirable."

"They've been loyal to me for many years. I wanted to provide a stable environment for their families. I believe you get back from the universe as much as you put in." She smiled as Jack came and entwined his arms around her. "The key to happiness is to remember

325

surface wounds are painful, but they heal. Dig deep and focus on who and what's important."

Fran hesitated at the door and waited for Jack and Ava to leave. She watched Lauren humming while she checked her lists and counted trays. "You're certainly in your element."

Lauren braced herself for the impending criticism. "Please don't say anything negative about Casi. I won't engage in the conversation anymore. She's changed my life for the better, and I owe her a huge debt of gratitude."

"Including reconnecting you with your father? I suspect she had a hand in the reunion. She can never leave anything alone, always prying into other people's business." Fran crossed her arms over her chest. "I'm sure it brought her great joy to meddle, like she did with your brother. He has no right to be involved in this hotel."

"He has every right!" Lauren set down her clipboard. "He's a brilliant designer who brought our vision to life. What does it matter if he's gay? I don't care about Dad's preference either."

Fran's eyes welled with tears. "I knew my children would villainize me in the end. After everything I sacrificed, someone else is always the hero. Your father is misunderstood and Casi is a super-star."

Lauren smiled. "You're a wonderful mother who always put us kids first. I'm finally a mom and I truly understand everything you did to protect us. Madison is barely eight months old and I feel like I'm failing her continuously." She exhaled. "I stayed with Dalton because I wanted her to have two parents, but now I comprehend I must put her safety and well-being first." She waved a hand around the kitchen. "Casi provided an opportunity for me to accomplish everything I always wanted."

"As long as she keeps Kyle. Smart woman."

"Kyle never loved me. I hated how much he adored her, and it killed me to see him swoon." Lauren shrugged. "We were meant to be great friends, not husband and wife. Maybe one day I'll find real romance, but I'm thrilled to cherish the incredible elements in my life." She embraced Fran. "Including you. Thank you for raising me by yourself. I want Dad in my adult world but it doesn't erase your dedication to bringing up three wonderful children. The only thing I ask is for you to remove the barrier between you and Lance. He's my brother and it hurts me to witness your neglect of him."

Fran twisted her hands. "He probably doesn't want anything to do with me. Now he knows the truth about your father, he'll use it as ammunition for all the ways I failed him."

"He loves you. Let it be enough. Your work is done in molding us. Lia and I want to raise our kids in a community who supports us."

Fran furrowed her brow as two men walked in. "Hello, Maury." She clenched her jaw. "Ronaldo."

Maury's eyes softened as he surveyed her. "Fran, thank you for raising our children. They are lovely, and it does my heart good to see them working together."

"I tried my best."

"You excelled." He approached her with a smile. "Our secret has run its course. Maybe it's time we move on to being friends."

Fran glanced at Lauren's hopeful expression. "Probably."

Maury nodded, and Ronaldo held out a hand. "May I assist you to your seat while Maury tends to Lia?"

Fran slid her hand through the crook of his arm. "I can't walk fast. My knee is still giving me trouble."

"I understand aches and pains." Ronaldo smiled. "Maury with his back and me with bad feet. Endless complaints for two old men and it's getting worse." He led her through the garden gate and settled her in a chair in the front row while the guests smiled and nodded to them.

The music began, and everyone stood. Kyle walked down the aisle with Casi on his arm while they directed six adorable children to toss rose petals. Jake and Anna followed and redirected Austin's attention from tugging at his sister's bow on her dress. Tommy ran ahead and waved to the people he knew until Kyle grasped his hand to stand at the altar. Fran smiled at Lauren and Lance and wiped a tear as they passed. Lance winked, and her heart melted in the resolution of love for her son.

Lia glowed with happiness as she floated down the aisle on her father's arm. She grinned at the chaos of the adults wrangling the children while she handed her bouquet to Lauren and whispered, "It's so much better when you're totally in love with your husband."

"I'm looking forward to the experience." Lauren surveyed the landscaped grounds with a view of the lake. "I'm satisfied to wait for the real thing. I have a lot to occupy my time."

"Daddy, I have to go potty," a tiny voice stated as she bounced beside Shane.

Gail sprung to her feet and held out a hand. "I'll take her."

Georgia smiled and patted Gail's hand as she walked by. "You're a wonderful caregiver to these children. They're blessed to attend the amazing school you created."

Gail beamed. "I love every minute. Who knew my life would take such an unbelievable turn?"

Shane glanced at Katie's family before he said his vows and her mother nodded. He turned back to Lia and smiled. "I don't regret the road I traveled before it led me to you. I've had the support of family and friends on my journey. My daughters are part of who I am, and I honor your commitment to your children." He smiled at Jake behind him. "I'm humbled by the love your tribe has shown me, and I vow to take care of you and our family. We're not kids making empty promises. We've both seen disappointment and heartbreak, but with you by my side, I know our future is bright. I love you with all my heart and I cherish the person you are." He leaned in and kissed her. "We're in for a wild ride. You had better fasten your seatbelt."

The ceremony concluded, and the children were released to run free while the adults socialized, and appetizers were served with cocktails. Casi embraced Lia and smoothed a hand over her silky locks. "You look radiant. Was the ceremony what you hoped for?"

Lia smiled at Jake. "So much better than Vegas."

Jake clutched his chest. "How hurtful."

"Your wedding at the lake was lovely. I wanted the children included, and to not stress about party favors." She turned to Casi. "I reflected on your special day in Hawaii and it changed my opinion. I experienced what it's like to be completely in love and only want to celebrate with people who care about you."

"I hope you don't mind a few hundred people attending the grand opening." Casi glanced at her watch.

"That's the best part. A private ceremony and a killer party afterward with zero effort required from me." Lia smiled.

"Just like my wedding," Casi laughed. She waved Dylan over and hugged him tightly. "Where's princess excessive names?"

Dylan rolled his eyes. "Snappy sarcasm from someone who looks like she climbed out of bed after a hot sex session."

Casi shrugged. "I'm a mature woman in a loving relationship. This is my look, and I embrace every wrinkle and gray hair."

"Um, wisdom highlights." Dylan snapped his fingers. He turned and smiled as Brian arrived with Grace and the baby. "Come to Uncle, my little sugar snap pea."

Lauren smiled and smoothed Madison's dress. "Maybe in a few years our girls can be friends."

"We signed Fiona up for Gail's preschool. We haven't been thrilled with the overcrowded daycare in Seattle, and Anna wants the girls to be together. We're fighting over who gets to bring her in the morning because we've heard the coffee bar has sensational baked goods." Grace nodded to Lia.

"I hope you'll come for dinner a few nights." Lauren smiled at Brian. "It's been nice having you involved with the finances. You're not only brilliant, but we can trust you to protect our best interests."

"I suspect I'll be here a lot since the forecast is extremely positive for huge profits." Brian leaned closer. "The bookings Casi secured this summer already has us in the black!"

"She has a head for business," Lauren agreed.

"Babe, spectacular location!" Alix strolled in like a movie star greeting fans on the red carpet with Chase as his shadow.

Mary slid an arm around Casi's waist. "Baby Girl, you pulled it off! I couldn't have predicted a wisp of a thing with a sassy personality could accomplish so much!"

"The spa came out well, didn't it?" Casi beamed. "We have our first international clients next week."

"Another brilliant idea. Bring the business to you rather than traipsing all over the world and exhausting yourself," Mary said.

"I'll look forward to the annual visits, but I'm excited about being home more." Casi surveyed the hotel. "This project allowed everyone to prosper and create something special. What I realized is I already had the best things in life, and I needed to alter my career to fit." She embraced Mary and grasped Ava's hand to join them. "Thank you for believing in me and being my best cheerleaders. I learned it takes more than a mother to nurture us."

Kyle came behind Casi and wrapped his arms around her. "You are a dream weaver of magical proportions." He regarded the guests mingling. "Who would believe I met a self-absorbed goddess in LA, and she turned out to be the salvation for everyone."

"Is that a compliment?" Casi laughed.

Kyle pointed to the group of friends nearby. "You don't merely exist for yourself. Your gift is bringing out the best in others, even when they don't have faith in themselves." He smiled at Amber, laughing with Chase. "No one was overlooked by your compassionate heart."

"It makes me happy to bring joy to others."

"We've had an amazing love story."

"No past tense." Casi smiled. "We're starting a new chapter."

"I believe the Blackberry Falls resort might be the beginning of our next adventure." Kyle grasped her chin and turned her face toward the sky as a symphony of excitement radiated from the garden. "Northern lights! Have you ever seen anything so beautiful?"

Casi brought her lips to his. "It's what I envision when you kiss me. It's absolute proof our love will stand the test of time and bloom for an eternity."

"And a day." Kyle smiled as he kissed her tenderly.

Always and Forever

ALWAYS AND FOREVER CAKE

Serves 12

1 cup cake flour

3/4 cup sugar

1 teaspoon baking powder

1/4 cup vegetable oil

4 large eggs, room temperature

1/3 cup whole milk

1/2 teaspoon salt

1/4 teaspoon cream of tartar

1 teaspoon pure vanilla extract

1 tablespoon Dutch-process cocoa powder, sifted

Red food coloring

¼ cup raspberry preserves

1 cup raspberries

1. Line a sheet pan with parchment paper and spray with pan spray. Preheat an oven to 350 degrees.
2. In a medium bowl, whisk together flour, 1/4 cup sugar, baking powder, oil, egg yolks, and milk until it has increased in volume and is pale in color.
3. In the bowl of a mixer fitted with the whisk attachment, combine egg whites, salt, cream of tartar, and vanilla. Whisk on medium speed until foamy, about 1 minute. Slowly add remaining 1/2 cup sugar. Increase mixer speed to high and continue whisking until stiff, glossy peaks form, about 5 minutes more.

4. Stir about one-third of egg-white mixture into flour mixture to lighten, then gently fold in remaining egg-white mixture in three additions.

5. Transfer 1 cup batter to two small bowls and gently fold in cocoa in one and red food color in the other.

6. Using an offset spatula, spread vanilla cake batter in prepared pan, stopping about one inch from the sides of the pan, being careful not to deflate batter.

7. Drop teaspoons of chocolate and red batter evenly across surface of vanilla batter, then swirl into hearts.

8. Bake until lightly golden brown and center of cake springs back when lightly pressed, about 18 minutes.

9. Let cool about 5 minutes. Invert cake onto a sheet of parchment paper and remove the paper used for cooking. Start at a long end and roll up cake. Let cool completely, seam-side down.

10. Unroll cake and spread with a thin layer of raspberry preserves and top with Chambord filling. Reroll the cake carefully, brushing away crumbs and browned cake to reveal the pattern. Transfer, seam-side down, to a serving platter to maintain cylindrical shape.

11. Slice and serve over raspberry coulis and garnish with raspberries.

CHAMBORD BUTTERCREAM

Makes 3 cups

1/3 cup water

1/3 cup Chambord

1 cup sugar

8 large egg yolks

12 ounces salted butter, softened

1. Pour the water and Chambord with sugar in a medium saucepan and bring to a boil. Reduce by about half (the mixture should have a syrup consistency).

2. In the bowl of a stand mixer fitted with a whisk attachment, beat the egg yolks until pale and thick, about 10 minutes.

3. With the mixer running on medium, carefully drizzle the hot syrup into the yolks and whisk until room temperature, about 10 minutes.

4. Begin adding the butter a little at a time until it is fully incorporated. Continue to whisk the buttercream until it is smooth.

RASPBERRY COULIS

Makes 2 cups

1 1/2 pounds fresh raspberries (or frozen)

1/4 cup white sugar

1 tablespoon Chambord

2 teaspoons lemon juice

1. Combine raspberries, sugar, Chambord, and lemon juice in a saucepan over medium heat; cook and stir until raspberries break down, sugar dissolves, and sauce is heated through, 3 to 7 minutes.
2. Remove from heat and press sauce through a fine-mesh strainer to remove seeds. Cool to room temperature, cover the bowl with plastic wrap, and refrigerate until chilled, at least 45 minutes.

A WORD FROM THE AUTHOR

Is this the end for Catwalk? I believe the Blackberry Falls Resort has a few secrets and surprises still to tell.

Stay up to date on upcoming releases, short stories, recipes, behind-the-scenes photos, and travel by joining our monthly mailing list at sqorpin.com and following me on social media.

Feel free to email with questions or vote for which character you would enjoy reading about in a spin-off.

Standalone novels are planned for characters whose stories could not be contained within this series. Next in line is Ava's heartbreakingly beautiful backstory, Bittersweet. Due to be released in early 2021.

Thank you for reading the Catwalk Series, and I hope you enjoyed the Contemporary Women's Fiction.

Reviews on Amazon are always appreciated!

Canadian-born author, Suzy Quenneville-Orpin, has always had a vivid imagination and a keen desire to write. Suzy views the world through her own narrative, weaving in the fascinating challenges, triumphs, and lifestyles of the people she meets. An unapologetic daydreamer, Suzy's early experiences in Toronto, Ontario provided the perfect upbringing to fuel her creativity and discover the wonder of the roads less traveled. A move to the west coast brought new opportunities and a deep appreciation for the Pacific Northwest.

Follow Suzy to discover more about what inspired the Catwalk Series and behind the scenes photos.

www.sqorpin.com
www.facebook.com/sqorpin
www.twitter.com/authorsqorpin
www.instagram.com/sqorpin
sqorpin@yahoo.com
www.Amazon.com/author/sqorpin